Killing Rommel

Steven Pressfield

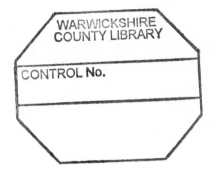

W F HOWES LTD

This large print edition published in 2008 by
W F Howes Ltd
Unit 4, Rearsby Business Park, Gaddesby Lane,
Rearsby, Leicester LE7 4YH

1 3 5 7 9 10 8 6 4 2

First published in the United Kingdom in 2008
by Doubleday

A CIP catalogue record for this book is available
from the British Library

ISBN 978 1 40741 954 1

Typeset by Palimpsest Book Production Limited,
Grangemouth, Stirlingshire
Printed and bound in Great Britain
by MPG Books Ltd, Bodmin, Cornwall

FSC
Mixed Sources
Product group from well-managed
forests and other controlled sources
Cert no. SGS-COC-2953
www.fsc.org
© 1996 Forest Stewardship Council

For Nancy

HISTORICAL NOTE

What follows is a work of fiction, but its basis in reality is fact.

All details of the trucks and tanks are historically accurate, as are desert geography and place names, campaigns of the war and timing of battles, equipment, weapons, nomenclature, and all wireless and operational protocols. All military units are real with the exception of T3 patrol of the LRDG and 'the Regiment' of 22nd Armoured Brigade, which are fictional. Everything about Rommel's history and death is true. All incidents concerning the reconnaissance and outflanking of the Mareth Line in late 1942-early 1943, excepting those involving T3 patrol, actually happened.

Patrol designations and commanders of the Long Range Desert Group are historically true, and their orders are as they were issued in fact. Where actual historical characters appear – Jake Easonsmith, Paddy Mayne, Nick Wilder, Ron Tinker, to cite the more prominent – all actions that they are said to perform before and after the central patrol are exactly as the real individuals performed them. Other characters are composites or inventions.

Only men who do not mind a hard life, with scanty food, little water and lots of discomfort, men who possess stamina and initiative, need apply.

From the initial British Army Circular, North Africa, summer 1940, seeking volunteers for what would become the Long Range Desert Group

PROLOGUE

When my dad died, his closest friend came forward as a mentor and surrogate father to me. This was not without its challenges since Chap – his full name was Richmond Lawrence Chapman – lived in England, while my family's home was in Manhattan. Chap's profession was publishing, so he got to New York regularly on business; I remember him taking me every winter to the Millrose Games at Madison Square Garden, in the days when the indoor track and field events were held in an arena so dense with cigarette smoke that you could barely see from one side to the other. Summers, I visited Chap and his wife, Rose, in London and at Rose's brother Jock's cottage at Golspie in Scotland. Chap and Rose had an adopted daughter Jessica who was exactly my age and two sons, Patrick and Tom, a couple of years older. The four of us were inseparable.

Chap had lost his own parents when he was quite young, so he was sensitive to the needs of a boy without a father. He took me trekking and fly fishing; he taught me how to brew tea and how to write a declarative sentence. Chap was quite a celebrated editor and publisher; it was not unusual to find writers like Harold Pinter and John Osborne sitting down to supper. Chap was also, though he never talked about it, a war hero. He had won a DSO for his service in North Africa during the Second World War. DSO stands for Distinguished Service Order. The only British decoration higher is the Victoria Cross, the equivalent of the US Medal of Honor. I was too young to understand much of this then, but I was impressed all the same.

I remember Rose showing me a photo album once at their flat in Knightsbridge. There was Rose, circa 1939, looking as glamorous as Gene Tierney in *Laura*. And young Lieutenant Chapman, as dashing as Tyrone Power. I squinted at yellowing snapshots of youthful Englishmen and New Zealanders of Chap's unit, the Long Range Desert Group, posing beside wilderness-rigged trucks armed with .30-caliber Brownings and twin .303 Vickers K machine guns. You could see the 'sand-channels' mounted on the vehicles' flanks – perforated steel tracks that the men used for extricating trucks stuck in the soft sand. Rose said that such patrols routinely crossed hundreds, even thousands, of miles of waterless, petrol-less desert, where there was no mercy and no hope of rescue if anything went wrong.

Some time in the early seventies, Chap began writing a memoir of this experience. I was eleven or twelve then; I remember Chap sending Jessica and me to the Public Record Office in Chancery Lane to look up army records for him. The documents had only recently become declassified; there was a stamp on the first page of each that read

MOST SECRET TILL 1972

Jessica and I got five pence apiece from Chap for copying these papers, which was big money in those days. Chap worked at home in his study, a tiny cubby littered with his war journals and diaries, correspondence with former comrades, maps of North Africa, and operations reports in English and German. I was fascinated. I plagued Chap with question after question, I'm afraid, most of which he was patient enough to answer.

It was not until the early nineties, however, when I became a historian myself that my thoughts returned seriously to Chap's memoir. I was visiting him and Rose in Scotland; Chap and I were playing the Struie golf course, next door to Royal Dornoch. I asked what had happened with the document. It was in a drawer at home, Chap said. He had finished it but never shown it to anyone except Rose. I asked if I could see it.

'No, no, it's a mess. Besides, I can't publish it.'

Chap expressed a number of reservations, largely about the personal nature of the material. He feared, he said, causing pain to the still-living widows and grown children of the men whose deaths he described in his pages. I could see that his own grief was deep and keenly felt. Still, as a writer, you can't let stuff like that stop you, and Chap knew it.

'Can you at least tell me what the book's about?'

'It's not even a book. Just . . . I don't know . . . an account.'

'Of what?'

'Nothing really. One patrol. Not even a successful one.'

I managed to drag out of Chap that the operation's objective had been to locate and kill Field Marshal Erwin Rommel, the legendary Desert Fox.

Now I was really hooked. I pressed Chap to show me a few pages. He wouldn't budge. I accused him of being a chicken writer. He was exhibiting, I said, all the symptoms of publication terror that he always told me his own writers showed.

'C'mon, Chap, you can't be tough on them while letting yourself off the hook.'

'They're professional writers,' he said. 'I'm not.'

Back in the States, I found myself unable to let go of curiosity about Chap's story. I began researching the era. The Long Range Desert Group, I discovered, was one of the first of those units that would come to be called 'special forces'. It had been based in Cairo and at various oases in the Libyan desert; its missions were raiding and reconnaissance behind enemy lines, against the Italians and Rommel's Afrika Korps. The LRDG was small and secret. Rommel himself had declared that man for man it had done more damage to the Axis cause than any other outfit in the North Africa campaign.

On August 31, 2002, Chap had a heart attack. He was OK; he recovered quickly. But on Christmas Day two years later he had another. I flew over. I was getting worried. Rose never left Chap's side. Three nights after Christmas, Chap took her hand. He said he didn't think he would see the New Year. By ten fifteen he was gone.

The funeral was at Magdalen College, Oxford. I was amazed at the turnout. Over four hundred mourners filled the quad and cloister, including three Booker Prize winners, all of whom Chap had either edited or published.

The morning before I had left New York, a parcel had arrived from Rose.

Chap wanted you to have this. He said he won't be a chicken writer any more.

It was the manuscript.

I read it on the flight over, then twice again over the next three days. You have to be careful when you take in something like that, to evaluate it object-ively and not get carried away by the emotion of the moment or by your personal affection for the writer. Still, I knew from the first page that this was special. It was all Chap, the best of him as I knew him, and other sides I'd never gotten a chance to know, including his love for Rose, which brought me to tears more than once. But best of all was its portrait of men and of the desert war. Chap's Englishmen and New Zealanders were by no means professional soldiers. They had not trained all their lives for war, as had many of their Axis enemies, yet they rose to the occasion when necessity demanded. Chap's own story was that of a civilian who, under exigency's law, embraced the virtues of war and was transformed by them.

Chap's memoir brought forward a second theme which was, to me, equally significant. This was the self-restraint, even chivalry, that distinguished the conduct of combatants on both sides throughout the North Africa campaign. Because the forces clashed in open desert far from civilian population centers, there was little if any of what we call today collateral damage. The flat, vacant waste, coupled with the extreme nature of the elements and the terrain, lent a sort of 'purity' to the conflict. Machine-gunners routinely held their fire when enemy soldiers bailed out of disabled tanks. Stretcher-bearers were permitted to dash into the open to evacuate the wounded. In front-line dressing stations, wounded men of Axis and Allied armies often received treatment side by side, on no few occasions from German and British medical officers working shoulder to shoulder. The leading exemplar of this code was Rommel himself. When orders from Hitler mandated the execution of captured British commandos, Rommel tossed the document into the trash. He insisted that Allied prisoners receive the same rations and medical care as he himself was given. He even wrote a book about the conflict called *Krieg Ohne Hass* (*War Without Hate*). Memoirs of the North Africa campaign attest that, fierce and brutal as much of the fighting was, relations between individual enemies retained a quality of forbearance that seems, today, almost impossible to imagine.

This chapter is the introduction to Chap's memoir. The full document follows. It was my decision not to render the text into American English but to leave it in the mother tongue as Chap wrote it. I have edited it slightly for US readers and have added a brief epilogue, the aim of which is to bring up to date the lives and deaths of the officers and men Chap wrote about since the time he completed his pages. To avoid using footnotes or a glossary, I have taken the liberty of blending into the text as unobtrusively as possible clarifications for such English-isms or shorthand as Chap occasionally employed – e.g., military acronyms such as KDG (for the King's Dragoon Guards, an armored car regiment). Where period slang appears, I've tried to shape the surrounding text so that the meaning is clear – or at least decipherable – from the context. These alterations excepted, the final text remains as close to Chap's original as I could make it.

BOOK I

AN ENGLISHMAN

CHAPTER 1

During the final months of 1942 and the early weeks of 1943, it was my extraordinary fortune to take part in an operation behind enemy lines, the aim of which was to locate and kill Field Marshal Erwin Rommel, commander-in-chief of German and Italian forces in North Africa.

The operation – the term 'raid' was never employed – was authorised by Lieutenant-General Bernard Law Montgomery, commanding Eighth Army; planned by the office of Lieutenant-Colonel John 'Shan' Hackett, of G Raiding Force; and carried out by elements of Lieutenant-Colonel David Stirling's SAS, the Special Air Service, reinforced by irregular troopers of Major Vladimir Peniakoff's No. 1 Demolition Squadron, more familiarly known as Popski's Private Army, as well as by officers and other ranks of the Long Range Desert Group. The operation placed its hopes of success not in firepower, since its heaviest vehicles were unarmoured 1½-ton Chevrolet trucks packing no armament bigger than .50-calibre aircraft Brownings and 20mm Breda guns, but on

11

cunning, audacity and surprise. Attempts on Rommel's life had been made before. These, however, had struck at lightly defended rear areas, to which their target had withdrawn temporarily for rest or recuperation. The operation in which I took part aimed to strike at the heart of the German Afrika Korps in the field.

If this scheme sounds driven by desperation, it was. At the moment of the operation's initial planning – summer '42 – Rommel and Panzerarmee Afrika had just finished routing the British Eighth Army in a series of battles in the Western Desert. German armour had driven our tanks and men across all Libya, over the Egyptian frontier to the very gates of Alexandria. Churchill had just sacked the army's commanders. In Cairo, the code books were being burned. Rommel stood one push from Suez and the Middle East oilfields. Russia was then reeling under attack from a hundred and sixty-six Nazi divisions. With Arab oil, Hitler's war machine could break the Red Army's back. Nor would rescue quickly come from America. The US had barely entered the war; full mobilisation lay months away. The Allies were staring global defeat in the face.

Could a commando raid in North Africa make a difference? It could, the planners in Cairo believed, if it could eliminate Rommel. Rommel was the heart and soul of Axis forces in the desert. 'The Jerries have no general who can replace him,' said Major Jake Easonsmith, our commander, at the initial briefing. 'Kill him and the beast dies.'

But could such a strike succeed? It might, paradoxically, because of Rommel's own personal bravery and his audacious style of command. The Desert Fox led from the front. His mode of leadership was to place himself physically wherever the action was hottest, heedless of his own safety. 'Rommel isn't reckless,' declared Easonsmith. 'He has simply found that in mobile warfare the commander's presence at the point of action is essential.'

Rommel was notorious among his own junior officers, we were told, for materialising unannounced at forward positions, stepping down from his Fieseler Storch scout plane or his 'Mammoth' armoured command vehicle, or occasionally from a tank or a staff car or even a motorcycle upon which he had hitched a ride. It was not exceptional for Rommel to issue orders directly to his regimental commanders or even, in the heat of the moment, to take personal command of units as small as infantry companies.

Such boldness had nearly got Rommel killed more than once. He set his plane down by accident one time amongst an Allied formation and winged away, barely, with bullets whizzing round his head. Another time he escaped capture when he ran out of fuel on the frontier wire, again amidst Commonwealth troops. He was rescued a third time by the staff car carrying one of his own generals, who happened, emulating his mentor, to be as far forward as Rommel was.

Rommel's trademark aggressiveness, it was hoped, could render him vulnerable to a surprise thrust. If Allied raiders could use the deep desert routes to move undetected into the German rear; if they could manoeuvre forward undiscovered; if they could fix Rommel's position . . . if a skilled and daring party could do all this, they might be able to land a blow that would change the course of the war.

My name is Chapman, Richmond Lawrence. In September 1942 I was a lieutenant in the 22nd Armoured Brigade, 7th Armoured Division. I was a tank officer. In theory I commanded a 'recce' (reconnaissance) troop of four A-15 Crusaders. I say 'in theory' because in action the turnover was so swift and violent, both from enemy fire and from mechanical breakdowns, that a troop could be down to two tanks or even one of its original kind, then reconstituted overnight with different types fresh from the repair depots – American Grants, British Crusaders, and the US-built aircraft-engined Stuarts that their crews called Honeys. The turnover among the men could be similarly brutal. That is another story. The point for this tale is that, at that time, circumstances conspired to export me from the Armoured Division and translate me into the Long Range Desert Group.

My presence amongst this company was in a technical capacity only; I had been PTDed ('personnel temporarily detached') to the formation with an

14

eye to assessing 'the going' over which the patrols would travel – meaning the terrain's suitability to bear tanks and heavy transport. I was by no means the first troop leader so assigned. Advisers from the Royal Armoured Corps regularly hitchhiked on LRDG patrols for similar purposes; Royal Air Force officers did the same, scouting out potential landing grounds in the inner desert.

The mission of the Long Range Desert Group was raiding and reconnaissance in the enemy's rear. At the time I joined it, the unit operated in patrols of five or six trucks, with one officer and fifteen to twenty men. Patrols were entirely self-contained, carrying all their own petrol, water, rations, ammunition and spare parts. In addition to its own combat operations, the Long Range Desert Group conveyed spies and agents on covert assignments and provided transport and naviga-tion for assault parties of the SAS and other commando outfits. The group's greatest joy, however, was to work 'beat-ups', their slang term for attacks on enemy airfields, motor assembly areas and convoy routes.

At the time of the British retreat to Alamein in summer '42, the LRDG had been in business for almost two years. Its raids had destroyed and damaged hundreds of Axis aircraft and caused thou-sands of German and Italian troops to be pulled out of the front lines and re-deployed to provide rear-area security. The formation had acquired a certain swashbuckling glamour. Volunteers queued by the hundreds. Getting in was no easy matter, however. From one batch of seven hundred applicants, the LRDG took only twelve. Criteria for selection were less wild and woolly than one might imagine. The group was not seeking buccaneers or assassins; what its officers wanted was the solid, mature sort – the type of chap who could think for himself under pressure, work in close quarters with others, and handle extremes not only of danger but of tedium, hardship and privation. The virtues of resourcefulness, self-composure, patience and hardiness, not to mention a sense of humour, were prized as highly as those of bravery, aggressiveness and raw martial rigour.

In this I believe the LRDG was spot on. One of the factors that has kept me until now from writing of my own experiences under fire is the uneasiness I have felt about the genre of war literature. Tales of heroes, the nobility of sacrifice and so forth have always made me uneasy. They run counter to my experience. From what I've seen, the operations of war are constituted less of glorious attacks and valiant defences and more of an ongoing succession of mundane and often excruciating balls-ups. The patrol of which I write, typical of so many, achieved little heroic beyond its own survival, save at the very end, and then less by military or tactical brilliance than by luck and its protagonists' stubborn, even mulish, refusal to quit. Those actions of its men that may legitimately claim the name of gallantry came about largely from attempts at self-extrication from peril, most of which we got ourselves into by our own overzealousness, and were generally performed either in the heat of instinct or the frenzy of blood terror. The men who performed these heroics often could not recall them in the aftermath.

Let me say this about courage in combat. In my experience valour in action counts for far less than simply *performing one's commonplace task without cocking it up*. This is by no means as simple as it sounds. In many ways it's the most difficult thing in the world. Certainly for every glorious death memorialised in despatches, one could count twenty others that were the product of fatigue, confusion, inattention, over- or under-assertion of authority, panic, timidity, hesitation, honest errors or mis-calculations, mishaps and accidents, collisions, mechanical breakdowns, lost or forgotten spare parts, intelligence deficiencies, mistranslated codes, late or inadequate medical care, not to say bollocksed-up orders (or the failure to grasp and implement proper orders), misdirected fire from one's own troops or allies, and general all-around muddling, sometimes the fault of the dead trooper himself. The role of the officer in my experience is nothing grander than to stand sentinel over himself and his men, towards the end of keeping them from forgetting who they are and what their objective is, how to get there, and what equipment they're supposed to have when they arrive.

Oh, and getting back. That's the tricky part. Such success as the Long Range Desert Group enjoyed may be credited in no small measure to the superior leadership of Colonel Ralph Bagnold and Lieutenant-Colonel Guy Prendergast, its founder and follow-on OC, for whom the applications of preparation and thoroughness far surpassed those of courage and intrepidity.

Before being seconded to the Long Range Desert Group, I served, as I said, with the 22nd Armoured Brigade of the 7th Armoured Division – the famous 'Desert Rats'. Our regiment was brought forward from the Delta in April and May 1942 as replacement crews during the chaos of the battles of Gazala and the Cauldron. 22nd Armoured Brigade had begun the campaign as part of First Armoured Division but was taken under command of Seventh Armoured Division in the emergency. Her sister armoured regiments (which at that point had been reduced to composite formations) were the 3rd and 4th County of London Yeomanry and the 2nd Royal Gloucestershire Hussars. We too were a Yeomanry regiment, that is, a home formation of the Territorial Army – cavalry recently mechanised and converted to armour.

To the civilian (and to me as well, before I became familiar with them), tanks appear to be invulnerable behemoths beneath the massive bulk of their armour, their great guns, and the deafening clamour of their engines. In reality, a tank

18

is as fragile as a flower. A three-foot slit-trench can snap a track; a too-tight turn can shred the pins that link the treads. An armoured column guzzles petrol; unreplenished, it can stay in action no more than two and a half hours, less over rough going or at speed. The range of a British Matilda was seventy miles; under battle conditions American Stuarts had to fill up every forty.

Tanks advance tethered to their B-echelon vehicles – the unarmoured lorries and trucks that carry the petrol and rations, water, lubricants and ammunition without which the monsters they serve become nothing but clumsy and stationary targets.

A tank depends utterly upon its supporting combat arms. Without infantry to protect its flanks and rear, to knock out anti-tank guns and to clear minefields, a tank is vulnerable to all manner of evils. Without artillery and anti-tank fire to shield it from the enemy's armour, without aircraft to sling bombs and cannon fire at the foe advancing outside its field of vision, the tank is a plum, a bull's-eye, a sitting duck. High-explosive shells can junk its suspension and tracks, armour-piercing rounds rip through its turret. Anti-tank guns can penetrate its armour at two thousand yards. In a tank, fighter planes and bombers are on top of you before you can hear them. You're deaf and blind in a tank.

The commander in a Crusader or an American Grant rides directly above the gearbox and engine, whose combined din screams at such ungodly volume that an enemy shell can explode thirty feet away and you can't hear it. At speed over uneven ground, the tank commander bangs and lurches within the cylinder of his cupola, eyes fixed to his field glasses, ears fastened to his headset, concentrating hour after hour not only upon the flats, hummocks, ravines, wadis, and dead ground of the desert on all sides of him – and of course upon the enemy manoeuvring, lurking and darting over it – but also and without let-up upon the crackling cacophony of his squadron and regimental wireless nets, over which come his orders and his relief, of which he must miss nothing, as his own life and those of his men depend on it. Then there's the heat. Captain James Mattoon, my original squadron leader and a mechanical engineer in civilian life, calculated that an external temperature of 10 degrees Celsius (50 Fahrenheit) was ideal for a tank on the move. At 10 outside, you rode at 20 inside (70 Fahrenheit). For every degree-Fahrenheit rise outside, interior temperature rose a degree and a half. Seventy out was 100 in; 90, 120. At 100 outside – and the thermometer reached and exceeded that every summer day in the desert – you were broiling inside at 135.

Still, I loved tanks. I loved the Armoured Division. What I hated, what we all abhorred, were the vain and courage-crazy tactics which obsolete doctrine and our own undergunned and under-armoured tanks compelled us to employ. While

Rommel's Mark III and Mark IV Panzers advanced in self-covering leapfrogs, backed by crack motorised infantry and screens of lethal 88mm and 50mm anti-tank guns, our Crusaders, Grants and Honeys found themselves again and again on their own, isolated and exposed. Outranged by a thousand yards by the Mark IV's long-barrelled 75s (and nearly as far by the Mark IIIs), our squadrons had no alternative but to dash from one spot of cover to the next, when and if such sites could be discovered, seeking either to flank the foe or to charge at him head-on, usually across open ground, in a desperate attempt to get within gun range before he or his anti-tank screens turned us into flamers or 'brew-ups'. The enemy knew this of course and exploited it with feigned retreats, flanking manoeuvres, and ambushes into which we blundered time and again.

The retreat to the Egyptian frontier in summer 1942 culminated for me in a fiasco on a sandy track alongside the Cairo–Mersa Matruh railway line. My troop of four tanks had been reduced to one Crusader and one American Grant, our squadron having lost, over the preceding twenty-one days, no fewer than nineteen others – Valentines, Honeys, A-10 and A-13 Cruisers, even a pair of captured Italian M-13s. Some had been brought up from the repair shops as replacements, others salvaged intact or refitted in the field, along with their crews, who were cycled through so quickly owing to wounds, death or capture that most barely learnt my name nor I theirs before their place was taken by the next round fresh from the pool companies. On the twenty-first day I found myself separated from my squadron (who were a mile or two ahead), bottlenecked on the track west of Fuka in a hundred-mile traffic jam, still that distance short of Alexandria, with a hundred more to Cairo. My wife Rose was a Navy telegrapher in Alexandria; she was pregnant with our first child. I was desperate to get her evacuated before Rommel and Panzerarmee Afrika overran Egypt all the way to Suez. Suddenly I spotted a break in the line of lorries, with clear sailing ahead, cross-country, at least enough to get round the jam and rejoin my squadron. 'Driver, hard right,' I commanded. Off we rumbled, steamrolling a wire barrier, directly on to a Mark IV mine.

No one was hurt but my right track and front ventilator were blown to hell. Under favourable conditions, the crew can refit a shed track by locking the steering on the unspooled side, railway-tracking spare plates beneath the spooled side, then using the power of the still-shod track to inch forward over this newly cobbled sheath, while the fitters on the ground manhandle the heavy plates into position, replace the blown ones with spares, and re-pin them. That option was out of the question in the middle of a minefield. Meanwhile the mortification grew more excruciating by the moment. Before the unstifled glee of several hundred onlooking officers and other ranks, I baled out with my crew, intending to back-track on foot out of the minefield, where I would take over my other, still-mobile tank. The humiliation was unalleviated by the spectacle of driver, gunner and wireless operator emerging from our tank, arms laden with tins of apricots, cigarettes and Italian ham, not to mention half a dozen bottles of Boar's Head gin, all looted on the retreat. Our commanding officer, a colonel with whom I had had a run-in several days earlier in the desert, chose that moment to appear on the shoulder of the track and, standing tall within the turret of his Grant, commanded me and my crew to return to our disabled tank and climb back aboard. He indicated a signboard poking up beside what was left of the wire. 'I say, Lieutenant, can you read that posting?'

I replied that I could.

'What does it say?'

'It says "minefield", sir.'

'Whose minefield?'

'Ours, sir.'

'Then what, upon Christ's twisted Cross, are you doing in it?'

He demanded my name and unit, though he knew both well, and instructed his adjutant by signal to report me. I and my crew were to stay put until a squad of sappers could be called to carve us a way out.

But I have got ahead of my story. I must reverse and set down the approach march, so to speak, without which this tale will make no sense, to the reader or to me. If this were a work of fiction, and I its editor, I would urge the writer to dramatise such events as hold significance for the narrative's thesis. But I have no patience for such stuff in my own memoir, so the reader will forgive me, I hope, if I simply lay out the essentials overtly, as they were and as they felt to me.

CHAPTER 2

I am a product of the English public school system. I state this neither as a badge of honour nor as a blot of shame, only as a foundation in fact, from which I venture the thesis that this often nasty, brutish, and peculiarly British institution, whatever its other shortcomings, must be given credit for producing a type of citizen who came into his own during the war, in the officer corps of all theatres, but specifically, in my own experience, in the Western Desert.

What is it about featureless wastes that appeals so powerfully to the Anglo-Saxon soul? William Kennedy Shaw, who served from its inception as intelligence officer of the Long Range Desert Group, relates the tale of a captured German officer transported from Kufra to Cairo by one of the LRDG's patrols, nearly seven hundred miles in unarmoured Chevrolet trucks across such appalling wilderness that even native Senussi tribesmen rarely dared venture into it. After several days of observing the Long Range Desert Group's Tommies and Kiwis imperturbably at their labours, the prisoner confided to his captors, 'We Germans could never pull off this trick as you do, wandering about on your own, miles from anywhere. We lack the individual initiative. We prefer to run in a pack.'

What appeared as unendurable hardship to soldiers of other nationalities produced a species of exhilaration in our lads, raised on a diet of Kipling and institutional porridge. Some time after the war I ran into a school chum, a pilot, Flight-Lieutenant S., who had been shot down over Holland in 1940 and had endured the better part of four years in Oflag Luft III, most notorious of the camps for Allied fliers. When I asked him to describe the experience, he replied, 'A bit like Marlborough, only with better breakfasts.'

The English educational system for the privileged classes of that era was made up of two tiers – public school and university. When war came, a third tier was appended, the regimental, so that a young man might be identified as, say, Harrow/Oxford/Scots Greys or Ampleforth/-Cambridge/the Guards, which venues of passage cast, or reinforced, the graduate in a sliver of social hierarchy from which no earthly intervention could extract him – Old Rich, New Rich, Newly Ruined, Anciently Impoverished. My own family was Old Rich Freshly Ruined on my father's side and Never Rich At All on my mother's.

At Winchester when I was thirteen there were three heating stoves, two half-sized baths and one WC in a boarding house housing thirty pupils. We used chamber pots at night. In winter, water froze in our drinking pitchers. Winchester boys were called 'commoners'. We wore ties in the classroom and caps and gowns on examination days. Twenty cigarettes cost a shilling with a penny back in the packet. We read in Greek Xenophon's *March of the Ten Thousand* and in Latin Livy's history of Rome, not to mention all of Chaucer, Milton and Shakespeare, and the main freight of Marlowe, Coleridge, Hardy, Arnold, Tennyson, Thackeray, Dickens and Conrad, while participating in all weathers in football, rugby, cricket, rowing, riding and track and field, as well as attending religious services, usually Anglican, not once on Sunday but five times a week.

Many boys saw their parents at the holidays only; some not even then. They raised each other like feral beasts with all the outrages and excesses that such an upbringing implies. For most, it worked. The public schools of that era produced a type of young man who was keen but not academic, athletic but not muscle-bound, gay of heart and confident of mien, a solid chap, the sort who would sooner die than let the side down. Put another way, the system turned out the kind of individual who frequently displayed boredom or feckless complacency during times of prosperity, but shone through in hours of trial. I have often wondered of comrades who fell as heroes during the war whether, in the fatal instant, they weren't privately relieved to do so, dreading a deadly post-war normality more than the bullets and cannon shells of the foe.

★   ★   ★

When I was twelve, my mother was killed in a motor accident. I am not a subscriber to the theory of traumatic psychopathology. It is humbug, in my view, to isolate some episode from childhood and extrapolate from it an aberration of character, indelible for the remainder of one's life. That said, some wounds go deep. My father, who had been driving at the time of the accident, suffered far worse than I. He could not overcome his grief and guilt. He soon withdrew, first from work, then from family, at last by his own hand from life itself. I have three sisters: Edna, Charlotte, and Margaret Anne. After the deaths of my mother and father, our two uncles, my father's brothers, in whose care we children were placed, thought it best that we be sent to boarding schools. My sisters were enrolled in St Catherine's, an Anglican academy in Herefordshire near the town of Hay-on-Wye. I was sent to Winchester.

The night of my father and mother's accident, my sisters and I were driven to the hospital by our neighbours in their 1924 Humber sedan, a car I adored because it had a jump-seat in the back, which folded up from the floor. My sisters disdained this as undignified, which was a joy to me as I got it all to myself. No one had told us yet what had happened or where we were going. We could scent the wind, however, and this cast a pall over the ride. My sisters were weeping already.

At the hospital a nurse instructed us to wait in

an area of wooden benches. My sisters obeyed gravely; our neighbours, an elderly couple, sat up with us. At the end of the hallway stood two wide, handleless doors, through which from time to time nurses pushed trolleys. On the far side of these, our mother lay in surgery. The doctors were labouring heroically, we were told, to save her. Our father's injuries were less severe; he was being treated in another wing.

We waited. How long would the operation take? No one could tell us. Hours seemed to pass. Our caretakers would not let me go outside so I excused myself to find the lavatory. I poked down a hallway. A passage opened on to a corridor of patients' rooms, from which a nurse chased me. A dim space led to a kind of anteroom. I entered. In the corner sat a surgical trolley. On it was my mother's body.

The bloody clothes from the accident had been wadded into a ball and dumped on to the trolley shelf below. My mother herself lay beneath a white surgical sheet, which had fallen partly free, exposing her nakedness from waist to neck. She lay on her side, with her right arm dangling grotesquely. Her mouth was agape; she was already going stiff. No one was about. The institutional custodians had just left her there.

A child sees and understands far more than grown-ups believe. I knew at once that this was death. My mother was gone; this inert object was not she. She was with Jesus or amongst the stars. I didn't believe any of that, but I repeated it to myself as I imagined I ought. I told myself I should not be angry. The hospital had many patients besides my mother whose needs were urgent. At times, the overtaxed staff had no alternative but to stick a dead person temporarily out of the way so that they could get on to other emergencies. The nurses would return soon, I was certain, and restore my mother to dignity.

But I knew this was rubbish. I hated the authorities for leaving her like this, even for a moment. And I was furious with them for not telling my sisters and me. For how long did the hospital intend to hold us in suspense, believing that our mother might yet survive, when in truth her cold corpse had been dumped and forgotten in this shameful siding? I crossed to the trolley and repaired my mother's modesty. I worked the rings off her fingers and put them in my pocket. I didn't want the staff stealing them.

My sisters told me later that I reappeared in the corridor in a state such as they had never seen. 'Your face was scarlet,' Edna said. 'Tears were streaming down your cheeks.' The surgeons, a young man and a senior, had just that moment emerged from the rear doors. 'Without a word, you sprinted the length of the hall and hurled yourself upon them, kicking and punching.' In the end, my sisters told me, I had to be given a sedative and carried physically to the car. I have no recollection of that. What does remain, with blazing clarity, is this.

My mother's death was my fault.

I knew this instinctively and with every cell of my body. I had caused her end. How? By being too young and too small to protect her. Had I been driving the car instead of my father, no accident would have happened. Had I been with them even as a passenger, somehow I would have preserved her. But I wasn't there. Because of my absence, my mother was dead.

A child does not understand with reason. Later at university we studied Freud, Adler and Jung. I could grasp intellectually the preposterousness of this childish belief. But rationality is powerless against emotion.

Not long after that night, my uncles' influence got me into Winchester. Before then I had never been in trouble at school; from that date I was rarely out of it. I got into scrapes daily, with the other boys and with the masters. I hated them all. I despised the school and every sham rite and cruel tradition it prided itself upon. The house I was assigned to was called Kingsgate. Each house had three prefects. These were sixth-formers who received privileges in return for acting as counsellors and maintaining order. Our prefects were Tallicott, Martin, and Zachary Stein. Stein was a Jew. Rumour declared him a poet. I knew only that he was tall and rich and spent a lot of time in his room. He had an American Schwinn bicycle, with an illustration of a Red Indian on the chain-guard, which he rode in all weathers.

I came in with two other boys whose names I forget. We were all thirteen. The older youths at once gave us the treatment. I had no experience of boarding school and was not prepared for this. In addition I was both a 'muley' (an orphan) and a 'duff' (a hardship case), meaning I inhabited the absolute basement of the pecking order. The other two new boys alternated between rage and despair as each new indignity was heaped upon us. They hated the older boys and burned with murderous fantasies; that, or worshipped them shamelessly. I would do neither. I held in contempt the seniors who inflicted these abuses upon us. They perceived this of course and gave it to me twice over.

By then I was having a recurring nightmare. In the dream I found myself beside a lake at twilight. A mist stood on the water. My mother's body lay on a barge, swathed in silk and flowers; her eyes were closed, hands folded across her breast. Yet I was certain she was alive. Suddenly the barge was either pushed or began to move of its own accord, away from shore and into the mist, which I understood to mean oblivion. I had to save her! In a state of desperation I plunged into the lake, hands stretching for the boat to pull it back. A great weight of iron – a garment of some kind – dragged me down. My mother's sleeping form slipped from my grasp. I woke in a state of dread and consternation.

The culmination of the initiation ordeals at Winchester is a rite called the 'freeze-out'. This was a tradition at the school. Upon a bitterly frigid night, we new boys were stripped of mufflers and overcoats and locked out in the storm. We had been told by one of the more kindly sixth-formers that the torture would not last all night. The seniors would observe us in secret; when we had turned blue enough to satisfy the demands of the trial, they would fetch us back indoors. My fellow sufferers clung together, overacting their misery. I despised them. I would not give our tormentors the satisfaction.

I began walking. I was going home.

I made my way to the railway station. The place was deserted. I set off down the tracks. How far I marched, I don't know. At some point I lay down in the snow.

Stein, the prefect, saved me. He told me later he had sensed the freeze-out coming, but had been fooled by the older boys, who had made pillow-dummies of me and the other two and put them in our beds. Stein didn't realise what had happened till the frozen pair were brought back indoors. How did he find me? From my tracks in the snow and his own imagination. The train station. Home. He was a poet; he could figure it out.

I was lying on my side on the tracks when I heard the tinny bell of Stein's American Schwinn. 'Chapman! Where in damnation are you?' I had never heard a sixth-former employ such language. Stein pedalled up. He was frightened; he thought I was dead. He wrapped me in a woollen blanket.

Close behind him came the master's assistant in an ancient Peugeot. The assistant pulled up on the road that paralleled the tracks. Stein carried me through the woods to the car.

'You better not pop off, you little sod,' the master's assistant said as he bundled me through the passenger door and up against the machine's feeble heater. Stein wrapped me in the blanket and his own greatcoat, cursing when the assistant botched the clutch and stalled. 'Is this little twit going to croak?' the fellow demanded.

Stein produced a silver flask. 'He'll be fine,' he said, lifting the whisky to my lips. 'He just wants a stiff belt.'

CHAPTER 3

At Oxford, Stein was my tutor. For those unfamiliar with the tutorial system, it works like this. A student at university acquires his education by attending lectures and seminars given by dons. Attendance is voluntary. Theoretically you could duck every lecture – as some did, myself amongst them, passing the hours playing croquet on the lawns behind Magdalen, my college – and still graduate with a First. But you must be examined and demonstrate mastery of the material.

To assist the student in this, the university assigns him a tutor. Tutors are usually shaggy, ill-groomed junior dons who smoke and drink to excess and never leave their rooms except for illicit sexual liaisons or to replenish their stocks of tobacco and spirits. A good tutor can make one's college experience a revolutionary passage, to life as well as to literature; a bad one can make it misery. The college provides accommodation for each tutor, usually in double suites with another tutor (Stein's rooms were actually at Trinity College, where he was pursuing his own doctorate) with a kitchen and bath/WC, two sleeping rooms, and a sitting room between. The latter was invariably a hellhole, overheated in winter to a point barely shy of combustion, and knee-deep in texts, papers and the usual detritus of the academic life. I loved Stein's sitting room. It was the first home I'd had since my mother died.

I went up to Oxford because of Stein. His letters and testimonials got me in. Stein had eight or nine other pupils, among whom was Alan 'Jock' McCall of Golspie, Sutherland. Jock became my closest friend. In those days, to be an all-round chap was the ideal. Jock was that – a crack quarter-miler, brilliant essayist, undergraduate editor of the *Cherwell* in his second year, an unheard-of honour – though I abhorred his politics, which were thoroughly military and imperialist. Jock's sister Rose became my bride, to whom I have been blissfully wed for more than thirty years. But again I'm getting ahead of my story.

Stein was five years my senior. He was twenty-four when I arrived at Oxford and already a published poet. Beyond his own studies in Milton, in which field he was known even then as an authority, he was working on a novel. This impressed me even more. Stein refused to show pages to anyone or even to reveal his subject. Rumours, however, declared it homoerotic and political. 'So,' Jock used to ask me as he arrived for his tutorial, immediately after mine, 'what have you and Oscar Wilde been chatting about today?'

Stein's tone towards me was one of affectionate irony. He teased me constantly, usually over my 'black Irish', meaning the moodiness that descended upon me with such regularity, which I had acquired, Stein speculated, from my Irish mother.

Stein had a theory that there was a difference between Jewish despair and Irish despair. 'Jewish despair arises from want and can be cured by surfeit. Give a penniless Jew fifty quid and he perks right up. Irish despair is different. Nothing relieves Irish despair. The Irishman's complaint lies not with his circumstances, which might be rendered brilliant by labour or luck, but with the injustice of existence itself. Death! How could a benevolent Deity gift us with life, only to set such a cruel term upon it? Irish despair knows no remedy. Money doesn't help. Love fades; fame is fleeting. The only cures are booze and sentiment. That's why the Irish are such noble drunks and glorious poets. No one sings like the Irish or mourns like them. Why? Because they're angels imprisoned in vessels of flesh.'

When I told Stein of my recurring nightmare, his immediate question was, 'What garment of iron are you wearing that drags you down?' When I described it, he said at once: 'Armour.' I had never thought of that.

Stein's conclusion was that I was at heart a knight and that the mystery of my life could never be solved without taking into account the centrality of that vocation.

Stein lifted my gloom. His example gave me permission to seek my truest self. He assigned me readings far beyond the scope of university instruction. With Jock and others, we talked of literature for hours. Under Stein's tutelage, I blossomed both as a writer and as a critic of writing. I lost my fear of seeming smart, of standing out or appearing different.

Amongst the many qualities I admired in Stein, foremost was his refusal to be anything other than who he was. In those days to be a homosexual, even in a university setting, was something one dared not speak of. It was against the law. You could go to prison. Certainly your career could be impeded. Stein didn't give a damn. 'A Jew, a poet and a poof,' he declared of himself. 'The hat trick of social undesirability!'

Once, in the dining hall, Jock and I got into a row over Stein. Jock respected Stein but avoided him in public. A too-close association, he believed, could do harm to one's standing. 'Balls,' I told him. 'Stein's keener than half these bloody dons, he's twice the writer, works three times as hard; he's the only one who actually takes time for his pupils, and he's got the courage to speak his mind, unlike these other careerist bootlickers.'

Stein's politics were left and radical. He was wildly rich. I visited the family estate once in the West Riding of Yorkshire; the grounds covered seven hundred acres. Stein was related to the Rothschilds on his father's side; his mother was descended from Benjamin Disraeli's niece. The family fortune came from wool. The Lederers, Stein's mother's family, owned mills at Bradford, Leeds and Bingley. Stein's great-grandfather Hyman had pioneered the concept of the factory village. He provided housing, education and medical care for his workers, of a standard surpassing anything of the time. His essay 'On the Perfectibility of Human Nature' was required reading in my Natural Sciences course.

In those days at Oxford, the social roost was ruled by an elect spawned of the wealthiest and most ancient families, who possessed or affected the following constellation of virtues: athletic prowess, especially if acquired without apparent effort; capacity for alcohol consumption; reckless physical daring, particularly involving horses, heights or motor cars; contempt for all affairs of religion, politics or commerce; and a withering disdain for academia and academic achievement. The scions of this elite by no means despised Hitler; many applauded the Munich Pact of 1938. They viewed with scorn the 'red' opponents of appeasement. In their eyes Churchill was little better – an arch-conservative jingoist and warmonger.

I hated these bastards. So did Stein. At Winchester he had been famous for abhorring the twentieth century. He refused to learn to drive. He believed in reincarnation. Asked what religion he followed, he answered 'Hindu'. He spoke and read French, German and Italian and could translate classical Greek and Latin as fast as he could read them. The more anti-Semitism he observed in government and in the press, however, the more he identified with his co-religionists and the more outspoken he became on their behalf. He penned letters to the editor; he wrote cheques to all sorts of causes. By the time I reached Oxford, Stein was reading six newspapers a day. I know because he sent me down to the newsagent to pick them up. Stein demonstrated with the Communists outside Parliament. He was arrested. In the late thirties, as I said, there was tremendous pro-German and pro-National Socialist feeling in England. Stein's hair was too long, his dress too unkempt. He was 'not the right sort'. Rumours began. Stein laughed them off, declaring that such calumnies were the same as those levelled against Socrates – inventing new gods and corrupting the young.

Stein's downfall came about because of an undergraduate I shall call B. (B., a fine rugby wing, became a Royal Marine and was killed piloting an assault craft at Gold Beach on D-Day, 6 June 1944.) B. fell in love with Stein. But he never told him. He confined his passion to entries in his private diary, no doubt terrified of the consequences, should he dare act upon his impulses. Somehow B.'s father, a prominent solicitor, learnt of this. The next thing anyone knew, two police inspectors appeared at Stein's door. Stein assumed that his offence was connected to his activities on behalf of refugee Jews.

'It's the Amendment Act,' said the policemen.

This was a charge of 'gross indecency' and 'solicitation of unnatural vice'. Stein was arrested for having seduced a boy he had never met. In the end, the charges were dropped for want of evidence. Not, however, before Stein had become notorious. In those days such a scandal might have been weathered by a tenured don; for a tutor it was fatal.

Worse were the consequences for Stein's novel. B.'s father, it seems, was not content with running Stein out of Oxford; he made it his business to finish him in the world of letters as well. At that time, there were only a handful of houses with the intrepidity to publish the type of novel Stein was writing; it was no chore for B.'s father to persuade them of the inadvisability of such a course. Stein went to the man and confronted him. I went with him to back him up. This was at B.'s father's offices in Great Titchfield Street. The old man had us thrown out.

Throughout it all, Stein affected to be aloof and amused. But we who knew him could see that he took the affair hard – the meanness of it and the bitter, small-minded malice. 'It's literature's loss,' declared one of our fellow pupils one night in Stein's rooms.

Stein laughed. 'Not to mention England's.'

Of course none of us had read his manuscript. Stein had shown it to no one.

The caucus broke up. We students felt like the

disciples at Gethsemane. When Stein asked me to stick around, I imagined he wished to discuss my work in Milton, which was faltering. The rooms cleared out. Stein poured sherry.

'Chap, would you consider taking a squint at my manuscript?'

I was speechless.

'It would have to be tonight,' said Stein. 'You'll need to read it here. I have no other copy, and I can't let you take the pages away.'

It would be my privilege, I said. I only hoped I'd prove worthy.

'Don't disparage your capacity, Chap. You've a keen mind. I can think of no one whose opinion I should value more.'

I stayed up all night. I read the manuscript straight through, returning to critical passages twice and even three times. The book was far more political than sexual. It was Swift, not Rabelais. Stein's reach was fearless; the work bore ambition beyond anything I had anticipated. And it was funny. I was terrified of offering some boneheaded critique, particularly now that Stein had demonstrated such faith in me. The tower bell tolled six; I asked Stein if I could have the rest of the morning to order my thoughts. 'No,' he said. 'It has to be now.'

We walked down by the river. I proffered reams of conventional praise. Stein chafed. He was getting angry. We had stopped at a bench beneath a row of hornbeam trees. Stein drew on his dead-coals pipe. I took a breath.

'The book is too good, Stein. Too true, too brave. Too far ahead of anything the public will tolerate. No publisher will have the guts to bring it out, and if they did, the critics would savage it and crucify you.'

I had dreaded offering this assessment, which I was certain was accurate and which I feared would devastate Stein. Instead he threw back his head and loosed a great, roaring whoop. 'Chapman, my friend, let's get bloody, stinking pissed!'

My review, it turned out, had been precisely what Stein had hoped for.

'By God, if you had offered tamer praise, I'd have leapt in the flipping river.'

I couldn't get drunk with Stein that day; I had two examinations and a rowing club meeting to attend. 'Why,' I asked him, 'did you need me to read this so fast?'

'Because,' he said, 'I've joined the army.'

He took the train to Aldershot that afternoon. The date was February 1939. War with Hitler was only half a year away.

CHAPTER 4

S tein enlisted as a private soldier but was soon summoned forth and commissioned. The army assigned him to the Royal Horse Artillery, the smartest of the gunnery regiments. We celebrated one night in late summer at a pub called the Melbourne in Knightsbridge; Jock with his sweetheart Sheila, I with Jock's sister Rose. Stein was fresh out of OCTU – Officer Cadet Training Unit – at Sandhurst. He looked fit and military in his RHA uniform with its single second lieutenant's pip.

'Do you really have horses,' Rose teased, 'in the Royal Horse Artillery?'

'Horses? We're lucky to have artillery!'

Stein had orders for Egypt. Wavell's Army of the Nile was defending Cairo and the Canal from thirteen divisions of Mussolini's *fascisti*, who were building up in Cyrenaica and out-numbered our fellows by between five and ten to one. Stein entertained us with tales of his training as a FOO, a forward observation officer whose role it was to direct the gunnery of his battery of 25-pounders. He talked of 'surveys' and 'time on target'. All this was Greek to me but Stein, to his own surprise as well as mine and Jock's, seemed to be thriving on it. His ship sailed in twenty days; he would spend his embarkation leave with his family in Yorkshire.

'Will you look after something for me, Chap?'

And he produced his manuscript.

Rose frowned. 'There's nothing morbid in this overture, is there, Stein? For I won't stand you forecasting some dire fate for yourself.'

'My dear,' said he, 'I shall outlive you all.'

Rose, as I said, was Jock's younger sister. During our first terms at Magdalen, Sheila would take the train from London at the weekend. Rose came along to keep the thing from appearing unseemly. Inevitably she and I were thrown together.

If it is possible to be a double, or even triple, virgin, such was my state at that time. The concept of sex, let alone love, seemed absolutely unreachable. I had never known a woman, save my mother, to see past my surface presentation – and certainly none who actually believed in me. Rose changed that. From the first instant, I felt that she saw through to *me* – to a 'me' that I was but could not yet grasp. She saw that 'me' and all future 'me's and believed in them all. As for her, the first time I saw her, I thought she was the most ravishing creature I had ever set eyes upon. And she had wit. I had never known a girl who made me laugh. Rose feared no one and was kind to all, especially to me, a phenomenon I could not begin to make sense of. I could not imagine being worthy of her and would no more have pressed my physical attentions upon her than flown to the moon. Rather, the emotion I felt towards her was one of fierce protectiveness. She seemed, from the first, so precious that I would have hurled myself into fire in her defence.

When you're young and without resources, you have no place to go. Rose and I had no private rooms, no car, no way out of the weather. It seemed we were outdoors all the time. It was wonderful. Only Stein took us in. He made pots of tea and sat up with us till all hours, talking politics and poetry.

Rose and I corresponded by mail. I still had not kissed her. It took me weeks to summon the temerity simply to upgrade my salutation from 'Dear Miss McCall' to 'My dear Miss McCall'. At the same time, I knew with absolute certainty that she and I would be married. I never said a word, nor did she. But we both knew it, and we knew that we knew it. At Oxford each college has its own rowing club short of the varsity Blues. I rowed in Magdalen's. There is a competition in the early summer called Eights Week, a rather smart event in the university calendar. Rose came up to cheer me on. I can't remember what place our boat took, but in the warm evening afterwards, when Rose and I as usual had no place to go, we walked with another couple along the river. A storm had got up; the four of us ducked for shelter into one of the boathouses. The other couple immediately began having it off in the one dry corner, an act that in those days was audacious beyond belief. Rose and I were mortified. We slipped out under the eaves. Our companions' passion continued unabated. We gave up waiting and simply set off into the rain. I was so in love, I could barely draw breath. Suddenly I felt Rose take my hand. The rush of blood nearly made me faint.

We began a romance. I fell into it like a man dropping off the edge of the earth. The innocence of our lovemaking would strain the credulity of today's youth. Yet chastity did not preclude passion. We found places for trysts. Hideouts in the woods, back seats of cars. We took hotel rooms, registering as husband and wife.

One night Jock caught Rose and me emerging from rooms above a pub on the High Street, in front of a pharmacy that's no longer there called Saxon Chemists. Jock was with Sheila; clearly they'd been doing the same thing and probably a lot more. 'Damn you, Chapman! Where have you been with my sister?'

Jock was a skilled amateur boxer. In a flash his fists went up; I tackled him to keep him from swinging. The scene devolved into low burlesque, with the pair of us crashing together into the rows of bicycles parked along the pavement while our young ladies beat our backs with their handbags, clamouring for us to stop. Two policemen pulled us apart. Jock was hauling Rose away. She jerked free. 'Piss off, Jock!'

She crossed to me; I took her under my arm.

Jock goggled in consternation. 'Bloody hell, Rose! Is this the kind of language you've caught from him?' He glared at me. 'What have you to say, you damned sod?'

I took a breath. 'Your sister's with me, Jock. That's it.'

Rose's arms tightened round my waist. I had never been happier in my life.

For months, Jock wouldn't speak to me. This was at the moment in Stein's scandal when the college was physically evicting him. I had read Stein's novel by then. When Stein left for the army, I took it upon myself to see the book published, if I had to bring it out myself, hand printed and hand bound. Rose backed me up. We spent days at a time in London, resubmitting the manuscript to every house that had turned it down. An editor at Lion's Gate mulled it briefly, imagining war breaking out and Stein dying as a hero. Novels by gallantly fallen authors sell better. 'We'll speak to Stein,' said Rose. 'Perhaps we can arrange to have him catch it precisely upon date of publication.'

Rose was living at home then. Her father, a Territorial Army colonel, took a dim view of her liaison with a penniless, academically faltering university student. He ordered Rose 'confined to quarters'. She sneaked out anyway. We'd meet in tube stations and news arcades, riding for hours on buses or the underground. Just before the autumn term, Rose left school and moved out on her own. She found a flat at Shepherd's Bush and a job in a print shop. 'It's positively Dickensian.' She loved it. We planned to marry. I was set to return to Oxford. Then came 1 September 1939.

Hitler invades Poland! Two days later the nation was at war.

There was no question but that I would enlist. What astonished me was the intensity of my reaction. At once, all clouds lifted. Clarity returned. I loved Rose and I was going off to fight. The only question was where to enlist and in what capacity.

Of all people, it was B. who decided my course – the unfortunate fellow whose infatuation with Stein had kicked off this whole debacle. He had come to Stein at the height of the scandal and apologised. Astonishingly he and Stein became friends. I liked him too. It was B. who suggested that he and I enlist as private soldiers. We drove to the recruiting station in Kensington in the rain in his '32 Standard. B. was ecstatic. 'Tell me, Chapman, do you feel as I do? I'm overwhelmed by relief. I feel as if I've been waiting for something all my life and now it's here.' This was the moment, he declared. 'History. Great events.'

At Kensington, the various regiments had set up tables on the pavement under awnings, each manned by a senior NCO and each with a queue of young men waiting before it in the rain. B. went straight for the Royal Marines. I set out seeking the Staffordshire Yeomanry, in which my father and uncles had served. The recruiting sergeant informed me that a young man with my qualifications – that is, more than two years of university – would be enrolled at once in OCTU and sent straight to Sandhurst. This, I knew from Stein and other friends, could mean, with specialised training afterwards, a year or longer before getting into action. I baulked. Behind the adjacent table sat a lean sergeant major of about forty. He had been talking to two potential enlistees, but I could see that with one ear he had been keeping tabs on my conversation as well. Propped before him, half sodden in the drizzle, stood a recruiting poster depicting that armoured clanker I would come to know at Bovington as a Nuffield Cruiser A-9. A name plate said:

SGT-MAJ STREETER, ROYAL TANK REGIMENT

'Why walk,' he said, 'when you can ride?'

He promised that if I took the King's shilling that day, he'd have me on my way to battling the Hun in twenty-six weeks.

Rose was the only one who approved of my decision. My uncles were apoplectic. Rose herself had signed to be a Volunteer Air Warden and was applying for training as an ambulance driver. We all felt that way then. We would have drained our blood for England.

Jock and I repaired our friendship some months later. Jock had enlisted with the Cameron Highlanders, his family's regiment for five generations. He could not forgive me for the 'liberties I had taken' with his sister. 'But,' he wrote, 'it's my own fault for putting her in harm's way.' He added that he would give me two choices for the war ahead – get killed or marry Rose.

The platform at Victoria Station was packed with enlistees and their sweethearts seeing them off for the various training depots. The mood was not brash and gay as it had been in our fathers' time, the Great War. Neither was it grave, as it ought to have been. Rather, as B. had said, the sensation was one of overwhelming relief. One felt released from a state of excruciating suspense and set free on to the field of action.

At last, I thought, I am neither too small nor too young to defend my country and the woman I love.

CHAPTER 5

The training depot of the Royal Armoured Corps, as it was then coming to be called, was at Bovington Camp in Dorset. The place was packed with enlistees and conscripts; by the time the contingent I was with arrived, there was no room for us in barracks. We were housed instead in twelve-man tents with plank floors and one three-hole latrine for every four tents. After initial 'square-bashing', the driver's course was sixteen weeks. We practised first on light 15-hundredweight trucks, then 30-hundred-weights, then 3-tonners, learning to operate on paved roads, cross-country and over obstacle courses. After six weeks we graduated to tracked vehicles: first Bren carriers, then light tanks. We learnt to ford streams, surmount stone walls; we drilled at binding fascines (great bundles of timber or pipe) and using them to cross anti-tank ditches. When it came time to train on full-sized tanks, the depot had so few that we had to use dummies fabricated from original Holt Caterpillar farm tractors, the old DCMs from the Great War. A shell of wood and canvas was mounted over the steering station so that the learning driver could not see ahead. Above and behind him sat a second recruit, the 'tank commander', who possessed a view over the top of the cab. The commander shouted directions – 'Driver, advance! Driver, hard left!' – while the poor bugger in the blind-box heaved against the steering levers and wrestled the massive clutch, simultaneously working the two throttles and clanging through the gears of the unsynchronised double-clutch crash-box. You turn a tank not with a wheel but by levers and pedals, retarding one track while advancing the other. This is not easy. Turn too tight and you snap the track pins; the track comes spooling off its sprockets like toilet tissue from a thrown roll. When this happens, the crew have to sort the mess out themselves.

Dearest Rose,
    I should not be enjoying myself as much as I am, I know, given the desperate state of affairs in Europe. Still, I am having fun! The commanding officer of our training regiment has called me out for officer training, as the army has every man with even ten minutes at university, but he says I must learn to drive a tank in any event, so I might as well stay and finish the course.

The training got easier when we moved to Lulworth to practise on A-9s and 10s – real tanks

– and the new A-13s, the first of that series to be called Crusaders. If you were a driver/operator, as all of us were, you learnt to work the wireless as well. We had to master every skill in the tank, so that a loader could stand in for a driver or a wireless operator and all at a pinch could take over as commander. In addition we were required to learn maintenance. The instructors, most of whom were fitters drafted out of civilian garages, taught us by deliberately putting vehicles out of action – disabling cooling-systems, clogging fuel lines and so forth. We were supposed to diagnose the problem and come up with the fix, while our teachers ranted in our ears, 'What's the hold-up, cock? Set the bleeder right, can't you?' Physical training consisted of three-mile and five-mile trots with steel helmets, laden rucksacks, and rifles at port arms. One morning on a run my legs gave out beneath me. An ambulance took me to hospital, where an Indian major who spoke the most flawless English I had ever heard examined me sole to crown. 'I'm sorry,' he said. 'You've got polio.'

In those days, a diagnosis of infantile paralysis was the most frightful finding a patient could hear. The disease was virulent, infectious, and incurable. Paralysis started in the legs, then worked up into the torso, eventually reaching the lungs, so that the victim could not even breathe without the aid of a monstrous mechanical contraption called an iron lung, in which he was imprisoned, immobile and flat on his back. Yet, terrified as I was by the medical side of the calamity, the thought of dropping out of training was even worse. Why was this so important to me? I can't say, even today. I doubt that many of my contemporaries could either. We were simply driven to get into the fight or, perhaps more to the point, to *not be left out*. Absurd as it sounds, for me the dread of spending the rest of my life as an invalid paled alongside the agony of being shunted to the sidelines, unable to aid England while she stood in mortal peril.

The army quarantined me and shipped me off-depot to a civilian polio ward. Rose came on the run. She refused to accept the diagnosis. She got into a table-banging row with my second or third doctor, I forget which; he would not discharge me for fear of infection in the community, while Rose would not hear of my staying on the ward, where I would almost certainly be stricken if I wasn't already. At the same time she began her own independent research of medical journals, physicians' articles and case histories; she made herself an expert on all forms of viral disorder, particularly those which attack the sheaths of the nerve canals. In the end I was passed through six wards in three hospitals, each time receiving a different diagnosis. By now I had lost motor function below the waist and was running a fever of 103. My commanding officer, a decent chap, visited me in hospital to congratulate me on my acceptance to

OCTU. The course started in ten days. 'We'll hold a place for you, Chapman,' he said with a look that communicated that he never expected to see me again.

I was placed on convalescent leave. Rose took me home to her sister's family's farm at Golspie. We were married from there, at Dornoch Cathedral, with me in a wheelchair and my two weeks' army pay packet – one pound six shillings – in my pocket. I shall never forget the faith and kindness of Rose's family, particularly her sister Evelyn and brother-in-law Angus, whose cottage we lived in all that winter, spring and summer. They took me in as if I were their own blood. There was a disease similar to polio, Rose had learnt, called transverse myelitis. The doctors confirmed this. It was sometimes called 'false polio'.

With Rose's aid, I struggled to walk. I hobbled first on crutches, in leg braces, just the fifty yards out to the farm steading. Later we struck for the post box, about a hundred and fifty yards. The day I could climb the hill to the house – a full furlong – we all got gloriously drunk.

The town golf course at Golspie runs along Dornoch Firth; I began walking there morning and evening with Rose and a local hound named Jack who had adopted us and met us without fail at the first tee. Till then I had known nothing about golf. I thought it an old man's game. But as Rose and I trekked back and forth day after day, the brusque great-heartedness of the local players, mostly veterans of Great War vintage, touched me and made me appreciate the dour beauty of the game. I still could not swing a club. I would come home from walking three or four holes, so exhausted that I could not mount the steps to the house. Inside, I collapsed into a chair as if dead.

Throughout this period, letters came from Stein in North Africa. He had been wounded in action against Graziani's Italians, promoted to first lieutenant and mentioned in despatches. He was a hero. Jock had been in France and barely got out at Dunkirk. I envied them desperately, as I did every man who could stand and walk and do his bit. On the farm, all chores revolved round supplying the troops. The barley crop, which before the war had gone for Scotch whisky distilled locally at Glenmorangie, was now contracted to the Office of Procurement for cereal, soup and fodder. Spitfire pilots were training at Nairn; we'd see them practising 'touch-and-goes' from the fairways there and at Royal Dornoch. A coast watch was on night and day; ammunition bunkers were going in at Brora and every twenty miles along the road to John o' Groats.

By midsummer I could walk thirty-six holes. The Royal Armoured Corps would not take me back till I had passed the PHT, the physical hardiness test, a sort of obstacle course that all applicants for Officer Cadet Training Unit must complete in under a certain time. By luck, the scorer assigned to my group was Sergeant-Major Streeter, the same man who had recruited me at his pavement table at Kensington. My tally was 47 out of a possible 50. I was in. Years later I ran into Streeter on a platform at Waterloo Station; he confessed that my real score had been 27, failure. 'My pencil slipped, I reckon.'

In the end my diagnosis was confirmed as false polio. It retreated the way it had come, from trunk to thighs to calves and, at last, entirely.

France fell while I was recuperating; the Battle of Britain raged; Hitler was preparing his invasion of Russia. By spring 1941, when I had at last completed OCTU, Rommel had arrived in Tunisia with the Afrika Korps. His first onslaught had caught our Western Desert Force off guard and driven it east nearly to Alexandria; then Rommel himself fell back before Auchinleck's counter-thrust of Operation Crusader. (Western Desert Force had by then become Eighth Army.) When I arrived in Palestine at the turn of the year, Rommel was building up to his next attack out of his bastion at El Agheila.

My regiment, as I said, was a Yeomanry forma-tion, meaning horse cavalry mechanised and converted to tanks. I was a second lieutenant, healthy again and dead keen to get into the fight. The regiment was in no such hurry. The officers' mess was a two-tiered affair, comprising the Old Boys, who had been with the unit in its eques-trian days (or whose fathers and grandfathers had been) and the New Sods like me who cared nothing for such humbug and burned simply to get on with it. When it became clear that no action was coming for at least six months, I put in for No. 11 Scottish Commando, several of whose officers I knew from Golspie and Dornoch. Surely, I reasoned, the regiment could take no exception to an officer eager to serve. Indeed it could. When our commanding officer, Colonel L., learnt of my application, he called me on the mat and gave me a blistering rocket. Apparently such attempted defection reflected poorly on the regiment. He ordered me to recall my papers. I refused. From that hour I became in L.'s mind a bomb-throwing Bolshevik.

I hated Palestine. We trained and trained and went nowhere. In all that country, the only thing that lifted my spirits was Jerusalem. Every weekend that I could get away, I caught the No. 11 Qama bus, a multi-hued, tassel-bedecked Citroën crammed with chickens and squalling Arab urchins, often riding on the roof or clinging, standing, to the rear rails. I spent my days at the Jewish bookstore across from the King David Hotel or walking the stones that Jesus and the prophets had trodden. I felt like a Jew myself, an outcast who fitted in nowhere. These excursions, of course, only alienated me further from my brother officers, who thought me antisocial and unclubbable, and particularly from Colonel L., in whose eyes I was a first-rate Riot Acter or, worse, an intellectual – in his phrase, 'someone who reads books' – the most damning appraisal that could be made of a junior lieutenant.

Rose meanwhile had followed me to the Middle East. She came out to Egypt by ship, in a convoy loaded with army troops and their stores, crossing the Atlantic from Glasgow to Rio de Janeiro, then back again, round the Cape to Durban and up the east coast of Africa, twelve thousand miles in six weeks. She landed at Tewfiq, the port of Suez, riding from there down to Cairo ('down' meaning north in Nile lexicon) in the back of a post van with six other girls who had pulled the same stunt for the same reason. When I think of this now, the daring seems beyond belief. The young are mad. Nor, as I said, was Rose alone. Scores of other young wives and fiancées made such jaunts, and thousands more would have done so if they could.

How did Rose engineer this adventure? Her sister Jemima was chums with Randolph Churchill, son of the Prime Minister. Through him Rose secured an interview with a general of Royal Signals. 'My child,' declared this officer in kindness, 'I would no more despatch you to Egypt than put you on a rocket to the moon.' Before dismissing her, however, he mentioned in passing the Navy's shortage of civilian telegraphers. Rose went straight to the Admiralty. Within five weeks she had mastered civilian and naval code and had passed the telegrapher's test. Nineteen weeks later she was in

Alexandria, working sixty hours a week for Naval Intelligence at Raz-el-Tin and drawing both overseas and danger money.

I was still in Palestine. I still hadn't seen her. The month was March 1942. Spring floods had temporarily stalled operations in the desert, but everyone knew that action would resume soon. Either Rommel would attack us or we would attack him. Other formations kept getting called but never ours. A sheet had been posted in our orderly room called the Sugar List; it was for individual officers to volunteer as pool replacements for other units. My name stood on top every week. No call came. I continued applying for special forces. I volunteered for Advance 'A' force and for SOE, Special Operations Executive. I got as far as clearance for parachute training with 'L' detachment, SAS, before a notice from division scratched this, declaring tank officers too critical to be spared. Despite this, I secured an interview with Jake Easonsmith, then a captain, of the Long Range Desert Group. I flew from Lydda in Palestine to Heliopolis at Cairo, catching a lift in a Bombay bomber, only to find that duties had called Captain Easonsmith away. I left a letter, in truth a plea, then couldn't find a friendly flight out; I wound up taking two days getting back by bus, missing pay parade and nearly being declared absent without leave. My punishment, with another tardy subaltern, was to be made cinema officer. We ran the nightly screenings of American westerns and pre-war gangster films. The men called us the Warner Brothers.

In April the regiment was called forward to Egypt. Finally we were going 'up the Blue', meaning into the Western Desert, whose vast, featureless surface and flat, cloudless skies rendered the experience of being upon it more like being at sea than on land. Our formation became part of 22nd Armoured Brigade, which had been under 7th Armoured Division but was now under 1st. All regiments were being re-organised after the heavy attrition of the previous year's Operation Crusader. Then, in February, Rommel attacked. Bursting from his bastion at El Agheila, he drove our side back all the way to Gazala. A line of defensive positions held the Desert Fox for the moment. But everyone knew he would strike again – and soon.

Stein was up front somewhere. He was a FOO, a forward observation officer, with 4RHA – the Fourth Regiment Royal Horse Artillery. His batteries of 25-pounders were on the move constantly as part of various 'Jock columns', mobile formations of armour, infantry and artillery that ranged the desert, striking when and where they could.

As for our regiment, we were transported via Kabrit to Abbassia Barracks, the Royal Armoured Corps base outside Cairo. At last we had tanks: reconditioned American Stuarts, called Honeys; upgunned A-13 and A-15 Crusaders; and new heavy American Grants. Even then we didn't see action. We continued to train and to man defensive positions.

Our post was called a 'box'. This was a wired and mined-in stronghold in the desert south of Mersa Matruh. Tied in with other boxes, ours formed a defensive line protecting a deep band of minefields and anti-tank ditches, the lanes between which were covered by artillery, with infantry companies and anti-tank batteries at selected strategic points, and mobile armoured columns arrayed in reserve. My command was a troop of four A-15 Crusaders, the 'recce' or reconnaissance unit of a squadron of three troops, which itself was part of our regiment of four squadrons. We spent our days in dust-churning exercises, exactly as in Palestine, racing from one sector of the box to another, rehearsing our role as mobile reserve. This was preferable to what the infantry was doing, enduring hordes of stinging flies and digging slit trenches all day long in the parched, stony earth.

The only action was the occasional 'demonstration' or 'reconnaissance in force'. A vacant zone of over two hundred miles still existed between our rear defensive line and the actual front at Gazala. Into this void our squadrons probed and patrolled.

This experience, though of no tactical significance, proved invaluable for us untested crews. We ventured past Sidi Barrani and Buq Buq and round the escarpment at Halfaya, darting as far west as Sidi Omar and Gabr Saleh. We found ourselves at times behind the patrolling Germans and they behind us. We loosed the odd pot-shot and even got into a few fox chases. And we learnt crucial skills: where to look to find loot in abandoned vehicles (Bavarian chocolate, bottles of Liebfraumilch and cases of Macedonian cigarettes); how to brew up tea under field conditions, using a petrol stove or a hot engine block; and the proper technique for wolfing down a meal of bully burgoo (beef and biscuits mashed together) without losing half to the omnipresent swarms of flies. But the most powerful impressions acquired during these forays were, first, the monumental scale of mobilisation of both Axis and Allies, the vast numbers of vehicles that were being brought up by rail and transporter and under their own power; and, second, the colossal magnitude of the destruction of last summer and autumn, particularly south of Fort Capuzzo and along the Trigh el Abd highway, where mile upon mile was strewn with hulks and derelicts and the graves of the luckless men who didn't get away.

On 26 May, Rommel attacked the Gazala Line. Finally our regiment was called up. My squadron had been temporarily pulled back to the mobile repair shops at Fuka to have new tracks fitted. The rest of the formation remained forward at Mersa Matruh. In other words, we were split up.

The Gazala Line was a series of defensive boxes about two hundred miles forward of Mersa Matruh and three hundred from Alexandria. The line ran from the coast south, through a box called Knightsbridge and several others, thence to Bir Hacheim, its southern pivot. This position was crucial because Rommel would inevitably try to run a right hook round it. If he succeeded, the whole line would collapse. Bir Hacheim was manned by Free French and Foreign Legionnaires. They would hold to the last man, we were told, to restore in the world's eyes the honour of France.

Back at Fuka, my squadron was moving heaven and earth to get moving. We still didn't have our tracks. When they came, they had the wrong pins. Each night the BBC reported more furious clashes along the Gazala Line. Rommel's Panzers had broken through; our fellows had pushed them back; the Afrika Korps was trapped within vast minefields; no, they were breaking out. Hour by hour, I and my squadron-mates grew more agitated. We had been training for weeks in the art of loading tanks on to special trucks called transporters. Now, with our tracks finally fitted, only half of these 'low-loaders' showed up, the remainder having been assigned in some administrative balls-up to other regiments. The result was that our squadron of sixteen tanks set out for Gazala first on railway cars, then under their own power. It took us three days to reach Sollum, the first twenty-four hours travelling cross-country. By the time we rejoined the coast road, troops and squadrons had become hopelessly separated from one another and from higher command. My troop of four tanks fell to three and then two, as first one suspension failed, then an engine blew. No matter; we picked up two strays and pressed on.

The tactical unit of a British armoured regiment is the squadron. A squadron at full strength is four troops of four tanks each and a fourth headquarters troop of four or five tanks. The squadron leader is a major, sometimes a captain. A lieutenant commands each troop, taking one tank as his own, with the other two or three commanded by the troop sergeant and one or two corporals. Above the squadron is the regiment, which is three squadrons and a headquarters squadron, fifty-two tanks in all, on paper at any rate. Attached to each regiment are an 'A' and a 'B' echelon. These are the supply units, the lorries and trucks that shuttle between the rear depots and the fighting front, bringing up fuel and ammunition, oil, rations and water.

By the time my troop reached Sollum, a town on the coastal plain at the base of the escarpment that rises to the inland plateau, we had lost contact with battalion, brigade and division. Wireless contact was hopeless with the short range of our sets and the massive overload of the nets and their changing frequencies and protocols. The road at Sollum ascends in a six-hundred-foot serpentine to the raised desert above; here luck got two of our tanks rides on transporters, while the other pair were forced to grind uphill in creeper gear, making about a mile per gallon. In the crush I spotted a familiar command pennant and scrambled on foot to the Grant belonging to Major Mike Mallory, our regimental second in command, who retained his fitter's truck, two HQ tanks, and nothing else. 'Hell, Chapman, you're the first familiar face I've seen in forty-eight hours!' Mallory crayoned my map, indicating Sidi Rezegh and Bir el Gubi in the desert ahead as objectives, marking positions with yellow for enemy and red for friendly.

'Of course that was yesterday,' he said. 'The colours may have switched round by today.'

From the frontier wire a few miles ahead, Mallory said, we were still eighty miles out of the fight which was raging round Bir Hacheim, the French-defended southern anchor of the Gazala Line. The Fighting French and the Legionnaires were putting up a heroic defence, but Rommel's 21st and 15th Panzer divisions, along with the Italian Ariete ('Battering Ram') armoured division, were pounding them relentlessly, seeking to get round to the south. If this succeeded, the French would have no choice but to withdraw. That was all Mallory knew, except that our orders were to find Rommel's Panzers and stop them, if it meant sacrificing every tank we had.

Two days later my troop, following a line of markers, at last stumbled into a formation we recognised. The regiment lay in a dispersed formation, spread over miles, just east of El Adem in the rugged escarpment country west of Sidi

Rezegh. Tanks, armoured cars, infantry lorries and 'B' vehicles straggled in continually from the rear, altering the shape of the disposition as they came up and worked themselves in, so that it took most of a day to locate my post, refuel, and carve out a few hours to replenish oil and fluids, tighten tracks, and snatch a spot of grub and sleep. My troop sergeant, Hammond, had badly smashed both hands when a hatch crashed on to them; he was evacuated to the rear, his place taken by a corporal named Pease from 5RTR, the Fifth Royal Tank Regiment whom we had picked up en route along with his A-13 and who was the closest thing to a veteran we could muster. The squadron leader was Major Patrick McCaughey, whom I had known at Magdalen. He told me that 22nd Armoured Brigade was no longer part of first Armoured Division; we had been taken under command of 7th Armoured Division. We were now officially 'Desert Rats'.

The first dawn our regiment was called forward to that area called the Cauldron, between the Knightsbridge box and Bir Hacheim. The 7th Armoured Division at that time had only one armoured brigade, the Fourth. By the time the we reached it, two of its three tank regiments had been wiped out – meaning the entire division was down to one armoured regiment, 3RTR, which itself was barely holding together, under constant attack by the Luftwaffe. Now we were in the same fix. For three days our squadrons were strafed and bombed by Messerschmitt 110s, Stukas and Italian Savoia-Marchettis. Our sister regiment, the 2nd Royal Gloucestershire Hussars, lost half its tanks and its commanding officer and adjutant. The 10th Indian Brigade was destroyed. By now units were scrambled together from all over. On 10 June our squadron and one other from 6RTR were ordered south to protect the unarmoured columns of the 7th Motor Brigade, which were trying to bring aid to the Fighting French and the Legionnaires. Before we had gone ten miles, a signal came that Rommel's right hook had out-flanked the French.

Bir Hacheim fell.

The 15th and 21st Panzer divisions were racing round our flank.

From that hour, the retreat started. It didn't end till Rommel was beating at the gates of Alexandria.

In the cinema it's always the tanks that advance first. In real armoured warfare, the form was the opposite. First came the enemy scout infantry on sidecar motorcycles. After the bikes you saw armoured cars, the four- and eight-wheeled SdKfz-222s and 234s that served as screens and recce units for the armour and as assault elements against foot troops and unarmoured transport. Behind these came the motorised infantry, on trucks and in armoured half-tracks. The Afrika Korps's infantry's role was to take on our unar-moured gun crews and transport – anti-tank guns, artillery, echelon vehicles – and to protect their

69

own weaponry, the low-slung Pak38s and the high-profile, long-barrelled 88s. The latter were enormous, with barrels as long as entire tanks; they sat high, ten feet off the desert floor, and were manned by crews of seven. Once you heard the sound of an 88, you never forgot it. The gun had been designed originally as an anti-aircraft weapon. It fired an extremely high-velocity, flat-trajectory shot that could penetrate 150mm of armour at two thousand yards. The thickest steel we had, on heavy Matilda infantry tanks, wasn't even 100mm. An 88 could knock out a Crusader with one shot at a mile and a half. The killing range of the guns on our Honey and Crusader tanks was closer to five hundred yards. The 88s and Paks advanced and dug in, using ridges and folds in the ground for cover. Only then did you see the Panzers.

We new troops had been prepared for this; we had been trained to appreciate such tactics and to recognise them in action. But it took the real thing to make you a believer. Two days after El Adem, in rolling featureless country west of Bir el Gubi, my recce troop of four tanks was out in front of the battalion, mounting the reverse slope of a ridge, to peep over the brow, when our left-most Crusader – Pease's A-13 – spotted two German Mark IIIs withdrawing at speed directly in front of us. A tank's most vulnerable part is its rear end; we couldn't pass up such a target. Up and over we went, hounds after the fox. Before we had dropped a hundred feet down the slope, two of our four tanks had been hit and stopped in their tracks, the crews of both baling out madly (a third, my own, though holed, remained drivable), while tungsten-steel armour-piercing rounds slammed into the stationary hulls. We never even saw the 88s. As we reversed flat out, leaving one Crusader and a Honey smoking on the sand and my Crusader hobbling for the repair shop, I could see the German commander in the turret of his Mark III, giving us a wave.

For the next five days our troops and squadrons waged what historians would later call the battle of El Adem and Knightsbridge but to us felt like a succession of isolated and maddeningly inconclusive skirmishes. We would be ordered by brigade to take up a position in anticipation of being immediately attacked. We would scurry to the trig point and set up. No enemy would appear. For hours we would squat, broiling in the sun, hull-down along a ridgeline with our sister squadrons on either flank and HQ and 'B' vehicles echeloned back for miles to the rear. Suddenly headphones would blare with reports of German columns advancing round our flank. We would decamp in a mad scramble, only to dash again into vacant waste.

A typical action, Day Four, reconstructed from my diary. The skipper's voice crackles over the wireless. 'Hello, all stations JUMA, JUMA calling. Friends [meaning our forward screen of armoured cars] report enemy tanks, figures four zero, approaching from south-west, at range figures three zero zero zero. Orders: Three [meaning Three Troop, i.e. us], observe but do not engage until all units come on line. Others conform to my movements. We will advance and hold for orders. Off.'

Forward goes my troop of four, reconstituted from the repair shops. It's noon and the heat haze reduces visibility to a thousand yards. We rattle over one ridgeline, spread out at a three-hundred-yard interval, one tank on point, two on the wings. Trailing us by five hundred yards, Major McCaughey brings up the other troops of our squadron; he's in the centre rear. Through my earphones I hear him deploying his other troops and reporting to regiment on what the armoured cars are seeing up front. We don't know this then, but the enemy are tuned in too. The Germans have Signal Intercept trucks manned by operators who speak English as well as we do and whose detection skills are so keen that they can recognise the voices of our individual commanders down to squadron and even troop level. Already they're reporting our movements and formation numbers to the column of Panzers advancing against us. Now comes report from battalion that the enemy have stopped.

'JUMA Three, JUMA calling. Keep going. Report what you see. Off to you.'

That's us. In my bucking, heaving turret, pressing the small of my back into the rim of the hatch with one knee braced against the rack that holds my Mills bombs, my spare glasses and the four books I'm reading, and the other wedged against the side of the breech guard of our 2-pounder, I wave Corporal Pease in the point tank forward. We're advancing at about five miles an hour. My binoculars are riveted to my eye sockets. The ride is like a small boat at sea. Petrol and machine oil reek. The surface of the turret is so hot from the sun than it burns my elbows through my shirt. Inside the tank, the temperature is well into triple figures.

Now I see our 'friends', two armoured cars of 3KDG, 3rd King's Dragoon Guards, darting back towards us, hollow to hollow, like water boatmen. I can't see the cars themselves, only their dust, which I recognise. We're all learning, day by day. I wish I were a seasoned tank commander. I'm not. I'm faking 50 per cent of everything. The enemy's skills are leagues beyond ours, as are his tactics and equipment. We know it and so does he. I'm not frightened – there's no time for that; too much concentration is required. But I'm keenly aware of my own deficiencies and those of my crew and my guns and my commanders. It is not a reassuring feeling.

Ahead lies a ridge with a hollow into which a tank can slip without exposing itself on the skyline. I order Pease to take the wing; I advance myself into this pocket. 'Driver, halt.' So I can see. A breeze clears the vantage south. External temperature is

110 Fahrenheit. Through the binoculars I can make out two columns of dust, advancing south-east round our flank. The first is tanks; the trailing column, five miles back, is enemy MT – motor transport – petrol and ammunition trucks. 'Hello JUMA, JUMA Three calling.' I report what I see.

'Hello JUMA Three, JUMA answering. Hold where you are. Wait for orders.'

Up the ridge in front of us scuttles a water boatman, one of our KDG armoured cars. It zips up alongside and stops. On its prow is painted 'Tink 21' above an excellent rendering of a bathing beauty straddling a Breda gun. Its driver is a sergeant I don't recognise. He grins up at me. 'Haven't got a smoke, have you, guv?' I toss him a pack of four horrible Chelseas from the clutch I keep in the wireless rack. 'What's up front?' I ask. He lights two cigs and passes one overhand to his driver, through the port. 'Half the bloody Hun army.' He has had to beat it, he says, from lorried infantry and big German 8-wheelers, armoured cars, coming up at the same time as at least fifty Mark IIIs and IVs. 'A sight,' says the sergeant, 'to make me piss me bleedin' pants.'

Enemy infantry up front means they're protecting anti-tank guns, which means trouble for us.

'Hello, all stations JUMA, JUMA calling. Orders: wheel south, come on line, and engage enemy supply column. Off.'

We do. Now the stopped German tanks start rolling forward; they burst through our vacated position before our follow-on elements can advance into place to counter them. South on the flat, the German supply column breaks away long before we reach it, warned by our dust and, no doubt, wireless intercepts. Our attack buckles in the face of a screen of furious anti-tank fire; we are compelled to retreat yet again when the west-leading column of Panzers comes about and threatens to cut us off. I lose Pease's tank when a high-explosive round turns its right track and suspension into spare parts, and I lose its driver to a broken jaw when a round of solid shot opens up one side of his turret. Darkness approaches. Corporal Ledgard is my number three tank commander. As he and I take the crew off and hurry back to the protective perimeter of vehicles and infantry that we call a night leaguer, we can see two Mark IIIs closing in to claim the prize of Pease's A-13. By midnight German salvage crews will have towed it back to a mobile repair shop. In five days we'll see it again, with a black cross painted on its flank and an Axis crew inside.

The day is over. We're alive, we haven't been put in the bag, haven't disgraced ourselves. But we haven't accomplished a damn thing either, and in fact we're about to sit down twenty miles east of where we started. As darkness descends and our squadrons retire in weary, dust-caked columns, we know the enemy are not reeling as we are, but remain keen and eager, anticipating the dawn when they will throw their formations upon us again and we will face them with our same inferior tactics, armour and weaponry.

It's a sickening feeling, knowing the enemy has your number. We can feel the force of Rommel's genius. He calls the tune, we dance – and always one step behind. Rommel concentrates his armour; we fritter ours away in dribs and drabs. His Panzers never attack but in mass. When you see Axis tanks, you see columns and phalanxes; it looks as if the whole world is coming at you. The enemy's style is ripping, audacious. They are all little Rommels. Opening the merest breach, they exploit it ruthlessly and without hesitation. They turn small victories into big ones. On our side, we're bold but not smart; our rushes are like the Charge of the Light Brigade, all flash and no sense. Now in night leaguer troop and squadron commanders assemble at Colonel L.'s command truck, ducking through the blackout blanket into the cigarette- and pipe-smoke-dense interior. We can sense control slipping. The field is too broad, the enemy too swift and unpredictable. Squadron commanders ask L. for the Germans' position. He doesn't know. Brigade doesn't know. Division doesn't know.

Days of disorder follow. We have no answer for Rommel's armour, firepower or speed. The Afrika Korps's tactics are to throw tanks and anti-tank guns forward in tandem, either to seize some strategic ground that threatens our flank or route of withdrawal, or to advance frontally in such strength that we must counter or be overrun. Since the range of our guns won't let us slug it out at long distance, we have no choice but to close with the enemy. This is exactly what he wants. We fling our outgunned, underarmoured Honeys and Crusaders at Rommel's Mark IIIs and IVs, which immediately reverse out of range, leaving us to run on to his dug-in, diabolically sited 88s and Pak38s. The anti-tank guns tear us apart. When the enemy officers spot enough flamers and gun-downs, their Panzers reappear. With every clash, we lose more men and more tanks.

Our line falls back again and again. In the confusion, elements scatter. Regiments crack up. Brigades break apart. Entire squadrons go missing. The civilian may react with incredulity. How can vehicles as massive as tanks get separated from one another in flat, open desert? But a brigade on the move spreads out over scores of miles. When the terrain is broken, when sand- and dust-storms get up, when midday glare obscures vision or the tanks must move in darkness, if the column comes under fire and individual elements must move swiftly in attack or retreat, not only is it the easiest thing in the world to get separated but in fact it requires tremendous concentration and presence of mind *not* to get separated. The norm is to be separated. One learns how to arc tracer fire, 'toffee apples', into the night sky to show your mates where you are so they can help you navigate by wireless as you grope your way home.

In the Cauldron clashes, as these battles have

come to be called after the name of the minefields round Knightsbridge, our squadron loses eight tanks out of sixteen; at King's Cross south of Tobruk, my troop of four drops down to one, then zero. Pease has had four tanks shot out from under him; I've had three. As refits come up after dark, each troop commander grabs what he can. Faces cycle through as fast as machines. In column rumbling into night leaguer, we run into fellows we have never seen before – individual tanks separated from their squadrons, regiments, brigades. Day Seven since the fall of Bir Hacheim, it happens to us. We're lost. I have two strange tanks and all strange crews; our scratch lot end up with what remains of 4th Armoured Brigade, who have themselves been tossed in with unallied companies of Indian and South African infantry.

As organisation breaks down across the vast and muddled field, improvisation becomes the order of the day. Proper radio protocol requires tank troop and squadron commanders to communicate only within their own regiment; it's a court-martial offence to go over or round. Now commanders are poaching on to any net they can break into, seeking aid from any allies they can find. Day Nine, retreating to a defensive line thrown together on the Tobruk-El Adem track, I'm tapping into an artillery net when I hear a familiar voice. 'Hell's bells, is that Chapman from Magdalen?'

'Who's this?'

It's Stein. His two batteries of 25-pounders (or such sections as remain intact and functioning) have somehow thrown in with those elements of our regiment that still cling together. Two nights later he and I find each other in leaguer, outside Colonel L.'s command truck.

Stein is a captain now, an acting major. I barely recognise him. A grisly burn scar paints one side of his face. Shrapnel, another officer tells me, has left one of his knees half frozen. Stein is cut about but flying high. Captains and lieutenants defer to him; he's their chief and they love him.

Something extraordinary is happening. Under the stress of withdrawal and dislocation, with the chain of command cast into anarchy through wounds and deaths, vacuums of leadership have begun to appear. Many commanding officers rise brilliantly to the occasion, but others falter, fail or in effect abdicate. In numerous formations, seconds in command are compelled to step forward. This is the case with Stein. He's only a captain but he's running the show of a colonel. He does it so smoothly we barely notice. From his demeanour and the confidence with which he issues orders, not to mention the alacrity with which they are obeyed, I assume his post is battery commander. It takes a night or two before I realise his name isn't even on the top sheet of the War Establishment. He has simply taken over, or rather been called forth by the moment.

Stein has always been a brilliant teacher. He employs this faculty now. Earlier in the retreat, when batteries of 25-pounders have come under fire, they have simply packed their kit and poodled off. Most are still doing so. Stein puts a stop to this. He has two batteries; he alternates them, forward and rear, keeping one up front with the tanks, firing over open sights if necessary, the outfit so far forward that at times they're actually out in front of the armour. He drills his gun crews to 'set up, sight up, light up' – then fall back to a new position and do it again. Stein recruits forward observation personnel from displaced infantry, ambulatory wounded and from 'B' echelon troopers whose trucks have broken down or been shot up, giving them patched-together wirelesses and salvaged Bren carriers or Morris pickups and teaching them how to call in fire-orders. He keeps his object simple: 'Make life bloody for Rommel's 88s.'

We have an officer like him in our own regiment. This is Major Mike Mallory, second in command under Colonel L., whom I ran into on the Sollum serpentine. Mallory had been a theatrical producer in London (he had had a hit with Irene Cawley in *Her Sweet Fancy* just before the war). Whether this background in some way prepared Mallory for command, no one can say. We know this, though: L. will not get us out of this fix. Impelled by instinct for survival, the junior officers rally to Mallory. We listen to him. We do what he says. He becomes de facto regimental commander, with Stein and two or three other captains and majors of Allied arms in support.

High command has lost control of the field. Brigade can't locate its constituent elements on a map, let alone find the enemy, or work out what to do with either. My diary records a run of four days when either no orders at all come in, or they do and are so out of touch with affairs on the ground that to obey them would produce an even graver tragedy than what is already happening. 'I can't make head or tail of this, can you?' says Mallory of one particularly egregious signal. When he bins it, all hands cheer.

Mallory issues his cardinal order. 'From this hour, all heroism is forbidden. If I hear of one officer making some valiant "charge" or taking some gallant "stand", by heaven, I'll find him myself and wring his bloody neck.'

Mallory outlaws all undisciplined retreat. 'One cannot simply pack up and piss off. It's bad manners.'

Our new leader restores order. He gives us heart. He defines the problem and provides a solution. 'The enemy attack with tanks and anti-tank guns working together. He advances in massed order, while we hurl ourselves at him in penny packets. This is suicide. From now on, we advance and withdraw as one unit, supporting one another.'

Except the Grants with their 75mms, Eighth Army has no tank gun that can fire a high-explosive shell, the kind you need to knock out

Rommel's 88s and their crews. The solid shot of our Honeys and Crusaders is worthless against such targets.

This is where Stein comes in. Working with Mallory, he brings up his 25-pounders, which *can* fire HE, and he keeps them close. This is a desperately risky business, for such artillery are hell to move out in a hurry; it takes minutes for them to limber up and flee, should Rommel's gunners get their range or his infantry bring them under fire. So we tanks must stay with them. Stein's 25-pounders are the only weapons we have against the Afrika Korps's 88s and Paks, and the only guns that can take on Mark IIIs and IVs beyond a thousand yards. We are in this together. This is not tactics: it's life and death.

'Listen to me, gentlemen,' Mallory instructs us in night leaguer. 'One act I will never stand for is leaving our fellows behind. Bugger military protocol or lofty notions of honour. I can't live with running out on a pal, and I won't let any of you do it either.'

This is the sort of stuff we need to hear.

Our condition is preposterous, really. We are like civilians seeking to bring common sense to bear upon problems that we should have been trained for but have not been. Worse, we must get our new lads up to speed, sometimes during the very night preceding their first action, while we ourselves are nearly as green as they. Fresh 'bods' come up from the rear and are made corpses almost before we learn their names. Stein takes this hard. All our young officers do.

Night Thirteen, Stein and I get a few minutes together, after each has completed his duties of the evening. We perch on the tailboard of a fitter's truck and share cold tea and rum from the very flask that Stein had revived me with that night at Winchester. I ask if he's still writing poetry.

'No, by heaven, and I shan't ever again.' He indicates the tanks and men round about. 'Stuff like this calls for prose, Chap. Short sentences, pithy and lean.'

I tell Stein how impressed I am with him – and how different he seems from our days at university.

'Not actually. All that's changed is we've switched from men of words to men of action. And a damn relief too!'

Stein tells me that when he first got out to Egypt he applied for the Long Range Desert Group. 'It seemed like what Lawrence would have done.' He means T. E. Lawrence, Lawrence of Arabia, our fellow Oxford man.

I tell Stein of my own failed application to the LRDG. 'Did they accept you?'

'Division squashed the deal. Said they couldn't spare artillery officers. The fools! I'd have been damn smart out there among the prophets and the scorpions.' Stein laughs. 'I must tell you something, Chap, that I daren't confess to another soul. I'm having the time of my life.' He shakes his head. 'It's outrageous to declare such a thing, I know, with dear friends getting blown to pieces and England's own survival hanging by a thread. But by God, life is brilliant out here, isn't it?'

He asks if I've ever had a premonition of my own death. I tell him I follow the advice of my drill sergeant from Bovington: stay dumb and don't think.

'Will you take this for me, my friend?' And he slips a folded envelope into my breast pocket.

'What is it?'

'It makes you executor of my estate.'

'Don't joke around, Stein.'

He's serious. He asks if I recall our conversations about the twentieth century and how much he abhors it. 'All that is behind us, Chap. We're living in the time before Christ.' He laughs and indicates the desert round our camp. 'We're a tribe. We've become that. The Huns too. The poor bastards.'

He hoists the flask. 'Do you know,' he says, 'I used to feel apart from men of the trades, as my father would call them. Other ranks. No more. Out here I've come to love them. Officers too. Hell's bells, I even love the Jerries, the bloody swine.'

He says if he writes anything in future, it will be damn serious. Life and death. But it'll be funny. The gods themselves laugh, he says. 'And not darkly, but with joy.'

Mallory comes up, our leader. 'What are you two on about?'

'Nothing you'd understand,' says Stein, passing him the flask.

'Well, break off for a bit, will you?' Mallory indicates the command truck, at which other officers are now collecting, apparently for a late-hour change in orders. 'Let's see if we can conjure a way out of this mess for one more day.'

CHAPTER 6

June 21, Tobruk falls. With that, Rommel acquires a seaport within three hundred miles of Alexandria – and we lose our last stronghold in Cyrenaica. The gallop is on, back to Cairo.

Two episodes give the flavour of the retreat. The first involves Colonel L. Our commander is painfully aware of his displacement in the men's hearts by Mallory. He feels shame over this and takes to reasserting his authority by spasms. Falling back in the desert between Sidi Aziz and Fort Capuzzo, our troop of 'A' squadron is ordered by L. to take up a defensive position at a feature identified on the map as Hill 99. We arrive with our sister troops, eleven tanks in all, and set up hull-down along the ridgeline, facing west. Within minutes shells begin dropping amongst us, first the air-burst high explosive that 88s use for ranging; then straight HE, possibly from Mark IV Panzers, though we can't see; then even bigger shells that Pease identifies as 105s from field guns. This fire is coming not from in front, where the enemy are supposed to be, but from behind and left. What the hell is going on?

86

I drive with my troop sergeant, 'Tick' Haskell, and a lieutenant called Marsden, nicknamed 'Duke', commander of the adjacent troop, to the brow of the ridge; we peer over to where our infantry are supposed to be dug in, awaiting the foe. The infantry's dug in all right, but they're firing at *us*. It's the Germans. Either the map is in error or we're on the wrong feature. I raise battalion, report the situation, and request permission to attack the infantry. 'Hold your position,' declares Colonel L. 'No movement without my orders.'

It takes no imagination to reckon that our neighbours of the Afrika Korps will not sit tight; they'll be in our laps any moment, packing Panzerfaust anti-tank weapons and satchel charges. Worse, Rommel's artillery has got our range. I call in to battalion again, asking clearance to move out. Let us do something: go forward or back. Negative, replies L., appending aspersions on my manhood. Marsden chimes in and gets a dose of the same. One of the Crusaders in his troop takes a direct hit and becomes a flamer; we can see the crew baling out as black smoke pours from the engine compartment. Haskell is pointing to our southern flank. A phalanx of dark shapes can be seen at three thousand yards, rumbling in our direction. I report this, with Haskell adding another ten to the figures, just spotted on a farther ridgeline. Meanwhile nasty air-bursts from the 105s are creeping closer. Shrapnel is pinging off our hulls;

the sand has acquired a carpet of smoking shards of steel. L. still won't let us move. 'Bugger this,' Haskell declares off the air. 'I'm not sticking it here till Jerry comes galloping down our cheese-holes.' An instant later an armour-piercing shell, a ricochet, comes pin-wheeling past us, three feet off the sand at two hundred miles an hour, screaming like a cat. Its passage sucks the air right out of our lungs.

'"A" squadron, withdraw in good order,' barks Mallory over the blower. We get the hell out before L. can countermand him.

This is how command passes from a weak officer to a stronger. No rank alters; no papers are filed. Without a word, every man understands.

That night L. and Mallory vanish into L.'s command truck. We can hear raised voices. 'It's Bligh and Mr Christian,' says Marsden, when I relieve him as duty officer at 2200. Stein comes over with tea. When Mallory exits L.'s truck, red-faced, L. appears in the blackout doorway. 'Show's over,' he says to Stein sharply. Of me, he demands to know if I still have idle time to read books. Next night, L. delivers a particularly vicious tongue-lashing to a gallant and exhausted troop commander I'll call Q. At the peak of L.'s tirade, the young officer, without any ill intention, chances to let his hand fall toward his sidearm. 'Go ahead!' bellows L. 'It's what the lot of you want, isn't it?'

We fall back to the Wire on the Egyptian frontier. We are learning belatedly the lessons our elders of the veteran brigades have acquired before us. We grasp the difference between being 'tied in' and 'in the air'.

A unit is 'tied in' when it has contact with friendly formations right and left. A unit is 'in the air' when it is cut off, alone.

A force that is tied in will hold.

A force in the air will run.

The skill to desert warfare, we begin to comprehend, is to put the other fellow in the air while keeping your own side tied in. This is what Rommel is so brilliant at. His armour appears out of nowhere in massed strength; by bold thrust or clever misdirection, he achieves a breach. Into this he pours his Panzers. The penetrated front is now broken into two sections. Both are in the air.

Inevitably we run. This is not bolting as in cowardice; it is re-deployment to get tied in again. The last real scrape our troop gets into is in defence of a ridge near Sofafi, east of Halfaya Pass. Aussie infantry holds one extremity of this otherwise featureless drumlin, while three or four troops of British tanks assemble turret-down on the other wing. The enemy have attacked this ridge once in the morning and been repelled, then again at midday; now they are coming at it again. The assault is supported by heavy guns, with 88s and long-barrelled Mark IVs lobbing in shells from closer range.

Behind these, we knew though we couldn't see, waited a massed formation of faster, more mobile

Mark IIIs, with motorised infantry immediately to their rear. At some point the foe would mass this force and hurl it at some vulnerable point on the ridge. Stein had one of his two batteries of 25-pounders several miles to the rear, laying down a strong fire of HE, trying to keep Rommel's 88s at bay. He himself was up front with the other battery. To direct the long-range fire, Stein had forward observers zipping from one vantage to another, before the enemy could zero in on them – two in tanks, two others in armoured cars, with Bren infantry carriers and several truck-mounted combat teams to protect them. My troop, which was then two Crusaders and an A-9, was forward too, covering this screen. I had a new corporal, Wicks, in the other Crusader, and Pease in the A-9. We were all low on fuel and ammunition and all exhausted. Two hours remained till dark. All after-noon we had been seeking a lull to pull back and replenish, or a break in the fire when the supply trucks could get up to us.

Suddenly an urgent signal squalled over the headset. One of the Bren carriers had been hit. These are open-top vehicles, notoriously under-armoured, designed for multiple purposes, mostly transport of infantry. This one protected one of Stein's OPs. It was unclear what had happened but, whatever it was, men were badly wounded. Our troop was ordered to pick them up. Wicks in our scout tank took the lead. We could see the Bren carrier, at the foot of a column of dense black smoke. Now Stein's rear batteries started adding smoke shells of their own to protect the carrier. At this moment, the German attack broke. There was a sort of bowl northwest of the ridge-line and into this, from the north, rumbled a mass of dark armour. I could hear Duke Marsden reporting, '. . . figures five zero Mark IIIs and IVs, I say again five zero.' This mob was rolling straight towards the burning carrier, about four thousand yards away. The tanks did not advance as a whole but by elements; one section would halt and fire while another rolled forward; then the one that had halted would charge ahead, while its cohort drew up, sighted, and loosed its volley. Just as Wicks got to the Bren carrier, he was hit too, an HE round slap on top of his engine compartment. I shouted to him over the wireless. I could hear Wicks calling to his men inside the tank; clearly one or more had been hit: the interior was in chaos. Pease and I were about three hundred yards behind when I saw another flash of HE and the mass of Wicks's tank dropped belly-down, the way armoured vehicles do when their suspension collapses.

Stein's post was at the south-east shoulder of the ridgeline; he could see all this happening directly in front of him. (I only learnt this later from Mallory; I was too busy with my own prob-lems at the moment.) Apparently Stein reckoned that this sweep of enemy armour was the main attack; that this spot on the ridge was what the

Afrika Korps commanders called the *Schwerpunkt*, the critical point. Stein could see that no British armour, other than my light troop and Marsden's, both of which were about to get vaporised, was in position to respond. The black shapes were at thirty-five hundred yards now. Stein ordered his forward battery up, using whatever cover they could find. A 25-pounder is not a big gun. Its muzzle shield stands little higher than a man's shoulder; three muscular crewmen can easily manhandle it on its wheels. But it shoots fast, fires true and packs a bang. Stein began engaging the Panzers at three thousand yards. I couldn't hear him through my headset; he was on a different net. But Mallory told me later Stein was simultaneously directing the fire of his forward battery, exhorting the fire of his rear battery, and crying the alarm for help from any source who could hear him.

By now my Crusader was within a hundred yards of Wicks. Flames were jetting from the deck of his engine box. I called to him over the wireless to get his crew out at once. From inside the tank he might not be aware of the danger he was in, of the blaze creeping towards his ammunition or of smoke asphyxiating him. 'They're dropping stones all over me,' Wicks called back, meaning he was coming under machine-gun fire. I sent Pease after the men in the Bren carrier; I took my own tank to cover Wicks. Now we were hearing a rattle on our roof too. The fire was coming from the left so I ordered the driver to pull in on that side of Wicks, to screen him, at the same time lighting off my own smoke generators. Black soot billowed. I heard a titanic wallop and felt all forward motion cease. We're hit, I thought. But no, we had crashed into Wicks's tank amidst the smoke. I could feel the tank corkscrewing under us as one track found traction and the other hung on something, probably Wicks's tank, whose radio had now packed up as well, so that I could no longer reach him. I thought: this is a damn ridiculous way to cop it.

I popped the hatch and clambered out, but I had forgotten to cut off the smoke candles. They were spewing black petrol-stinking clouds that my lungs sucked in as I shouted for Wicks. I was hoping his crew would have baled out, but apparently something was preventing this. Through gaps in the smoke, I could see Wicks helping his gunner out of the forward hatch. Flames from their engine compartment were flaring up behind them. If Wicks's tank blew, we would all be seeing the red light. I scrambled down from my turret to help him get his crew clear. It didn't seem a particularly dangerous proposition, as both tanks were obscured by Stygian murk, and my own vehicle screened me from the enemy machine gun. My primary emotion was outrage at the Germans, for throughout all prior clashes in the desert campaign, chivalry had dictated that gunners hold fire when men were baling out of tanks. At any event I leapt down, grabbed the kit rail on the left of Wicks's turret, above which his crew's ruck-sacks and bedding were blazing like Yule logs, to haul myself up and take his gunner. I couldn't understand why those stones continued rattling round us. Then I realised there was a second weapon. At least one other machine gun was raking both tanks from the opposite direction. In the end, the gun turned out to be one of ours, whose gunner was severely reprimanded in the aftermath, not so much for shooting at his own men as for shooting at *any* men in that position.

By this point I was halfway up Wicks's flank with ricochets of .30-calibre rounds banging off the hulls of both our tanks, and tracers skipping and popping all round me, Wicks and his gunner. Now the wind changed. In the time it takes to say the words, all smoke blew away, leaving us revealed in the gunsights of two machine guns. Shame primarily, coupled with Wicks's gallantry and the shared peril to us all, as well as rage at the enemy for shooting at us under these conditions, prevented me from plunging right back into the hole I had just leapt out of. To cut a long tale short, Pease came up with his A-9, with the survivors of the Bren carrier burrowing frantically into every nook of cover they could find, and somehow we got Wicks's crew clear and into mine and beat it out of there. His tank never blew. In fact we encountered it four days later (its name was 'Mad Martha', stencilled in big white letters), still in action but now being used by the enemy.

At the same time as this spectacle was unfolding, Stein, on the ridgeline, was single-handedly holding off the main German assault. What one must understand about the 25-pounder gun is its defencelessness when used in this desperate, exposed fashion. The crew, covered only by the gun shield, has no protection against machine-gun fire or HE, and both were thundering in from the advancing Panzers and the 88s and 105s. The hell of it was that none of this should have been happening at all, if Eighth Army had been properly equipped and possessed of effective tactics. The enemy had guns that could fire armour piercing *and* high explosive. Why didn't we? Why was it up to our fellows to improvise? Why must our gunners make up in valour for deficiencies that should have and could have been remedied months ago? Why did it take someone like Stein to use unarmoured, slow-poking artillery in the place of tanks and *against* tanks? The whole stunt was madness. That it worked, which it did, long enough at least for the Aussies and a couple of squadrons of Grants to trundle on-line and convince the enemy to try again later, was the product of luck and gallantry alone, a fine saga for the regimental archives but a bloody travesty in terms of fighting a war. Stein lost six brave men and four guns. Incredibly he himself came off without a scratch. The tally of Panzers taken out by his guns, five, sounds less than spectacular – but his actions and those of his men saved the line and held the position. We would have lost scores, if not the whole formation, without him.

In the after-action, Mallory put Stein in for a DSO and four of his men for Military Medals, three posthumously. Wicks and I wound up getting mentioned in despatches. When I went to Mallory and told him the real story, that for my part I probably deserved a dressing-down more than a citation, he laughed and said, 'Take it anyway, it'll look good in your obituary.'

Eighth Army continued to fall back. When you saw the wrecks of Crusaders or Grants or Honeys, the cause was rarely enemy fire. Typically the tanks packed up owing to mechanical breakdowns, collisions or mishaps, or they ran out of fuel. When a tank became disabled, its crew's standing orders were to destroy it so that it could not be salvaged by the enemy. But it's no small chore to scupper a tank, even your own when it's sitting still. Half the time our lads simply made off with the breech blocks and code papers, bashed in the wirelesses, then sluiced petrol into the engine box and chucked in a lighted match. Many didn't do even that. They just 'ditched the bitch' and pissed off. German salvage crews towed off scores of functioning tanks and hundreds of lorries and guns. It was a scandal. Even the correspondents covered it up. Every intact Grant or Honey our retreating column rolled past elicited storms of profanity from troopers who knew they'd be facing these same machines again in a matter of days, with Axis crews manning them.

Our squadrons fell back along the coast road. My fears at that point were not for myself. I still believed, like every other imbecile, that I was bullet- and shell-proof. I feared for Rose, for her safety, and wanted to let her know that I was all right. I was certain that the Navy would have evacuated her from Alexandria along with the intelligence office where she worked. But even in Cairo she would not be completely safe. I tried reaching her by phone each time we passed an outpost that still had wire communications. It was hopeless. Cairo was in panic; civilian and even military switchboards had ceased to function. On the coast road we had no idea who was in charge and no notion of any plan except to point our noses east and keep buggering on.

1430, 26/6/42. Somewhere W of El Daba. Smoke, fire far as eye can see. Stukas dive-bombing all day, Henschels and Italian Macchis all night under flares. They fly right over the roadway. Why not? We are sitting ducks to them.

The retreat had become the world's champion traffic jam. For a hundred miles, the tarmac was nose-to-tail with lorries and guns, 'quad' tractors and 2-pounders on portees, ambulances, armoured cars, open trucks and jeeps, tanks rumbling on transporters and under their own power.

In the jam, we hear rumours of Rommel sightings.

One that proves true has the survivors of a British battery surrounded and refusing to surrender. The German captain who holds them besieged has captured a ranking British officer, Desmond Young (who later, as a brigadier, will write an outstanding book about Rommel), and is demanding at gunpoint that Young order these troops to lay down their arms. Young tells him to stuff it. Suddenly: a storm of dust, a staff car . . . Rommel himself appears. The captain spits out the story. The Desert Fox considers. 'No,' says he. 'Such a demand runs counter to chivalry and stands in opposition to the honourable conventions of war.' He tells the captain to solve the problem some other way, then shares with the captive Young a draught of cold tea with lemon from his own water bottle.

0800, 27/6/42. Shunted off track by traffic control, mired behind vehicles in uncountable numbers. Downpour. Arabs sell us eggs. They want aluminium foil, I can't imagine why, and become ecstatic at the slightest scrap from our ration packing. Thank heaven for the RAF. Without them, the Luftwaffe would turn this road into a 100-mile graveyard.

More rumours of Rommel sightings. He's leading the Panzer assault in person, we hear, hard on our heels. 'Why don't we despatch some of our

bleedin' commando types to pot the bastard?'
Such is the anthem of every trooper in the column.
'Stonk the bugger! Let's see some action!'

> 1630, 27/6/42. Pease's A-9 out of petrol.
> We siphon from an over turned lorry. A
> major pulls rank but I buy him out with 2
> fivers and the Breitling watch my grand-
> father gave me. We get 12 gallons. Enough for
> 3 tanks to go 4 miles.

I still can't get through to Rose but manage to raise Jock on an infantry net. His Camerons, I learn, have been taken prisoner at Tobruk but Jock has got out with a convoy of Coldstreamers; he's in the same column we are, only a few miles east. Our HQers in Cairo, Jock says, are burning their code books; Mussolini himself has flown in from Italy, primed to enter the city in triumph like a Roman emperor.

Is defeat so close? Will Cairo fall? If Rommel takes Suez, Britain will be cut off from India and the Far East. Two hundred thousand men will go into the bag. Worse, Hitler will get his hands on the oilfields of Iraq and Arabia. Russia could fall or seek terms. The war could be lost at one swoop.

The only good news, says Jock, is that the farther the Germans push us east, the lengthier their own supply lines stretch from the port of Tripoli in the west. Tobruk, under attack by the RAF, is not yet operational. 'Rommel has to truck his fuel over a thousand miles. Not even he can keep this advance up for ever.'

2200, 28/6/42. More rain. Five miles in 13 hours. Ahead: minefields and the defensive box at El Alamein. Eighth Army will make its stand here, rumours say. Word is that Rommel has pulled up and stopped, 75 miles back. He's out of petrol too.

CHAPTER 7

It took me ten days to reach Rose. I could not get leave, or even an overnight pass into Cairo. Eighth Army was being reorganised top to bottom. What was left of our regiment remained under 22nd Armoured Brigade but was thrown in with an anti-tank company, a battery of 25-pounders and two depleted battalions of motorised infantry to make a new formation. We would be among a number of like units held in mobile reserve for when Rommel resumed his assault. What this meant immediately was new tanks, new crews and new training. I was stuck and so was everyone else. This was at Kabrit, where the Armoured Division was temporarily headquartered. Jock was there too. We ran into each other one night at a fuelling point called Dixie Eleven. Jock was a captain now, with a Military Cross on the way for his heroism in the breakout from Tobruk. He had spoken to Rose by phone two nights earlier. 'She's well and I've told her you are too.'

To hear Rose was close made me even more desperate to see her. 'Where is she?'

'Still at Naval Intelligence. They've moved the

101

office from Alex to Grey Pillars in Cairo. Don't worry. I've reassured her that you're fine and that she'll see you soon.'

'Will they evacuate her?'

'I don't know.'

The fuelling point was nothing but a half-circle of tankers parked under blackout lamps on a flat beneath the Muqattam hills, with queues of tanks, lorries, quads and Bren carriers snaking round hoping to suck up a few gallons. Petrol was supposed to be dispensed only by requisition and only at appointed hours, but a new order had arisen with the imminence of Rommel's assault; currency had become whisky and cigarettes, English pounds (not Egyptian currency), and running into friends who actually had requisitions and would let you pump a few gallons on their ticket before the indignation of others made them stop.

I asked Jock if Rose had told him anything about the baby. My wife, as I said, was pregnant – nearly six months. 'She's fine, Chap. Better than we are.' Jock's citation for valour had come with a twelve-hour pass. He gave it to me, to use to try to reach Rose.

I got through by phone the next morning; we made plans to meet at Shepheard's Hotel in Cairo in two days. As for Rose's own safety, she begged me not to be anxious; her section was being withdrawn to Haifa as soon as transport could be arranged.

Jock's pass turned out to be useless. You had to be cleared by your commanding officer. I couldn't get another. Phone lines had now been restricted to emergency calls only. Four more days went by; finally on the fifth, still unable to get through by telephone, I caught a ride in to Shepheard's, hoping against hope that Rose had left me a note.

She was there.

Everything they say about wartime romance is true. When I saw my bride, she was in the most unravishing pose possible – slouched against the wall in a windowless alcove, with both shoes off and her hair, which had become dishevelled when she had taken off her hat to adjust it, falling across one eye. She was in civilian clothes. She hadn't seen me yet. Shepheard's at that time was one of the most glamorous hotels in the world. The atmosphere of peril had been screwed to an almost unbearable pitch by Rommel's approach, rendering every sound and sensation precious. Amidst this stood Rose. I suppose every fellow must believe his sweetheart the most beautiful in the world. I rushed to her. We crashed together and hung on for dear life. 'How long have you been here?'

'Every night. I knew you wouldn't be able to get a phone line.' We kissed crazily. 'Are you all right, darling?'

'Me? Are *you*?'

She said she had got us a room. I pulled her to me. I felt her resist. For a moment I thought it was because of the baby. 'There's something I have to tell you.' She took a breath and straightened. 'It's Stein.'

I felt the floor open beneath me.

'He's dead,' Rose said. 'The report came across my desk. I saw it.'

I felt as if all the air had suddenly been sucked out of the room. Rose told me she had tried to get a carbon of the report, but regulations forbade removing anything from the office.

'Let's get out of here,' I said.

We worked through the crush of the main salon. Some colonel was playing the grand piano. A group was singing a university song. Outside, the terrace was mobbed with drunken Aussies and South Africans. Gharries and taxis were coming and going. Two New Zealand majors, noting Rose's swollen belly and her state of agitation, stood at once and offered their table. When I shook their hands, I was trembling.

Stein had been killed, Rose said, at a place called Bir Hamet, south of Fuka. A high-explosive shell had taken him and two others. 'I tracked down the reporting officer and made him confirm that he'd seen the event with his own eyes. I verified the name and checked it against all the rosters in Eighth Army. Captain Zachary Aaron Stein. There's no other.'

I put my arms round Rose. We downed two brandies as if they were water. Rose said that she had told Jock of Stein's death; he had known when he ran into me at the fuelling point. 'He told me that when he saw you, he couldn't make himself deliver the news.'

My gallant Rose. 'You're braver than any soldier.'

That Stein could die was a possibility I had never even considered. He was my mentor. He had saved my life. 'It's like . . .' I said, 'like losing the war.'

The most important thing now was getting Rose out of harm's way. Palestine was no safer than Egypt. If Cairo fell, no place in the Middle East would be secure. I told Rose she must resign her post in the code office. She must go home.

She refused. She was needed here. 'Do you imagine,' she said, 'that home is any safer?'

She told me that Stein's remains were being held in the temporary morgue at Ksar-el-Nil barracks in the city centre. We decided to go. I am one of those who fends off shock by activity. I must see Stein's body. Identify it. I must get through to Stein's family and execute their wishes as soon as and as best I could. The hour was eight in the evening. Would the morgue even be open?

There are two public telephones at Shepheard's in the corridor outside the bar. Queues of officers waited for both. One of them was Colonel L. Balls, I thought, this is all I need! L. had seen us. I introduced Rose. There was no getting out of it. When L. asked what errand we were on, there seemed no option but to tell him.

To my astonishment L. offered immediately to help. He had a car and driver; he would take us to Ksar-el-Nil straight away. He did, brushing aside the duty sergeant who tried to make us come back the next morning.

The morgue was two vast mess tents jiggered together in a square that had formerly been used for cavalry exercises. Only uniformed personnel were allowed in. L. offered to stay with Rose. I entered alone, escorted by a Graves Registry corporal. Two enormous diesel refrigeration units stood outside each entry. They had been switched off at night, the clerk said, to conserve fuel.

The dead, all officers, were laid out on tables and cots – any surface that could be put to use. 'We had litters,' said the corporal, 'but the Ambulance Corps took 'em.' He led me to two wrong corpses before finally locating Stein.

My friend's remains were laid out on a perforated steel sand-channel, the kind used by trucks and armoured cars to extricate themselves from bog-downs in the desert. A hospital sheet covered him.

I thought: this is just like my mother.

It took no time to make the identification. The high explosive had incinerated half of Stein's face, leaving the other half more or less undamaged. 'Your mate's in for a DSO,' said the clerk, indicating the registry card. 'He'll get it too. The board never turns down a PH.'

'PH?'

'Posthumous.'

L. offered a smoke when I got back outside. He was telling Rose of Stein's heroism at El Duda.

Outside he hailed a cab for us and paid for it; he had an appointment and needed his car. I held out my hand; L. took it.

'I owe you, sir, for far more than your kindness this night. I have served you ill in the field, and for that I am deeply sorry. Please forgive me. From this hour, I shall bend heaven and earth to serve to my fullest capacity.'

The power was off when Rose and I got back to Shepheard's. The fans wouldn't work in our room. We sat on the bed in the dark, smoking and drinking warm champagne from the bottle. Rose had brought Stein's manuscript; I had left it with her for safekeeping. She put it in my rucksack. The typewritten pages were in a velveteen case with the word 'Macédoine' in script. A trade name of porcelain or something.

We stayed up all night. I told Rose everything I could remember of Stein during the fall-back to Cairo. I was not the only one, I said, who thought the world of him. 'Do you remember how solid he was in every crisis at Magdalen? That was how he was in the desert. He hadn't changed. I can't tell you how frightening, exhausting, and nerve-racking it was out there, and how close we all got to out-and-out breakdown. Stein held all the wires together. When he appeared among a circle of officers, you could almost hear the expulsion of breath. "Stein's here," we all thought. "We'll be all right."'

I told Rose how Stein would sit patiently

teaching young corporals how to call in fire-orders, when he himself had gone for nights on only a few hours' sleep. 'We had our tanks to jump into when the shells started coming in. But Stein with his 25-pounders was out in the open. I asked him once if he was afraid. "Bloody petrified," he said. "But one can't show it, can one?"'

I told Rose that despite all the blood and death of the past thirty days, the experience of war had until now remained unreal to me. 'I was just watching it, like a film, or something that was happening to somebody else.'

In the morning Rose and I ordered croques-madame on the hotel terrace and chased them down with pots of strong Egyptian coffee. I discovered a boxed scarf in my jacket pocket, a gift for her that I had forgotten. Today was her birthday. She was twenty years old.

'I know you're worried about me, darling,' she said, 'and I love you for it. But I'll be all right, I promise, and I'll bring our child safely into this world.'

Rose made it clear that I was never again to speak of sending her home. 'I won't go. Don't ask me. I have my job, as you do. Our child will be born here. Maybe that's how it should be.'

Our taxi dropped Rose at Grey Pillars. She had to get in to the code office and I had to go back to camp. Our parting kiss was on the pavement in front of the sandbagged guard post. 'I came out here from England for you, my love,' Rose said. 'It was a game to me then too. A romance, a grand adventure. But it has become something other, hasn't it?'

Three weeks later Rose was evacuated with her office to Haifa. Eighth Army's new commanders, Alexander and Montgomery, had now assumed their posts. The line at El Alamein was holding.

Stalemate followed as both sides built up supplies for the inevitable all-out clash. I trained with my new formation through to the end of August. One morning, just before the turn of the month, I was sent with reports to Saladin's Citadel, the great Arabian Nights complex where the Royal Armoured Corps then had its headquarters. On the stairs I ran into Mike Mallory. He was just returning from the ceremony in which he had received his DSO; he still had the citation box in his hand. Better yet, he said, he had been kicked up to acting lieutenant-colonel. He was taking over a regiment of the 1st Armoured Division.

'I requested you,' he said, meaning he had put my name in to serve under him at his new posting. 'But it seems GHQ has got you down for the Long Range Desert Group.'

'What?'

He shook my hand in congratulation. 'Apparently Colonel L. has put in a word for us both. I'm off for "the Blue" and you for the bush.'

BOOK II

THE LONG RANGE DESERT GROUP

CHAPTER 8

The Long Range Desert Group was, as I said, one of the 'special forces' units to which I had applied unsuccessfully during the previous winter in Palestine. I had long since given up hope of hearing back from them and certainly never expected to receive orders to report. The news electrified me.

Here at last was a unit that was small and personal, where a single individual might make a difference. The LRDG operated on its own, behind enemy lines, hundreds of miles beyond centralised command. Risk was high, but so was the chance to strike a blow. If I'm honest, though, there was something far deeper to my desire to serve with this group of men. It had to do with the desert, the inner desert. I wanted to go there. I wanted to break clear of the crowded, corrupted coastal strip and get south five hundred, a thousand miles into the raw interior.

Did this have to do with Stein's death? I couldn't have answered. I knew only that I needed to place myself past where others had been, beyond where I had been myself. I needed to be tested. The war had little to do with it. I didn't hate the Germans. I bore no burning desire to inflict injury or death. But I wanted to strike. I wanted to deal a blow.

How disappointed was I, four days later when my orders at last arrived, to discover that Eighth Army was not sending me to join the LRDG but only to be temporarily attached? I would 'serve in a technical capacity'.

> TASK: To accompany a patrol of the Long Range Desert Group for the purpose of assessing 'the going', in a quadrant to be specified, for its suitability of passage for a force of all arms.

In other words, I would help find routes through the inner desert that could be driven over by tanks, guns and heavy equipment.

That was good enough.

That would do.

I report to LRDG headquarters at Faiyoum oasis on 7 September, ten days short of my twenty-second birthday. I have been PTDed, as I said, for the duration of one desert patrol.

Faiyoum is a made-over resort sited along a string of salt lakes an hour's ride south of Cairo. The place is enormous. Elements of 4th and 7th Royal Tank Regiments are here training on the new American Shermans, as are formations of 2nd County of London Yeomanry and the Staffordshire

Yeomanry, my father and uncles' old outfit. Rommel is expected to attack El Alamein at any moment. Queues of transporters line the broiling tarmac, waiting to carry tanks back to the fight. My own reconfigured formation is already in defensive positions at Alam Halfa.

It's 1330 when I locate the Orderly Room. The thermometer reads 110. Major Jake Easonsmith, to whom I am to report, greets me cordially and hands me over to Sergeant Malcolm McCool, a New Zealander, who signs me in and walks me across to my quarters, a bungalow in what had been the bathing area of the disused resort. I'll share two rooms with a second lieutenant named Tinker, who is absent on patrol. McCool asks if I've had lunch; when I say no, he takes me over to the common mess (officers and other ranks dine together in the LRDG), a Nissen hut with mirages of heat radiating off its roof and portable floor fans blowing at both ends. I am to report back to Easonsmith's office at 1630, McCool says. 'You'll get your books then.'

'Books?'

'Lots to learn, sir.' And he grins and leaves me to it.

The mess is empty when I enter except for six fellows sitting together at a table beneath the curving corrugated roof. I have never seen men so brown and fit. They are SAS. They keep their weapons within hand's reach – two Thompson sub-machine guns, three Brens, and a heavy machine gun which turns out to be a German Spandau. Only one is an officer. I recognise him. He is Paddy Mayne, the legendary Irish rugby wing forward, who was my idol when I was at school. Mayne is in his late twenties but looks older, six foot three and as powerful as Ajax. I'd be less nervous meeting the King. But he and his men welcome me warmly. They don't know my name but have been told to expect an officer of the Royal Armoured Corps. We are to train together for an unspecified but extremely brief length of time, then set off on some sort of 'beat-up', which I take to mean a raid. I try to act as if this is not news to me. 'Do you have any idea where we'll be going?'

'Somewhere fun,' says a sergeant.

It's dark by the time I get in to see Major Easonsmith. He is matter-of-fact but welcoming. I hand him my orders, which he scans in seconds, then tosses aside. I start to ask about my assignment.

'You needn't worry about that,' says he. 'And please, call me Jake.'

Jake explains my duties in the vaguest terms. For now, they will be simply to train and get up to speed on LRDG protocol. 'You'll have to absorb six weeks' work in less than two. I hope that suits you.' Before I can answer he indicates a stack of a dozen books on a table at the back of the room. 'Read these. Learn everything that's in them. You must not fail, because no one else will get a look at them.'

He taps my orders dossier and congratulates me on my evaluation.

'Sir?'

'Your colonel's appraisal of your performance as an officer. According to him, you can walk on water.'

So: my parting gift from L.

I have been selected for this assignment as well, Easonsmith tells me, because my service record indicates that I speak German. I explain that at the peak of my powers, several university terms in the past, the best I could do was struggle through the front page of the *Frankfurter Allgemeine Zeitung*.

'It'll come back,' Jake assures me. He gives me a peaked Wehrmacht cap. 'In case you need it.'

He stands. 'Oh, by the way, the books can't leave this office. You'll have to study them here after the day's training.' He raps me warmly on the shoulder and strides for the door. 'It goes without saying: you may speak a word of this to no one.'

Dearest Rose,

Well, I'm here. Can't tell you where, but it's picturesque as hell and about the same temperature. The unit is unlike any I've served with. Officers wear no insignia and are called by their Christian names. When there's manual labour to be done, everyone mucks in. I like it.

Throughout the first days of training, the battle that would come to be called Alamein I rages along the coast. Rommel is hurling everything he's got against Montgomery's dug-in tanks and artillery along the defensive line at El Alamein. Each night while my new mates are glued to the BBC for news of this clash, I'm in Jake's office reading. The books are about Rommel. Jake has numbered them in order of priority. First is the Field Marshal's bestseller, *Infantrie Greift An* (*Infantry in the Attack*), a serious, almost scholarly account of his exploits as a lieutenant during the Great War. I am astonished at the number of actions Rommel has participated in under fire, well over a hundred, and at the extent of his audacity and fearlessness. In the Carpathian campaign he and a handful of troopers ford an icy river under shellfire, taking almost a thousand prisoners. Rommel breaks through defensive lines, captures fortified peaks, single-handedly turns battles. It's all true and written not with ego or grandiosity but in the spirit only of a teacher seeking to share his experience with the next generation of infantry officers. On the cover of the book is an illustration of Germany's highest decoration for valour, the Pour le Mérite, of which Rommel is his country's youngest recipient. In addition to this book, I read Most Secret wireless intercepts of communications between Rommel and Kesselring, his immediate superior, and between him and Hitler. I study the operations

118

report of a British commando raid, mounted last year on Rommel's rear headquarters at Beda Littoria. The raiders burst at night into what they thought was the general's living quarters, machine-gunning rooms on the first floor before being shot up themselves and driven out by defending troops. In the end, intelligence on the house proved faulty; the site was not Rommel's quarters and he himself had been nowhere near it for a fortnight. I study articles and war college lectures by and about Rommel, as well as tracts on tank tactics by General Heinz Guderian, his boss during the blitzkrieg of France, and essays on the employment of armour by our own countrymen, J. F. C. Fuller and B. H. Liddell Hart. I read *Mein Kampf*.

Still no word on our mission, its date or objective.

All day I drill with the SAS men. We train among sandhills near the Pyramids. Our instructors are Willets and Enders, Kiwi NCOs with over forty LRDG patrols between them. They school us in explosives and demolitions. We learn about fuses, primers, 'sticky bombs' (a mixture of plastic explosive, motor oil and incendiary thermite, used to blow up parked aircraft), 'time pencils' (a type of detonator, the size of a test tube, which is activated by snapping its glass shell in two, thus releasing an acid that then eats through a copper electrical wire), igniters and 'daisy chains' (for multiple, simultaneous or sequential explosions). This stuff is old hat to the

SAS but brand new to me. Together we learn desert driving skills: techniques of extrication from sand; formations for travel; defence against aircraft; vehicle maintenance and repair; land navigation using the sun compass and the theodolite. Two hours each day are spent in weapons training, with particular stress on keeping the guns free of sand and grit. Each truck in an LRDG patrol has at least two machine gun – .30- or .50-calibre aircraft Brownings and twin .303 Vickers Ks. One truck in each patrol is a weapons vehicle, packing a 20mm Italian Breda gun that can blow down the wall of a house. We study first aid. Wireless and code. Physical conditioning is restricted to the pre-dawn hours, because of the heat and because the SAS men are already as fit as greyhounds.

For the driving work we're overseen by Corporal Hank Lincoln, another New Zealander, who has become something of a celebrity for his twenty-nine-day walking escape from a POW cage at Agedabia, his account of which has been published to considerable acclaim. He's a cheery sort, who calls everyone Bub or Topper, and is enormously knowledgeable in gunnery and navigation as well as in driving. He teaches us sand-motoring technique: how to mount and descend hummocks and razorback dunes; tyre inflation; recognition of salt marshes and quicksand. He schools us down to the actual grains of sand which, we learn, are coarser at the crests of minor dunes than at the peaks of big ones. What this means is you have to drive differently up the great three-hundred-foot Sand Sea combers. In these the individual grains have settled over centuries into a geometric configuration whose surface is as fragile as the skin on a pot of rice pudding. One assaults these giant dunes head-on, Lincoln tutors us, bringing all the speed one can carry. We're rolling at forty with the gearbox howling, topped out in second, when the front tyres strike the 'apron' and the nose of the truck tilts upwards. 'Steady throttle!' Lincoln roars. Punch too hard and the spin of the wheels ruptures the membrane of surface tension; you plunge through and sink to your axles. Too slow and you belly out. You can't change gear or you lose traction. Meanwhile the glaring, featureless face of the dune masks all sensation of motion; your engine's screaming but you feel as if you're sitting still. Suddenly: the crest. 'Hard ninety!' cries Lincoln, meaning turn left or right, deliberately bogging down on top of the razorback. If you let the front tyres nose over by so much as eighteen inches, the truck will plunge and flip.

Dearest Rose,

Still in the dark about our mission. We train and eat, train and sleep. The men's conversations are composed entirely of speculation. 'Where are we going? When? With what orders?'

121

The clashes at Alamein continue. What none of our fellows can work out is what the brass hats have in mind for an outfit as tiny as ours. What can our few trucks and machine guns accomplish when every Allied tank and gun is already engaged in the battle that will decide the fate of Egypt, the Persian and Arabian oilfields, and perhaps the war itself?

Days pass. Though the mission's objective remains unspecified, its composition begins to become more clear. Two additional units have arrived. First is LRDG's 'T1' patrol of five trucks and sixteen men, freshly returned from a raid on the Axis airfield at Barce. T1 is commanded by Captain Nick Wilder, a New Zealander. Wilder himself is straight out of hospital, having been shot through both legs during the raid, in addition to suffering a concussion from ramming his truck into two Italian L3 tanks which had blocked his patrol's single lane of escape. The raid destroyed twenty German aircraft on the ground and blew up a number of warehouses and repair shops; Wilder has been awarded a DSO for his actions under fire. He gimps about with a cane now but is getting nimbler every day.

The second addition is Major Vladimir Peniakoff, called Popski after the cartoon character. Popski's outfit consists of an indeterminate number of Arabs, Commonwealth officers and NCOs of obscure provenance, and a white dog named Bella. The formation is referred to in official documentation as PPA, Popski's Private Army. Popski himself is a Belgian national of White Russian extraction, a businessman in Egypt before the war who, I am told, speaks innumerable Arab dialects and loves England more than Milton, Shakespeare and Churchill combined. He's about fifty, podgy as a doughnut, with a dome as innocent of hair as an ostrich egg. Three Senussi tribesmen accompany him at all times (one reputed to be a sheikh), speaking to him alone and refusing to sleep indoors.

As for our SAS contingent, they, it seems, are all champion boozers and rugby players. One night in the mess their commander, Major Mayne, takes up a post empty-handed in the centre of the hall and challenges any four men to tackle him and take him down. Ten strapping blokes take turns for half an hour. Mayne remains upright, grinning the while.

Without question the leader of the outfit is Jake Easonsmith. I have met no officer like him. He commands by example alone, or more accurately by a kind of focus and gravity that elevates each act he performs and inspires all beneath him to emulation. One would sooner cut off one's own hand than disappoint Jake, though no one I have questioned can state exactly why. In the special forces, I'm beginning to understand, an officer rarely issues orders. The men are ahead of him. Whatever the task, they set about it before their superiors can command them and have it half done before the officer even knows they've plunged in. Discipline is not externally imposed, as in the Armoured Division. Here it's self-discipline.

'A good desert hand,' declares Jake, instructing the SAS men and me on a training patrol, 'needs a bit of the ascetic. He must enjoy deprivation and thrive on hardship.'

Jake is a rangy chap in his early thirties with a mane of dense unruly brush that seems permanently nested with dust and sand. He's not a military type; he was a wine merchant in Bristol in civilian life. I have heard Bach's cantatas coming from his room. He rules with the lightest of touches, appearing during training at ghost hours and staying only moments, yet every man including Mayne and Popski jumps to please him. The solitary personal exchange I have shared with him, one evening on a practice patrol, concerned the subject of the imagination. I had muttered something about the desert being a place where a man's mind could wander.

'It'd better not, Chapman. The desert demands one's focus at every moment.'

Jake has assigned me to prepare a document on Rommel and on the defensive dispositions employed by the Afrika Korps in the field. At the same time, other papers are being prepared by other officers. On the morning of their distribution, Jake shuts down the LRDG sector of the base. Corporal Arnem-Butler of the orderly office passes the word: all officers and senior NCOs of patrols R1, T1 and

T3 including navigators and medical personnel will assemble for a briefing at 1300 hours. 'Is this it?' I ask the corporal.

He grins and says nothing.

CHAPTER 9

The briefing takes place in the motor repair shop of the Heavy Section, that branch of the LRDG whose role is to supply petrol, ammunition and rations to the fighting patrols. The shop is the only space that has windproof walls (to keep dust out of the newly machined engines) and is big enough and cool enough for comfort. It is called 'the barn'. Three officers preside: Major Easonsmith, commanding the operation as a whole; Captain Bill Kennedy Shaw, LRDG Intelligence Officer; and Major Mayne, commanding the SAS.

Present are all LRDG patrol officers and their senior NCOs: Captain Wilder commanding T1 patrol, Lieutenant Warren commanding T3 (Jake himself will take R1). T2, under Second Lieutenant Tinker, is absent on another operation. Major Peniakoff – Popski – takes a seat on a bench alongside his second in command, Lieutenant Yunnie. I find a place on the side. At the front are the patrols' medical officer, Captain Dick Lawson, and its RAF adjunct, Flight-Lieutenant Higge-Evert, who will accompany

126

Wilder's patrol as adviser and air liaison. Near Major Mayne sit his three NCO mainstays, Reg Seekings, Johnny Cooper and Mike Sadler, the navigator, along with Mayne's single fellow officer, Captain Alexander 'Sandy' Scratchley. The feel of the briefing is extremely casual. There are no chairs, so the fellows perch on test stands or benches or simply camp on the floor with their knees up and their arms round their bare legs. The uniform is shorts and shirts, with chaplies, the box-toed sandals that the men favour over boots because they're cooler in the heat and because scorpions and spiders can't hide inside them.

A sergeant named Collier closes the big sliding shop doors. At the front, Kennedy Shaw pins a blow-up photo to a presentation stand. The photo is of Rommel.

I glance round to see if any of the officers appear surprised. If they are, they don't show it. Sergeant Collier comes back and takes the seat beside me on a wooden crate of .303 ammunition.

'The Desert Fox,' says Kennedy Shaw, indicating the photo. 'For nearly two years every man in this room has burned to get a crack at him. Well,' he says, 'soon you shall.'

Briefly Kennedy Shaw goes over Rommel's early career – his spectacular success as an infantry officer in the Great War, his winning of the Pour le Mérite, the triumph of his book

127

Infantry in the Attack. Kennedy Shaw is trying to give us a sense of the man. 'Rommel's physical courage is beyond question. The hallmark of his fighting style is audacity and aggressiveness.'

In the invasion of France in 1940, Rommel commands the crack 7th Panzer Division. This formation spearheads the blitzkrieg breakthrough of the Ardennes, the blow that breaks France's back. Rommel's reward is command of DAK, the Deutsches Afrika Korps, and all German troops and armour in Tunisia and Libya.

Now elevated to lieutenant-general, Rommel lands at Tripoli in February 1941. In his first campaign, before half his men and tanks have arrived from Europe, he chases Western Desert Force out of Cyrenaica, driving our armoured divisions back a thousand miles to the frontier of Egypt. The British press in effect knight him by bestowing the title 'Desert Fox'. Churchill himself declares: 'We have a very daring and skilful opponent against us, and, may I say across the havoc of war, a great general.'

'No one has to tell this to the British soldiers,' says Kennedy Shaw. So powerful is Rommel's hold over our Tommies' imagination that General Auchinleck, commander-in-chief of Eighth Army, felt it necessary last spring to publish the following directive:

There exists a real danger that our friend Rommel is becoming a kind of magician or bogey-man to our troops, who are talking far too much about him. He is by no means a superman and it is highly undesirable that our men should credit him with supernatural powers . . . We must refer to 'the Germans' or 'the Axis powers' . . . and not always keep harping on Rommel. Please impress upon all commanders that, from a psychological point of view, this is a matter of the highest importance.

'What makes the Rommel myth even thornier to contend with,' Kennedy Shaw continues, 'is the fact that he fits neither the stereotype of the rapacious Hun nor that of the brutish, doctrinaire Nazi. He is not a member of the party and never has been. His code of soldierly honour was shaped by the era of Prussian arms before the rise of National Socialism. He is, we are told, a warrior from a bygone era, an old-fashioned knight for whom the virtues of chivalry and respect for the foe are indivisible from the passion for victory. In other words,' says Kennedy Shaw, 'you can't even hate the bastard!'

Rommel's men worship him, Kennedy Shaw declares. He is unique, essential, indispensable. No German general can replace him. This is the strength of the Rommel phenomenon and its weakness.

'Eliminate this one man,' says Kennedy Shaw, 'and you drive a stake through the Axis's heart in North Africa.' He indicates the photo of the Desert Fox. 'That, my friends, is where you come in.'

Kennedy Shaw turns the briefing over to Major Easonsmith. Jake thanks him and comes forward, with a sly look towards his audience. 'Do I have your attention, gentlemen?'

For the first time, laughter breaks up the concentration.

'I know what you're thinking,' says Jake. '"The job can't be done. And we're just the fellows to do it."'

More laughter. A coffee flask is passed round. Cigarettes are lit. Next to me, Sergeant Collier tamps his Sherlock Holmes pipe and re-fires it.

Jake begins, describing Rommel's style of command. Rommel leads from the front. 'He's got guts, give him that. He doesn't manage the battle by telephone.' As Jake speaks, he distributes a number of Afrika Korps propaganda photos depicting Rommel in various front-line environments – in staff cars, on Mark IV Panzers and so forth. Rommel's aggressive instincts, Jake says, have made him thrust himself again and again into the thick of the fight.

'In other words, gentlemen, the single most important enemy personage, upon whom the outcome of the entire North African war depends, will not be sitting safely hundreds of miles behind the lines, where we have no hope of getting at him, but will in all probability be placing himself deliberately out in front, in broad daylight, protected by nothing stouter than an open command car. All we have to do is find him.'

The men are given photos of the vehicles that comprise Rommel's mobile headquarters, his *Gefechtsstaffel*, whose identifying characteristics we are to study and commit to memory. A field marshal's command post, Jake reminds the men, will stand out amidst acres of other vehicles by virtue of its concentration of wireless aerials, the steady traffic of couriers funnelling to it, and the beefed-up security round about. These factors, too, will enlarge our chances of success.

This produces the briefing's second laugh. A sergeant pipes up: 'What are we supposed to do, sir, go swanning about the desert hoping to run into the bastard?'

'Sigint has learnt,' Jake responds (meaning Signals Intelligence, our radio-intercept fellows), 'that each night when circumstances prevent Rommel from returning to his proper HQ in the rear, his wireless operator sends a single coded signal at a specific hour, different each night, informing his headquarters staff of their commander-in-chief's whereabouts.'

Our spies, Jake says, have acquired this schedule. He indicates the words 'Desert Fox' on the chalkboard.

'What this means is that the DF can be DFd' – located by radio Directional Finding. 'By no means does this warrant that Rommel will stay put. Where he sets down at 1900 may not be where he remains at 1930. That's where you fellows come in. Major Mayne, will you take over?'

Paddy Mayne steps forward. To those of his era, no introduction would be necessary, but for later readers let me say only that Mayne had been a rugby star before the war on a par with the great champions of any epoch; he is a Cambridge man and a solicitor; by war's end he will become Britain's most highly decorated soldier and, with the exception only of his commanding officer in the SAS, David Stirling, the most celebrated British commando of the North Africa war.

'What does this mean, sir?' A voice addresses the major. 'That we pinhole Rommel and go in with all guns blazing?'

Mayne smiles. 'I wish it did, lads. But it looks as if the RAF will be getting all the glory.'

The first groan ascends.

Our ground party's assignment, Mayne explains, is to penetrate the enemy's defences, getting close enough to the target either to fix its bearings or, if possible, to mark Rommel's location with red smoke. Fighter planes of the Royal Air Force will take care of the kill. Our role is to clean up anything left over, then get the hell out.

At this, the briefing breaks into muttered indignation. For my part, though by war's end I will have participated in a number of such Orders Group, during which outlandish assignments are imparted with absolutely straight faces, and during which I invariably feel my blood run cold, I cannot fail to be astonished at the keen and cheerful fervour with which this near-suicidal mission is embraced.

'Rotten luck,' says Mayne. 'The air force boys have beaten us this time. Still, our turn should be damn brisk sport. Don't give up hope, lads. I've seen these aviation types come up empty more than once. If they kick it, we'll get our shot.'

The briefing breaks up in high spirits. The men, who all know each other from their units and from prior operations, move off into their various groups to work out the details of their individual assignments. I find myself alone, picturing in my mind the vast expanse of the Western Desert and the tens of thousands of soldiers, tanks and guns of the Afrika Korps. Is it just me, or is this operation as preposterous as it sounds?

I turn to the Kiwi sergeant, Collier, who has been perched on an ammunition crate beside me throughout the briefing. He looks the athletic sort, who on civvy street has probably been a rugby player or a mountaineer, as so many NZedders are.

'What do you make of this show, Sergeant?'

The New Zealander turns to me with a grin. 'Sounds like a dodgy do to me, sir.'

CHAPTER 10

That afternoon comes the load-out.

Orders are issued at 1400. All passes are cancelled and all mail and phone privileges cut off. Instructions to the patrol commanders are to outfit their vehicles with fuel, oil, water, rations and ammunition for thirty days.

T3 patrol – the one I'll ride with – has at the last instant lost its commander, Lieutenant Warren, to an emergency appendectomy. Sergeant Collier is placed in command. The eleven other men are all New Zealanders except Miller, the medical orderly, who's a Yorkshireman from Bradford. We have five SAS troopers who will travel with us.

The trucks are loaded in a yard that's off-limits to all but LRDG personnel. The men are given the afternoon and night to pack the vehicles; I keep close but out of the troopers' way.

In honour of the New Zealand composition of T3 patrol, the trucks all bear Maori names. I will ride in Te Aroha IV. Patrol commanders' vehicles are American Willys jeeps, reserved for the LRDG from the rare and highly prized few that Eighth

Army has managed to lay hands on, so that these officers can scout ahead over rough going. The other vehicles are all full-size 30-hundredweight trucks. The crew of Te Aroha IV, or 'Four' as she is called, are me, Trooper L. G. Oliphant as driver, Corporal Jack Standage as one gunner and Trooper 'Punch' Danger (pronounced DAN-gurr, with a hard g) as the other. We'll have one SAS man, Sergeant Pokorny, as a passenger; he'll handle his own weapon, a Bren gun. Sergeant Wannamaker commands Te Rangi V, the wireless vehicle, with Trooper Frank Grainger as his operator, gunner Marks and fitter Durrance. Corporal Conyngham runs the weapons truck, Tirau VI, with gunners Midge and Hornsby and the medical orderly, Miller. They'll carry two SAS team members each. The LRDG men are all New Zealanders, as I said, and all, except two privates, Holden and Davies, older than I by at least seven years. In civilian life they are farm appraisers, stockmen, fitters and joiners. They have families and own farms. Oliphant's family's is ten thousand acres.

The load-out takes place under the eaves of the motor shop. Supplies are laid out on tarpaulins alongside. Wilder and Easonsmith oversee the labours. Every requisitioned item seems to be on hand with the exception of T3's petrol, which has been delayed coming from the quartermaster. T1 and R1 have theirs. I watch Easonsmith's and Wilder's patrols finish up and tarp over (the covers are for not rain but sand and dust), then roll the trucks into their parking slots, ready for tomorrow. Our fuel, T3's, still hasn't shown up. It's dark now. At last our lorry arrives, a White 10-tonner, stacked to the gunwales with petrol tins. Our fellows offload the boxes labelled

SHELL

MT

BENZINE.

This White and a Mack NR9 will accompany the patrols for the first two hundred and fifty miles, acting as rolling petrol dumps.

A thirty-hundredweight truck is supposed to take a load no greater than a ton and a half. Added leaf springs can beef that up to 3,300 pounds, though Collier tells me that at a pinch he's packed on as much as two tons. You load a truck with petrol tins first. T1 and R1 patrols' fuel comes in tight, leakproof jerry cans (captured from the Germans and valued almost as highly as US jeeps) – forty-five per truck. Eight jerry cans apiece go to Wilder's and Easonsmith's jeeps and to the three others set aside for Major Mayne, his infiltration teams and for Popski. But the Q has ballsed-up T3 patrol's fuel ration; instead of jerry cans we get 'flimsies', the notorious four-gallon containers made of metal so thin you can practically puncture it with a fingernail. Flimsies come two to a case, packed in cardboard. Of seventy-six that Collier's crew take down from the Mack, twenty-one are leaking at the seams; eleven have drained half to nil. 'A lot of work with the funnel,' says our sergeant. He and I conspire. The shortage is made up by a bit of light pillaging, in the form of three forty-four-gallon drums, which Punch and Grainger under my direction spirit out from the shop stores and which all three of us roll up ramps in the dark into the trailers. The solution is so satisfactory that we help ourselves to two more drums, leaving the piles of leaking flimsies for the quartermaster. We stow the drums aft of the cab; counting the topped-up twenty-gallon fuel tank, each truck is now loaded with about a hundred and eighty gallons, or a little over half a ton.

The remaining two thousand pounds is water, rations and cooking gear, POL (petroleum, oil, lubricants), ammunition, bedding and kit, sand-channels and mats, wireless, batteries, and guns and men themselves. In addition, for this operation only, each patrol commander's truck will carry a short-range 'A' radio, like the kind used in tanks. The 'A' set uses voice, not code, and will be employed to communicate among patrol commanders and with the jeeps of the SAS infiltration teams. The fitter's truck carries spare axles and radiators, extra clutch plates, steering rods and assemblies, and all manner of hoses, belts and fittings. Twenty-six tins of petrol are stowed directly behind each cab in four rows of six each across with the remaining two on top. Directly aft of this stands the mount for the Browning. Pipe stanchions at the four corners of the truckbed provide supplementary mounts. Ammunition boxes, wood with rope handles on each end, form a floor for the gunner to stand on, with a wall of tins rising directly behind the petrol. In the gaps go sleeping-tarpaulins, coats, caps, web gear and each man's personal bedding, rucksack, and bale-out kit. Rations and cooking gear (and the ceramic jugs of rum marked 'SRD', which stands for Supply Reserve Depot but which all hands translate as 'Seldom Reaches Destination') are secured just inside the tailboard, so that the cook, or whoever is acting in such capacity, can drop the plank and get at the 'conner' fast when men are hungry. Drinking water is carried in tins identical to those used for petrol, with their caps soldered shut to prevent leakage, and marked with a big white X. 'This,' declares Sergeant Wannamaker, 'is so that officers can tell which tin to drink out of.'

A Mills bomb is what the Yanks call a hand grenade. Oliphant and Holden pack them for all four of T3's vehicles. The elements go in separate boxes – explosives in one, fuses and detonators in another. The boxes are wood, which Oliphant explains is handy, as we can break them up to make fires for a brew-up of tea.

By ten at night the trucks are loaded. (A last-minute change in orders pulls Popski and his Arabs from the operation; rumour says they will kick off

139

with Tinker, when he returns with T2 patrol, on a different mission.) Wrapped and tarped, the vehicles glisten like Christmas packages. I have only helped a little but I feel proud and satisfied. A quick feed, a smoke with Collier and Oliphant, and I'm off for the bunk.

I can't sleep. Midnight comes and goes. I'm thinking about my shaving kit. Why have I packed a razor? There'll be no water to shave with. Hairbrush? Pistol? Saved weight would add a pint of petrol. Books. Those I *will* need. I lay out half a dozen, including *Paradise Lost*, *The Sun Also Rises*, and Stein's manuscript, which I carry for luck. At 0245 I'm up and pacing. I shave one last time, dress and start on foot for the motor yard.

The vehicle park is blacked out, not even electric torches permitted. Desert nights are bright though; the trucks cast shadows, even in starlight. Four new vehicles have arrived since I went for dinner – German Kübelwagen jeeps with camouflage paint and Afrika Korps markings. No one has told me about these; they must be for the SAS infiltration teams. I walk round the trucks. You can smell the gunblack on the Brownings and the Vickerses, even under their canvas covers. The vehicles stink of petrol and rubber, motor oil and grease. They're cold in the night; condensation beads on their mudguards and trickles down their frames. Along their flanks ride the perforated steel sand-channels. Beside these are mounted the sectioned poles for the Wyndom aerials; spades and axes; extra leaf springs. Clearance between tyres and mudguards had been over eighteen inches when we started; now with the load it's under six. No doors on these trucks, just canvas dust-flaps, and no roofs or windscreens except open-car-style 'aeros', covered in canvas so their glass doesn't flash in the sun. Seats and steering wheels are swathed in blankets to keep off the wet tonight and the sun tomorrow. The trucks have no ignition keys; you just step on the starter. I'm finishing a walk-round of Te Aroha IV when a lanky form materialises from the corner of the shop.

It's Easonsmith. For an instant I consider ducking from sight; he's such a daunting presence to me. He spots me, though, and comes forward. 'Can't sleep, eh, Chapman?'

'No, sir.'

'Neither can I. Never can, the night before a push-off.'

We exchange good-mornings and chat informally for several moments. He asks about my notes and orders. Do I have everything I need? Do I understand what will be required of me?

I assure him I do.

'Yes,' says Easonsmith, 'I always lied too.'

Jake regards me thoughtfully. He wears a Hebron fleece greatcoat; I'm shivering in a new Tropel.

'I'm glad we've run into each other, Chapman. I have something to say to you.'

I brace for the lecture about Special Operations being different from the regular army,
which I have heard already half a dozen times
from Kennedy Shaw, Willets and Enders and
the other instructors. But that's not what Jake
has in mind.

'You're in a bit of a ticklish situation here,
Chapman – an officer in a patrol whose
commander is an NCO. I mean Sergeant Collier.
It's unfortunate, Lieutenant Warren being taken
ill so suddenly, but there you have it. Collie, I
assure you, is top-shelf, an old desert hand. You
understand that I can't place you, a seconded
officer with no inner-desert experience, in
command of a specialised unit whose men have
served together under this particular leader for
over a year. As you know, we have an RAF officer
in Captain Wilder's patrol; I've handled his
placement the same as yours.'

I assure Jake that I understand.

'That being said, you are by no means a mere
passenger.' He draws on his pipe, which he holds
upside down for blackout protocol, and nods
towards the desert. 'The one thing you can count
upon in operations like these is that something
will go wrong. When it does, a second balls-up
invariably follows. Before you know it, all your
cherished plans have unravelled down to the
ground.'

I respond yessir.

'You think I haven't been watching you.

Chapman, but I have. I've been waiting for you to find your place. Sink or swim.'

I tell him I'm swimming as hard as I can.

'Try swimming less hard.'

Footfalls sound from the far side of the vehicle park – Major Mayne and Mike Sadler, the SAS navigator, come to give a onceover to their vehicles. Jake greets them across the space with a half-salute, then turns back to me.

'Hell could break loose on this operation, Chapman. Be ready when you're needed.'

I acknowledge, with my bones rattling inside my light coat.

'Here,' says Jake, 'you're freezing.'

He strips off his greatcoat and wraps it round my shoulders. 'Don't worry,' he says. 'I've got another.'

Now I'm thoroughly confused. Am I in favour or on the mat?

Easonsmith beats the bowl of his pipe against the heel of his boot, then grinds out the embers in the dust. He straightens, ready to move off.

'Don't mind this little lecture, Chapman. Keyed up, that's all. Chattering as much for my own benefit as for yours.'

He raps me once on the shoulder, then nods towards the paperback in my pocket.

'What're you reading there?'

'You mean this book, sir?

Jake smiles. 'You *do* read, don't you, Chapman?'

With sinking heart I confess to ploughing

143

through Bertie Nevins's *The Chrome Castle*. Detective pulp. Absolute drivel.

'Excellent!' declares my commander. 'For a moment I was afraid you might say Livy or Lucretius.'

BOOK III

THE INNER DESERT

CHAPTER 11

I'm looking over the windscreen-less bonnet. The speedometer reads 35. As far as sight can carry, the plain is as flat as a billiard table and as white as an ocean of salt. No need for goggles; the heavy sand grains raised by our tyres are whipped away by the wind before they get a foot high. The air beating past our brows is pellucid; Adam himself breathed nothing purer. Were it noon, we'd be squinting across the surface of a mirage-lake, with heat-shimmer rising fifty feet into the air. But the trucks can't travel at noon; the shadow is too short to give a bearing on the sun compass. The lads lie up instead in the shade beneath the undercarriages of their trucks, in sun-scorch so fierce that it wicks the moisture off the surface of your eyeballs and sucks the air and its water content out of your lungs. It's 0900 now though and the day still clings to its last breath of cool. We skim over a surface as smooth as tarmac. Not a bush, not a hummock. A teacup set on the sand would show up five miles away.

Over the Chev's bonnet I can see T1 and R1 patrols, speeding ahead in third gear, six trucks each

147

in diamond formation, with patrol commanders out in front in their jeeps, the lot dispersed in case of air attack – two hundred yards between each vehicle and half a mile between patrols. Collie's jeep lays down tracks ahead; over my tailboard I see our trailing Chevs. They look like torpedo boats at sea. Our truck's plume blasts behind like a shallow wake; the two to our rear throw up their own miniature cockerel tails. The trail blows away to the north. It's gorgeous. We sport like lads set loose in the grandest of amusement parks. Punch grins from behind the wheel. 'Fun, ain't it?' He's already got a two-day start on his beard.

The patrols' route from Faiyoum has been south to Beni Suef, past the poor-relation pyramids of Hawara and El Lahun, and on to the Assyut road. Our departure is supposed to be secret but when we bundle through the gharry- and donkey cart-congested bazaar at Nazir el Wab, the boys who sell melons and dates off street-barrows are waiting in the lanes as if they've known we were coming for days. The patrols have pooled their piastres under Sergeant Kehoe of T1; he stocks up as we weave through the crush at a pace slower than a walking man, buying eggs and dates, lubia beans and fresh oranges. This is the last place that paper money will be good. By ten we have cleared 'the cultivation' and left civilisation behind.

The other ranks have still not been briefed on the mission. That will come in the next few days, whenever Jake feels ready. What all have been told is that the usual routes into the desert can no longer be taken. Rommel's forces now hold Siwa oasis, the old LRDG base. From there the Germans can patrol by air and ground for hundreds of miles. Other enemy units have either physically blocked the tracks via the Qattara Depression or are scouring them too frequently for any Allied formation to take a chance on using them. As for us, we'll be swinging far to the south, beyond the range of Axis patrol planes, then making west across the theoretically impassable waste of the Great Egyptian Sand Sea. For me this is tremendously exciting.

Dearest Rose,
Finally I am where I want to be. Insignificant as our tiny formation may be numerically, I feel for the first time a part of great things. We shall be crossing stretches of wilderness that no motorised expedition, other than prior LRDG patrols, has ever traversed, and seeing sights that few, if any, Europeans have ever seen.

The track into the desert comes up suddenly at the end of an irrigated patch of melons. There's a stone cairn and a battered tin sign with the seal of the Royal Egyptian Automobile Club:

SIWA 500 KM

The column turns off the road. A ragged two-tyre track runs straight ahead. It's hotter away from the river. The temperature jumps ten degrees in the space of a hundred yards, becoming a parched, furnace-like blast that's oddly invigorating. The trucks bang across choppy but good going. I feel elation. I start to turn round for a last glimpse at civilisation. Punch stops me. 'Don't look back, sir. Bad luck.'

The track runs dead straight, a washboard that rattles your brain in its pan and wrenches your molars in their sockets. Punch handles the wheel skilfully, though; he finds the speed that skims us crest to crest. Other trucks swing off the verges, seeking smoother going. The wind beats out of the south, our left hand as we speed west, making each trailing vehicle decline in that direction to avoid the dust of the ones ahead. It's a thrilling sight, this desert-camouflaged armada zipping along at forty miles an hour.

Ninety minutes out, at a formation called Needle Rock, our White 10-tonner and Mack NR9 are waiting for us with fuel. A tall Bedford flatbed squats by the rock as well, carrying under tarpaulins the four Afrika Korps jeeps that I had noted back at Faiyoum. My watch says 1100. Punch logs the temp as 122, though it doesn't feel that hot. The men are lying up under the lorries, making a lunch of tinned salmon, melons and eggfruit. The RASC driver off-loads the jeeps, refusing all assistance. He wears welder's gloves. Even under the tarps the metal surfaces are too sizzling to touch. The men eye the swastika-and-palm-tree insignias of the Afrika Korps on the Kübelwagens' bonnets. 'Who're we after on this beat-up, Lieutenant?' calls a trooper as I pass, heading for a pow-wow at Jake's truck. I stay quiet and keep moving.

Supper that evening is at a place called Mushroom Rock which, not surprisingly, looks exactly like a mushroom; then a long second day over soft, deep sand, with trucks again and again bellying into that spirit-deflating nose-dive stop, like driving into a vat of tapioca. Out come the sand mats and channels. The labour is excruciating at 120-plus but the men's hearts remain high; they treat the crossing as a contest – which driver can get stuck least? – and chaff each other with merry profanity when a rival hits the soup.

It's much drier here than along the coast. My photo of Rose curls up like a leaf in a flame. Spines of paperbacks warp; the stitches in your boots parch and pull apart. Still, we're a long way from true inner desert. Signs of human passage are everywhere. The sand is scored with tyre tracks by the hundred. Markers line the trail: iron posts, stone cairns, empty petrol tins weighted with sand to keep them from blowing away. Every twenty miles we pass a dump of fuel and rations, water tins and spare parts. We haven't had to do any navigation yet. Just follow the tracks and the dust of the trucks in front. Late in the second day, I ask Collie where the Sand Sea begins.

'Don't worry, Chap. You won't miss it.'

I'm keeping a diary. It'll help with the 'going' reports I must file, but I want it as well to keep my thoughts in order. It's easy to drift off out here. Late in the afternoon of Day Two, we stop at a well called Bir el Aden, which is nothing but a circle of stones in the middle of a hundred miles of sand. An iron pipe has been topped with a pair of petrol tins as a marker; there's a pulley and two buckets. Will we camp here? No, comes the word from Jake, we've still got two hours of daylight. The trucks and jeeps take on all the water they can carry, emptying all partially full containers. It seems mad, pouring good drinking water into the sand, but you can't put new in with old. If the old is bad, it'll contaminate the new. All hands re-balance their loads, checking guns, tyres, fluids. Jake comes by and asks if all is well; I say yes. Do I need anything? Any reason to go back?

At 1030 on the third day the patrols enter the broad gravel basin in which lies Ain Dalla, our first real landmark. *Ain* means spring in Arabic. A patch of good going appears. We fly over it. Up ahead one of the trucks has stopped. Puncture. Our vehicles sweep past at forty miles per hour. The bogged truck is Sergeant Kehoe's, of T1, Wilder's patrol. All four crewmen are out working with patch kits and jack. I can see two fellows pulling the inner tube out of the tyre as we speed by. No other vehicle has halted to help them. This is policy, straight from the manual. Still, it's unnerving, waving and watching Kehoe's truck recede, all alone in this vast nothing. I ask Punch, 'What if they can't get moving again?'

'They will.'

Time reads 1111 when we come over a rise and there's Ain Dalla. Jake's and Nick's patrols are already on-site setting up for the midday siesta when our three T3 trucks and jeep clatter in. I swear every nut and bolt is rattling and every rivet straining to pop from its seat; the poor steering rods have taken such a pounding that Durrance, the fitter, has to wait till the steel cools before beating them back into true; if he hammers the rods while they're still hot, he says, they'll bend like rubber.

I look round as we drive in. Ain Dalla is population zero, a few date palms and a sandhill with the spring at mid-slope and a six-inch pipe feeding the excellent, cool water into a splash pool hammered out of discarded petrol tins. A queue of a dozen men waits to snatch a quick skull-scrub and whore's bath.

Each patrol establishes its own midday camp, dispersed in case of air attack. The men finish off the fresh fruit. Punch reminds me that this is the last time we'll have extra water, so shave and wash now because we won't get a chance again. The 10-tonner fuel lorry will top up all our tanks, then head back to Faiyoum. As Standage and Oliphant rig our lie-up, Collier and I drive forward to catch up with Nick and Jake. Jake's crew are setting up the Wyndom aerial to radio back to base at Cairo. The two masts are seventeen feet tall, supported by guy lines, with the aerial suspended in between. Pints of water are being dispensed when we come up. The fellows pool them for noon tea. Wilder walks up at the same time.

'How do you like the real desert, Chapman?'

I tell him I thought it was supposed to cool off in September.

'This *is* cool.' He laughs. 'C'mon, let's have a chinwag.'

Officers and NCOs assemble in the shade beneath a fly sheet alongside Jake's weapons truck. The vehicle radiates heat like a foundry. Jake reviews the scheme for the postnoon, quickly so we can rest, and so Nick and Collier and I can get back to our tea and a feed. I watch the faces. How competent they are! How relaxed! The fellows might as well be convening on the railway platform at Wimbledon.

'What happened with Kehoe back there?' Jake asks.

'Puncture.'

Jake's navigator, Corporal Erskine, goes over the form for tackling the Sand Sea, whose eastern-most rampart, I gather as he speaks, is only five hours ahead. We'll camp short tonight and attack the dunes early; you need shadows to judge ascents and crests. Jake still hasn't called a war council. The fellows, however, have pretty well worked out the scheme. They're excited. I am too.

154

So far there's no sense of danger. The scale and isolation of the landscape is so overwhelming that, if you ran into other humans, your instinct would be to hail them in for a smoke and a cup of tea. The emptiness humbles you. When Punch speaks, or Collie or Oliphant, it's often in a whisper. I catch myself doing the same.

> Dearest Rose,
> One would think that the imagination would run riot in a place so blank and devoid of stimuli. But the case is the opposite. The creative faculty shuts down.

I don't think of Rose till we're in camp at night. Jake was right; one expends all one's energy simply trying to focus. 'A man lives like a reptile out here,' says Punch as we spool across good gravel at twenty miles per hour, squinting ahead for sign of the Sand Sea. 'Conserve everything, even the air in your lungs.' He shows me how to breathe through the nostrils, never the mouth. 'You'll lose three pints a day, just out of your gizzard.'

CHAPTER 12

Three days into the Sand Sea now. The dunes tower as high as thirty-storey buildings; we speed up their faces in our rolling-bomb trucks with tyres half flat for traction and the accelerator pressed to the floorboard. It's like climbing mountains of sugar. One skates over a surface of grain geometry so fragile that it tears like silk at the slightest mistread. Ten times a day we dig ourselves out of bogs in sun like a furnace blast and air so scorching it sears your lungs just to breathe.

I've decided to combine my diary into a sort of running letter to Rose. Might as well, since we can't mail anything till we get back. The Sand Sea lives up to its reputation. The terrain is like the surface of Mars – devoid of life, perfectly geometric, shaped only by forces of wind, gravity, and time. Once you are in it, the landscape dominates your attention utterly. To stand on a razorback ridge with a plume of sand blowing off it sideways, squinting into eternity at the ranks of endless,

156

rolling combers, each coloured a different shade of pastel as the distance recedes, must be like what George Leigh Mallory felt at the summit of Everest if he ever got there. Then you slide down into the trough between the crests – and slide is the word, for the descent is more like skiing than driving, with all four tyres useless except as skids and no amount of wheel-turning altering your course one jot. The emotion changes from other-worldly exaltation to something deep, maternal and cocoon-like. You feel safe. Striking the floor of the trough, when your front tyres at last find purchase on the sandy but drivable flat between giant dunes, and your hearing and sense of touch return with the grind of your engine and the feel of the pedals starting again to respond, you are enveloped by a feeling of release that is prehistoric, primordial, other-terrestrial. You understand why holy men seek out desert places. The great dunes seem to collect and concentrate some immense cosmic energy and focus it on to the boulevard down which you now glide. It mesmerises you. Counteracting this, the men revert to their profane soldier selves. Our Kiwis, most mature of troopers, curse and jabber; they make engines rev and gears grind. Orders are shouted and a great hubbub is made of resettling, reorganising, refitting. The flat between dunes can be two or three miles wide. Here the lads pump up the tyres from 10 psi to 40 (they'll go to 60 later over hard gravel serir); drivers and fitters slide beneath their undercarriages to sweep out the sand which has worked itself into every joint and crevice, abrading oil from lubrication points and burnishing the undersides of propeller shafts as if they'd been scoured with steel wool.

All day we follow the tracks of the patrols ahead of us. The parties try to keep together but it's impossible; the skilled desert hands inevitably outpace the newcomers. By midday of the third day, Jake's and Nick's tailboards have sailed from sight over the massive sand swells. In T3 patrol we rotate drivers, seeking ones with the big-dune touch. Punch turns out to be a thorough hand. He takes over from Oliphant. Holden does fine, leading in Collie's jeep, but Marks in the third Chev can't get the hang of it and Hornsby in the Breda truck – 'Guns', as the fellows call it – is setting new records for B&B, bogging down and boiling over. Miller, the medic, takes over. I relieve Punch when he starts to wear down. I'm happy to contribute. I feel less like a passenger. When we halt at noon on the second day, Standage shows me a trick for refreshment: a tot of rum with water and lime powder in a shallow saucer. 'Set it here,' he says, placing the cocktail on the crown of a tyre in the shade of the mudguard, 'where the breeze can work on it.' Sure enough, five minutes produce a brilliant cool drink. Standage sips his like a colonel beside the pool at the Gezira Sporting Club.

My 'going' reports read the same every night:

Impassable to MT

Motor Transport – meaning tanks and artillery – can't cross the Sand Sea. Even our specially rigged trucks can barely handle the extreme terrain – and then thanks only to the skill and patience of their crews.

Ahead, Jake's and Nick's formations have split up. They have to, to avoid driving over sand displaced and weakened by the trucks of other patrols crossing the dunes ahead of them. Vehicles fan out, seeking firm going. Trailing Jake and Nick's wake, we can see scarred dune faces where trucks have bellied and had to be dug out. On the third night, our patrol camps alone. I've been looking forward to this all day, but now, when we stop, an eerie emotion overtakes me. The same dunes that had seemed so welcoming and maternal yesterday have turned ghoulish and uncanny. No one else seems to feel it. The lads set to in brisk fashion; soon they have a pretty camp going. We're in a vale between two-hundred-foot combers; a narrow avenue extends north-east round one corner and south-west round another. It's like sitting in the bottom of a bottle.

I'm getting claustrophobic. The world has turned lunar and, with the descent of darkness, freezing. The sensation is like being on another planet, in a bad way, as if you've gone so far out you can never come back. I can feel my breath coming shallow and my heart hammering in my chest. What's wrong with me? The others are yarning and laughing; three campfires blaze gaily. To make matters worse, a weird, otherworldly keening now rises from beyond the shoulder of the dunes. I have never heard anything so ghostly. I eye Pokorny, the SAS sergeant; he hears it too. The sound rises in pitch, drops, then returns louder. Engines? Human voices? 'What the hell is that?' Pokorny asks.

'Sand,' says Grainger nonchalantly, crossing from the wireless truck and taking a seat with his back against the right rear tyre of Guns. 'When the day's been blowy like today and the wind drops at night, the grains on the surface settle and rub against one another.'

'That's what's making that sound?'

'Spooky, ain't it?'

The old hands get a chuckle; watching us new men find our legs. Punch grins across the fire and gestures in my direction.

'Now, take Mr Chapman here. Content as a clam he is, out in the Tall Sand! Ain't you, sir, away from all that bumf back in the regular army – fatigues and drills, parades every time you turn round and always some lofty bugger jumping down your neck 'cause you got the wrong button or the seams of your drill shorts don't match. I was with Second New Zealand in Operation Battleaxe before I got away to here, thank heaven. The desert was like bloody Piccadilly at

160

rush hour – lorries and guns, tanks and carriers. Not out here! This is the life!' Punch gestures to the endless dunes and sky. 'No officers – or only decent ones who know the score – and nothing to bother you except the odd scorpion in your boot or black-snake crawling up your arse in your sleep.'

Day Four, I get a moment to speak alone with Sergeant Collier. It's midday; the trucks are lying up waiting for the sun to fall from its zenith. On foot Collie and I have climbed a skyscraper dune and are peering ahead through binoculars, seeking tracks that may be Jake's or Nick's. Collie offers me a smoke. His birthday, it turns out, is 17 September, same as mine. He's twenty-seven, five years older than I. In civilian life, he tells me, he's a farm appraiser. He's got a wife named Nola, short for Eleanor, and three daughters. He volunteered for 2NZ Division and, from there, for LRDG. He's one of the original volunteers who were in from the start, when Colonel Bagnold founded the outfit. 'It was called the LRP then, the Long Range Patrols.'

I note his thick red-blond forearms as he raises his cigarette case to shield a light. On one side is a hand-drawn 'Swee' Pea' over a sketch of Popeye, Olive Oyl, and their baby. His eldest, Susannah, did it for him when he shipped out.

I admire him. I think of Rose and our life to come. In a way Collier is who I want to be.

A straight-ahead chap, decent and true, with no humbug about him.

All afternoon we assault dune after dune, executing 90-degree turns at each summit to halt and peer ahead through glasses, seeking a glimmer of Nick or Jake. No exertion has drained me like this. We get stuck again and again. Finally, with my watch reading 1600, we ski down the face of the last razorback and we're through!

The Sand Sea is behind us. An endless gravel plain stretches west. Where are Jake and Nick? Collie and I split the patrol into two-truck sections and take off in opposite directions. My party finds tyre tracks just before dark. I fire a Verey flare to bring Collie in.

Together we follow the trail into the setting sun. Dark comes fast, this far south. We're groping lights-out across a pan strewn with sharp black stones the size of crab apples. Guns has lost third gear and the wireless truck labours with a cracked sump; it's leaking oil so fast we have to stop every fifteen minutes to refill. Collie and Punch go ahead. An hour passes. Finally we catch a glittering, which grows to a gleam, then a solitary light and at last divides in two and becomes the headlamps of Collie's Chev coming back to guide us in. The crabapple plain turns to pebbly gravel, broken at intervals by low crescent dunes. Jake's and Nick's trucks camp round petrol-tin fires at the base of one.

We come in to no ceremony. One of Jake's

corporals indicates the area where Punch's truck has already set up and where we are to make camp as well. Collie passes the word to all hands: no tea and no supper till the trucks' needs have been seen to, all weapons cleaned, oiled and re-covered, and loads re-balanced after the day's jouncing and jostling. He makes straight to Jake to report, with me in train.

I'm expecting a rocket for our tardiness. But Jake is fine. When he offers tea, Collie declines till our fellows have had theirs. I feel immense relief. We've made it! The day could easily have devolved into calamity. But here we are, in one piece and still rolling.

Then we cross to our little camp and Oliphant comes up with a sick look. 'We were sorting the loads for tomorrow . . .'

'What is it?' asks Collie.

'. . . when we got to the forty-four-gallon fuel drums. They've been under tarpaulins, remember . . .'

'What's wrong?'

'Diesel.'

Collie's face changes. Three forty-four-gallon drums is more than half our patrol's reserves. If they're diesel fuel, our trucks' petrol engines can't use them.

Loading in the dark back at Faiyoum, we must have somehow put up the wrong drums.

'How many?' Collie asks.

'Three out of five.'

The bottom drops out of my stomach. Three

163

drums equals 132 gallons: 1,320 miles. In other words, T3 doesn't have enough fuel even to reach its objective, let alone get back.

'I was the one who loaded the drums,' I say. 'It's my fault.'

CHAPTER 13

There's nothing for it but to go straight to Jake.

Collie and I cross over together. 'Well,' Jake says when I finish my confession, 'you'll just have to go back.'

There's a fuel dump nearby at a place called Big Cairn, Jake says, but its petrol has been used up by other patrols. He has confirmed this, just this evening, with Cairo on the wireless. The desert base two hundred miles south at Kufra can't help us; German and Italian air patrols have been terrorising every track in and out.

'You'll go back to Dalla and replenish from the dump there.'

We're standing beside Jake's weapons truck. Collie is trying to take responsibility for the balls-up. I won't let him. Blame is the last thing on Jake's mind; his focus is on the mission. Meanwhile men of all three patrols and the SAS are converging on Jake's jeep for the briefing at which the Rommel operation will finally be laid out. By now news of the diesel debacle has worked through the camp. I feel an inch tall.

'We can't wait for you,' Jake is telling me. 'You'll have to go back across the Sand Sea on your own and catch us up on your return.' .

I tell him I'll leave tonight.

'Like hell you will.'

The men assemble for the briefing. Groundsheets have been spread, one flat on the sand to sit on, the other lashed upright to the flanks of the parked trucks to form a windbreak. The men have been grilling rissoles for supper; they sizzle tantalisingly in their skillets and smell delicious on the chill desert air. Mugs of tea are passed round. Men take their seats. NCOs have brought notebooks; officers open their map cases.

Jake and Major Mayne run down the operation, much as they and Kennedy Shaw did for officers and NCOs in the prelim at Faiyoum. The troopers know most of the plan already, having wormed it days past from one source or another. They're fired up. I try to listen but I'm sick with my blunder and the toll it could take on the operation. Already I'm plotting how to cross and re-cross the Sand Sea as fast as possible. Jake is telling the men the latest intelligence on Rommel's whereabouts.

'As you know, gentlemen, a hell of a dust-up is about to kick off at El Alamein. Monty's brought up everything but the kitchen sink and is getting set to throw it all at Rommel. If it works, the Jerries'll have to pull back.' Wherever the enemy stops, Jake says, our group will go in from behind. Sigint continues undetected by the foe; our radio-intercept fellows are still delivering their nightly bead on Rommel's whereabouts. With luck, says Jake, we'll be in place to do some damage in as few as ten days.

The briefing finishes. I'm told to sit tight. Jake and Nick Wilder confer with Major Mayne and the SAS team leaders in private. I'm called forward again, with Collie. Jake says he's changed his mind about sending me back to Ain Dalla across the Sand Sea.

He spreads a map on the bonnet of his jeep. There are fuel dumps at Gravel Cairn and Two Hills, he says, on this side of the Sand Sea. 'But both are tricky to find, and I don't want you swanning about on your final fumes. You'll go here instead: the dump at South Cairn. It's about a hundred and sixty miles, good going most of the way; and it won't require a re-crossing of the Sand Sea.'

Jake tells Collie he can't spare him for this errand; he, Collier, will continue north with the full outfit, taking his jeep and Guns, the weapons truck. As for me, I'll take the two others – my own truck with Punch, Standage and Oliphant, and the wireless truck with Sergeant Wannamaker.

South Cairn? My heart sinks. What can this be but a postage stamp in the middle of a thousand-mile waste?

'The reason I'm not sending you back across the Sand Sea,' says Jake, 'is not that I don't think you can make it. With Punch and Oliphant, you will. I'm more afraid that your tracks or the patrol itself will be spotted from the air. We've been lucky so far. I don't want to press our good fortune. It'll be dicey enough at South Cairn, with the Jerries and Italians poking round Kufra. Be careful.'

I understand that Jake is not angry with me, either personally or professionally. His focus is entirely on the mission. 'Have you got anything in your stomach?' he asks. When I say no, he makes sure his own cook puts something together for me. And a round of rum for everyone. He dismisses Collie with a warm handclasp, then leads me, alone, to the far side of his jeep.

'You've been taught as an officer, Chapman, never to pretend to know something you don't. Now I'll give you a corollary: never try to make up for one mistake by committing a greater one.' He sets a friendly hand on my shoulder. 'Get to South Cairn, load up, and get back. It's like trotting down to the newsagent for a *Daily Express*.'

I try to thank him but he won't have it.

'In an odd way,' he says, 'your making a hash of this has brought you into the club. We've all committed our share of balls-ups. What counts is setting them right and pressing on.'

CHAPTER 14

Jake personally supervises the stripping of our two trucks that will set out for South Cairn. It's dawn. He orders all unneccessary ammunition and explosives transferred to his own vehicles, both to save weight and because he can put them to better use than we can. He rehearses me and Sergeant Wannamaker on recognition signals and on routes north to the RV, the rendezvous point – a place called Garet Chod – where we will reconnect with the full patrol once we're back from South Cairn. Jake gives us five days to get there. We are allotted enough fuel to reach South Cairn with a few gallons to spare. This should provide a measure of incentive,' Jake says without a grin. He needs all excess here for the primary operation. But at the last minute, as we're waiting for the sun to climb, Nick Wilder and Sergeant Kehoe slip us a couple of full jerry cans, which we stow in the truckbed, next to the spare tyre mounted behind the patrol commander's seat.

My crew on Te Aroha IV are Punch and Standage. Oliphant and the SAS gunner Pokorny will stay with the main outfit, partly to save weight and partly because Pokorny has taken it badly, being left out of the real action. The wireless truck's crew are Wannamaker, Grainger and Durrance. Jake has taken Marks, a crack gunner, for himself. We make a breakfast of bacon, biscuits, tinned peaches and hot sweet tea whitened with condensed milk, then set off as soon as the sun's high enough to throw a shadow on the sun compass.

Navigation in the desert is like navigation at sea. Since there are few features or landmarks, you have to use the sky. The same techniques are employed by desert travellers as by sailors – compass headings and dead reckoning while in motion, sun and star shots when you're stopped. Standage is our navigator; Punch takes the guns. I drive. The sun compass is a disc about three inches across, marked off into 360 degrees and set horizontally in a mount between driver and navigator on the crown of the dash. A thin metal rod rises vertically in the disc's centre; it casts a shadow like a sundial. The navigator aligns the disc so that the shadow falls on the desired heading. Every half hour he adjusts the disc a few degrees to match the sun's true course across the sky. The driver's job is to steer the truck so the shadow doesn't move. It's not as easy as it sounds. Standage is an ace navigator, trained under Mike Sadler – the best ever, I've been told – who's heading north now with Major Mayne. What's tricky about dead reckoning in the desert is that the ground is never entirely flat; you can't maintain a bearing the way a ship can at sea. A desert navigator has to compensate mentally and mathematically as his truck jinks round hills and salt marshes, across wadis and dune lines. One degree out in a run of a hundred miles will put you off target by three miles. That could be life and death. Standage stays glued to sun compass, speedometer and watch. X minutes on heading Y at speed Z equals our position, more or less. Each time I veer half a degree out, he shoots me a sharp look.

'It's the tyres that knock you out of true,' Punch says when we stop to repair a puncture and to equalise inflation. He means that the sun's heat and the friction of running over stovetop-hot ground make the air in the tubes expand; psi goes up but not uniformly, so that one tyre will read 40, another 60. Standage times the re-start to the second. I wait with my foot on the accelerator. 'Now,' he says, and off we go. Sergeant Wannamaker in the wireless truck keeps his own nav log, also recording heading, time and distance.

I have never seen terrain this level. It's like driving on linoleum. The featureless flat gives no sense of velocity. Time goes elastic. A minute feels like an hour and vice versa.

I'm talking to Standage about Einstein. Relativity. I took a course in college on Special Theory. 'A man rides in a lift which is falling at the speed of light. In his hand is an electric torch, turned off, which he aims at the floor. Now the question:

when the man switches the torch on, how fast will the light travel to the floor?'

'Light plus light,' says Standage.

I tell him that was my answer too. But no, nothing can go faster than the speed of light, even travelling at the speed of light.

'Balls,' he declares.

On we hum. The desert is broken now by low basalt ridges, against one flank of which long sand slopes have been built up by the wind. We skirt these, not in wide swooping curves, but by geometrics – 'squaring round' – to keep our reckoning true. Twenty miles on, the ridges become higher and sharper, forming barriers in which we must find gaps and low saddles. Speed and direction keep changing. Fatigue becomes a factor. You can't tell how hot you're getting with a breeze on you and humidity near zero. Our brains are probably cooking under our Arab headgear, or what we've fashioned out of rags and straps to make keffiyehs. I can hear the petrol sloshing in the two jerry cans Nick Wilder and Sergeant Kehoe gave us, on the truckbed just behind my seat. My gaze is riveted to the sun compass. In desert this flat and empty, you don't need to look ahead. I'm reviewing time and fuel in my head. One hundred and sixty miles to South Cairn at twenty per makes eight hours. We kicked off at 0815. Figuring a one-hour lie-up at midday and a half-hour to brew up at teatime, we should be closing in on our goal by 1745. Sunset is 1851 for 29 September. That gives us an hour of daylight to search the area. My foot presses the accelerator.

'Sir.'

It's Standage, noting the speedo.

'Sorry.' I ease off.

'You can goose 'er, Chap. Just lemme know first.'

By ten the sun is up full. It is impossible to convey the heat of the Libyan desert to one who hasn't experienced it. This is fever unearthly; it is heat as one might imagine it on Venus. We have come up on a track used years ago by the Italians. It angles off to the south-west, towards Kufra oasis, but Standage has the heading from maps made by earlier LRDG patrols so, he assures me, we can use it and not throw out our calculations. The trace itself consists of two double tyre tracks. Iron boundary stakes mark the route at intervals of a kilometre. We speed past in the mounting heat haze. Something small and round sits in the tiny square of shade at the bottom of each post.

'What are those, Punch?'

'Birds.'

I squint.

'The little buggers migrate over this mess. Them's the weak ones that fell out.' They've got no chance, Punch says. 'They just sit and wait to die. Then the wind blows 'em away.'

Standage's log ticks over at eighty miles. The mirage surrounds us. Wannamaker on the wireless truck is waving for us to make our midday lie-up.

The shadow on the sun compass has become too short to navigate by.

We draw up in the centre of a pan shimmering with sunblast. This is no longer Venus heat; it is Mercury heat. Surface-of-the-sun heat. The mirage is so extreme that a division of tanks could drive past half a mile out and we wouldn't see them. For the past two hours no one has thought of a thing except the pint of water he'll get here. The men rig the tarpaulins for shade and turn to their individual tasks.

Standage's job is to fix the patrol's position by 'shooting the sun' with the theodolite. Grainger assists on the chronometer. It's basic nautical navigation and it works. Punch looks to drinking water and checks the covers protecting the guns and the blankets that will shield the seats and steering wheel from the heat of the sun. My bit as driver is to inspect engine and tyres, oil, water, radiators and belts. In this heat, rubber melts and metal expands so much that you have to watch things you never would do in a temperate climate. Tyres work off their rims; tie rods warp; leaf springs blow their bindings. Every gasket has to be checked to be sure it still holds its seal.

Finished, I stride back to Wannamaker, Grainger and Durrance to be sure they're all right and to stretch my legs. The No. 11 wireless set is mounted behind the cab in an outboard compartment on the right-hand flank of the truck; a drop board folds down to make a writing surface. Wannamaker and Durrance assemble and erect the poles for the Wyndom aerial; when it's up, Grainger checks in with Jake on the wireless. Jake's patrols will have halted for midday too. Signals are sent by key in code. 'One seven' means 'Safe and stopped'. Grainger taps it out in under a second. In a few moments, 'Nine nine' comes back: 'Message received, carry on.' Then another 'Nine': 'No further instructions.' Back go the poles into their cradles on the side of the truck; Grainger unhooks the aerial wires and stows them.

We plunge into the shade under the trucks. Punch's thermo reads 128. 'Not that bad,' he says.

'Hello,' says Standage. 'Who's this?'

Two birds have alighted. They touch down on the sand alongside our left front tyre and hop into the shade under the chassis, where we three lie on a groundsheet, propped on our elbows. We perk up at the appearance of these visitors. The birds are past fear; when Punch sets out a canteen cap of water, they tread right over our hands to get it.

'Don't wanna go back out into that heat, do ya, mate?'

The second bird drinks from the palm of Standage's hand.

'Ride along with us then. Be our mascots.'

But a minute later we look round and they're gone.

'Makes you feel sad, don't it?' says Punch.

The two trucks are parked side by side so that we can talk, both crews, without having to get out into the sun.

I go over our position with Wannamaker and Standage. Eighty miles to South Cairn. If we get rolling again by 1300 and keep our speed near twenty, we should strike the AOP, the area of probability, with an hour and a half of daylight. I've decided to skip the teatime brew stop. To the others, I broach the notion that when we get moving again, we take our speed up as fast as we can without overheating. 'What we burn up in fuel, we save in minutes of daylight. I don't want to be groping round in the dark, trying to find tins of petrol buried under boulders. Everyone agree?'

Grainger scrambles under with tins of meat, which he passes round with a wink and a grimace.

LIBBY'S
Corned Beef
Product of Brazil

Can we really face beef in this heat?

With his knife, Grainger pokes a hole in his tin to break the vacuum. He snaps the key off the bottom, notches it into the nib of the sealing strip, then winds this back round the tin's equator till the bottom half, which is wider than the top for just this purpose, comes off. A tap with the heel of his hand and a slab of gelatin-sided, pinkish-grey meat plonks on to his mess plate.

'Biscuits. Corned beef. What more does a man need?'

Wannamaker concurs with my suggestion of getting to the dump early. 'Nothing's ever where you think it is in this desert. And it can get damn spooky after dark. Patrols have shot at their own mates more than once.'

By 1315 we're ready to go. But the sun is too close to directly overhead to throw a good shadow on the sun compass. I tell Standage to set our course magnetically and we start anyway. The delay kills half an hour. Terrain has become ragged now; we're tacking round a series of basalt ridges. Each zig makes our navigation more iffy. My over-heated brain starts working. What happens if we don't find the dump? We'll be out of fuel, five hundred miles on the wrong side of the Sand Sea and over three hundred from Jake and Nick. How dependent we are on these fragile and fallible machines! I find my ears straining at the tiniest irregularity. Punch grins down from his box seat. 'A bloke never listens so hard to a motor as he does out here, eh, Mr Chapman?'

He's caught me.

'I swear,' he says, 'sometimes I can hear the tick of each tappet.'

We jink round another ridgeline.

'What kind of work do you do back home, Punch?'

'Raise ducks. Serious operation; five breeding ponds, a hatchery.'

'Who's looking after it?'

'Brother. Wife.' As he speaks, Punch keeps his

eyes peeled for aircraft. He says he's got three brothers in the service, one here in North Africa in the RASC, two in the Navy. The last one at home, excused from service, looks after all their affairs.

'You miss home?'

'Can't think about stuff like that, sir. Drive yourself daft if you do.'

1400. The day gets hotter as the sun descends. I find my thoughts running to something Stein said in night leaguer during the Gazala battle, not long before he was killed. He asked if I was still having that dream about my mother on the lake. I said I was, but lately with a curious alteration. 'I'm not weighted down by the iron garment any more. Remember, the one you interpreted as a knight's armour. What do you think? Is that progress?'

Stein has a theory about inner evolution. A man matures, he believes, from archetype to archetype: from Son to Wanderer to Warrior and from there, if he's lucky, to Lover, Husband, Father; King, Sage and Mystic.

'It could be,' Stein says, considering the evolution of my dream, 'that your journey no longer requires the knight's armour, since you're living it out in the flesh.' He gestures round our leaguer to the tanks and armoured vehicles. 'You're "in armour" now, aren't you?' And he laughs. 'What could come next but Ascetic, Anchorite, Renunciant?' Stein predicts I'll be drawn to the inner desert, another metaphor. Now, I think, here I am.

Is there anything to this stuff? Is the soul really governed by such interior architecture, and if so, to what end?

I'm snapped out of this reverie by the thwack-thwack of a fan belt shredding. The water-temperature needle buries itself in the red. We coast to a stop and turn the radiator into the wind. Wannamaker, two hundred yards to the right, carries on a quarter of a mile to the shoulder of a ridge and there takes up a position where he can see all around and provide cover.

When we catch up, ten minutes later, Wannamaker has dismounted beside some tyre tracks he doesn't like the look of.

Germans?

'Armoured cars,' he says. 'Two of 'em.'

He can't tell how fresh the tracks are. Could be two days or two hours. Meanwhile our wireless truck has developed a hiccup of its own, a bent steering-rod, making the front wheels track in a hard wobble. If we don't stop and hammer the thing straight, we'll have tyres blowing all the way back.

'That's the least of our worries,' says Punch. He means petrol. We're fifteen miles out from South Cairn with ninety minutes of light remaining. 'Let's get what we came for.'

We press on cautiously to the five-mile mark. Where's the dump? Punch has been here before and so has Grainger. I put them both up front in the cabs, standing. We prowl forward, four hundred yards apart.

Terrain has changed again, into a washboard of gullies and dry ravines, with numerous tyre tracks converging like motorways. A ridge of low dunes runs north and south, looking like the Cornish coast. Have we overshot? At twenty minutes Grainger sings out, indicating a hummock several hundred yards on the right.

I have both trucks take up posts hull-down behind ridges, north of the site. I can't send Grainger forward; he's too valuable as wireless operator. Punch and Durrance go in on foot. We kill both engines so we can hear.

A wind comes up at sunset in the desert, as the air cools above the still-searing sand. If the tracks we saw earlier are fresh, the armoured cars that made them could be nosing round anywhere.

I can see Punch and Durrance scanning for the dump marker; they spot something, then slip from sight behind a dune. When they re-emerge, Punch holds both arms out, palms up, as if to say we're buggered.

He comes back.

'Some bleeders have beat us to it.'

We go in while there's still daylight. The dump is an L of slit trenches carved in the stony ground and covered with sand and boulders. About sixty jerry cans and the same number of flimsies sit neatly in rows. Durrance treads above them, banging each with a stick as he passes. Hollow, hollow, hollow. 'Only fifteen with petrol.'

A fast calculation says we've got just enough to get back. If it weren't for the two jerry cans Nick Wilder gave us, we couldn't make it at all.

'The bastards could have at least shown manners and left a note,' says Grainger. 'We've got supper, anyway.' And he holds up six jars of Palestinian honey he has found. We stock the dump with our diesel; the fuel may save someone's life some day, even the enemy's. 'Whoever took the petrol,' says Wannamaker, 'could still be about.'

We look at each other.

'Top up the tanks,' I say. 'Let's get moving.'

The desert gets very dark before moonrise. That suits us fine. We're all spooked by the tracks and the looted dump. It makes no difference if the culprits are Germans, Italians or our own Tommies or Kiwis; in the dark, they'll all take a crack at us.

We skim north along a different track from the one we came in on. Twice tyres on Wannamaker's truck blow, caused by that bad front wobble. Finally, when the moon rises we halt and hammer the steering-rod back into shape. The racket must carry twenty miles. We chug on. The night crackles frostily under starlight bright enough to drive by; we're wrapped up in wool caps and greatcoats. At 2200 we camp. No fires. Cold rations. We've been driving fourteen hours. A double tot of rum fortifies us mightily. We rig the aerial and try to raise Jake. Too late. He'll be tuned to London and the

Overseas Service. Ten in Libya is nine at home. We lock on to the BBC too. Alvar Lidell's baritone squawks from Grainger's earphones, set up like tiny speakers at the edge of the drop shelf that makes his writing surface. Standage and Grainger shoot the stars with the theodolite. I ask Standage how close he can come to fixing our position exactly.

'Do you play golf?'

'A little.'

'Within a niblick.' And he grins.

There's no danger of air attack so the trucks squat side by side, with all guns under their canvas wraps. We spread groundsheets, scooping out hip-holes, and lay our bedrolls on the stony serir.

Suddenly in the distance: an engine.

All hands spring to the guns. Covers are torn free, safeties clicked off, cocking levers pulled. I can hear Punch's breath whistling in his nose.

The engine sound recedes.

Silence.

'Bloody hell,' says Durrance.

We stand down. Two minutes later: engine noise again. All hands leap back to alert.

Again a phantom.

'Blast this place! What the hell's going on?'

Durrance and Standage grab Tommy guns and trot out from the trucks, straining their ears into the distance. The rest of us stand by the Vickers and the two Brownings, listening like dogs.

'There,' says Punch.

He pads to the tailboard of our truck.

'It's the flippin' rum jar.'

We cluster round.

The wind blowing across the mouth of the ceramic jar makes a sound exactly like a truck engine.

I whistle Durrance and Standage back. We're all twice as nervy now. We settle but can't sleep. It's no good, sitting here working ourselves into a state. The track north is flat; no wadis or unseen drop-offs to plunge into. 'Pack up,' I say. 'Let's put some miles under our belt.'

We run, lights out, navigating by the Pole Star. Who cares how tired we are? If armoured cars catch us in daylight, they'll make mincemeat of us. I lead, with Wannamaker a hundred yards behind and to the side so we don't smash into each other if one of us drifts off. Every twenty minutes we switch leaders. The trucks make five miles, ten. Then we start seeing lights.

Headlights? Stars?

'See 'em?'

We all do. Except none of us trusts his imagination any more. The lights roll steadily northwards, to our west, paralleling our route. This makes no sense. An enemy stalking us would run lights-out. The sight must be a phantom. I pull alongside Wannamaker at ten mph. We're both peering through binos. The lights look about two thousand yards out. Just within machine-gun range.

'Speed up,' I say.

The lights stay with us.

We slow down. The lights don't go away.

Now: a second set. Farther out but also running parallel.

'Sod these buggers,' says Punch. 'Let's have a run at 'em.'

I veto this. The lights may not even be real. They could be an atmospheric anomaly. The way they mirror our movements makes me think so.

'They're getting closer,' says Standage.

'Everyone,' I say, 'keep your wits about you.'

I order both trucks to turn to the flank, drive ninety degrees away from the lights. Will they follow? All eyes strain over the tailboard. Then: 'Where's Wannamaker?'

We've lost the wireless truck!

I brake and switch off. We listen. A truck in the cold doesn't go silent at once; our suspension and undercarriage groan and squeal. 'I can't hear a bleedin' thing,' says Punch.

A shape.

Engine sound.

Punch snicks his safety off.

It's Wannamaker.

'Damn you lot!' Durrance hisses from their truck. 'We almost blasted you.'

Curses stream from both vehicles.

'Shut up, everyone!' I'm furious. I unload a stream of abuse at both crews, including Wannamaker. The men stare. I'm not even technically their commander; I have no right to blister them like this. But all hands

184

seem to respond positively to my tirade. I know it helps *me*. When I finish, my nerves are steady and my mind clear.

What concerns me most about the phantom lights is the possibility that they may be our own fellows'. Another patrol on a different mission.

To engage an unknown force in the dark is madness. But we can't keep on like this; we'll drive ourselves batty.

We turn north again.

The lights keep tracking us. It's too much.

'All right,' I say. 'Let's have a go at 'em.'

I position our trucks flank-on to the lights, fifty yards apart. We'll close on an angle till we're fifteen hundred yards out, then open up with the Vickers and both Brownings. The guns have tracers every fifth round. On my command, open fire; on my command, cease.

'Light 'em up.'

The instant the guns fire, everything changes. The alteration in the men's spirits is immediate and miraculous. The great ripping din of the muzzle blast; the smoking barrels; belts burning through the receivers on the Brownings; the Vickers's drums screaming round; tracers arcing in great two-thousand-yard parabolas; the pinging of the spent cartridge cases as they eject on to the truckbeds, and the satisfying way the vehicles rock from the recoil of the gun mounts. All irresolution is dispelled by taking the initiative. 'Cease fire!'

Are the enemy shooting back? In the blinding

dazzle of our own muzzle flash, we haven't seen a thing. Is anyone even out there?

The lights have vanished. None of our fellows is hit.

Punch's Browning looses one final burst for good measure. 'Let's see if we got 'em!'

Absolutely not.

I order the trucks north. We push all night, navigating by the stars and the outlier dunes of the Sand Sea on our right. Several times I think I smell spilt petrol but I put it down to imagination, like the spectral lights. Two hours after sunrise, when at last we link with Jake's No. 3 and No. 5 trucks in charge of Sergeant Thoroughgood, which have waited for us at Landing Ground 210 in the notch between the Egyptian and the Kalansho sand seas, I inspect the jerry cans of fuel in the truckbed behind the commander's seat. Two neat bullet holes have been punched in the upper rims of each.

CHAPTER 15

Sergeant Thoroughgood commands the two trucks left behind to take us on. To my immense relief he's got petrol for us, from another of Jake's trucks which has broken down and had to be abandoned. Jake has stripped the vehicle of guns, ammunition and fuel and left it under cover, in case it can be salvaged later.

Thoroughgood puts us in the picture as to T1 and R1. Both patrols have crossed the neck between the sand seas and are now two hundred miles north. Thoroughgood will lead us to rendezvous with them.

'Any chance of getting our heads down?' asks Punch. We're all exhausted.

Thoroughgood says no; Jake's orders are to take us north the moment we appear. We are to establish a base for the other patrols, who will be conducting raids on Axis supply routes. 'Oh,' says the sergeant, 'I almost forgot. Signal last night from HQ: Rommel's been evacuated to Germany. The mission's off.'

We stare. Is this a joke?

'The bugger's ill, flown over to hospital. How's that

187

for a twist of the winkle?' The news, Throughgood tells us, is more than a week old. 'Intelligence learnt it from the BBC. Brilliant work, eh?'

I can't tell whether I'm relieved or disappointed. I'm too tired to think. While the men get a brew on and top up the fuel tanks, Thoroughgood takes me through a swift map briefing: instead of progressing north beyond the range of patrols out of the Axis-occupied oases of Jarabub and Siwa, then turning east to get directly into Rommel's rear, as had been the original plan, we have been redirected north and west towards Sidi Omar and Sidi Aziz. Jake, Nick and Major Mayne have already established a base camp halfway there at a place called Hatiet el Etla. From that site they will push north and begin ambushing German and Italian convoys on the Trigh el Abd and Trigh Capuzzo. I gulp a mug of hot sweet tea and climb back on the truck. We're off!

It takes two days to cross the sand seas to Garet Chod, about sixty miles west of Jarabub. The new moon is approaching; we're six days into October. Thoroughgood guides us across the Garbada track, a desolate stone-bounded trace following the upper rim of the sand seas, then north across hard flat serir towards the RV. Signals from Cairo update the news on Rommel. Apparently the Field Marshal's medical staff has ordered him evacuated to a hospital in Semmering, near Vienna. Jaundice, with intestinal complications. General Georg Stumme, whom none of us has heard of, now commands Panzerarmee Afrika.

Three more hard days carry us across a band of salt marshes called balats. The trucks are breaking down with dispiriting regularity. They're worn out and so are we. By the fifth noon, we're back gratefully among sandy, undulating duneland. That night we reach Hatiet el Etla. Jake isn't there. Neither is Nick Wilder. Both patrols have gone north on raids. So have Major Mayne and the SAS. The only trucks are Collier's two and one of Jake's under repair. Collie's waiting for us; he comes forwards with a broad grin. The intensity of emotion, on his part and mine, takes me aback. I barely know the man; we've only served together a few days – but now we clasp hands like brothers. The inner desert truly is like the sea. When you make port, the weight of the world falls from your shoulders.

Collie has hot coffee for us, and boxes of biscotti scrounged from the hulks of Italian trucks nearby. 'Heard about the operation being scratched?' Collie tells us that another LRDG patrol, Spicer's Y1, has been sent from Kufra with fuel, ammunition and spare parts for us. We're to wait for it and for orders. 'Hell's bells,' Collie says, eyeing Punch, Standage and Grainger, 'you buggers look like you just crawled out of the sausage machine.'

Spicer's patrol appears four days later. My diary reports us passing the next six repairing vehicles and serving as a rear base for the other patrols' operations. Hatiet el Etla is nothing grander than a colony of sand mounds and wadis but, judging by the welter of camel and tyre tracks round about, it's a regular caravanserai for roving Tommies and Arabs. We have to move for safety, then move again after that. Too many tribesmen nosing about. 'They're friendly,' observes Collie, 'but you never know.'

The full moon is now two days away. It takes no genius to reckon that Monty will launch his all-out attack that night. The only question is will the Jerries strike first?

On the ninth day a signal from Jake sends us hurrying north to a site called Bir Golan in the desert south of the Trigh el Abd and west of the Sidi Omar–Fort Maddalena track. By the time we find it, just before dawn on 23 October, the BBC is reporting the commencement of the mightiest artillery barrage of the war so far. The battle of El Alamein has begun.

Jake and Nick's patrols are waiting at Bir Golan. They eagerly offload the petrol and ammunition we've brought from Spicer. I ask Jake if he and Nick have been waiting only for us.

'No,' says our commander. 'For the infiltration teams.'

Three SAS teams, with Major Mayne in charge, have set off two nights ago to raid the Afrika Korps supply depot at Sidi Suleiman. They haven't come back. That's the hold-up. Jake has sent a wireless truck forward each night to recall them, but they must have advanced beyond the range of their 'A' radios.

'Could they have been captured?' I ask.

'That, or dead,' says Jake.

Nick asks Jake how long he'll wait for the SAS teams.

'Tonight's it,' Jake answers. 'We'll leave two trucks for one more day, but the rest of us have got to get on.'

The night passes. Nothing from the infiltration teams.

Jake lingers till noon.

At 1300 a weak signal comes. Jake recalls the teams. They acknowledge. But now they can't find us. Another night passes. All three wireless trucks are sent forward seeking contact.

Again nothing.

Twice we move camp. Storches and Me-110s are over all the time now. We're seeing Italian Macchi fighters and Savoia-Marchetti bombers. Once, a patrol of Italian scout cars passes within fifteen hundred yards. I have stopped keeping a diary, in case we're captured. No point in giving the enemy any more info than they've already got. The hours drag. Weather has turned cold and rotten. We take cover under the trucks, not to get out of the sun but to shelter from the rain. I haven't bathed since Faiyoum or moved my bowels since the Sand Sea. Desert sores plague all of us, caused by nicks and scratches filling with oil, grit, sand and grease. They become infected and must be bandaged. They hurt like hell.

Night descends. We're freezing. At ten those still

awake gather, bundled in our greatcoats, to hear the BBC news. At Stalingrad the Russians are holding strong. Then this:

> From North Africa comes an unconfirmed report that Nazi ground commander Georg Stumme has been killed in an artillery barrage. Stumme is the general who replaced Field Marshal Rommel less than ten days ago. Rommel has been evacuated to Austria to undergo medical treatment.

At 0400 Collie shakes me awake. When we get to Jake's truck, Major Mayne and two of the SAS teams have returned. Nick and Sergeants Kehoe and Wannamaker hurry in sleepily from their trucks. Jake holds a lined notepad sheet, the kind upon which wireless signals from Cairo headquarters are written down and decoded. He reads: 'Stumme dead. Rommel returns. Carry on operation.'

The group stares, still groggy from the sudden wake-up. Jake passes the page to Mayne, who scans it and hands it to Wilder.

'What does this mean, Jake?'

'It means Rommel's flying back to North Africa. Resuming command.' Jake takes the note sheet. 'It means we're back in business.'

BOOK IV

THE DESERT FOX

CHAPTER 16

The operation returns to its original plan: strike east, penetrating from the rear the German and Italian formations west of Alamein.

One day's travel, cut short by a sandstorm, takes us to Bir al Khamsa south of Sofafi; a day in place for repairs, then two nights over good going (daytime is too dangerous now; the skies are solid with Axis fighters and bombers) carry the patrols to Bir el Ensor, forty miles south of Fuka, marked on LRDG maps as 'Sore Thumb' for its jutting limestone outcrop. Here, Jake establishes a base with two trucks from his own R1 patrol, including the medical vehicle with Captain Lawson and one wireless truck that has stripped second and third gears and must be repaired anyway. The heavy-weight clashes at Alamein lie forty miles east along the thirty-mile front between the Qattara Depression and the sea. With nightfall, we can see the big guns flashing along the horizon. Jake passes the word for all patrol commanders and NCOs to assemble.

For the first time, I am called forward and asked

to contribute. Our assault parties, Jake says, will move up this night into their advanced positions; the men will be penetrating Axis formations within forty-eight hours. 'Give us an idea of the types of security formations we're likely to run into, and your best surmise as to where Rommel will be and what he'll do.'

Briefly I describe the tactics and configurations employed by the Afrika Korps in advance and retreat when they leaguer at night. I have already prepared a document on this subject, as I noted earlier, which was distributed to these same officers and NCOs back at night Faiyoum. Most of them probably studied it then but have forgotten the body of it by now. So I go through it again. I describe how Axis supply columns come up after dark, replenishing the tanks and artillery in the forward positions. Mayne confirms this from his recent penetration. He's getting impatient. He wants to know where Rommel will be. When I answer, 'Up front,' he laughs and observes that we didn't need a tankie to tell us that.

The whole idea of a formal plan strikes Mayne as ludicrous. His notion is to brazen it out. Broad daylight. Go in big as life.

His teams had no trouble infiltrating in their recent forays, Mayne says, and once inside the German and Italian formations they roamed at will. 'If our Directional Finding chaps can put us on to Rommel, by hell, we'll make sure he gets a hero's funeral.'

'That's your plan?' Jake asks. 'A bit vague, isn't it?'

'Vague is good,' says Mayne. 'The vaguer the better.'

He's got a point. Flexibility. Improvisation.

'It's going to be one big balls-up anyway, Jake. Let our men go in and take a rip at it.'

At midnight, the three patrols start east. By dawn Jake has got them within fifteen miles of the front, spread out and netted-over on a ridge that he describes as a 'prominent feature' but that Punch calls 'a knoll the size of a tit'. Jake sites our T3 vehicles on the southern shoulder. His design is this:

At moonrise, seven of the nine trucks – Jake's and Nick's patrols, plus Collie's jeep and Conyngham's Guns truck from ours – will continue east until they have set up immediately in the enemy rear. Mayne and his SAS teams will have gone ahead; they'll already be there. At the last minute Collie decides to switch with Conyngham, giving Conyngham and Holden the jeep and taking the weapons vehicle for himself. From here on, he says, firepower will be more crucial to the mission than mobility. The remaining two trucks in our T3 patrol, mine and Grainger's wireless (minus Sergeant Wannamaker, who will go forward with the main party, and Standage, who'll man the Breda gun on Collie's truck), will establish a covering position, here where we are. Our role will be to serve as a combination rallying point and mobile reserve, to provide cover for all vehicles fleeing to Sore Thumb and to pick up any stragglers whose trucks get shot up or disabled in the getaway.

Jake's and Nick's patrols and Collie make ready in the moonlight. After a feed and a brew and a final wireless exchange with HQ, they start up and roll out in two columns. We wish them God speed. Their dust and the sound of their engines recede into the dark.

My truck and Grainger's are alone now. I've got Punch and Oliphant; Grainger has Marks and Durrance. We dig in on the reverse slope, scraping out a shallow gun pit, into which both trucks burrow and over which we rig camouflage netting and as much brush as we can gather. The trucks' business ends are their rears, over the tailboards, where the guns can fire most effectively. These we position facing east. We clear boulders from the pit rim to protect against ricochets, then bank the parapet with bagged sand, the best shock absorber for bullets or artillery shells. Grainger erects the aerial thirty feet downslope. No enemy had better creep up behind us in daylight because the damn thing will be visible for five miles. We must be in wireless contact, though, not only with Jake and Nick but also with HQ and possibly even with the RAF.

As the stars come out, I gather the men and go over scenarios. A stew of bully and rice is chased by hot sweet tea and lime cocktail with a double tot of rum. The men are ready. I send Punch and

Oliphant down the east face of the ridge to find a way forward and mark it, so we don't nose-dive over some unseen drop if we have to race to somebody's rescue. Grainger and I scout a getaway lane to the west. I order all guns cleaned and oiled one last time, belts and magazines checked, all rounds aligned. We go over jam drills. I stress again that when action starts, firepower is everything. 'Keep shooting. Maintain controlled, well-aimed bursts. Don't burn up the barrels. But, no matter what, keep firing.'

These are the kinds of orders men like to hear. This is good. I'm happy. A bond is forming between me and Punch and Grainger and Oliphant. It's happening in this moment. I can feel it. As the first watch stands to, I sit with two blankets round my shoulders and my back resting against a rear tyre of Te Aroha IV, with a mug of hot tea on the sand and my notebook on my lap.

> Dearest Rose,
> Nestled on a desert knoll which on a proper evening would make a delightful picnic site. Unfortunately this night we're freezing our backsides . . .

I assign myself the last watch and bed down under the stars. I wake on my own, one minute before Oliphant shakes my shoulder. The moon is down. I'm so cold I can barely move. Time for the wireless.

'Wake Grainger. Tell him to get his ears on.'

All hands are astir by 0430. A thick mist muffles sound. The men huddle in their greatcoats with wool caps pulled tight over their ears. I mount to the ridge with Punch and Oliphant; we strain like owls into the fog.

The terrain is rolling scrub with numerous low ridges, of which ours is the most prominent, rising about thirty feet from the desert floor. False crests abound, leaving great swaths of dead ground. Tamarisk and creosote bushes grow with some density, broken by stony depressions, stripped by the wind, which stand out almost as if they were paved. You could snug down a regiment among the folds. Oliphant is just asking if he can risk a smoke under cover when we hear engines.

'Quiet!'

Grainger kills the radio.

'Which direction?'

We can't tell.

'Our blokes?'

'East,' says Oliphant, pointing in the direction our Eighth Army will be coming from. The problem is Rommel's Panzers will be coming from there too. Engine sound swells and fades. If it's diesel, it's German. We can't tell yet. A thousand yards and getting louder. I send Oliphant and Durrance to pack up the aerial, chop-chop. The other four of us hurry to our guns. My heart is hammering. If the approaching force is German, do we shoot it out and get ourselves killed or elect the better part of valour and beat it out of here? I order both engines started and all camouflage lines tugged loose, ready to run. We crank all four guns round towards the advancing motor sound.

'There!' cries Oliphant.

Headlights. Blackouts with cat's-eye slits. A motorcycle and sidecar bucks over a crest a hundred and fifty yards south. Oliphant and Durrance are caught in the open. In the dark, the bike doesn't see them. It roars on, followed by another and another.

'BMWs,' says Punch. 'I know the sound.'

'Are you sure?' I sign to hold fire.

'Seven-fifties, horizontal twins. German as sauerkraut.'

Oliphant and Durrance have plunged flat on the sand. The seventeen-foot aerial masts tower over them.

A motorcycle column churns past, each bike following the others' tracks without glancing right or left.

'Get that aerial down!' As Oliphant and Durrance scramble, we hear a new rumble from the southern end of the ridge. Before any of us can react, another motorcycle and sidecar heaves into view, sees us and makes straight for us. The bike roars up and brakes in a cyclone of dust. The machine, I note, is not a chain-drive but shaft-driven. Cycle and riders are caked with grit and look done in. The driver tugs his goggles back.

'*Wohin sind sie gefahren?*' he demands. Where have they gone?

I cup a hand to my ear. '*Was?*'

'*In welche Richtung sind die Krads gefahren?*'

I point west. Driver and gunner take off.

A German scout car bucks past, three hundred yards south, then another the same distance north. Daimlers, with their bowler-hat crowns. Oliphant and Durrance scamper back to the wireless truck, breaking down the aerial masts and stowing them into their carrying cradles. We can see more scout cars to the south, rumbling cautiously across the undulating, still-dark ground. Punch and I peer east over the crest. Mist obscures all sight beyond a few hundred yards, but there's no mistaking the growl of diesel engines – big ones, Mark III and IV Panzers, not the light Mark IIs that sound like trucks. I order camouflage nets down and stuffed into the truckbed. 'Stand by, ready to move.'

There's nowhere to go.

Within minutes, the area round our post has become a hive of Afrika Korps troops and transport. The build-up happens so suddenly and so matter-of-factly that we almost feel like Germans ourselves. At least a dozen lorries, half of them captured British Bedfords, roll past our site, following the trail broken by the motorcyclists. Behind them appear more waves of trucks and guns.

Oliphant mans his Browning. 'What the hell do we do now?'

'Move with them.'

To fight is suicide. Sitting still will only get us spotted.

'Find a cloud of dust and get inside it.'

We rumble several miles in convoy. Every vehicle but ours is stencilled with the palm-tree-and-swastika insignia of the Afrika Korps. Thank God for the dust and the pre-dawn murk. Suddenly the column begins slowing. German military police have laid out a stop line; with hand signals they are directing units into positions. 'They're setting up,' calls Punch.

'Set up with them. Find a spot.'

Here come the tanks we heard before. We can see them as the mist disperses, advancing in column on the flat to the south. Thirty, forty, fifty of them. Round us and in front of us, Afrika Korps NCOs have dismounted from their vehicles; they're selecting positions, manoeuvring trucks and gun tractors, directing their men to dig in. Signalmen run wire between posts. Anti-tank guns appear – enormous, wicked-looking 88s and squat, lethal Pak38s, towed by half-track lorries and tractors.

We're hunting for a spot to blend in. 'There?' asks Punch.

A Spandau machine-gun crew beat us to it.

'Go left.'

More infantry digging in.

'There!'

We squat down between two hummocks. 'Now what?' calls Oliphant.

'Play along.'

We dismount. Whatever Rommel's troopers are doing, we do too. A mortar crew begin setting up a hundred yards to our rear; a machine-gun post appears fifty yards on our flank. In minutes both have set up and sandbagged. In front, the crew of an 88, joined by mates from a half-track towing vehicle and a three-ton ammo truck, are digging a gun pit and rigging camouflage nets. We net up too. I smell sausages. Punch points.

'Look there, sir. The bastards are cooking breakfast.'

We smell porridge and ersatz coffee. The Germans, we note, fry up using the same kind of sand-and-petrol stoves we do.

'Do the same, Punch.'

'Sir?'

'Work up some grub. Act natural.'

What preserves us in the midst of the enemy camp is the universal desert garb worn by both sides – greatcoats and khaki trousers in the chill, with peaked caps, scarves and sand goggles. In addition, both armies have captured and put into service so many enemy vehicles that our Chevrolets look no more out of place than the Afrika Korps-ised Fords, Macks and Marmon-Herringtons that trundle past us, left, right and centre. Ours look like theirs and theirs look like ours.

Still, we're scared witless. Somehow getting found out seems worse than being killed in action. Simultaneously the fright is offset by the theatricality, even absurdity, of the situation. We feel like schoolboys pulling a prank. As the minutes pass and we sizzle up our bacon with no enemy catching us out or even taking any notice of us, an odd sort of exhilaration begins to take hold. 'Hell,' says Grainger, 'do I dare have a crap?' And he does – 'taking a spade for a walk' between our post and the 88 gun position two hundred yards ahead.

At 0630 exactly the British barrage begins. This clearly is why the Germans are withdrawing. The shells land at first harmlessly in vacant desert, then begin walking westwards, towards us. These are not little 25-pounders but serious stuff – medium and heavy guns. No one moves. The foe have dug in and snugged down. 'Damn!' says Punch. 'How long d'you reckon these heroes are going to sit tight?'

I've got another concern. Clearly this pullback will alter Rommel's location – and that of Jake and Nick and our SAS teams. My role was to man a position covering our men's withdrawal. All that has changed now. What must we do? How can we help? Plan A is obviously obsolete.

I wave Oliphant and Grainger over. 'Get ready to move. Look official, as though we just got orders. We'll go in three minutes.'

Grainger stops. 'Where are we going?'

'I haven't a clue.'

I'm turning towards Punch to repeat these instructions, when an Afrika Korps NCO in a

Kübelwagen jeep rolls up to the 88 crew two hundred yards to our east and orders them to pack their kit and get ready to move. He reaches us next, shouting the same command. All along the line, gun limbers are being readied and engines are kicking over.

'It's about mucking time,' says Oliphant.

The whole position is being dismantled and pulled back.

'Balls and glory,' says Punch. 'The Huns ain't as dumb as I thought.'

Twenty minutes later our trucks are grinding north across country alongside a dust-billowing column of 88s towed by armoured half-tracks. Bucking over a hummock, Punch lifts a buttock and looses a spectacular trumpet.

'Damn!' he says. 'I'm even farting like a Kraut.'

CHAPTER 17

Three hours pass. The sun blazes. We have stripped to the waist except for Wehrmacht caps and goggles. Storms of alkali roil on a blistering west wind. The German column has halted and scattered three times, all false alarms, once when a front of tanks, which turned out to be their own, appeared on a ridge to the east; once when British fighters screamed overhead; a third time for no reason at all. It's reassuring to see that the foe are not supermen but fuddled troopers muddling along, as deaf and blind as we are.

'Jump on the blower?' Grainger asks amid the dust of the second halt. He means do we dare radio our position and report what we've seen. I've been chewing this over since the first scatter. Is the information worth more to Eighth Army than our mission? I decide it isn't. We've seen our own planes overhead. What report can we make that the aircrews haven't radioed in already? Then there's Jake and Nick and Major Mayne. To break wireless silence risks them and the whole operation, not to mention ourselves.

On the other hand, we may have stumbled on to something. The operation's objective is to penetrate enemy lines. We've certainly done that. I decide that our aim is to stay cool and keep our eyes open. After the third scatter, we make off to the flank, away from the heaviest concentration of vehicles. No one notices. We're paralleling the southernmost column, a fleet of ammunition lorries, miles from our original post. My watch tells me it's ten o'clock when, just as the midday haze begins fogging all vision, we cross a spur of some nameless desert highway and enter a broad valley cut by numerous defiles and wadis. Axis scout cars and bikes can be glimpsed ahead. The supply vehicles are being funnelled into single-file columns by military police with death's-head insignia on chains round their necks. Taped lanes lead the way through a minefield. The provosts wave us through too. A vast marshalling area spreads before us. It must hold a division.

Punch drives. I've taken the commander's slot, so I can perch on the rail and take in as much as possible. I've changed my mind about signalling HQ. This massing of enemy armour is too important. Oliphant stands at my shoulder, on the Vickers, industriously de-gritting its receiver with a paintbrush. I'm fumbling with the map in the wind when Grainger on the wireless truck shoots me a whistle.

He points west. A hundred-foot escarpment

parallels our route. At its brink sits an enormous camouflage-painted vehicle, towering over several staff and scout cars parked adjacent to it. The vehicle is scrim-netted and dug in for concealment. But it's so huge you can't miss it. A forest of aerials rises several hundred feet away, no doubt planted at that distance so as not to appear like a headquarters concentration. The hair stands up on my neck.

'Rommel?' I call to Grainger.

'If it ain't, it's his bloody uncle.'

I tell Punch to slow down but keep moving. Our two-truck convoy continues traversing, about a mile out, on a line parallel to the scarp and a hundred feet below it. We're in a broad, sandy valley, across which spread scores of infantry, mortar and anti-tank positions; in fact we're on the trace used by supply lorries to service them. On top of the scarp, I count a dozen soft-skinned vehicles, but no tanks.

'There,' calls Oliphant, indicating the base of the slope. Six or seven Mark IIIs squat in line abreast. Hatches are open; crews lounge about, looking to their housekeeping. Bivvy flaps have been rigged for shade. I see one fellow shaving over a canvas basin. We're passing a thousand yards in front of them. No one pays us any attention. The place looks like a happy village, with denizens in no hurry crossing hither and thither.

Through glasses I peer at the oversize vehicle. It is definitely a Dorchester, the type of captured

British ACV that Rommel calls a Mammoth. Should I go on the air? I've forgotten all about alerting HQ. What counts now is Jake, Nick, and Major Mayne. They have to know what we've run into.

'Punch, I'm putting up the fishpole.'

He can't hear with the engine noise. I go ahead. I cross to the cradle on the rear of the truckbed and loose the six-foot antenna for the 'A' set, the short-range wireless. It springs skyward with a great whoomp-whoomp. I'm thinking: if the caravan on top of the scarp is indeed Rommel's Mammoth, Rommel himself will almost certainly not be in it. He'll be in a staff car, roaming the front somewhere. I would gain nothing by going on air. To do so could queer the whole mission if the Germans intercept.

On the other hand, Rommel could be here. This could be it. To stumble on to such luck and do nothing . . .

The 'A' set sits under a steel shell behind the driver's seat in my patrol commander's truck. Oliphant has already dug out the headset and chest mike. He switches the radio on. I take the gear and kneel beside the set, balancing myself between a spare wheel and a stack of ammunition cases. I lift the backing plate on the radio and reach my hand in to feel the vacuum tubes; when they're warm, the set will be ready. I pull the phones over my peaked cap. What I'm about to do is potentially the most momentous act of my life.

Forget codes and protocol. I'm going up in the clear.

'Hello Jake, Chap calling. Objective in sight. I say again: I'm looking at what we came for. Over.'

The headset fills with static. Nothing. I realise I have not thought beyond the sending of this signal. I have no clue what to do next except continue to report. I repeat: 'Hello Jake and Nick, Chap calling. Objective in sight. Over.'

No answer. I'm half relieved. How many more times can I transmit before some German intercept truck picks us up? I'm just depressing the mike button when Punch raps me hard. Ahead on the sand road, a Fiat 3-tonner is ploughing straight at us, with more trucks behind.

'Smile and wave,' I tell him.

The Italians pass, singing. Ammo vehicles. Two more roll by in a storm of powder. My headphones come alive:

'Hello Chap, this is Jake. I see you. Shut up and get in a hole. I say again: shut down and find a hole. Out.'

The last Fiat buffets past, swamping our cab in dust. I pull the headset off and turn to Punch and Oliphant. 'Jake's here.'

They react as electrified as I.

'Keep going.' I sign to Grainger on the wireless truck to follow.

I'm expecting the whole camp to erupt into action. Surely our signals have been overheard; in seconds we will come under fire. But nothing happens. We continue rumbling across the flat. Oliphant scribbles

JAKE

on a pad and holds it up for Grainger, Marks and Durrance in the wireless truck. They sign back that they understand. My skull is revving. Have I done the right thing? Where's Jake? What's the form? The track our trucks are on leads past some kind of mobile repair shop. A safe spot. No infantry. Punch sees it and puts us on a beeline.

We buck past a pair of parked transporters. Their drivers smoke in the shade beside the first cab. I swing my glasses back towards the scarp. Tank crews are packing up. Men clamber up over the kit rails of their vehicles; plumes of diesel smoke belch from exhausts.

Has my signal been intercepted? Is this the cause of the pack-up? It can't be. No massed formation can react that fast. What should we do? If Jake is here. Nick must be too, and Mayne's SAS. Have they signalled the RAF? Will Mayne and Jake attack on their own?

All round us, enemy outfits are loading up, engines cranking. The transporter drivers peer in our direction. Not suspiciously; more like they're confused by the mobilisation and want to check with us, their comrades, to see if we know what's going on. One of them starts towards us on foot. I turn to Oliphant on the Vickers guns.

'I see him,' he says.

The German keeps coming. Sixty yards out.

'Punch, get us rolling.' I sign to Grainger to do the same. At my shoulder, Oliphant pulls both cocking levers. The enemy driver keeps approaching.

'Chap,' says Oliphant, 'let me take him now.'

'No.'

The wireless truck fires up. Punch stalls. 'Grainger, get moving!' The driver sees our No. 2 start up; he lengthens stride to head it off. Punch wrestles with the choke. I can smell the carburettor flood. The German is within fifty feet now. He stops.

'He's on to us,' says Oliphant.

The driver squints hard in our direction.

Suddenly he turns and bolts. I see the back of his shirt and the soles of his boots. At that instant, the earth erupts.

A blizzard of destruction rolls directly over the man. For an instant I think it's Oliphant on the Vickers. Then the shock wave hits. Shadows streak above us; a blast like a bomb nearly bowls me out of the truck.

Two RAF fighter planes boom overhead at two hundred miles an hour, strafing everything in their path. Cannon fire rips the sand. Two stripes fifty feet wide roar forward at impossible speed.

'Jesus Christ!' cries Punch.

The Hurricanes thunder away. The concussion of their engines deafens us. We have not even heard them coming.

Out on the sand the transporter driver, who has been knocked prone, scrambles to his feet and sprints for all he's worth. Somehow the cannon fire has missed him. As I turn to check on myself and my men, two more Hurricanes drop out of nowhere and scream down the axis of the valley, machine-gunning the enemy tanks and trucks at the base of the ridge. Where the planes' fire strikes, the earth explodes in a storm of rock and dust. The fighters blast over the scarp at the height of a clothes line.

Punch is cursing our stalled engine. The second pair of Hurricanes has boomed overhead so fast the eye can't catch up with them. In the killing zone, German trucks and transports are shredding like toys in a gale. The ground still shakes beneath us.

Impulse makes me look at my wristwatch. To this day I can see that face, a Wittnauer Elysian with squarish numerals and radium arms that I bought on the Rue Fouad el Awal in Cairo after bartering my grandfather's Breitling for fuel on the retreat to El Alamein. In an instant I understand everything.

'This is it!'

The attack. It's happening now. This is why Jake has ordered us to find a hole and get in it.

The planes scream over the scarp and roar skyward into a steep, banking climb. It takes moments before our skulls stop ringing, so overwhelmed are we by the suddenness of the aircrafts' appearance and by the impact of their speed and power. In moments the second pair of Hurricanes have climbed a thousand feet and are banking into the turn that will bring them back again over the target. We can see the trails of their exhaust hanging in the air. On the summit of the scarp a surprisingly small number of enemy vehicles are blazing. Men are racing in all directions.

We're moving too. Punch has got our truck started. I'm peering through glasses at the Mammoth. Nothing has touched it. It hasn't moved. I can see armed men rallying to it and others, without weapons, exiting its side and rear doors. They do so in neither panic nor urgency but looking a bit muddled, as if they thought something had happened but weren't sure exactly what it was.

'Go for the target!'

We're picking up speed now, straight down the axis of the valley. I have climbed back into the truckbed and am wrestling the tarpaulin off the Browning. Oliphant is already blazing away with the Vickers. The twin barrels fire so fast, nine hundred and fifty rounds per minute, that they burn through a ninety-six-round drum in seconds, howling with a piercing, blood-freezing squeal. The Mammoth perches a thousand yards away and a hundred feet up the scarp. We're crossing directly in front of it. Dead ahead of us squats the repair bay. Fitters are streaming out into daylight.

Some dash towards slit trenches, others congregate nonchalantly as if they're about to ask their comrades for a smoke. As we accelerate to go round the repair tent, a 10-tonner pulls out broadside, inadvertently blocking our route. Oliphant swivels the Vickers. The truck lights up with hits. I have never seen a motor vehicle get out of the way so fast.

We're past the repair shops now. I can feel Punch engage third gear. The truck bucks like a wild beast. We still haven't seen Jake, Nick or Major Mayne. The Germans have seen us though. Along both sides of the track, enemy troopers dash to positions. Oliphant shreds one fellow before a wall of sandbags. I'm shouting to him to put his fire on the Mammoth. I look behind. A truck chases us. I'm swinging the Browning round to engage it, when I realise it's Collie.

He's standing on the bed of Guns, hanging on to the mount of the 20mm Breda gun and pointing in frustration at the summit of the scarp. The heavy Breda faces rearward and can't be rotated forward past 90 degrees. Standage is braced beside Collie, draped in belts of ammunition. Midge is driving; Hornsby mans the fore-mounted Browning. I can't see the jeep with Conyngham and Holden anywhere. Collie's truck speeds ahead, apparently seeking some spot where it can pull up with its rear end facing the summit and cut loose for at least a few moments. We barrel past two Afrika Korps infantrymen carrying spades, no doubt returning from heeding nature's call. They gape like tourists. Oliphant holds his fire though they're sitting ducks.

Collie's truck turns off the track, angling towards the scarp. We veer with him. Adrenalin floods through me. I look in Oliphant's eyes and see the same. He's changing drums; both barrels of his Vickers pour smoke as if they were on fire. We bounce off the main trace at forty miles an hour.

On the summit of the scarp, two storms of dust are racing towards the Mammoth. Tracer fire streaks from both. This can only be Jake and Nick or Mayne's SAS. It's too far to see and impossible to use field glasses at this jarring, molar-rattling clip, but the vehicles, whoever they are, are racing along the crest of the scarp, throwing up great plumes of dust and chalk. Down on the flat, our column of three produces its own cyclone. Impossible as it sounds, no one has fired at us. We're moving so fast we're outrunning the alarm.

Something makes me look up. What I see stops my heart. Two Hurricanes are diving straight at us. I can see their propellers like giant windmills and the flashes of the cannons on the leading edges of their wings. They're firing at us. The dust we're raising must have drawn the pilots' eyes. This realisation comes in a fraction of a second. Then the rounds strike. I have never heard anything, including solid shot from Mark

IV Panzers, to match the violence of those cannon shells as they hit and explode in front, on both sides, and behind us. The sound is like the end of the world. The Hurricanes roar overhead so low that their wingtips seem to scrape the sand.

'We're your own blokes!' Punch is howling at them, appending a raft of obscenities. Oliphant shouts something I can't hear and points at the planes as they bank away and begin to climb. I understand. He means they'll be coming back.

On the crest of the scarp, though we will only learn this later, the same sort of chaos has played out. The dust we saw was indeed Jake and Nick and Major Mayne. The two other Hurricane pilots must have seen it too. Have they mistaken it for the red signal smoke, meant to mark the target? Or are these pilots as adrenalin-addled as we are and blasting away at the first thing that moves?

I can't see Grainger's truck any more. Collie races ahead. Every gun in the camp, it seems, is firing at the planes. Suddenly we're among, an infantry encampment. Enemy soldiers are diving out of our path. Punch flattens a tent kitchen. Our right mudguard blasts through the flue and tank of a camp stove; the blazing fuel explodes in all directions, painting us as we speed past. We're on fire. I'm on the truckbed, wrestling the Browning, as flaming liquid lacquers a stack of wooden ammunition cases and coats two boxes of Mills bombs. The hair on my arms incinerates; my beard catches. I grab a tarpaulin and beat myself like a madman, then plunge on top of the ammo boxes, trying to smother the blaze. Now the tarp itself catches fire. Oliphant's focus is on finding the Mammoth, whose camouflage netting is a lot more effective from this low angle; he has no idea that our truck is about to go up like a Roman candle. We're directly below the scarp now, four hundred yards out.

'Where is that bastard?' Oliphant curses in frustration.

Now the Mark IIIs at the base of the ridge spot us. Flashes blaze from their 7.92s. As I beat at the flames on the ammunition cases, splinters of wood tear into my right cheek and ear – slivers from the truck's flank being shredded by machine-gun fire. If I had stayed standing, I'd have been cut in half.

Oliphant continues cursing. Blown grit has fouled one of his drum magazines; he can't get it seated on the gun. He still doesn't know the truck's on fire. By now I've hurled the burning tarpaulin overboard. I can't get the ammo cases doused so I'm heaving them out, on fire. A wooden case of .303 ball ammunition weighs over fifty pounds. I'm flinging them out as if they were crumpets. Meanwhile the truck is weaving so violently that I fear Punch has been hit at the wheel. I dive over the forewall into the cab. Punch has the accelerator to the floor. 'I'm fine!' he shouts.

Now the planes come back.

One pair takes the scarp, the other the flat. I see Collie's truck, a hundred yards ahead and angling diagonally away from the summit, so its rear-facing Breda gun can get off at least a few rounds where they'll do some damage. Collie fires the gun, Standage feeds the oversize belt; Midge and Hornsby are up front. The Hurricanes dive on us and on them.

In slow motion I see a double stitching of cannon fire rip the sand in front of Collie. The right-hand stitch rolls over the long axis of his truck. The vehicle is a rolling bomb, packed with explosives. I see the rear half disintegrate. Midge at the wheel is attempting a hard right to evade the cannon fire. As the truck's hind end explodes, the frame and forechassis cartwheel into a series of high, bounding flips. I see the undercarriage ten feet in the air, then the engine, somersaulting over. The Breda gun drops dead-weight, seven hundred pounds, on to Standage. The Hurricanes pass with a shock wave that nearly floors us.

Later, Nick will tell of the parallel bedlam taking place on the summit. Before the first strafing run, one of the SAS jeeps has succeeded in getting close enough to the Mammoth to mark it with red smoke as planned. But somehow the Hurricanes don't see this. Their first pass misses everything. At the same time the Mammoth's defenders, recognising the purpose of the smoke, cleverly snatch up smoke grenades of their own and begin marking every vehicle and position within two hundred yards.

The Mammoth, like all staff command centres, is protected by its own combat team; these troops have now taken up defensive positions and are plastering our fellows' vehicles with machine-gun fire. Neither Jake nor Nick sees what happens to the first SAS teams in the assault, but it can be nothing but death or capture. Now come the Hurricanes on their second pass. By this time the trucks and jeeps of Jake, Nick and Major Mayne have been located by the enemy and are being engaged in an all-out firefight. The Hurricanes' third pass attacks this. Nick tells us later that he is firing his Thompson into a lane of Axis staff vehicles, sited shrewdly away from the Mammoth and pointing in the opposite direction, when he hears the planes dropping on to him. In an instant the bonnet of his truck vaporises, along with both front tyres, the radiator, and half the engine. Motor oil scalds his face, blinding him. The Chev nose-dives into the sand. Nick is certain that his number is up. But the truck simply stops, settles upright, and he and his driver and gunner dismount, 'like stepping out of a taxi in Grosvenor Square'. The Hurricanes have shot up everything on the summit except the Mammoth. 'I can see the bloody thing,' says Nick later, 'fat as Aunt Fanny's arse and not a scratch on it.' One of Mayne's jeeps picks up Nick and his men. In the end they flee down the reverse slope of the scarp, chased by the machine guns and cannons of enemy armoured cars.

Down on the flat, Punch has got our truck flat-out, racing for the wreck of Collie's. We can see Collie, charred black but on his feet, along with Standage, whose left leg hangs limp. Collie supports him. We can't find Midge or Hornsby. As our truck barrels towards Collie and Standage, another vehicle appears on our right – an Afrika Korps van, racing towards the wreck at top speed. I shout to Oliphant to take the German out. The camp is pandemonium, with men and trucks criss-crossing madly and smoke and dust everywhere. Oliphant swings the Vickers. Then I see: the enemy van is an ambulance! The Germans obviously think the shot-up truck is one of theirs. Why wouldn't they, when it's just been strafed by two British Hurricanes? Oliphant sees the red cross and holds fire. Only one thought animates us – get to our comrades first and haul them out of there.

Punch ploughs to a stop alongside Collie and Standage. Oliphant and I dash to them on foot. The ambulance men are racing up as well – two young stretcher-bearers, barely more than boys, and an officer in shorts and peaked cap who looks as if he might be a doctor. Now we spot Midge and Hornsby. Midge's jaw has been shot away. His shorts and shirt have burned off. He is naked, his chest, arms and legs charred black.

He rises from the spot where he had been flung. His eyes look clear. Hornsby lies face-down in the sand. Midge is trying to speak. Blood rises in bubbles from where his mouth used to be. I feel as if I'm in hell. The magnitude of the horror is more than one's senses can bear. At the same time a part of me remains lucid. That part remembers the Hurricanes. In moments they will be back to rake the earth with another fusillade. Oliphant and I get to Midge just as the doctor scampers up. He takes our comrade under one arm. '*Hilf dem Anderen!*' he shouts. Help the other one!

More soldiers are racing up from other units. They still don't realise we're the enemy. Collie gets Standage aboard our truck. Punch hauls him up. Oliphant and I drop beside Hornsby. When we turn him over, he looks OK. Maybe the crash has just knocked him cold. Then we see the pool forming at the base of his skull. The stretcher-bearers have got Midge now. I'm thinking, How can we get him away? The ambulance driver has backed round to take our men aboard. A medic hauls the rear doors wide; we can see the hangers for litters inside. The doctor comes up before me. I see his face change. For a moment he freezes. Then, in perfect English: 'Save yourselves!' He indicates Hornsby. 'Leave your wounded with me!'

I glance to Oliphant, then to Punch and Collie.

'Both will die if you move them,' says the medical officer.

I wish I could say that I got the man's name or at least shook his hand. But I couldn't make myself say or do anything, only glance in agony at Midge and Hornsby, then bolt like hell for the truck.

Ten minutes later the Hurricanes have gone and so have we, tearing south into the desert. Grainger's truck and Conyngham's jeep are missing. We have no idea what has happened to Jake or Nick or to Major Mayne and the SAS men.

CHAPTER 18

It takes forty-eight hours, travelling by night and lying up by day, to reach the rallying point at Bir el Ensor, Sore Thumb. We have barely closed an eye the entire way.

Two miles into the desert, fleeing the enemy, Te Aroha IV's engine begins pouring smoke. Five hours of daylight remain; we can see the dust of Axis armoured cars several miles behind us and hear aircraft engines east and west, searching for us and the others. Luck stays with us. The enemy, it seems, have been tardy in realising that the raid was truck-borne as well as from the air. Our vehicles, barrelling across the camp, were mistaken by the Germans for their own, evading the planes. By the time they reckon what's what, we've got a start on them. At nightfall, our first halt to draw breath, Punch discovers a heavy-calibre rip through the sump and a crack in the block you can stick your little finger into. 'I told you,' says Punch. 'She's been running on two cylinders for twenty miles.'

The truck pushes on, leaking and overheating. Standage groans in the back. His wounds are in both legs. The right is mostly burns and abrasions, but the left has been nearly severed at the knee; the bottom half is bound to the top only by strips of bloody gristle, for which trauma we can do nothing except bind the mess as tightly as we can and shoot Standage full of morphia. Punch and Collie have cleared a space for him among spare wheels and petrol tins and set him on our combined bedding, which, we discover when we unbundle it, has been set alight by tracer fire and charred half to rags. None the less we pack this under and round Standage, trying to make him as comfortable as possible. His only complaint is the cold. Funny, when a man is hit, you call him by his nickname. Standage has become 'Stan' and now 'Standy'. Collie donates his syrette of morphia though he needs it badly for his own burns. I contribute mine too. Standage's courage humbles us. Collie himself is burnt across his back and neck and the right side of his face. His beard has been singed crisp. The truck gasps and wheezes across the plain. The radiator keeps boiling over. Its overflow tank has been holed and continues to drain despite patch after patch. We refill using the 'honey jar' of our week's urine, saved for just such an emergency. I'm worried about Collie going into shock. He deflects my concern. 'Plenty of time,' he says, 'to fag out tomorrow.'

When the engine becomes too hot to run, we shut down in neutral and push. The labour strains us nearly to our limit, but we have no other option. If we abandon the truck, we'll have to carry on our backs water, food, ammunition and guns, not to mention Standage, on whom the passage will be a lot easier reclining on blankets than carried in a litter. In fact, mercifully he conks out under the morphine. We push till the engine cools, then start up and drive till we smell steam and gaskets smoking. Push and drive, push and drive. Our 'A' set has got wrecked some time during the escape. Worse, the theodolite has been shattered. We can't transmit or receive and we can't navigate. Some time around 2200 we notice the truck getting easier to push. A downhill. We're so addled with the hangover of adrenalin, fear, and exhaustion that we begin laughing. We give the truck a rousing shove, then leap aboard and coast. It's sport. The truck is picking up speed. The night is moonless; it's like driving through ink. No one is even at the wheel. What could we possibly run into in the middle of the desert? Suddenly Punch cries, 'Brake!' Next thing we know, Te Aroha IV's nose is in midair and the frame is crashing like a bomb on to the stone rim of a fifty-foot escarpment. The truck hangs half over the precipice. Standage shoots upright with a howl. The rest of us grab any handhold we can find and, hauling with every sinew, manage to manhandle the vehicle back from the brink. Standage is in agony from the jolt. We swaddle him with every scrap of blanket we've got, imploring his forgiveness and promising never to let it happen again. 'Bugger!' says Stan. 'I woke and thought I was dead.'

We're spent and freezing. I call a rest and break out the rum. We're mad to risk a flame to brew up but I've got to get something hot and sweet into my men's stomachs. We're just sharing out the tea when Grainger's truck appears out of the darkness.

He's been nosing along the same scarp for an hour, having nearly gone over the edge several times himself. The truck trundles up, preceded by wary long-distance halloos. By heaven, we're relieved to find each other! Grainger's wireless is still working and so is his engine. He takes us in tow. His men Marks and Durrance are alive and unhurt, but Corporal Conyngham and Holden and the jeep are still missing. 'The Jerries probably grabbed them,' says Grainger, 'back there in the shoot-up.'

By dawn we've got both trucks under netting in a shallow wash. We snooze on and off all day, doing maintenance on the weapons and improvising seals and plugs for the various points of leakage in the engine's lines and hoses. Collie claims his burns are only a nuisance. I'm not so sure. We scrounge up every bit of margarine to grease him down and even use motor oil, which at least is sterile coming straight from the tin. We prop him in a hammock alongside Standage and try to keep him warm. Grainger's truck has two more morphine stickers, which we save for

Standage. It's extraordinary how lucid he remains. He asks me to read to him. From my rucksack I produce *Paradise Lost*.

Standage can't take it. I try the Bible; that doesn't work either. I wind up reading from Stein's manuscript. Standage likes it. The homosexual allusions sail right over his head. I've forgotten how good the book is. It lifts me too. When we get tired, I tell Standage about Stein and how he died. He tells me about his daughter in New Zealand. She's a piano prodigy. In the farming community outside Wellington where Standage and his family live, there's no teacher capable of taking his daughter to the level that he and his wife believe she's capable of achieving. Standage and his brothers have pitched in so that the young girl can live and study in town. 'I miss her badly,' says Standage, 'but when a girl's got a gift . . .'

As he's telling me this, the oddest thing happens. I realise what I want to do with my life. My civilian life, that is, if I ever get back to one. I want to be a publisher. Not a writer. I lack the gift and I'm not cut out for the loneliness.

A publisher. I'll have my own house and bring out writers. Why hadn't I thought of this sooner?

In a flash, I see myself and Rose, our children, our life. I will find young writers, help them find their voice. I will champion their careers.

I tell this to Standy. He gets it right away. 'Stuff comes to you at the strangest times, don't it, Skip?'

Patrol commander is not my post; it's Collie's.

229

But the others take note of Standage's slip of the tongue. He's lying under camouflage netting with his bad leg bound and splinted and his head pillowed on the oak block we use to brace the jack on. I glance to Collie, who rests on his side in the back of the truck on an improvised hammock with his back, neck and face bandaged. He meets my eye. So do Punch and Grainger.

By this silent ratification, I have become patrol commander.

Enemy scout planes overfly us all day, Henschels and Storches and, mid-afternoon, a flight of Italian Macchi fighters. Around dusk we hear a lone engine circling. Punch and I take the Browning and creep up to the crown of the wadi we're lying up in. A Storch scout plane with black Axis crosses on both wings sets down on the flat, stopping two hundred yards in front of us.

The hatch opens; out pops the pilot. He's alone. Punch fixes him in his gunsights. The flier has no idea we're here. He drops his trousers, grabs hold of a wing strut and unloads a defecation that would make a plough horse proud. Punch's finger tightens on the trigger; I stop him with a hand on his shoulder.

'If that plane doesn't return to its base tonight, the Jerries'll send ten more looking for it tomorrow.'

Reluctantly Punch backs off.

The pilot climbs into his Storch and wings away.

'I'd love to run into that bastard some day,' says Punch, 'just to tell him how close he came.'

The following night, riding and being towed, we limp in to our base at Sore Thumb. Nick Wilder is waiting with the remains of T1 patrol, two trucks and six men. What's left of Jake's R1 is there too, with Captain Lawson, the medical officer. Jake himself has been evacuated twenty-four hours earlier with a broken collarbone, along with six other wounded LRDG men. A signal from Cairo has ordered them to retire to Bir al Khamsa; another patrol will be despatched to pick them up. Jake has asked Doctor Lawson to remain, anticipating serious casualties among the later-arriving parties.

While we newcomers scratch out a camp, Major Mayne straggles in with three jeeps and six troopers, including Cooper, Seekings and Mike Sadler. Four of his men are missing. Mayne plans to rest only long enough to get a meal and a brew; then he'll turn back with his surviving team members to look for the missing. He will not leave them on foot with the enemy hunting them.

Bir is Arabic for well. Our lie-up is typical of these flyblown oases: a patch of stunted palms, a few scattered outbuildings and the well itself – a circle of mortared stones with an iron cover called a *meit*, pronounced 'mate', to keep out the drifting sand. A flap-door allows a bucket through; when the *bir* is dry, the tribesmen haul the cover off and rope themselves down into the void, seeking a trickle. Campsites lie here and there among the camel thorn. This night, in addition to our lot, several kin-groups of Senussi Arabs have set up shop. You can smell their camels and hear the jingling of the bells on their sheep and goats.

Two crosses mark fresh graves. Nick tells me that three others of our fellows have been buried in haste during halts on the getaway. One was Malcom McCool, the Kiwi sergeant who showed me my quarters the first day I joined the unit. Another was Corporal Mickey Lukich, an Olympic gymnast who came into the SAS as a driver for its founder, David Stirling, and won the Military Medal for heroism in the first raid on Benghazi.

It's sombre, settling in. Captain Lawson has rigged the rear of his truck as a one-tent hospital. We give up Standage to his much-welcomed ministrations. Collie only wants grease or butter for his burns; he sets off with Punch to buy or barter some from the Arabs. A motor repair shop has been set up. Grainger brings our trucks in. I report to Nick and Major Mayne, who both call me 'Chap' and shake my hand with surprising affection. God knows, I am glad to see them.

The patrols have been out for more than a month now. Every man wears a beard. Here at the *bir*, there's water for a shave. No one wants it. The matted growth has become a badge of honour; to scrape it off would somehow devalue the sacrifice of our fallen comrades.

Before he goes seeking the missing, Major Mayne calls a council. For several minutes the talk is of the men we've lost and those who've been brought out wounded. Jake's party, Mayne speculates, will be halfway to Bir al Khamsa by now. While he's speaking, a signal comes in from HQ informing Mayne, who has assumed command since Jake's evacuation, that three Bombay bombers equipped as ambulances will be sent from Cairo to LG 119, an emergency landing ground that is farther away than Khamsa but over better going. This signal will be sent to Jake at his next scheduled check-in. With luck, our commander and his wounded will be on clean sheets at Heliopolis in three days.

What about us? Jake's truck and jeep have taken as little petrol as possible to complete their passage, but even this modest measure depletes the overall stock, leaving the remaining vehicles low. The patrols have water now from the *bir*, but ammunition is short, both fitters' stocks of spare parts have been lost, and we don't have a single vehicle without mechanical problems of one sort or another. Speculation follows on what retribution Rommel will seek when he learns that raiders have targeted him personally.

What do we do now?

Have we had it?

Do we turn back?

The council is held in the lee of Nick Wilder's wireless truck. The fitters, Durrance and Lister, give their report. They'll need another day, possibly two, to put the trucks right. Captain

233

Lawson expresses concern for the wounded. Standage must be transported to aid. Two of Mayne's SAS men need attention too. All three must be put on trucks, as soon as the vehicles can be made mechanically sound, and evacuated to LG 119 or to wherever Cairo designates. Should Lawson accompany them? Leaving the patrols without a medical officer? Do we all go back?

Mayne wants to know first what damage our raid has done. Nick and I with Sergeants Kehoe and Wannamaker and the SAS NCOs give our assessments. The conclusion is damn little. Mayne is furious with us and with himself. While the council debates, a signal comes in from Cairo. Both patrols are to withdraw to refit and await orders.

'Balls,' says Mayne.

He wants to go back after Rommel.

Someone asks if he's serious.

Mayne spreads a map and points to Alamein. 'Monty will break through the Jerries any minute. Rommel will fall back. Hell, he's falling back already.' Mayne indicates the open desert south of Mersa Matruh and Sidi Barrani. 'Wherever Rommel goes, we'll get there before he does. We'll be waiting for him.'

We can get there ahead of him, says Mayne. We can be waiting for him.

I look to Nick Wilder. He's grinning. So are Reg Seekings, Johnny Cooper and the SAS men. Are they out of their bloody minds? Sergeant Wannamaker attempts to restore sanity. He cites the enemy ground and air patrols scouring the desert right now. Do we imagine the whole Afrika Korps isn't on high alert, hunting for us? We don't have Directional Finding any more and we don't have the RAF.

'Screw the RAF,' says Mayne. 'This whole show has been too complicated from the start. We should've taken on the Huns on our own and not mucked about.'

There's truth to this, the men acknowledge.

'We've buried five good men,' says Major Mayne, 'and sent nine others home in pieces. I'm not arguing for throwing good money after bad, but, hell's bells, the rest of us are still on our feet. We've still got punch.'

Someone asks what we do about HQ's orders.

'What orders?' says Mayne.

Planning begins. The men know this is lunacy. But Mayne is right. The enemy expect us to run; they'll throw all their pursuit parties on to the tracks along which we're likely to flee. They know we'd be crazy to go the opposite way.

'Crazy,' says Paddy Mayne, 'is our business.'

CHAPTER 19

The patrols take two more days bringing in the missing (all of whom are recovered unharmed), repairing the trucks and allowing the men time to rest and recuperate. The remaining wounded, including Standage but not Collie who refuses to be evacuated, will make for Landing Ground 119, about ninety miles northeast of Jarabub oasis and a hundred and twenty south of Halfaya, as soon as vehicles can be made ready to transport them. Sergeant Wannamaker, who is suffering from dysentery and must go back anyway, will lead the party.

Major Mayne orders the camp moved from Bir el Ensor, which as it turns out takes a pasting from Me-110s ten hours after we get away. The patrols move twelve miles east the first night, as far as the trucks can go in their shaky state, and south another fifteen the next.

The scheme has changed. Monty and our Eighth Army are breaking through at Alamein more powerfully than anyone had anticipated. Rommel is pulling back fast. The Allies could reach Mersa Matruh in a matter of days; Tobruk could be liberated soon after. New orders dispatch us even further west. Intelligence reports that Rommel's intestinal disorder still plagues him; short of Tripoli, five hundred miles away, only Benghazi possesses proper medical facilities. The Desert Fox will go there, HQ believes. We will too.

Our party has been joined by a third patrol. Second Lieutenant Tinker with T2 has come out from Faiyoum via Kufra, crossing the neck of the sand seas where we did, at Garet Chod and swinging east, avoiding Jarabub. One of Tinker's trucks takes our wounded aboard; another tows our most damaged vehicle. In this ragtag column we cover fifty miles to a good safe camp at Gadd el Ahmar, which is far enough south to be out of range of Axis scout planes and far enough west to be within a day's hard drive of LG 119. Tinker is the officer I shared a room with at training camp, though we never met because he was on patrol. With him are twelve men in three trucks and two jeeps carrying our White Russian friend Popski with two savage-looking Senussi guides and a couple of French-speaking Bren gunners who look like no serving soldiers I've ever seen. 'Who are these fellows?' I ask Nick.

'Never ask Popski his business. I promise this though: these buggers can slit a throat.'

It was Tinker and Popski, we now learn, who beat Wannamaker and me to the petrol dump at South Cairn. Their headlights were the ones tracking us in the dark. One of Popski's tribesmen shows me the holes our Vickers put in the side of their jeep. I give him a tour of our patched jerry cans. Having shot at each other creates a bond. At once we are the best of mates.

As for Tinker, I'm delighted to make his acquaintance. He's a Kiwi like Nick, twenty-nine years old, a handsome devil with a thick jet-black beard that gives him the gravity of a man ten years older. Tinker, his mates testify, is the best navigator in the LRDG (though he has moved beyond this, becoming a patrol commander) and a crack desert hand. When I ask him why he ran his trucks with their headlights on when they were stalking us, he responds with a Cheshire-cat grin. 'To draw your fire. We had the moon behind us; we could see the glint off your bonnets but couldn't make out who you were. There weren't supposed to be any friendly patrols in that area so we reckoned you were Jerries.'

His intention, Tinker says, once we opened fire, was to douse his lights and scatter, returning fire using our muzzle flashes as aiming points. 'But your shooters were too good,' he laughs. 'We got off one burst and had to run for it.'

Tinker is another of those chaps, like Mayne and Wilder, who are born warriors. Mayne, the rugby star, is a formidable, even frightening, example of this type. Tinker's patrol sergeant Garven has told me of a raid last year on the German aerodrome at Berka. Mayne led the SAS team that infiltrated on foot at night to plant incendiary bombs on parked aircraft. Once inside the wire, the raiders realised that each plane was guarded by an armed sentry. Mayne killed seven of them, one by one, with his knife, in the dark, going round the field planting his explosives.

At the same time Mayne, to us his comrades, is the kindest, most generous companion, one who will seek out the fellow in distress and spare no effort to make him feel part of the group. Tales of Mayne's drunken excesses are legendary. Yet he's an accomplished scholar – a Cambridge man from a fine family in Ulster, and a solicitor into the bargain. Mayne possesses an odd delicacy of speech; he will swear like a trooper, but without ever employing the ubiquitous term for fornication, which most soldiers use every tenth word, or any obscene term for a woman or a female anatomical part.

The camp at Gadd el Ahmar is a warren of wadis with plenty of cover and good water from an ancient Roman cistern. A number of Arab parties have collected, having learnt through the desert grapevine of Popski's arrival. The Senussi tribesmen of Libya hate the Italians, who drove them into the desert from their fertile grazing lands along the coast and whose favoured method of executing any Arab suspected of collaborating with the British is to hang him by a hook underneath the jaw. With the fall of darkness we are safe from aircraft; the tribesmen, cronies of Popski, will protect and not betray us.

Tea is brewed, stew boiled in the billy. What's so powerful about the desert is its timelessness. I wriggle a seat in the sand with my shoulders draped in the fleece greatcoat Jake gave me and my back set comfortably against a tyre. I peer about the camp to the men industriously at their labours, the trucks and jeeps dispersed among the camel thorn; to the Arabs and their flocks, the firelight, the vault of heaven. I am an ordinary Englishman, barely out of my university years. Yet here I sit, in the vastness of the African night, surrounded by companions who could have stepped from Caesar's legions or Alexander's phalanx. So primal are the surroundings that I would not be surprised to see Scipio Africanus emerge from the gloom and take a seat upon a hammered-out petrol tin. Wannamaker is setting a watch against our light-fingered neighbours, as Ptolemy or Hannibal no doubt did twenty-three hundred years ago. Dear comrades have been slain; I myself may meet my end tomorrow. Yet this only adds to the savour of being, ourselves, still alive. The smells about are of scrub acacia and motor oil, sweat and sheep dung and gunblack. The joy of this hour, of being in this place with these men, is so keen it makes my eyes smart. Can I write this to Rose? Would I only cause her distress?

At the same time I realise another thing: I myself am not a warrior. Not like these fellows. I am not a Paddy Mayne, nor a Nick Wilder or a Jake

Easonsmith or a Ron Tinker. Of Mayne certainly it can be said that if he could be translated across the centuries, he would fit in with the hardest of the Romans or Macedonians. And the others would not be far behind.

These fellows are different from me. I admire them; I wish I could be like them. They are men of action, warriors and man-killers. I'm not.

This apprehension is, paradoxically, the beginning of my true vocation as an officer. All genuine epiphanies seem to follow this model: their defining quality is the relinquishment of delusion. The initial fear is that one has lost something. A cherished self-conception must be given up, and one feels diminished by it. This is mistaken, however. A person discovers that he has been made stronger by the jettisoning of this sham and disadvantageous baggage. In fact he has become more 'himself' by aligning his self-concept more closely with fact.

Indeed, I was a flawed officer in the Armoured Division. I lacked empathy; I could not lead men. By war's end, however, I had become quite an able commander, which I define by the following criteria. First, from the point of view of my superiors, I could be counted upon to perform the mission they had assigned me, or, if that was unworkable, to improvise and turn my men's exertions upon a secondary undertaking as good as or better than the first. Second, from the point of view of those serving beneath me, I had become someone they could look to for leadership and direction, who would shield them from meddling from above, and would ask no act of them that he wasn't prepared to perform himself. I provided for my men a framework within which they were freed to use their own qualities of courage, resourcefulness and tenacity.

Tinker comes over and flops down beside me. His orders, after resupplying us, he says, are to reconnoitre 'the going' south and west of Tripoli. The mission comes from Eighth Army, from Montgomery himself. Our commander-in-chief is thinking ahead to hooking left round Rommel's flank. But Monty must first be certain that the terrain is passable in this season for heavy armour. Tinker's assignment is critical. But as soon as he hears of Mayne's plan to raid Benghazi, he wants in.

Mayne rejects this. He and Tinker have a proper dust-up over it, with Tinker making the case that not only has he been in Benghazi on prior raids, as Mayne has, but he also knows his way round the Hotel d'Italia, the site used in the past for Rommel's *Kampfstaffel*, the Field Marshal's rear Headquarters Group. Tinker can lead us to it, he says. Mayne rules against this. Tinker already has orders. But Mayne gets him to draw a map and to describe in detail how to find the site.

By the second night, Collie has recovered enough from his burns to return to duty. At least that's what he claims. His shoulders are still slathered with sheep grease, which he has got from the Arabs, but he swears the burns are not as bad as they look. I don't believe this, but I'll not be the one to send him back against his will. Standage is clinging grimly to life. Doctor Lawson has sawn off Standy's left leg at the knee and splinted the right. We of the patrol have made our comrade as comfortable as possible in a bed on the back of Sergeant Wannamaker's truck, renamed the 'Homeward Bound', and have all taken turns keeping him company at night.

Dawn Three, the patrols mount up. All will travel by separate routes. Nick's T1, combined now with Mayne's SAS teams and the surviving vehicles and men of Jake's R1, will proceed west through the desert via Msus to Solluch, coming up to Benghazi from the south. Tinker will bypass Benghazi entirely, swinging south and west past Agedabia and El Agheila towards Tripoli. Wannamaker will head for LG 119 with the wounded. Collie and I, in our two remaining trucks, will make a loop north and west into the Jebel Akhdar, the Green Hills. Our orders are to follow the highland tracks across the Jebel, sending reports of Axis traffic as we go. We'll rendezvous with T1 in five days at Bir el Qatal in the desert south of Benghazi, a site that everyone knows well but me. Oliphant will navigate us in, with Grainger on the wireless.

It's 0730, time to move out. I'm checking tyre pressures and finishing a smoke when Collie comes up but doesn't speak. 'What?' I ask.

It's Standage.

We bury him as our last act before departing.

'So long, mate,' says Punch as we toss shillings on to the canvas shroud. None of us is ashamed to weep. 'I was envying Standy,' says Punch. 'Getting back to Cairo.' Soldiers are superstitious. We beat it out of there fast.

Our trucks make only forty miles that day over stony going with soft dust beneath, with four punctures and one long stop for a carburettor rebuild. While we are lying up that night, a signal arrives from HQ. The Mammoth we attacked was not Rommel's after all. It was not even a command vehicle but the former living quarters for General Stumme, who had been killed weeks earlier. The Germans had converted it to a mobile dressing station. When our fellows shot at it, they were firing on sick and wounded men.

Rommel himself, we'll learn later, was not in that camp and never had been. At the time of our raid, he was with the 1st Panzer Division, somewhere west of Kidney Ridge, in the thick of the fighting at El Alamein.

CHAPTER 20

From Gadd el Ahmar, my truck and Collie's strike north-west towards Trigh el Abd, hoping to swing round the shoulder of the Jebel and turn west before any withdrawing Afrika Korps columns can make it too hot for us. But the place, as the Yanks might say, is crawling with Krauts. Rain has turned the desert to muck. Columns of Axis transport block ever track, mired up to their mud-guards. We're stuck too. We pass three days under scrim nets, with flights of Macchis and Me-110s overhead hourly. It's too risky to rig the Wyndom or make a fire; there's nothing for it but to lie up miserably under the trucks, passing the time reading and caring for our weapons.

Finally, on the fourth morning the skies clear; a cold wind descends from the north; the surface of the desert turns crusty and hard. We find cover and set up the aerial.

HQ signals that the enemy are falling back faster than anticipated. A gap is opening between Rommel withdrawing west and Monty pressing in pursuit. We receive new orders: proceed to

Benghazi via the tracks linking the Italian colonial settlements – Luigi di Savoia, Beda Littoria, D'Annunzio – or as close to them as we can prudently travel, and report what we see.

We work west and north all day over sandy but decent going, crossing scores of nameless tracks that pass through notches in the ridges breaking up the intervening pans. The desert is strewn with the wrecks of convoys and the graves of men. We are passing over battlefields from this summer and the winter and spring before. Along tracks with route markers in English as well as German and Italian lie the burnt-out hulks of tankers and supply lorries, ours and the enemies'. In cabs scorched to cinders, we glimpse the remains of drivers and convoy officers, the charred rags of their uniforms still clinging to their bones. For several hours we make time by running along a spur of the Trigh. We pass sites where supply columns came under attack. You can see where the tanks waited, hull-down in ambush, behind ridges a thousand yards to the flank. From there they charged in line abreast, scattering the trucks and armoured cars of the supply column; the victims' burnt and shot-up carcasses lie strewn about for miles.

When soldiers have been killed by high explosive, you find no bodies, just boots. The men have been blown out of them. Cresting north-south ridges, we can see the scooped-out pockets where in retreat the Honeys and Crusaders of the 7th Armoured

Division took up positions and made stands, seeking to slow down Rommel's advance. Where anti-tank guns were sited supporting the armour, we see now soldiers' junk, web gear and desert caps, the litter of campsites. Everything of value has been looted. German salvage crews are brilliant at turning rubbish into armament. What they miss, the Arabs make away with. The flats between ridges are studded with 'brew-ups', tanks incinerated with their crews inside. Only the really bad ones remain; Axis salvage crews have towed off all that can be repaired. Many of the brew-ups are US-made Grants, the tall heavy machines powered by aircraft engines that use high-octane aviation fuel. When these tanks idle in place, a halo of super-flammable vapours collects about them, so that an enemy shell needs only a near-miss to make the whole thing blow sky-high. The Germans and English mark their men's graves with an inverted rifle topped by a helmet; the Italians use a rifle and topi. The troops strip the bolts to make the rifles unusable, but the Arabs take them just the same; their expert gunsmiths can fabricate any weapon-part.

One would think that such grisly apparitions would sober us, but in fact we are cheerful. 'We're still breathing,' observes Punch. Nor are we superior to a little judicious pillaging. Oliphant sounds every petrol tank; it's remarkable how much juice you can recover with a simple siphon. We ransack the kit boxes of armoured cars and ammunition lorries, scrounge through the innards of tanks.

I forbid the men to loot corpses, but that doesn't keep them from rifling the pockets of loose tunics and greatcoats. The Germans' give up tobacco, chocolate, tinned sausages. Our own fellows' yield cigarettes, jam, boiled sweets. Italian lorries are the jackpots, producing such delicacies as tinned pears and cherries, cigars, Chianti and Frascati, Pellegrino water, even the odd split of champagne. We tuck away tins of cheese and sardines, packets of Fatimas or Players or Gallagher's Blues. Plum prizes are Luger pistols, swastika flags and Dienstglas binoculars. Finding a pair, I immediately dump my Taylor-Hobsons. Grainger finds a *Gott Mit Uns* belt buckle, which Marks trumps with a silver cigarette case, a gift to some major from his wife, bearing the sentiment

GOTT STRAFE ENGLAND

(God punish England).

In dead ground we come upon rucksacks overlooked by previous scavengers. The contents of these wrench the heart – diaries and paybooks, wallets, photos, letters from wives. We collect these articles, the enemies' as well as our own, and preserve them in a suitcase Punch has salvaged from a burnt-out Daimler scout car. We'll turn them in when we make contact with higher echelons; such personal effects may ease a young widow's grief or provide a cherished memento for a son or daughter.

By evening of the fifth day out of Gadd el Ahmar we're drawing near to the coast. Along the Martuba track tramp endless columns of Mussolini's infantry. The Germans have made off with all motor transport, leaving their allies to walk. The Italians have come a hundred miles and have two hundred to go. They march without order; all soldierly bearing has fled. We could put five thousand in the bag, but what would we do with them? We give them a wide berth and keep moving.

A failed big-end bearing immobilises us all the next day. I send Punch and Jenkins, who has replaced Durrance as fitter, to cannibalise wrecks. What we need most are hoses, inner tubes and gaskets. They come back with armloads, plus two radiators and a crankcase plate.

All that day enemy columns rumble past in the distance, withdrawing west. At night we watch the Panzers going into their leaguers and see the Verey lights they shoot off to guide stragglers in. The sea is only ten miles off; we can smell it. We can hear, across thousands of yards, the metallic banging of the enemy's field repair shops. A signal from HQ reports Wannamaker's convoy has reached Landing Ground 119 safely; our wounded have been taken out in Bombay bombers serving as air ambulances. We kill a bottle of cognac to celebrate.

We're starting to see Arabs. Normally as shy as gazelle, the tribesmen materialise now in parties of ten and twenty, on foot and on camels. They smell plunder. Dawn Seven out of Gadd el Ahmar, we skirt a freshly vacated German leaguer. Senussi pillagers carpet the site, hoovering up everything. They salute us, grinning. *'Inglesi! Inglesi!'*

We trade tea and sugar for eggs and boiled kid. The tribesmen are Obeidi from the Jebel south of Derna. They know Popski. When they learn he is out here and that we are his friends, our stock soars. One piratical-looking kipper swaps Punch a brand-new Luger, still in its case, for a wristwatch and a tin of fifty Woodbines. The sheikh is a lanky fellow with a nose like Disraeli and the whitest teeth I have ever seen. By sign and pidgin he communicates to us that these Germans, the ones who've just vacated this camp, are the last of Rommel's formations between here and Cairo. 'All flown,' says he, miming birds taking flight.

Sure enough, from the ridge where we stand, we can spot the dust of five columns receding.

The sheikh wants to join forces with us. He likes our trucks; they can carry more loot than camels or donkeys. I decline politely. Where, I ask, will he go now? He points north.

'Towns,' he says. And he grins.

CHAPTER 21

Derna is the first civilised settlement we enter. It's a good-sized town, on the coastal plain beneath the escarpment, made over into a temporary city by Rommel's occupation and now denuded in the Germans' and Italians' decampment. Our orders have routed us to the eastern shoulder of the Jebel Akhdar, the big bump jutting into the Mediterranean from Gazala to El Agheila. Benghazi is on the western side. We're on the north-east.

We have entered no-man's-land. The retreating Germans and Italians have moved out, but Monty and Eighth Army have not yet moved in. Approaching via the Martuba bypass we can see columns of black smoke from the top of the escarpment where fuel dumps of the aerodrome at El Ftaiah have been set alight by Axis engineers. Dull crumps resound from below on the plain; every article of value that can't be trucked away is being blown up so the advancing British can't make use of it. On the flat at the base of the scarp stand POW cages, their wire and guard towers still intact. Suddenly the whole hillside shudders; we squirt sideways into a shallow lay-by along the switchback descent. Billows of yellow-grey alkali ascend from below: demolition crews destroying the road. We give them half an hour to clear out, then work our way down over the blown sand and stone. The east side of town is the native quarter. From here on, roads and tracks will be mined; enemy engineers will be blasting bridges and culverts, rigging demolitions at every crossing that might delay a British column.

Derna appears to be a dirty town swallowed by an even dirtier military depot. Leaflets blow across potholed streets, announcing to the citizenry in German, Italian and Arabic that the administrative authority can no longer guarantee the safety of persons or property. A pretty white schoolhouse dazzles in the sun, stripped of everything but its flag. The playground is a welter of smashed filing cabinets and child-sized desks. Across one wall sprawls a heroic rendering of Mussolini:

VINCEREMO DUCE VINCEREMO

We enter the town proper. Fuel dumps and vehicle parks have been emptied and blown up. The grounds of a hospital have been made over into a tent city; now there's nothing left but rubbish and broken-up army cots. Every home and shop is shuttered. Native patriarchs are on guard before the unboarded ones. They've got camp chairs and beaten-up sofas, in which they lounge in the sun with Mausers and Enfields across their knees, backed by sons and brothers sporting various antique firearms. One old man sits cheerfully under a café umbrella: CINZANO. As quickly as the German engineers lay mines and pull out, the locals trot up and mark the sites – with barrels if they have them, with chairs and sticks and wire if they don't – to protect their children and themselves. When the townspeople realise we're Inglesi, they flag us down, wanting us to blow the mines for them. We're not trained or equipped for such a chore; we tell the locals to sit tight and wait for British engineers. In the Arab kin-groups you see no grown women, just girls under twelve, barefoot in headscarves. The boys look proud and defiant. Grainger translates a slogan beneath another mural of Il Duce:

CREDERE, OBBEDIRE, COMBATTERE

(Believe, Obey, Fight).
In the European quarter, pastel villas can be glimpsed with

CIVILIAN

painted on their courtyard walls. Roadsides out of town are littered with wrecked lorries and gun tractors. We detour to the harbour, reckoning that's where the loot is. There's a handsome hotel with its façade blown in. Broken-up cabin chairs pave a street; water taps don't work. There's no power. On lawns before cottages lie gashed-open mattresses, trampled lamps, punched-through wicker.

On the main drag beside the *prefettura* stands the shell of a cinema. A Tom Mix western is playing in German. We probe down jacaranda-lined lanes. Punch spots some kind of cloister: a convent, abandoned and unransacked. Maybe the enemy have spared it out of respect for the sisters. We break open the iron gate by backing the tail-board into it and enter, standing by all guns. Punch parks beneath a statue of the Virgin. I send him and our new fitter Jenkins to find us a kitchen with some grub or a garden where we might dig up the odd carrot or potato. Collie takes Oliphant and Miller, our Yorkshire-born medical orderly, to check some buildings at the back. If there's an infirmary we'll grab dressings and medicine. I stay with Grainger and the others on the trucks. We're wary. I watch Miller disappear into a courtyard off a colonnade. 'Watch for booby traps!'

He reappears almost at once, waving us forward. With Collie and Oliphant, we poke into the court. At the base of a wall lies a tangle of bodies. The stucco behind them has been stitched by bullets.

'Italians,' says Miller. He checks the corpses while the rest of us cover rooflines and lanes of approach.

'Looters, you reckon?' asks Oliphant.

Collie thinks they're deserters. 'More likely

blokes who tried to piss off.' The men's boots have been taken, probably by native youths; the corpses are all in stockinged feet.

'That's enough,' I say. 'Move out.'

The convent's refectory and infirmary have been rifled. Sacks of grain sag, knifed open; wine bottles and china have been smashed; contents of cabinets strewn over the floor, paraffin poured over them. We locate the sacristy; Punch searches through lockers. 'What the hell are you looking for?' Jenkins calls.

Punch surfaces with a bottle. 'Blood of Christ,' he grins.

Towns are hell on discipline. We've only been here an hour and we're already turning into tourists and pillagers. Time to clear out. I get us started up one of the wadi roads that lead to the good Italian-built bypass. Packs of Arab urchins swarm about our vehicles, begging for cigarettes and chocolate.

Abandoned farms and villas dot the hillsides out of town. The place looks like Italy. On hilltops you see red-tiled roofs and whitewashed walls. Everything is deserted. The farms are fortified compounds, with iron gates and pillboxes with gun embrasures.

Turning up the Martuba track, Collie spies a sedan approaching from the east. I get both our trucks off the road, sited to engage it. The car sees us and brakes in the middle of the road, five hundred yards out. Collie puts the binos on it.

'I'll be damned,' he says.

'What?'

'Journalists.'

Through my new German glasses I see pink faces and war correspondent uniforms.

'What are they doing?'

'Arguing.'

I have Grainger stand and wave a tin hat. Immediately we spot white handkerchiefs. The reporters have had us in their sights too. 'Canadian! South African!' they shout as their saloon pulls up on the road alongside us. The vehicle turns out to be an ancient Humber, loaded with newspaper and radio correspondents joyriding out from Eighth Army at freshly liberated Tobruk.

'Are you buggers daft?' calls Punch. 'The Jerries are only five miles up the road!'

The newsmen pile from three of the four doors (only the driver, a local, stays put), shaking our hands and declaring their delight at running into us. Each then makes for a different quadrant of the roadside, where he unbuttons and looses an exuberant stream. It's four in the afternoon and they're all pie-eyed. The Humber is a taxi. One of the correspondents hired it this morning, we are told; his colleagues piled in, determined not to let him beat them to a story. When the gang encountered no enemy, they kept pushing west. Now here there are, sixty miles in front of the furthermost Allied outpost. I ask if any of them carries a weapon.

'Just this,' says one, hoisting a half-bottle of brandy.

It isn't funny. The safety of these swashbucklers has now become my responsibility. I order them to follow us off the road, where they and we are less likely to get jumped by the Luftwaffe. Except one of our fellows has in the meantime blabbed about the massacre in the convent. The correspondents want to see it. I forbid this. The dean of the outfit turns out to be Don Munro of the CBC. I've heard of him. He's known as an outstanding reporter. 'What,' I ask, 'are you doing with these mad bandits?'

I can't turn our guests loose unescorted; they'll wind up captured or shot. If I order them back to Tobruk, they'll just wait till our trucks are out of sight, then carry on as they please. We certainly can't keep them with us. From our beards and vehicles they know who we are; if we offer up the first clue about where we're heading, the story will be on the air by tomorrow's tea.

In the end we invite them to supper. They've got a quarter-wheel of Reggiano cheese, liberated from an ice locker, with prosciutto and sweet sausage. 'It'll go bad,' Munro says, 'if we don't enjoy it.'

I'll give the reporters this: they know how to booze. Even without women, they crank up a spirited binge. I won't let them take over an abandoned farm, as they wish; it's more bad discipline. Instead I make them camp with us in the hills, in a position we can defend, with no fires after nightfall. From them I extract a promise that in return for our protection tonight they'll return to Tobruk tomorrow. When the sun goes down, our guests' bravado wears off. They're happy to huddle beneath our trucks and let us stand watch over them.

The correspondents turn out to be decent fellows. One of them, a South African named Van der Brucke, has a VC from the Great War. He was a cavalryman, his companions tell us. He owns his own newspaper now in Durban and could have happily stayed there, he says, filing stories off the wire.

'But I couldn't do it. The thought of boys like you out here haunted me.' Collie and Punch have gathered; something about the veteran draws them. He was a major, he says. Collie invites him to stay on. 'We could use you.'

It's a jest of course and the South African knows it. He chokes up anyway. 'I'd die happy alongside men like you.' He tells me I'm a good officer but too slack. 'You should've lit us up back there on the road.' How did I know, he asks, that he and the others weren't German agents?

Later I share a mug of tea with the Canadian, Munro. He's sober now and a bit chastened. He wants to help. He makes me spread out my map and, shielding an electric torch with the wing of his jacket, walks me over it. 'Monty expects no fight at Tripoli,' he says. 'The place can be flanked

258

via the Jebel Nefusa; Rommel might make a demonstration, but he'll fall back to here.' Munro taps a spot west of Medenine in Tunisia. 'The Mareth Line.'

'Stop a second,' I say. 'Let me fetch my sergeant and a couple of others.'

When Collie, Punch, Oliphant and Grainger arrive, Munro continues. He tells us about the Mareth Line. It was built by the French in the last war to keep the Italians out of Tunisia. No one knows exactly how many defensive emplacements it's got, how big its guns are, or how deep its minefields. 'But it's serious business. Forty miles end to end, blocking the gap between the sea and the mountains. If Rommel digs in behind that line with 15th and 21st Panzer Divisions, 90th Light Division, with the Italian Ariete and Centauro armoured divisions and the Folgore paratroopers – not to mention the reinforcements in armour and aircraft that Hitler is sure to ferry over in such an emergency – a raft of our fellows are going to get their tickets punched trying to push him out.'

Munro can tell from our expressions that this is news to us.

'Look,' he says, 'we all know who you fellows are and why you're here. I was having a beer with your boss Guy Prendergast the day he sent Tinker and Popski out after you. No one knows where Wilder and Easonsmith went last month so I assume they're with you or you with them.'

We're impressed.

'I can see from your faces,' Munro says, 'that you don't yet have orders for the Mareth Line. But you will.'

On the map he indicates the rugged country south of the Mareth Line – the Jebel Nefusa – and south-west the Grand Erg Oriental, an unmapped sand sea as vast as the Egyptian. 'Monty can't wade into that mess head-on. Some lucky bastards are going to get the job of scouting a way round for him. A left hook. That's Tinker and Popski's job now, is my guess.'

'Or ours soon?'

'All I'm saying is don't start counting the days till you're sipping John Collinses on the terrace at Shepheard's. You lads'll be out here till the show's over.'

Next morning we give Munro our mail to deliver to Eighth Army. I have twenty-seven letters for Rose. Munro promises to phone her in Haifa, if not look her up in person, and assure her that I'm well.

The last thing that happens on our way out of town is we capture an Italian. More accurately the fellow accosts us where the Derna road joins the Martuba bypass and won't take no till we accept his surrender. He's about forty, obviously an unwilling conscript, barefoot now and terrified, which leads Punch to speculate he's a deserter who somehow escaped a firing squad. By signs the fellow assures us he's an expert Fiat mechanic, but when we hoist the bonnet on Te Aroha IV his eyes pop as if he's never seen an engine in his life. At noon we halt and signal Cairo for instructions. Get rid of him, they say. They also tell us the attempt on Rommel's life at Benghazi is off, as is our assignment of reporting on enemy traffic on the settlement roads. Instead we are to rendezvous in three days with Nick Wilder and Major Mayne at Bir el Gamra in the Jebel south-east of Benina. We will receive new orders there.

We drop the Italian off two miles from an Arab encampment with a quart bottle of Pellegrino and a forage cap stuffed with cheese and ham. 'Bloody hell,' says Collie, watching the fellow recede over our tailboard, 'that's the sorriest excuse for a soldier I've ever seen.'

BOOK V

BENINA

CHAPTER 22

W e're moving, lights out, down the new bitumened road that runs from Benina to the Benghazi-Solluch railway line. It's night and raining. Two thousand yards north, Nick and Major Mayne's trucks and jeeps are advancing to raid the Axis airbase at Benina. My two trucks – with Collie, Grainger, Marks and Jenkins on one; myself, Punch, Oliphant and Miller on the other – are prowling towards an L-bend, where we will set up to cover their withdrawal. Already I can feel the whole show running queer.

Benina is an airfield and repair facility. Round the port of Benghazi are other satellite fields including Regima and two at Berka.

HQ has determined that the most effective use of our joint patrols' remaining firepower will be not against enemy personnel – i.e., Rommel – but against his aircraft and aircraft workshops. This is the type of job the SAS and the LRDG are set up for. So our orders have been changed to raid Benina.

As for our two-truck party, mine and Collie's, we have crossed from Dema in three nights, brazening it out on the good metalled road past Beda Littoria and D'Annunzio, descending the escarpment at Maddalena, then following the El Abiar railway cross-country south-west towards Benghazi on the coast. The second scarp, above the city, drops down within five miles of Benina, which is visible in daylight across a plain that would be planted in season with maize and melons but is now mud, criss-crossed by sloughs and silted-up irrigation ditches.

Rain is heavy and cold. With no roof or windscreen, we're drenched. Temperature has plunged to the forties. The guns are soaked, even under their canvas covers. I'm driving. The steering wheel with its grip ridges is handlable, but the steel pedals of the brake and clutch are both slick beneath my soles.

We're waiting to hear the first explosions. I've got a bad feeling. Rotten luck has plagued this operation since we started. Half a day out of Derna, Te Aroha IV began flooding and stalling; for two nights we've fought shorts in the electrical system, and the patches and bypasses we've rigged are not being helped by this rain. We're on our second and only spare propeller shaft, whose splines are already chattering. The list of ills for Collie's truck is just as long. At the same time our medical orderly, Miller, has come down with a fever of unknown origin. He's keen, but his hearing has been seriously impaired by the malady; he keeps drifting off mentally; twice he has called men by the wrong name, though he knows them as well as brothers by now. Collie has not fully recovered from his burns; he can hold himself together during the day, but at night his body-warmth flees so fast that I can't call on him to stand a watch; all he can do is wrap up in everything he owns and endure till the sun rises. The rest of us are afflicted by all the predictable ailments and inflammations of skin, bowels and stomach that assault men who've been too long away from fresh vegetables, clean sheets and decent medical care.

Nick and Major Mayne's journey has been as ill-starred as ours. Mayne's outfit were jumped by Macchi 202s two days ago descending the escarpment east of Solluch. The planes shot up three of his four vehicles. Casualties are two dead and two wounded, and though both injured fellows have been patched back to fighting trim, the loss of a pair of good men is devastating in such a small and tightly knit unit.

As for Nick Wilder, a sandstorm separated his patrol from Mayne's the day they set out. Groping blind, one truck has pitched headlong down a forty-foot wadi. Illness and mechanical breakdowns have stripped T1 of another 30-hundredweight and four other men. By the time my Chev and Collie's link with what's left of Nick's and Mayne's outfits at Saunnu oasis, our new rendezvous and fallback point, the combined force is down to nine vehicles, four of which are jeeps, and twenty-two men.

Our outfit is creeping down the dark tarmac now, seeking the L-bend. The road turns left there, according to the map – towards the airfield. Nick's trucks took this route thirty minutes ago. When they've lit the field up, they'll bolt back this same way. Our job, as I said, is to cover their withdrawal.

But where's the L? It's supposed to be half a mile but we've covered twice that and seen nothing. We pass a sign COLONIA ESPARZA. It's on our maps, just past the bend. Have we overshot it?

Suddenly from the west: an explosion. We strain, waiting for the fireball. It never comes. A second blast goes up and, moments later, a third. We're expecting alarms and searchlights. But there's nothing.

'What the hell's going on?'

We keep going. Another mile. There's the road-crossing. I roll through and turn left; Collie's truck follows.

But it's a T-junction, not an L-bend. There's no T on the map. Collie and I meet each other's eyes. The night is freezing but we're both sweating. Are we lost?

'Kill the engines,' I say.

We listen. Nothing. Suddenly the whole airfield goes up. Yellow fireballs wallop skywards, followed by massive, ground-shuddering explosions. We can hear machine-gun fire and see green and red tracers zinging in all directions. More minutes pass. Suddenly headlights appear, speeding towards us from the direction of the airfield. Our two trucks have taken up positions flanking the road, partially covered behind sand berms. We're expecting Nick's jeep and trucks to come racing out of the darkness.

Instead we hear the growl of diesels and the whap-whap of steel tracks on the tarmac. Three tanks churn past, an Italian M-13 and two Mark III Panzers. They don't see us. They turn right and rumble off, down the road we came in on. They're the first tanks I've seen since Cairo. I'm astounded at how huge they are and how terrifying. As soon as they pass, Collie and Grainger scurry to me. We can hear more diesels and see more headlights approaching.

'This road,' says Collie, 'is starting to lose its charm.'

We reverse farther back from the junction, seeking a spot from which we can cover all approaches but that won't leave us so visible. The trucks haven't gone fifty yards before my rear wheels nearly plunge into a six-foot-deep irrigation ditch. We're in melon and maize fields. I can see no way round the ditch. It's too deep to cross. We probe along its verges, seeking a culvert or crossover, but the muck we're driving through builds up so thickly on our tyres that we have to halt and scrape it off with spades. We can see headlights approaching from east and west. Suddenly a voice in Italian challenges us from the darkness.

Punch cocks the Browning. At once we hear the frantic overturning of mess tins, punctuated by furious Latin profanity.

'Fire!'

Punch lets loose. It's a thousand to one, hitting anything in this ink, but as always the din of the gun vaults us sky-high with adrenalin. When Punch cuts his burst, we can hear footfalls receding into the distance.

'That'll give the Wops some exercise,' says Punch.

We inch back towards the road. On the airfield, more bombs are going off. The buildings are hangars and repair facilities. The explosives will either have been detonated on delay-fuses, so that Nick's and Major Mayne's trucks may be fleeing or long gone by now. Or both raiding parties may still be on the field, planting explosives as they go.

Either way, we can't stay here. The Italians we have just stumbled upon may have a radio to call for help; they may signal by Verey flare or even recover their nerve and come back to snipe at us or to lob the wicked little grenades they call 'red devils'.

More blasts ascend from Benina. Sirens at last begin sounding; we can see and hear fire trucks and emergency vehicles speeding between build-ings, a number of which are now aflame. We have no choice but to pull away from the T-junction, back down the road we came in on. We can't go forward and risk getting cut off any more than we already have been, but we also can't abandon our assignment of covering our comrades' withdrawal.

By now my truck and Collie's have escaped the melon fields and are slogging on our mud-caked tyres back on to the solid shoulder. Suddenly Collie's truck nose-dives to the right and stops. I hear swearing. Somehow Collie has run over barbed wire; wreaths of the stuff have coiled round his front axle and right front tyre, which has been punctured in heaven knows how many places. Jenkins bangs through kit boxes, seeking the wire cutters. I hurry over. Collie radiates his usual calm.

'All right, lads, hang on to your water. I'll dismount the twins,' he says, meaning the Vickers K machine guns, 'and find a spot on the road to set up.' He pats the side of the truck. 'Jenkins and Marks, don't get your knickers in a twist. There's no enemy in sight. Shut up and get the bloody tyre off.'

I ask Collie how long till he can move.

'Ten minutes.'

I help him dismount the Vickers. We're both keenly aware of how tight our spot is. We must set up and man this position – but for how long? We've already witnessed an M-13 tank and the two Mark IIIs passing this post, heading south – in other words between us and our getaway route. Worse, as we've noted via our adventure in the melon patch, there must be scores of side tracks through and round the cultivation, known to the enemy but not to us – perimeter and airfield access

271

roads, fire and rescue lanes, not to mention the farm tracks that the Arabs use to get their donkey carts in and out of the fields. The infantrymen we bumped into will report our incursion soon, if they haven't already. How long till every track out of here is cut off?

In war, nothing ever works by the timetable you think it will. 'I'm going forward,' I tell Collie. 'We've got to know what's up front.' I leave him with the Vickers protecting the road and his truck. Punch, Oliphant, Miller and I press westward towards the airfield.

Rain continues sheeting. I'm rolling in second gear, lights out. Suddenly: a camel.

'Jesus!'

The beast looms out of nowhere, beam-on and big as a barn. I stand on the brakes. Punch, on his feet at the Browning, goes sailing over my shoulder, across the aero-screens, and lands with a crash on the bonnet. The momentum of the braking truck somehow keeps the surface beneath him. Two more camels appear. It's a string. None even looks up. The truck by now is into a slow-motion 180, all four tyres locked up and sliding on the rain-slick road. Punch is slung sideways on to the sand of the shoulder. Oliphant and Miller in the truckbed are hanging on for dear life. In a spume of spray the truck stops tail-on to the camels, who still haven't reacted in the slightest. Two Arabs materialise, tapping the animals' rumps with their sticks. In moments the caravan has melted back into the night. Miller dashes to Punch. Miraculously he's not hurt and the truck is OK.

Now we're completely frazzled. Punch is cursing my driving, Miller and Oliphant are cursing the camels, we're all cursing the Arabs. In the mêlée of braking, one of our spare wheels and all of our bedding, plus half our water and rations, have spilled over the rails on to the tarmac. As we're scrambling to fling it back aboard, Punch whistles:

'Headlights!'

We can see them coming from the north axis of the T. We heave our gear into the truckbed, but there's no time to get it all.

'Could be Nick.'

'Could be Collie.'

'Could be half the German army.'

It's the last. We buck off the road into the mush beside the cultivation. Before the truck gets a hundred yards, two four-wheeled armoured cars slew up on to the site we've just vacated. They brake, headlights blazing, spotting our debris in the road. We're in the salt-bush, big as life, with no cover except the darkness. I hear orders shouted in German.

In front of me the glass aero-screen disintegrates. Something hot and close passes under my seat. I hear the hammering of two MG34s. Punch replies with the Browning. I heave the wheel over and floor the accelerator. We're in mud. The wheels spin. The truck is fleeing at the speed of a tortoise.

I'm shouting to Punch to cease fire; the flash of his muzzle is giving our pursuers a target. He shuts down. We slide and slither for what feels like two minutes but is probably only fifteen seconds. The Germans have lost us in the dark; they're simply raking the fields with fire.

The armoured cars will be splitting up, each taking one direction to head us off. And they'll be radioing for help. We have to get round them and back to the road. But where is it? I'm certain I'm running parallel, but I have no idea how far I've gone. At any moment I'm expecting to plunge into an unseen ditch. I spot a donkey track at right angles. Does it lead to the road? I can feel the rain on my face mixing with the blood where the glass has hit. The rounds that passed underneath the seats have torn up the condenser. Boiling water is spraying over the bonnet on to my right arm and leg. I hit the donkey track and bury the accelerator. With a mad lurch the truck bucks over a runoff channel and on to an unpaved road. Where the hell are we now?

I turn hard right, lights out, and crash broadside into a forty-four-gallon oil drum, upright in the middle of the road. It's a roadblock. The truck rebounds off this first barricade (which is no doubt filled with sand) and ploughs headlong into another. I'm flung into the steering column. The vehicle stops dead. The wind has been knocked out of me by the collision. I'm aware that we're being fired upon from very close. The bonnet of the truck is levitating in a way that defies physics. I glimpse a guard shed at the side of the road. Yellow tracer rounds are ricocheting off the surface. I've got the accelerator flat on the floor. The truck crawls. The world has become a silent movie. A searing gale passes beneath me; I feel the floorboard disintegrate. In the left-hand seat, Miller has been flung face-first into the dashboard. 'I'm shot!' he cries. I turn towards him. The right side of his shoulder, arm, and ribcage has been ripped open so wide I can see the bone-ends and viscera; he drops hard left, out of the cab, so fast that when I lunge to catch him with my left hand, I grab only his belt. I haul him back. He's un-conscious and hangs, dead weight. I jam him into the seat, shouting at him to hold on, though I know he can't hear me.

I'm sensing rather than seeing a second vehicle approaching from the north. The machine skids up and stops, broadside across the road.

It's Collie.

I never see who is firing on us or what happens to them. I hear the ungodly shriek of Collie's Vickers Ks and the bang-bang of what must be Marks on the Browning. I'm still hanging on to Miller with my left arm.

Punch and Oliphant appear; they grab Miller. I turn back to the guard shed. Whoever was firing from there has vanished. This is cold comfort, as the racket and fireworks will bring every Axis trooper in the neighbourhood. I smell petrol and see flames behind me on the truckbed. Punch hauls Miller aboard Collie's truck. So much for covering Nick's withdrawal. There's only one option now and that's to get the hell out.

Miraculously my truck is still functioning. Punch and Oliphant climb on. They're kicking flaming petrol tins over the tailboard. I get the engine started; we follow Collie back to the main road.

Trouble, soldiers say, never comes in ones. Now: more headlights. Two fresh sets, speeding towards us from the south. Where are the armoured cars? We never find out. What's clear is there's no way round the approaching lights. They block our escape.

Collie's truck and mine brake in the middle of the road. Steam is pouring from beneath my shot-to-ribbons bonnet; smoke billows from under the cab; I've lost first but second and third seem to work. Jenkins is shouting that his Browning is tits-up. My truck is clearly on its last legs. Should I ditch it? I'm debating piling all eight of us aboard Collie's. But where can we run?

Our only chance is our guns.

The enemy headlights continue closing. They're a thousand yards out but already their high beams are flickering across the tarmac where we squat.

We wrestle both trucks off the road. 'Not far!' I'm shouting. If we get bogged down, we're sitting ducks. There's no cover. We slog at right angles away from the road, far enough to get clear of the approaching headlights but not so far that we can't dash back on to the road after they pass.

If they pass.

We halt, side by side, tails-on to the road. Every man dismounts and piles brush for cover.

Here come the headlights. We can hear the enemy engines now. Collie climbs back on the Vickers twins; Jenkins assists with the drums. Punch is on one Browning on my truck, Oliphant on the other. Marks seats a magazine in his Thompson. 'Hold fire till my order,' I say.

We can see the enemy clearly now.

Two trucks.

Fiat 3-tonners, the kind used to carry infantry.

The vehicles approach at twenty miles per hour, one a hundred feet behind the other. I can see a driver and an officer in the lead truck. Windscreen wipers beat. The officer still hasn't seen us. He's standing on the running board, hanging on to the outboard mirror strut. I see him point ahead.

The lead truck slows.

The second follows suit.

The officer sees us. He swings off the step on to the tarmac, gesturing to both trucks to stop. They do. The officer is very young and wears a Bersaglieri cap. He is pointing to us and shouting something in Italian.

What happens next takes no more than twenty seconds.

The Fiats are open-sided flatbeds with brown canvas covers keeping the rain off the soldiers in the back. The men ride shoulder to shoulder on wooden benches, one bench along each rail, facing inward. To dismount from the vehicles, the soldiers must stand and file to the back, drop the tailboard and leap down to the road. As they begin doing this, I shout, 'Fire!'

Collie opens up with the Vickers Ks. Punch and Oliphant join in on the Brownings, Marks on his tommy gun. I'm firing my own Thompson, which I have grabbed in a hurry from its cradle on the cab wall.

The Italians spill from the rear of the trucks, one and two at a time, like children jumping down from a school bus. The officer stands in the road. He has only a pistol. He is firing at us as Collie's Vickers puts a burst dead-centre into his chest. A Vickers K has twin barrels. Its rate of fire is nine hundred and fifty rounds a minute. The gun is designed to be mounted on fighter aircraft. Its intended targets are other planes, not unarmoured human flesh. What it does to the young Italian officer I will not describe, except to say that what had been solid in one instant is liquid the next.

The Brownings in Punch's and Oliphant's hands American designed .30 calibres chambered to take the British .303. Their rate of fire is six hundred rounds per minute. Mounted on Spitfire fighter planes, their original application, they are designed to take out targets at ranges beyond a thousand yards We, this night, are firing at no more than seventy-five feet. That is like saying point-blank.

Within seconds the first 3-tonner has disintegrated. The Vickers shreds its cab; the tyres rip and blow; the chassis crashes dead-weight on to the rims. Petrol spilling from the riddled tanks is ignited by our tracers; the Fiat goes up in a whoosh of orange flame. The second truck is reversing as fast as it can, back down the road. I am firing at it with my Thompson. I see the windscreen shatter. The vehicle lurches out of control, turns side-on and stops. Now the men tumble forth. Half the troopers in the first truck and a portion from the second have leapt to the road. Our machine guns cut them down, then elevate and traverse to take the others still in the trucks. In moments I have run through a fifty-round drum magazine. Punch's and Oliphant's belt-fed guns keep blazing. We are so close to the Italians that I can see the moustaches on their upper lips and the wedding rings on their fingers.

The volume of fire from the Vickers and the Brownings is so prodigious that it creates its own wind. The tarpaulins on the trucks blow and howl, then burst into flame. The Italians spill from the trucks in animal terror. Few have their weapons; none tries to turn and fire. Instead they dive for cover, seeking to burrow under the trucks or to use the frames and wheels as shelter. Our tracers and ball rounds pour into them. I can hear Punch's Browning banging, inches from my ear. Smoke seethes from its barrel. Our guns do not strip the foe of life with surgical strokes. They take them in a holocaust. The spectacle is not like the cinema, in which after a massacre the earth lies littered with forms clearly recognisable as human beings, possessed of heads and arms and legs. When we are done, the enemy are offal. I thank heaven that I glimpse this horror only by the light of the burning trucks and the tracers, and only for the instant I let myself look. One purpose is paramount in my mind. We must kill or incapacitate every man on the trucks. To permit even one to survive, in the darkness from which he can snipe or loose a machine-gun burst at my men, is unthinkable. These are armed enemy, who have hastened to this site with one object only: to take the lives of my comrades and me. I must take theirs first. No truth could be plainer. Yet at the same time nothing can alter the fact that beneath the fascist insignia of their uniforms, these men are fathers, husbands, sons.

I let it go on till it seems nothing can remain alive. 'Cease fire!'

I dash on foot to the shoulder of the road, peering north to a third, new set of headlights speeding towards us. I am shouting to Collie to get ready to run; we'll blow up my truck and take everybody aboard his. Suddenly the oncoming lights stop. A yellow Verey flare shoots skywards, followed by a red.

'It's Nick!'

In thirty seconds Wilder's patrol has reached us. They have two trucks of their own and an Italian Lancia. Without an order, Punch and Oliphant begin slinging our kit aboard. They pile the

Brownings over the rails, then the ammo boxes, water tins and jerry cans of petrol. Grainger sluices our own truckbed and tosses a match. Nick stares at the carnage along the roadside. 'Jesus,' he says, 'what a mess.'

I climb aboard the Lancia with the din of the massacre still booming in my ears. My last glimpse, as our trucks pull out, is of Punch dashing back to the now-blazing Te Aroha IV to grab our bedding and the jug of rum from its nest behind the tailboard.

CHAPTER 23

We reach the rally point at Saunnu to find it shot up and sodden under a downpour. The Benina raid has overturned the hornets' nest. German and Italian patrols cover all escape routes south and east; scout planes scour the flats and every patch of cover. Nick Wilder commands now and I'm glad of it.

For two days and nights we run. Rain makes the trucks hard to see from the air, but the desert surface is mush, and our tyres leave great livid scars. From these the enemy reckons our direction of flight; they send Macchis and Me-110s ahead. That's how they find the rally point.

Miller is dead. We've been unable to do anything for him; he has lost too much blood. Our lie-up the first night is tucked into the bank of a wide, stony wadi. We have learnt to site camps beneath gentle slopes, so we can get clear in a hurry if we have to. The post-adrenalin letdown has enervated us badly. We brew up by the heat of the engine block and knock back more rum than we ought. We wrap Miller's body in his greatcoat and belt it into a sand-channel which we lay flat on the truckbed of the Lancia. Miller had been chess champion of his Yorkshire outfit, the Green Howards; we tuck his miniature board and pieces under his shirt. We have not had a moment even to empty his pockets for his wife and children.

Nick calls for my damage report, which I can give in ten seconds: medical orderly dead, wireless truck destroyed. On the surviving truck: Browning disabled; cracked sump, two bent tie-rods, petrol for a hundred miles. Men either battered, shot, sick, or all three. Nick's T1 is in the same shape, except their wireless is still functioning. Like us, they too have no working navigation gear.

We reach the burnt-out RV at nightfall of the second day. Nick studies the site through binoculars, then orders us to pull back five miles to the secondary rendezvous designated before the patrols set out for Benina. Wrecks are sobering sights. Even in the fading light we can make out the hulks of our comrades' vehicles – Doc Lawson's, the fitters', Nick's second wireless truck – belly-down on bare rims with their tyres incinerated under them. The exposed engines are charred black, rubber vaporised, seats melted down to springs and frames. We can see the tracks where the Afrika Korps armoured cars came in, pasted our fellows, then rolled out. Sandbanks have been torn by the treads of half-tracks, the kind the Germans use to ferry motorised infantry. Farther back we can see the lanes carved by the wide desert tyres of the 3-tonners on which they carry ammo, rations and petrol. 'They're not out here on a picnic,' says Nick.

This time they mean to find us.

After dark, he takes two men and creeps in to inspect the RV. Returning, he reports three graves, one enemy and two of ours – Daventry and Porter, both New Zealanders, neither of whom I know.

'They buried them cleanly, give the Huns that.' Nick has taken the men's ID discs, which the Germans have left on wooden crosses on mounds rimmed with stones. He'll bring them home if he can. The enemy have marked two of our burnt-up trucks with paint:

288 MENTON

'Just to let us know who nailed us,' says Nick. 'It's their unit, whatever the hell the name means.'

Exhausted as both patrols are, we can't linger. We'd be safer splitting up – one group might reach safety and send aid to the other – but with only one wireless we have to stick together. Should we bury Miller here, beside the others? There's no time. We divide the remaining petrol and grub evenly among the four vehicles, sharing rum and cigs, tea and chocolate, in case one or two get shot up or mired. 'Luck,' says Nick. We're off.

All night we search for a way across the mudflats. Here at the southern end of the Jebel, the wadis all drain to the desert, forming the intermittent lakes called balats. The lakes are three feet deep in places, inches in others. Their bottoms are like mucilage. The patrols feel their way in the dark upon the high ground of natural causeways and grope along archipelagos elevated a few inches above the slough. Again and again one truck get bogged down, leaving the others to tow it clear. Clutches scorch and shudder. The labour proves an ordeal, as tyres become gummed with heavy, water-freighted mud, which can only be cleared by back-breaking spadework. The toil is exhausting; in the end we can't get clear of the balats. Dawn finds all four trucks slogging dejectedly back the way they came, west towards the foothills, while double lookouts scan the sky for the planes we know are coming.

0815. ME-110s overhead. Two with one spotter. We're lying up under camo nets in a notch of an escarpment. The MEs haven't spotted us yet. Their technique is to target one notch at a time and blast it top to bottom with cannon fire.

0900. MEs wing off, out of ammo. Spotter has found us though, stays with us, just out of MG range.

1145. Well, that was a hot hour and a half. MEs back, rearmed, wicked twin-engined monsters spitting fire from cannons and machine guns in the aircraft noses. Our lie-up is so far down the scarp, the planes can't have a real go or they'll crash into the cliff. It's a close thing, though, and we're pretty rattled.

By noon the Messerschmitts have flown off for the second time, returning to base to rearm and refuel. But now armoured cars have found us, probably the same pursuit force that shot up the rally point. No choice but to run. The worst of it is, these steady attacks leave us no interval to set up the Wyndom and signal HQ. Other friendly patrols may be within hailing distance. Tinker and Popski certainly. Nick says he's had signals informing him that at least two others, Lazarus's S1 and Spicer's Y1, may be within sixty miles, not to mention Major Mayne and the SAS, from or about whom we've heard nothing since Benina. Compounding the frustration: we don't know how far west the main British advance has pushed. That's where we want to go. Safety may be as close as a hundred miles, which we can reach, or as far as three hundred, which we can't.

Clearly our pursuers know this. They come at us from the east, cutting off all escape in that direction. Do they know we're the outfit that went after Rommel? Have they been sent after us specifically? 'There's an Iron Cross waiting,' Nick says, 'for any Hun lieutenant who brings in our scalps.'

My watch reads 1230 as our four trucks lurch from their hidey-holes and churn north along the base of the escarpment. Pursuing us are at least two armoured cars, a 4-wheeler and an eight, which we've glimpsed bulldozing through the brush, and one or more half-tracks carrying infantry. Our Chevs and even the Lancia could outrun the gang if they were in good repair, but with burnt clutches, patched sumps and punctured radiators, the convoy bangs and jounces like a Keystone Kops farce. Top speed never gets above ten miles an hour over salt-bush-thick sand and shingle, whose surface is cut every hundred feet by ditches and runnels, some capacious enough to swallow a jeep, others only a foot deep and two across. These are the worst. Into them the front axles plunge with an impact that beats the frame as if on an anvil and sends men and kit flying. Rain continues; visibility is down to fifty feet. We can't see the Germans and they can't see us. The armoured cars' cannons are useless in this gloom, so they simply rake the unseen ground ahead of them with bursts from their 7.92s. We can see tracers rebounding off the scree and hear the bullet strikes above us on the scarp. With dread, we're counting the minutes till the 110s come back. 'Maybe the buggers'll stop for lunch,' Punch shouts across at me as the Lancia bucks over the obstacle-course landscape with every bolt and rivet crying. The chase bumps along, devoid of excitement or even urgency. It just feels stupid. A futile, moronic way to die. After about an hour, our trucks gain enough of a lead for Nick to signal halt and set us up in an ambush position behind the shoulder of a ridge. At fifteen hundred yards, Collie's Vickers and two of Nick's Brownings get good bursts on to the 4-wheeler, which we catch in the open with both hatches up and its commander's and driver's heads high. Through the Dienstglas binos I can see the tracers spraying the armoured car like a garden hose; the German veers, plunges into a shallow wadi and stops with a bang. 'Got him!' cries Punch.

'Stay on him,' Nick shouts, 'till you knock him out.' For the first time I feel real rage towards the foe. I'm tired of being chased by these bastards. Guns from both our trucks pour fire on to the armoured car. But in a few seconds both hatches button up. The German grinds along laterally, using the wash as cover. Coming our way.

'Slowed him anyway,' says Collie.

We run for another hour, taking intermittent fire from the 4-wheeler (the eight appears to have fallen behind) and from two half-tracks, which we glimpse at intervals among the scrub, until a cracking Old Testament cloudburst saves us.

By dark we're fifteen miles farther on. The storm passes; the heavens clear. The night turns hard cold. We've been running all day north and west, 180 degrees from the direction we want. Night finds us making a hasty camp in a wadi at the base of the escarpment, fifty miles farther from safety than we were at dawn, with less than sixty miles of fuel remaining.

Worse, when Nick's operator sets up the aerial, the atmospherics are so bad he can't raise a peep. Collie, Punch and I scout out a high spot where we hope the next flood won't reach; we slip Miller's body underground, digging as silently as if with teaspoons, and set up a cairn with a cross of brushwood. We stand bare-headed over the Yorkshireman. We've got one beer, which at first we think to bury with him, then change our minds and share it out amongst ourselves. 'He'd have given us hell,' says Punch, 'if we'd wasted a good pint.'

Back in camp a rising mist has turned the night black and cold. 'I'm getting bloody tired of this,' I tell Nick as our patrols carve out a lie-up and try to get a brew on. It's clear to everyone that we cannot keep on this way. 'What now?' I ask.

Nick squints up the thirty-storey face ascending above us. 'I don't know what's on top of this bastard,' he says. 'But we either get up this scarp tonight or the Jerries'll finish us in the morning.'

CHAPTER 24

The escarpment looms three hundred feet over our heads, not much compared to the mighty coastal ascents at Sollum and Halfaya, but still damned daunting in the dark with four trucks at the breaking point and men pressed beyond exhaustion. Worse is the cold and wet. The face of the escarpment is like all others in the Jebel – limestone and marine conglomerate, sediment of some ancient sea. Wadis and ravines furrow the cliff, which steps back from base to summit, so that from the bottom you can't see the top. This is good; it means the slope should provide inlets and traverses that our vehicles can take advantage of.

Nick sends Punch and me in the Lancia north along the base of the scarp, seeking a way up. 'Don't dawdle,' he says. Half a mile out, Punch spots a natural ascent. I scramble ahead on foot with a spade and a torch; Punch churns at my heels in crawler gear. The Lancia bucks uphill by leaps and lurches. The scream of the winding engine seems as if it must carry for miles. The trail starts as a camel track, narrows to a goat path, then a trace, then nothing. It ends. Back down we go, with me at the wheel in reverse and Punch guiding by shouts. Already the brakes are overheating. I do the last forty feet free-wheeling, bouncing back on to the plain with Punch diving clear amid a storm of profanity.

We try three more tracks till we have to stop to spare the clutch a hundred feet from the top. 'This has to be the one,' declares Punch. We don't have the strength to try another. As we start down, red streaks flash across the cliffline; we hear thuds overhead; stones and shingle begin tumbling from above. My first thought is it's wild goats, even wolves.

'That's a bloody gun,' says Punch.

We can see tracers now and the pinpoints of muzzle flashes, far out on the plain below. The enemy haven't halted with nightfall; they've been trailing us, probably by our engine noise.

Back in camp, every man is on his feet with the trucks revved and ready. In the minutes it has taken Punch and me to get back, the enemy have found our lie-up and opened fire with a 20mm and two more MGs. At least three vehicles are out there in the dark, one of them an armoured car. 'How far,' Nick says, 'to this trail of yours?'

Of course we can't find it. I have marked the site by a limestone notch. Now this landmark refuses to show itself. Tracers, ball and incendiary continue streaking overhead and thumping into the cliff face. Nick calls us together. His idea is to duck our pursuers by bolting back the way we came. But it's too risky, he says, for all four trucks to try. 'Who's game for the scarp?'

I look to Collie.

'Hell with it,' he says. Meaning aye.

It violates protocol to split a patrol with only one wireless, but if we stick here together we're done for and there's no chance of four trucks getting up this cliff under fire. Whoever gets away first sends help for the others. 'Luck,' says Nick again. Again we touch hands all round.

Nick's trucks fake a runaway north, firing as they go, then cut their guns and beat it south into the dark.

Punch and I find a track that looks like our road and start up. The next five hours are surely the longest of my life – and that of every man in Collie's truck and the Lancia. As soon as we forsake the shelter of the cliff base, the Germans can hear our engines. As the moon ascends they can see us too.

The 20mm they're shelling us with is a Pak anti-aircraft gun, as big as a Breda. It fires cannon shells, not bullets. We start up the cliff with the Lancia in the lead, Punch driving. Oliphant and I go ahead on foot; Collie protects the space between the trucks. The trail takes us sixty feet up with no problems, then cuts back to another drivable slope. We can hear the growl of diesels approaching; our pursuers are bringing their guns up slap to the base of the scarp. By now every man we've got except the drivers is out in front with spades and mattocks. Dense brush chokes the route; we hack it away, road-building as we go. Fortune spares us momentarily when a twist in the track puts a shoulder of the slope between us and the 20mm. We're in dead ground. But now we hear the enemy troopers fanning out below, seeking an angle on us from the flank. They've loaded their belts tracer/ball/incendiary; we can see and hear the rounds, in crisp professional bursts, painting the cliff above us. A hundred and fifty feet up, a drivable chimney opens before us, but to get to it, the trucks have to negotiate a sharp zigzag ascent across a shelf no wider than the trucks themselves and with a 150-foot drop. Punch tries it in the Lancia with me outboard, hanging over the fall. As the Lancia's tyres dig, they tear the ledge away beneath. I can see the shingle spilling below my heel and hear the flat stones banging and clashing as they avalanche down the face. 'No good! We'll have to go up this next bit in reverse.'

It takes an hour for the trucks to get round the corner. We can hear German troopers below us, scrambling up the slope on foot. A burst or two from our guns and they think better of that notion. I post Oliphant and Grainger with the Vickers on a shelf where they can give our pursuers a welcome if they keep trying. Up we labour with the trucks. At one point, when the track has half sheared away, we find ourselves with a sand-channel spread across thin air and two men on spades bracing each extremity. The trucks inch into the dead end, then reverse up the slope above. We do this four times, climbing the next sixty feet. Each time we destroy the trail behind us so the enemy can't get vehicles up after us. By now the Germans have set up camp two hundred yards out on the flat and are pasting the hillside with everything they've got. We can hear them clearly. 'Come down, friends!' a voice calls in crisp upper-class English. 'We have hot broth for you!'

We've reached a shelf notched back from the face, safe for the moment.

'Who are you bloody buggers?' shouts Punch.

'Two Eight Eight Combat Team. Show sense, men, don't throw your lives away!'

Another hour carries us within thirty feet of the summit. Here the trail falls away completely. A twenty-foot chasm gapes. No way round. Do we blow the trucks, continue our flight on foot? Dawn is four hours off; the summit will be plastered by planes at first light. There's only one hope: fill the void with brush, then bridge it with sand-channels.

'There's another way,' says Jenkins. 'Show the white flag.'

Curses greet this. But Jenkins, who is no coward, is past caring. 'They won't kill us. So we're in a camp? Who cares?'

'That's enough,' I say.

I can see Jenkins is about to make an argument for his case, which in truth is not without merit.

In tank clashes throughout the desert campaign, Allied and Axis crews have routinely put their hands in the air when their machines were knocked out and they were cut off from aid. Little if any shame has attached to this. Generals on both sides have hoisted the white hanky; tales are legion of soldiers giving themselves up at one hour, only to have their captors surrender to them in the next when the tide of battle turns.

Tonight is different, though. The idea of giving in, embraced even for a moment, will sap our will and break us before morning. 'We'll have no more of that,' I tell Jenkins.

Whether it is something in my voice or eye, I can't say. At once, however, Jenkins backs off. He apologises.

'Forget it,' I say. 'Get back to work.'

All hands plunge into the chore of hacking brush and tying it into fascines. I have trained in this technique at Bovington. It's how tanks cross ditches. We bundle tamarisk and acacia into dense kindling-like rolls, then bind the mass with chains and ropes. The job takes hours. Throughout, my mind works. How, after Jenkins's lapse, can I restore the men's trust in him and his belief in himself?

At last the fascines have been wedged into place, sand-channels lashed across the top. The crews stare at their handiwork. A man would have to be mad to drive across this rickety span.

'Jenkins,' I say, 'show us the way.'

Jenkins understands. So does everyone. This is not to punish but to redeem.

He mounts the running board and slips behind the wheel. 'Tally ho!'

And across the gap he zips, as slick as a fox over a fence. The Lancia scurries to solid ground, halts to dig in, then hauls Collie's truck across with the tow chain. In a gang we bowl the fascines back down the slope so our pursuers can't use them to follow us once we're gone. On the summit, Collie and Punch pound Jenkins's back in congratulation. Oliphant and Grainger climb up from their rearguard post. We can hear the enemy below, still wooing us to surrender.

Collie stands at the brink with the Vickers. 'Who wants a go?' He means have a crack at the men below.

No takers.

The men are too tired and too relieved to find themselves still alive and uncaptured.

CHAPTER 25

We have hoped that the summit will prove easy going, but from the first fifty yards the trucks find themselves entangled in dense acacia and tamarisk. Both plants are tough and pulpy, impossible to hack through without keen axes, so that the men have no choice but to open what slender breaches they can with spades and their own shoulders, then bowl through by the push of the trucks. Progress is heartbreakingly slow, made even more frustrating because the man-high brush keeps us from seeing more than a few yards ahead. Again and again the trucks plunge into unseen creases. Even a shallow trench, a 2-footer, produces a frame-walloping crash that hammers our already battered tie-rods, steering boxes, axles, sumps and undercarriages. Blunder into one of these pits sideways and the whole truck teeters, necessitating a mad rush by all hands to save her from upending. To compound our ills, both Collie's truck and my Lancia now begin torturing us with minor breakdowns. Collie's engine overheats; we spend twenty minutes checking radiators, belts and hoses before discovering the stuck-closed thermostat. We pull it out and chuck it entirely. Next, the water pump fails on my Lancia; it has to be patched together, at the cost of half an hour.

The race is against daylight, not only to outstrip the Macchis and Messerschmitts that our friends in 288 will surely have called down on us for first light, but also to put miles between ourselves and the German armoured cars and motorised infantry working round the escarpment (which we know they will be doing because in their place we surely would) to beat us to the other side. They can't come over the summit unless they find another way up, so thoroughly have we wrecked our ascent behind us – and if they do somehow, they'll be thrashing through the same brush that's frustrating our progress.

Suddenly, more bad luck. After a mile or two of terrific labour, we hear the strangling sound of Collie's engine sucking dry. We've burned miles of fuel, just mounting the scarp. I call a pow-wow. 'All right. Who's got what?'

In the desert every vehicle holds its secret cache of juice. Punch and I have a full jerry can tucked behind the spare wheel. Collie coughs up another. Oliphant contributes two litres, stashed amongst his POL tins. We pool this reserve and press on.

Every man is exhausted. Nobody speaks. Yet our spirits remain strong. I discover a new capacity in myself. Without a word I can sense my comrades' state of mind. I feel the group's breaking point, individually and collectively, and my own as well. Have I at last become a commander? The elements of time, terrain and weather – I seem to know, almost without thought, whether they will be working for us or against us. I can gauge how long machines can carry on before they fail, or men before they crack. And I can sense their reserves, and my own, beyond that point. I can even, I realise with gratification, perceive the wider field – the theatre, the campaign, the war itself. As our patrol hacks its way across the summit plain, I grasp, despite the real and immediate peril to ourselves, that the greater enemy is on the run. Rommel himself, and all of Panzerarmee Afrika, is withdrawing before Montgomery's advance. This will do us of T3 patrol no good, of course, if we are killed or captured.

Still, I am at peace. Never have I felt so fully used or so at one with my companions. Not a patch of glory attaches to our endeavours in this hour. We crawl like beetles, marking progress not in miles but feet. Nor am I 'leading' in any way that the military manuals would recognise or commend. I'm just slogging miserably beside the others. But we are one, each giving his all. I catch a second wind, and I feel my brothers-in-arms catch theirs too.

By first light we have reached the western fall of the escarpment, which remains thankfully in deep shadow. Collie's brakes have packed up so we simply wrestle the truck down the slope, tow-chained to the Lancia, whose own drums have worn to bare metal and screech every yard of the way. By eight, we have reached the bottom and snuggled the trucks down in the deepest wadi we can find. The fellows weave brush and netting into masterpieces of camouflage, then collapse, all except the lookouts I post in one-hour aircraft watches. All day, enemy Storches and 110s scour the area but fail to spot us. At last with dark we give way to sleep. Surely nothing else can go wrong, at least till morning.

CHAPTER 26

I hear a roar and feel the earth break apart beneath me. Something cold and fierce jerks me awake. A gale howls. Am I dreaming? I hear Punch shout from up the slope, but his words are torn away in the wind. Then I see the flood.

The shock wave of air preceding it bowls me off my sleeping perch. In an instant, the foliage I have used as a mattress is sucked away, along with my Thompson, blankets, tarpaulin, and both my boots. Collie's truck is lifted like a toy. It shoots past me upside down and is swept from sight in the dark.

I'm half naked, scrambling frantically up the face of the wadi. Directly below, I hear the Lancia cartwheeling away on the surface of the flood. Oliphant and Collie have been sleeping in it. Jenkins too. I can't see them. I'm climbing hand over hand. The torrent howls, inches beneath my heels. It's tearing the bank out from under me. Punch catches me under one arm. Boulders and rafts of brush boom past beneath our feet. I realise that this is a flash flood. That's why there's no rain. Storms in another part of the Jebel have produced this torrent while we, here, have remained dry and unalerted.

In minutes the worst is over. It's remarkable how quickly your courage returns, the instant you know you're safe. Punch, Grainger and I have clambered on to a solid shelf. With each second, the fury-sound of the waters recedes. The torrent, whose depth has been twenty feet, shrinks to ten, five, then a very rapidly moving three or four. We are high, if not dry. Sections of slope continue to fall away beneath us into the still-churning flood. 'Collie! Oliphant!' We cry our comrades' names into the dark.

Now the rain comes, a frigid, drenching deluge in which the three of us hunker, mute and shivering. The scale of the calamity overwhelms us. What can we do?

Flood depth has dropped to three feet, still a wickedly lethal torrent. Our first imperative is to find any of our companions still alive and bring aid to those who have been hurt. Jenkins appears, preceded by a shout; then Oliphant, sluicing down the face, as mud-sodden and frozen as we are. His left knee is hurt but he claims it's nothing serious. We take stock of our resources – two coats and three blankets; one .303 Enfield with no ammunition but the six rounds in the single magazine that happened to be in the rifle when the flood struck; two one-litre water bottles. I've still got my rucksack, which I had lent to Punch to use as a pillow; it holds a shirt and a pair of trousers, along with Stein's manuscript and the remnants of my much-thumbed reading materials. The patrol's pooled supplies consist of two tins of sardines, half a handful of boiled sweets, a fountain pen, and two bayonets. Grainger still has his watch. We have no map, no tea, no electric torch, no Verey pistol, and, for Jenkins, Grainger and me, no shoes. We are missing two men.

An hour has passed since the flood. Time is 0320. Our party starts downstream, spread out in a skirmish line, calling Collie's and Marks's names. Snakes glide across the knee-high surface. They are as frightened of us as we are of them. Though the waters have receded to wading depth, the volume of the flood has produced pockets of quicksand. Into these we sink again and again; a cry and we haul one another out. A quarter of a mile down, we come upon Marks, alive, but with both legs so battered from the pummelling he has taken in the flood that he cannot stand, although it turns out no bones are broken. He's also taken a blow to the skull, possibly from a log or boulder, which has peeled the scalp back in a flap the size of a man's hand, exposing the bare bone. The wound bleeds profusely. Marks is in shock and shivering convulsively. We carry him on to dry land and warm him between our bodies, taking turns. Jenkins, who has replaced Miller as our medical orderly, gently draws the flap of scalp back into place and binds it down with a web belt. 'If we can find one of the trucks,' he says, 'it'll have a first-aid box with thread and a needle.' Jenkins volunteers to stay. I leave him to do his best to keep Marks warm; the rest of us push on.

A hundred yards downstream we find Collie's truck. The vehicle lies on its left side, sunk so deep that the only parts visible are the rear axle and the tyre mount behind the driver's door. Everything else is submerged in muck and brush, which has built up so thickly and in such a jumble, it's a miracle we discover the truck at all. I climb aboard via the axle. Every item of kit that was in the truckbed – guns, ammo, petrol and water tins – has been carried away. We call Collie's name. Nothing. The first-aid box remains in place. I send Oliphant back to Marks and Jenkins with it. Punch, Grainger and I push on along the wadi bottom.

Daylight. We still haven't found Collie. Back at the wreck of the truck, Oliphant and Jenkins have got Marks settled out of the wet, swathed in what clothing and blankets they've been able to retrieve. Jenkins has stitched Marks's scalp, but the poor fellow tosses miserably, shivering and semi-conscious. Oliphant's injured knee has swollen; he can barely hobble. We scratch out a camp above any potential flood line. When Marks recovers enough to speak, he can't stop apologising. He begs to be left behind; he can't stand the thought, he says, of his condition's putting his mates in danger. 'Shut the hell up,' Grainger commands him in a voice exquisitely tender.

I call a council. 'No one's leaving anyone,' I say. We have found two jerry cans of petrol and a tin of matches; between them it's enough to get a fire going, even of soaked driftwood. The risk of smoke has to be taken; we'll freeze to death without a blaze to dry our clothes and blankets. We have no billy and no tea. Punch produces two almost-dry cigarettes; we get one lit and share it amongst all. 'No hogging it, you blokes!' It is the most satisfying smoke any of us has ever had.

The final fallback plan imparted by Nick Wilder before his departure was to rendezvous at Bir Hemet on the track to Augila oasis. I go over this now with the men. 'We'll rest for the morning and dry out our kit. Punch and I will keep looking for Collie. In the afternoon we'll take one shot at digging out the truck. If it's hopeless, we'll sleep the night and start on foot to RV with Wilder's patrol as planned.'

CHAPTER 27

Midday: Punch and I find Collie and the Lancia. Both have been swept a mile down the wadi. Collie is suffering from exposure but he revives fast with the sight of his comrades and the warmth of the two dry blankets we have brought from the fire. He has survived the night under dirt and brush in an actual foxhole, having evicted the foxes. As for the Lancia, it lies upright, buried to its axles in smooth mud, with two tyres intact and two shredded.

I send Punch back to collect Marks and the others and to salvage what he can from the wreckage of Collie's truck. The vehicle itself is past repairing. By mid-afternoon all who are fit have made two trips, recovering three jerry cans of fuel and an armload of hoses, belts and fittings. The patrol assembles round the Lancia. A freezing rain has started; about three hours of daylight remain. We dig the vehicle out and manhandle it on to dry ground. Chocolate-coloured sludge sluices from every runway. 'Kick her over, Skip,' says Grainger. For the hell of it, I try. She starts immediately! I find myself weeping. Others jig and pound one another's backs. The engine stalls, but nobody cares. If she'll spark once, she'll do it again.

The party passes the night in a huddle, then turns to at first light. For tools we have only two fixed spanners and a single adjustable. No screwdrivers, no socket or plug spanners, no Allen keys, calipers or points. We have no tools to pull the head or replace it, no gaskets or material to fabricate them from, no tyre irons, no levers, no pump and no spare inner tubes, valves, or wheel braces to remove or replace wheel nuts. We have motor oil and petrol. We have water.

The most pressing issue is care for the wounded. Oliphant's knee is looking worse; Collie's burns, which have re-opened in the flood, are tormenting him; Marks's condition continues to deteriorate. The Lancia has to carry them. Grainger will be our navigator. He estimates Bir Hemet at seventy miles south by west. Walking and trucking the wounded, we might make it in three nights. But to navigate you must know your starting position; we can only guess at ours. The desert we must cross is cut by balats and seasonal mudflats that we'll have to square round, with no map and no means of shooting the stars or sun. It will take incredible luck to strike our objective and if we overrun it we'll have no way of knowing. Even if we get there, nothing guarantees that Nick Wilder's patrol will be waiting.

I think this but don't say it.

Everyone else, I imagine, is thinking it too.

All day the men toil, first disconnecting, flushing and drying all fuel, air and water lines; laboriously reconnecting their clamps using a bayonet point for a screwdriver; then cleaning and reassembling all pumps. Two desert foxes watch from a nearby outcrop. Their coats are the colour of sand, their brushes thin and scruffy. Half a dozen times the cry of 'Aircraft!' sends us scurrying. The foxes never budge. Each time, the enemy planes pass over.

We decide to name the spot Two Foxes. We'll put it on the map when we get back. This cheers us considerably.

The law of the Perversity of Physical Objects continues to frustrate us. Everything that can go wrong, does. During the flood the backing plate of the Lancia's differential has cracked open, exposing the innards, caking the gear train with sand and mud, and of course draining all fluid. Somehow Punch succeeds in sealing and rebolting it. But what can we use for lubrication? From a spiny cactus, we scrape the inner goo. Banana skins have been known to serve; perhaps this will too. Meanwhile Oliphant has taken the carburettor apart, picking out sand and sludge speck by speck. Jenkins works on the brake lines.

By nightfall we've sorted out everything but the tyres. Only two still hold air. Grainger supplies a trick he used on tractors back home: stuff them with brush. It works. Except now, removing the right front wheel housing, Grainger discovers the axle is broken. We have no spares. By now it's too dark to work. Suddenly our spectating foxes rise on their haunches and trot away. We hear growls in the distance.

Diesels.

Combat Group 288 returns.

We net the Lancia and deploy ourselves into a perimeter. The Germans approach in two parties, scouring the wadis as they go. Clearly our pursuers know we can have fled in only one direction and can have got only so far. We can see the beams of their torches and headlights, discovering Collie's truck a mile back up the wadi. Is the game up? Is this it at last?

Darkness saves us, followed by a fresh down-pour. Our fellows crouch miserably, hearing the enemy hastening to rig their own shelters. The foe pitch camp parallel to ours and a quarter of a mile out on to the flat, safely clear of the flood zone.

They haven't spotted us.

For the moment we're safe.

But Marks's state is getting desperate. Fever racks him. He thinks the voices from the German camp are ghosts of lost mates. He calls their names. Punch muffles him with a hand over the mouth but Marks, made frantic by this, gurgles louder and thrashes, trying to work free. Collie crosses swiftly to him, presses one palm over Marks's mouth and cracks him hard with the other fist – a solid shot, right between the eyes. Marks gags, blinks, then comes to himself. He shuts up. Collie cradles him, gently as a babe. 'My old man used to work that trick on me all the time.'

Rain abates, succeeded by a cold northerly gale. Our pursuers have set up their camp snug and tight. We can see the light of their fires, hear their laughter and smell their potatoes and sausages frying. I have assigned men in pairs to warm Marks with their bodies. When Grainger and my turn comes, our companion is shivering convulsively. Grainger's eyes search mine.

Shall we surrender?

The enemy may have a doctor or a medical orderly; for certain they have vehicles that can carry Marks to aid. They are not monsters; they will help.

Is this war? War is formations of armour, men and machines clashing in action. That's not this. We're just frightened, freezing men struggling to keep a comrade alive. 'Marks . . .' I say.

'Don't do it,' he answers.

Grainger and I press him more tightly between us. 'Don't be such a damn hero,' says Grainger.

There are moments for which no amount of training can prepare one. A man's life against a notion of honour. Who am I, at twenty-two years old, to make such a decision, to risk everything a man possesses or ever will possess, his wife, his children, their lives and future, against an abstract principle whose merit I am no more capable of gauging than he?

Two days ago I was moments from reaching for my pistol when Jenkins dared broach the prospect of showing the white flag. Now I don't care. Victory or defeat will come willy-nilly, determined by forces far greater than our meagre party. What matters now is this good man's life. I can save him with a simple shout into the dark. And if I don't? Shall we bury Marks at dawn, to join Standage and Miller, to be followed tomorrow by how many others of thirst or starvation, including myself?

But I can't do it.

'Can you hang on, Marksy?'

At dawn, our pursuers break camp. They perform a desultory search of the wadi, finding nothing, then form up round their lieutenant for final orders before departure. Shall I hail them? I see them plainly from my perch on the slope.

I let them go.

Our fellows emerge like foxes from their dens. We look like death. Collie's eyes meet mine. He has been thinking the same thing. Are we fools?

Hot water and biscuits do nothing to restore us, but Grainger overnight has hatched a ploy to get the Lancia moving again.

'Strip the front axle and rig a sledge in its place. A couple of logs lashed together will do, like the tail skid of an aeroplane. Then run in reverse. It won't be pretty,' he says, 'but it'll carry the wounded and water.'

No one congratulates Grainger. His comrades

just touch his shoulder or clap him lightly on the back as they get to work.

We rig a platform that Marks and Oliphant can be carried on. Collie wedges himself into the passenger seat. Punch drives. The advantage of having only the Lancia is that we're less likely to be spotted from the air. We keep two men up front on lookout for 288 and one in the rear scouring the sky. We walk for an hour, rest for fifteen minutes. After three hours, we stop for a bite and the last cig. Bir Hemet, if we reach it, will be the morning after next.

By mid-afternoon we have crossed the balats and entered a stony belt scored by limestone ridges in spectacular shapes. At one point our tyres crunch over a sward of shells, relics of some ancient sea floor.

We're seeing Arabs now – small groups at first, then longer trains on foot and camel. They're miles off and come no closer. The pan has become dead level between distant ranges of hills. Surely the tribesmen have seen us. But they make no move to approach. When we strike in their direction, they withdraw. Are they only being cautious, or do they harbour evil designs? The Germans will surely have posted rewards for our capture or threats of reprisal for furnishing us aid.

All day our party struggles towards the range of hills in the distance. This will be the Gilf Atar, the highland we must get round to strike the track to Bir Hemet. When we find solid going, we send the Lancia ahead, as fast as it can go. This is only three or four miles per hour but it cheers us. The hills crawl closer. By dark, the Lancia has reached them.

When the rest of us in the walking party straggle in, Marks, Oliphant, Collie and Punch are resting snugly in a cave above the ruins of a Roman cistern with good water in abundance. I call the lads round. Bir Hemet may be as close as forty miles. Shall we leave the wounded here with the weapons and the less strong men, while two or three of the ablest strike for the RV tonight on the Lancia?

We're debating this when three tribesmen appear on the plain below, on foot, leading a train of four camels. They return our hails; apparently they are heading for this same cave. Up they come. When Punch asks if they have goat's milk or eggs to sell, the tallest, a striking fellow, asks, 'Inglesi?'

'English, mate!' cries Punch. He begins blathering the names of every officer and patrol leader who might have crossed this patch of desolation: Wilder, Easonsmith, Mayne, Tinker, Vladimir Peniakoff. Popski.

At this, all three tribesmen light up. They know Popski. They love Popski. It has been their honour, they report, to have broken bread with Popski two nights past.

BOOK VI

WILDER'S GAP

CHAPTER 28

Twenty days later I am standing at attention in borrowed khaki drill trousers and tunic before a staff colonel and two majors at Advanced Headquarters Eighth Army, now at Marble Arch on the Gulf of Sirte, having been flown in via Zella from Jalo oasis. Tinker, Popski and Nick Wilder have been brought in from other quadrants. Tinker and I are interviewed together before even being permitted to file our reports to LRDG, then ordered immediately into hospital.

My bowels have been running liquid for the past two weeks. Amid far greater exigencies, I have simply endured the inconvenience, reckoning that my system will restore itself as soon as it acquires a few fresh vegetables. Now a friendly South African doctor gives me the diagnosis: pneumonia.

'You're a sick fellow, Chapman.' He shows me my chart.

Bacterial pneumonia (acute); bruised ribs and sternum; numerous ulcerated desert sores; possible malaria; possible worms.

I am stacked in a tent ward and pumped full of chalk and penicillin. My temperature, which the orderly won't tell me but which I read later on my chart, is 104. I have lost all my kit at Jalo, including the rucksack with my diary and Stein's manuscript. Where am I? What has happened?

After Popski's Arabs find us at the cistern cave, they lead us to a rendezvous with Tinker's T2 patrol at Bat el Agar, a complex of caverns west of the line of balats. Popski is there. Nick Wilder, he tells us, has got clear of our friends from Combat Group 288. His trucks are on their way to Landing Ground 125, an emergency evacuation strip in the desert south of Msus. Another LRDG patrol under Lieutenant Bernard Bruce appears that evening. Bruce is a wonderfully bawdy chap, who stands somewhere in line to become Lord Elgin and must, by the dictates of title protocol, file his reports not as 'Lieutenant' but as 'Lieutenant the Honourable'. He takes Marks aboard a truck evacuating his own wounded to Jalo oasis, now in British hands, from which an air ambulance will fly the men to hospital in Benghazi, also under a newly hoisted Union Jack. The rest of us will have to sit tight; Bruce can spare no other transport. 'Besides, thanks to your efforts,' he declares, 'the desert is lousy with Jerry patrols.' We can file reports, though. I put Collie, Punch and Grainger in for mentions in despatches.

For ten days our group lies up in caves out of the rain, waiting for transport to get clear. I have never been sicker. The Arabs succour us – generously, considering their own poor state – on eggs, dates and sour goat's milk with wild thyme, none of which I can keep down. Every ounce of fluid flushes from my body, leaving me limp as a stalk and burning with fever.

Collie nurses me through frightful dreams. I see Stein, dead on his sand-channel, and my mother in her barge. I see the Italians we massacred. This apparition is so real, complete with the stink of cordite and the banging of the guns, that my comrade has to shake me for seconds even after I'm awake. I'm seeing Standage and Miller too, our own dead. I keep apologising to them. They brush me off. 'It's nothing, Chap,' they say.

Each night we move camp. Popski's Arabs guide us. My guts are in a twist the whole time. We can travel only in darkness, which is freezing, with wet gales that knife through every blanket and rag you bundle round yourself. We slog afoot or on trucks for what feels like hours, only to end up in another dank grotto stinking of goat droppings and camel dung. Every cell in my body aches. Never have I been more excruciatingly aware of this physical envelope that is the flesh. How I long to escape it! How can one be so cold and so hot at the same time?

On the tenth night, three trucks of a patrol led

by a Lieutenant Birdwood (who himself is absent, recce-ing west) arrive and take us out. Collie, Punch and I are piled together on to the bed of their fitter's truck. The sergeant in command is named Chapman like me. There's a dressing station at Jalo, he tells us, under Captain Lawson. Chapman turns out to be a BBC buff; he has all the latest news. Eighth Army has taken Derna and Benghazi. Hurricanes of the RAF and the Royal South Africans are flying now out of Benina, the field where we shot up the Italians only, what . . . twenty days ago? Rommel's Panzers have evacuated Msus and Solluch and are pulling out of Antelat and Agedabia. All of Cyrenaica is in British hands. It's 10 December, Christmas is coming!

Rommel himself, Chapman says, has withdrawn all the way to his old defensive box at El Agheila, which, we will learn at Jalo, he vacates on the twelfth. Combat Group 288 serves as his rear-guard; our old friends are blowing bridges and mining wadis as Panzerarmee Afrika falls back on Tripoli.

The whole show is a blur to me. The front has shifted so far west so rapidly that the next likely action, I am told, will be not another Rommel counter-offensive but a head-on Allied assault, either against prepared Axis positions at Wadi Zem Zem east of Tripoli or farther west across the Tunisian frontier at the natural and man-made barrier of the Mareth Line. This is the old French skein of fortifications that Don Munro and the war correspondents told us about when we ran into them at Derna.

I'm too sick to visualise the campaign map. All I know as Sergeant Chapman transports us to Jalo is that I have to evacuate my bowels every quarter of an hour; the truck halts once every two. I have a quart dixie for a bedpan and part of a wet Arab newspaper. Downpours continue to drench us; Collie, Punch and I have no cover but what loose tarpaulins we can wrestle over our shoulders in the wind. Punch is sicker than I am. Every time he relieves himself, I follow suit; when I do, he does. How we hate this desert! What wouldn't we give for a dry room and a warm squat!

The brick through all this is Collie. Despite his own ills, he stands over us. We call him Sherlock for the stolid imperturbability with which he lights his Hound of the Baskervilles pipe upside down in the wind.

What do I know of Collie? Home again in New Zealand, if fortune bears him safely there, you could not pick him out from twenty others in a pew at the Anglican church or tinkering with his Norton on a weekend rideabout. But he is a hero. A bulwark of the empire. By rank this patrol may be mine, but he is its backbone and beating heart. He respects me. To him I am 'Sir', 'Skip', 'Lieutenant'. He won't call me 'Chap', though I have asked him to more than once and would take no offence if he did. If we meet for a pint when this mess is over, he'll still call me Skip and take his leave with the same awkward, half-embarrassed gait.

In real life I would never meet such a man either socially or professionally. Yet here we are closer than brothers. I consider it one of the signal honours of my life to serve beside him. No man could ask for finer.

At Jalo, our group is separated. Collie, Punch, Grainger, Oliphant and Jenkins will stay here with Doc Lawson; I am put on a Valentia and flown to Zella, then on a Bombay bomber to Marble Arch, Eighth Army HQ, where excitement and novelty carry me through a two-hour debriefing, of which I remember nothing and after which I faint on a bench outside the tent and must be hurried to hospital on a stretcher.

I lie for a day and night in a ward comprising four conjoined tents, part of a greater tent hospital that sprawls across acres of desert alongside the Via Balbia. The ward is theoretically for British and Commonwealth officers only, but so great is the number of casualties flooding in, Axis as well as Allied, that the MOs have stopped screening. Litters bearing the maimed and dying of both sides are set down under tent flies out of the rain or simply parked, stacked three and four high, in the ambulances and lorries that bring them. Under canvas, space is so tight that cots are butted together in islands of four with walkways round the peripheries. In the first twenty-four hours three Afrika Korps officers occupy in succession the bed adjoining mine. The first two are lieutenants named Schmidt – I note this from the white three-by-five cards (Allied cards are blue) that the orderlies pin to their blankets. Or maybe the admitting clerks call them Schmidt the way we'd say Tommy Atkins, and gift them with the honorific of *Leutnant* so they'll require less paperwork when they move on. At any rate, neither Schmidt can speak; both are too far gone.

The third officer is named Ehrlich, which means 'honourable'. He and I converse in German and English; he is a schoolteacher and ski instructor from Garmisch-Partenkirchen in the Bavarian Alps. He explains the difference between an *Oberleutnant*, equivalent to a British captain, and an *Oberstleutnant*, a lieutenant-colonel. I forget which one he is. He's a battery commander, like Stein. His pelvis has been shattered by .303 machine-gun rounds from a strafing Hurricane. 'My guts are soup,' he says. He gives me his wallet and paybook, which he asks me, in a whisper, to deliver to his wife when the war is over. With our meals come four-cig packs of Capstans and four-pellet boxes of chewing gum called Beechies. Ehrlich gives me his from breakfast. 'I shall be dead before luncheon.'

While he naps, an orderly comes in and says an officer of the Cameron Highlanders has been looking for me. A minute later the tent flap opens and Jock walks in. He asks what I've got. I tell him pneumonia.

He grins. 'Good enough.'

CHAPTER 29

I am a father. Rose has given birth. A daughter. Jock doesn't know the child's name. He tries to get me on a truck, but I won't leave Ehrlich.

'You've got a ticket out,' he says. 'I can get you back to Cairo, even Haifa. You're not going to play the hero, are you?'

Jock looks hale and trim. He's on division staff, he says. He draws up a petrol-tin stool and takes a seat. He has no more news of Rose, except that she's well and so is the baby. Word has come by victorygram, fifteen words maximum. We toast our new arrival.

'You look grand, Jock.'

He can stay only a minute, he says; he's hunting up a wounded officer of the Camerons. Seeking this man's name, he stumbled on to mine. Jock tells me he can pull strings, get me out of here, maybe even by hospital ship. 'Pneumonia's good for two weeks at Lady Lampson's rest house on the Nile and a month or more for recupe. For Rose to see you will mean the world.'

I ask Jock what's coming up for Eighth Army.

He confirms it will be the Mareth Line. We're

now in mid-December; by February Rommel will have consolidated his position round Gabès and Sfax in Tunisia. The Mareth Line protects these. If I'm healthy, Jock tells me, I'll be back with my old tank regiment and have become a cog in the assault, which looks like being a bloodbath. Jock says he'll find a way to get me out, to a staff job if he can; if not, then to some post out of harm's way.

My brother-in-law means well. I love him as a friend. Heaven knows he has earned the Military Cross on his lapel, fighting his way out of Tobruk behind fixed bayonets. But the more he speaks of getting me out, the more clearly I know I must go back.

Ehrlich listens. He understands. Later, when Jock has gone, he and I talk.

If I take this ticket out, the one Jock can arrange for me, I'll never see my comrades of the LRDG again. My regiment will catch me up. Am I daft to resist this? I tell Ehrlich of the Italians at Benina. He says nothing, which makes me believe he has experienced the same. 'They will pin a medal on you for this,' he says. I tell him of Standage and Miller. He understands that too.

An orderly appears to clean Ehrlich's wound and change his dressing. There are plenty of bandages, apparently, but no morphia – for him or for anybody. He lies very still for a long time, so long that I start to fear he has stopped breathing.

'Chapman . . .'

'Yes.' I roll towards him at once.

'Will you permit me an observation about your countrymen?'

I wish very much to hear this, because I suspect he will address my dilemma. But, I tell him, I can't stand to see him in pain from the exertion of speech. He smiles and rolls on to one elbow so that our eyes meet.

'You English are loath to embrace the virtues of the warrior. Such an act embarrasses you. You prefer to see yourselves as civilians summoned reluctantly to arms, as – what is the word? – "amateurs".' He chuckles at this term, which sends a stab of agony through his guts. Long moments pass before his breath returns.

'But you *are* warriors, you English. *You* are, Chapman. Trust me, who has faced you in the field.'

I tell him I don't understand.

'Do not be afraid,' Ehrlich says, 'to take that decision which a warrior would take – and for a warrior's reasons.' Something glints behind the smile in his eyes. 'Believe me, my friend, it will not turn you into a "lousy Kraut".'

He falls asleep. I do too. When I wake after dark, another wounded officer lies in Ehrlich's bed. Overnight two more, a Rhodesian and an Australian, take the cot and die in it. I have to get out of here. I decide simply to walk away. Find LRDG headquarters and report for duty. Let the army put me on a charge, I don't care. My only fear is that the system, when it can't find me, will notify Rose that I am missing or dead. How to prevent this? I hunt up the South African major who originally checked me in. I find him outside with two other physicians, between surgeries, grabbing a smoke. He understands my fix before I get out two sentences. 'Get on,' he says. 'I need the bed.'

He tells me where to pick up a victorygram sheet; the fifteen words will be delivered to anyone I want. The hospital, he says, is forty-eight hours behind on paperwork; that will be my head start. 'Travel from dressing station to dressing station. That way, if you fail, you won't just die by the side of the road.' I dash off the following to Rose:

In hospital saw Jock safe and sound cracking care love to you and baby.

The South African major is coming in as I head out. He stuffs a packet of pills into my fist. 'You're the one I saw before who had pneumonia, right?' He probes my belly and the ribs round my liver. 'You've got jaundice too.'

In a pile at the precinct entry are hundreds of boots, belts, headgear and coats – property apparently of men who no longer need them. I grab a pair of boots and a new tropel greatcoat. Two hours later I'm on a 3-tonner lurching towards the front.

CHAPTER 30

Before I take off, I go looking for Nick Wilder. He's gone. I can't find Tinker or Popski. Someone tells me the LRDG's forward base has been moved up to Zella oasis, where I flew in from, a hundred and fifty miles south-west of El Agheila. I bum a ride to Wadi Matratin on a five-ton Bedford loaded with tinned cherries and Christmas hams.

Every vehicle is moving west. Mussolini's Via Balbia is nose to tail with trucks and guns. At Matratin I run into a man I rowed with at Oxford named Jeffers, now a captain in the RASC; he gets me out of the rain into the cab of a 3-tonner. I gulp chalk solution like a pup on a teat. It does nothing. My bowels empty every twenty minutes. Half the troops in the trucks are in the same state. An orderly lectures us: 'Keep drinking. It's the dehydration that kills you.' He gives us salt tablets, so our systems don't short-circuit for want of elec- trolytes. We take a spade for a walk at every stop. One sees the same faces, so to speak, again and again.

As chaotic as the retreat to Cairo had been last

year, this advance is worse. Thousands of men have been separated from their units; entire columns of vehicles lumber aimlessly forward with no idea of their destination. All that the drivers know for certain is that there is only one road; the traffic is all going in the same direction; and no military policeman will put you on a charge for heading *towards* the front.

By midnight I'm beginning to wonder if I haven't made a serious blunder quitting the hospital. Two o'clock comes; I'm clinging to the bank seat in the cab of a canvas-sided lorry, freezing rain sheeting in through the zip-up window. I curl on to myself like a sick cat. Behind in the tarp-covered truckbed ride two squads of South African infantry, each man seated miserably on the inward-facing benches with his rifle upright between his knees and his tin-hatted head lolling on to his forearms, hanging on to the barrel of his Lee Enfield like a drunk on to a lamp post.

A matching image enters my mind and refuses to leave – a dark image, of the Italian soldiers we gunned down at Benina. I keep seeing them. I have never felt less like a military man. The insignia on my shoulder, the uniform I wear – beneath them I am still me. I cannot excuse my actions of that night by citing such notions as 'war' or 'enemy'. And yet this *is* war.

I realise that I am having a moral crisis. At the same time I'm so fevered that the experience seems to be happening to someone else. I strain to make my mind blank, but the insides of my eye-lids keep lighting up like cinema screens, playing the same newsreel over and over. My crisis is happening inverted. The army is trying to send me to the rear, where I can be with my wife and baby, that union which I desire more than anything in the world, yet here I am hastening, against all common sense and the expectations of my peers, towards the front. Why? Because I feel guilty for killing the enemy, which is exactly what I am supposed to do and what I agree I'm supposed to do. When I get to the front, how do I hope to redeem myself? By killing more enemy, or taking such actions as will lead directly or in-directly to the deaths of as many of the enemy as possible, as if by this further crime I will absolve all previous crimes, which are not crimes at all but actions for which my country will honour me and in which I in later years no doubt will take secret and perhaps not so secret satisfaction. Am I mad? Can I continue to serve?

On the one hand, I cannot and will not let myself believe that what I have ordered and performed at Benina is 'right'. It isn't and never can be. I can't simply block it out and carry on as if nothing has happened. At the same time I *must* carry on – for my mates, for England, for Rose and for our child. The alternative is unthinkable.

With this, I understand the perverse logic of war and the true tragedy of armed conflict. The enemy against whom we fight are human beings like ourselves, individuals with whom each of us might have been friends except for the deranged fictions of nation, doctrine, race and religion, and whom now we must murder (as they seek to murder us) in the name of those very same fictions. And yet, knowing all this and understanding it, still, in some depraved and ineluctable way, we and they must live it out to the bloody finish.

I have stopped keeping my diary. All I can do is mark each day with a tick. On the third tick – a bright, windy noon – I stagger into an ADS, an advanced dressing station, and simply sit down among the wounded. There are no tents, no beds, no shelter. Germans, English and Empire troops sprawl side by side across an open flat half the size of a football pitch. Someone gives me an injection. I have no clue what's in it but I feel better. I wake in the lee of a canvas windbreak where two bandaged Indian troopers are cooking chapatties on a flat stove made from a petrol tin. An orderly is noting my name from my AB64 pay book. The winter sun slants down. As far as sight can carry, the desert is littered with wrecked tanks, trucks and guns.

'What happened here?'

'The Jerries put up a scrap at every wadi.'

The road runs west along the coast. I can see a blown bridge; tapes mark a lane through a mine-field. A column of lorries low-gears up a freshly bulldozed sand ramp, where the bridge used to be, and back on to the highway. Thirty yards from me, on the desert side, lies a German Pak38 anti-tank gun with '288' stencilled on the gun shield. The weapon sprawls on its side amid acres of other junk, with its breech blasted and six white rings painted round its muzzle. Each ring represents an Allied tank or truck knocked out.

'Where are we?'

'Nofilia.'

'Is that all?' It has taken me three days to go forty miles.

The orderly looks into my eyes. He gives me another injection.

When I wake again, Sergeant Kehoe kneels beside me. Nick Wilder's chief NCO. 'You're supposed to be dead,' he says.

I'm so glad to see him. 'Where is everybody?'

CHAPTER 31

Zella is LRDG's new forward base. It's a ragged oasis two hundred miles into the desert. I ride in on Sergeant Kehoe's jeep. Kehoe has been sent to Nofilia not for me, but to pick up Jake Easonsmith, who was supposed to fly in from Cairo on a mission to the Americans, who have now landed in Algeria under Eisenhower and Patton, but instead flew directly to Marada and caught a truck the rest of the way.

The camp at Zella is three marquee tents and an under-construction Nissen hut serving as a motor repair shed, the lot ringed by slit trenches and sheltered by a berm topped with stunted date palms. There's water from a good well and even a ten-by-ten-foot pool for bathing, called Little Cleopatra. Trucks in various stages of refitting poke their noses under camouflage netting that pops and bucks in a hard, sandy gale. We pull in just at suppertime. Two sixty-foot wireless masts tower over the camp but there's no radio shack, just a pair of wireless trucks parked side by side behind a canvas windbreak, with desks on the sand and map boards taped to the trucks' flanks, under more camouflage nets, with a Cummins generator thumping away like a torpedo boat. I note Colonel Prendergast's single-engine WACO biplane with its wings tied down against the wind. 'Come on,' says Kehoe. 'Let's belly up to the trough.'

The mess is a single table under one wing of a marquee, beneath a fly sheet snapping in the gale. Grub is sandwiches in wax paper held down by stones. Each is, as the saying goes, 'more sand than wich'. I don't care. I have come back to life. Jake is here, with his shoulder wrapped, directing the show.

'Chapman,' says he, 'do you know I have orders to place you under arrest?'

But he grips my hand with warm emotion, which I return. 'Are you all right, sir?'

'Never better.'

The last time I saw Jake he had a broken collarbone – at Bir el Ensor, Sore Thumb, in the aftermath of the Rommel raid.

I ask after Collie, Punch, Oliphant and Grainger. 'Have you got a job for me, sir?'

Jake sends me to the medical tent instead. I'm given a bunk in the third of three shelters, alongside Lieutenant Ken Lazarus, whom I've never met and who is away on a patrol. I sleep for three days. Throughout this interval, trucks keep coming and going; patrols are mounted and sent out while others limp in, returning. A corporal named Hartley looks after me. He is best mates with one of the wireless operators. All signals are designated

Most Secret, but in a unit so small everyone knows everything. Hartley tells me that my old outfit is keen to retrieve me, now that my assignment with LRDG is over. Tank officers are in urgent demand for Monty's next westward push. At the same time, Hartley reports, XXX Corps has sent Jake a despatch announcing the arrival at Zella of two RAC lieutenants, to accompany patrols with an eye to evaluating the going between here and Tripoli. In other words, my original job! When I'm fit enough to get out of bed, I put this to Jake straight out.

'Jake, how can XXX Corps demand my return, when they're sending you two other tank officers on the identical assignment I'm here for already?'

'How do you know what XXX Corps wants?'

I clam up.

'Hell's bells, is there one bloody thing that stays secret round here?'

The next day Collie, Punch and Oliphant arrive from Jalo; we have a grand reunion. When they hear I'm being sent back to the Armoured Division, they demand to speak to Jake. I forbid this.

Then on Christmas Day, my seventh at Zella, an updated operations sheet is posted on the board in the company office. Below 'Wilder T1' and 'Tinker T2', I see:

Chapman T3

I make straight for Jake to thank him, but he's already gone, off to Algeria, having flown out at dawn. Bill Kennedy Shaw, now in command, shows me the signal Jake has sent to XXX Corps regarding my status.

Operation still in progress. Will restore officer immediately upon completion.

Now LRDG's Advance HQ moves forward from Zella to Hon. Another group of oases. We go with it. Patrols are being sent out from both sites. The first wave are to reconnoitre the going west of Sirte, Wadi Zem Zem and Misurata, scouting a left hook round Tripoli. The second will probe farther west – into Tunisia, seeking a way round Gabès and the Mareth Line.

The following, copied from the operations sheet, comes from my notes dated 26 December, '42. I can't remember why I took it all down, unless perhaps I sensed something historic in the offing. It names the patrol commanders and their patrols.

Wilder	T1
Tinker	T2
Chapman	T3
McLauchlan	R1
Talbot	R2
Lazarus	S1
Henry	S2
Spicer	Y1

Hunter	Y2
Bruce	G
Birdwood	Indian 2
Rand	Indian 3
Nangle	Indian 4

I am given three trucks and six new men, all elite infantry of the 6th Battalion Grenadier Guards, fresh from a training course at Faiyoum under our old schoolmasters Willets and Enders. The remainder will be our old crew: Collie, Punch, Grainger and Jenkins but not Oliphant, who has come down with an eye infection and been evacuated to Cairo.

Hon, to which we move on Boxing Day, is the plushest HQ yet – a colony of miniature oases that have been headquarters for the Auto-Saharan Company, the Italian counterpart of the LRDG. Hon has a barracks, a hospital and airfield, even a tennis court. Where is everyone?

Popski, I hear, has just arrived at Zella, preparing to join S1 patrol under Lieutenant Lazarus, my bunkmate, to reconnoitre the Jebel Nefusa south of Tripoli. Lieutenant Hunter with Y2 is there too, readying to depart immediately after New Year to recce the same left hook. Nick Wilder will set off from Zella as well, but bound for Tunisia. His T1 patrol will be the first to scout the Mareth Line. Tinker with T2 is still conducting a road watch east of Tripoli.

Eighth Army have sat down for Christmas just

west of Nofilia. Monty is short of petrol; his engineers are repairing the port of Benghazi and building all-weather airfields as fast as they can. Rommel, we are told, with 21st Panzer Division and 90th Light Division is preparing defensive positions at Beurat and Wadi Zem Zem. 15th Panzer Division remains forward.

Dearest Rose,

This may be the last letter I can post for a while, though of course I shall write every day and keep the lot till the next drop. I forgot to tell you, I still have Stein's manuscript! I left it behind at Jalo and believed it gone for ever. At Christmas, however, it found its way back to me, courtesy of Sergeant Collier, who discovered it with other items of my kit.

The men see 1943 in with an all-night boozer. After my bout with jaundice, I can't touch the stuff because of my liver. I don't mind. The weather has broken, as has my fever. I'm well except for desert sores on my legs and arms and a still-queasy stomach. I'm grateful these are the only things wrong with me. Days are windy now, nights ungodly cold.

As patrols are launched and others scurry about in preparation, everyone gets into everyone else's business. Officers grill officers for the latest griff; other ranks interrogate their own. We all want to know what's out there and how bad it's likely to be.

The first clue comes from Tinker, whose patrol limps in from Geddahiah a few days after Christmas. T2 has been shot up by planes and armoured cars, losing six men missing and two trucks. On nearly the same day in almost the same spot, Captain Tony Browne's patrol runs on to Teller mines and loses one officer killed and Browne himself gravely injured. He is replaced by Lieutenant Paddy McLauchlan who, a few days later, is ambushed near Wadi Tamet by German armoured cars; McLauchlan loses one truck and four men captured. A few days later, Hunter's Y2 will be plastered by Me-110s and armoured cars and have to turn back before it reaches its area of operation. 'Things are getting dicey out there,' says Kennedy Shaw, who relays the observation from Tinker's report that Tinker noted the numeral 288 on both 8-wheelers chasing him.

I've never seen an officers' mess more competitive than that of the Long Range Desert Group. On the one hand, patrol commanders readily hazard their lives to aid their brother officers, but at the same time they can't stand to think of a comrade getting one up on them. Each officer believes his patrol the best and himself the only man for the job.

My old bunkmate Tinker is the fiercest competitor of all. Nick Wilder's early start for the Mareth Line has put him into a blue-balled sweat.

Tinker is barely back in the barn before he begins lobbying to be sent out again. He gets his wish on 16 January when he and T2 depart Hon, escorting two 3-tonners carrying fuel and a mob of Popski's Arabs and demolition men (but not Popski himself, who is already at large somewhere round Wadi Zem Zem), with orders to deliver these bandits to their master, who will rendezvous with Tinker at a location of which Tinker will be advised by signal. Then Tinker and Popski will make for the Mareth Line together.

As for my own group, we're ready to roll by 3 January, with the addition of a new Willys jeep and Trooper Holden, Collie's original driver. But orders keep changing for another fortnight. I'm grateful for the delay; it's precious hours to regain weight and strength.

The Mareth Line mission has become everything to me. I spend hours each day poring over the nearly worthless French and Italian maps that are the only ones we have for Tunisia and conferring with the other patrol commanders and NCOs who are putting together their packages at the same time as I am. Kennedy Shaw and his two keen corporals are feverishly draughting their own maps, based on daily signals from those few patrols – mainly Nick Wilder's and David Stirling's of the SAS – that are out there recce-ing the area right now.

In a nutshell, our next wave of patrols will be operating three to four hundred miles behind the present front east of Tripoli. We'll proceed west across all Tripolitania, crossing into Tunisia south of the Jebel Nefusa, the great crescent-shaped ring of highlands whose northernmost range, narrowing in towards the sea south of Gabès, is called the Ksours de Mons, the Matmata Hills.

Our job is to find a way through those hills.

East of them lies the coastal plain, bottle-stoppered south of Gabès by the Mareth Line. West of the hills spreads a second plain, deserted and un-defended according to our French maps, that could lead round the entire defensive front.

This second plain is the one Monty wants to know about.

He wants to know if a thousand tanks and guns can get there. Are there routes through the hills? Has Rommel fortified the passes? How good is the going on the other side? Are the Germans there and, if so, in what strength?

Kennedy Shaw has sliced this pie into sections, each one half the size of Ireland. Our patrols will take a section apiece and explore it. Each will prepare a 'going map' of its assigned territory.

'This is it,' says Kennedy Shaw. 'This is the Big Show.'

CHAPTER 32

My patrol departs Hon on 16 January 1943.

The going is fast and firm on the short hop to the well at Socna (where our three trucks and one jeep, accompanied by one 3-tonner carrying fuel, top up with water as instructed) and excellent along the Italian-built track to the escarpment at Sciueref, which site we skirt when informed by signal from HQ that German motorised activity has been reported in the vicinity. Thence via the Mizda road – a good one, with a fast, firm crushed-rock surface – to Oswald's Dump, a petrol cache established by earlier patrols. We have exact map coordinates but, when we get there, we can't find the damn thing. I'm furious, recalling the diesel debacle at the Sand Sea, but Asquith, our new navigator, suspects a transposed numeral on the operation instructions and he's right. The dump appears, three miles from where it's supposed to be. We fill up mid-afternoon, leaving our empties, and press on till the last hour of winter light. We have been ordered to a rendezvous at latitude 29 degrees 30 minutes off the Mizda-Brach road. I'm anxious about Asquith but he reels us in on the dot.

The site is a complex of wadis beneath a rugged north-south escarpment. Tinker's T2 is already there. By morning, three other patrols have arrived – R2 under Sergeant Waetford (whose two officers, Lieutenants Talbot and Kinsman, have been captured by the enemy at Sciueref four days earlier), Y1 under Lieutenant Spicer and Y2 under Captain Hunter. The place looks like a Chevrolet truck convention. Popski is on his way, a signal says, ferried by Lazarus's S1, which has just got jumped by an Axis patrol at the north end of Wadi Zem Zem about fifty miles away and has had to turn back, reporting two captured, three missing, five trucks lost. Next morning, 20 January, Colonel Prendergast flies in in his WACO to issue instructions to the whole parliament.

Prendergast is commanding officer of the LRDG. Eighth Army, he informs us, is attacking Beurat this very morning, expecting to be in Tripoli in days. Monty is desperate for intelligence on the Mareth Line.

Then Prendergast drops his bombshell: Nick Wilder, he says, has found a pass through the Matmata Hills.

I'm standing next to Tinker when Tinker hears this. I have never seen the colour drain more swiftly from a man's cheek. All round, patrol commanders proffer a chorus of 'Hear, hear!' and 'Bloody brilliant!' Tinker is heartbroken. When

344

Prendergast recites map coordinates for Nick's discovery and instructs the group to inscribe the position on their maps as 'Wilder's Gap', Tinker's morale hits a new low.

Popski is laughing.

'Cheer up, you bastard. We're all on the same side!'

Tinker is inconsolable. What galls him most, I can tell, is that the name Wilder's Gap will be on maps of North Africa for ever. I observe aloud that it's not very sporting to begrudge a teammate his success, particularly a triumph earned fair and square.

'Screw sporting,' says Tinker.

Popski grins. 'War is hell.'

He asks Tinker how old he is.

'Twenty-nine.'

'And you, Chapman?'

'Twenty-two.'

Popski rubs his fifty-year-old dome and laughs even harder.

Tinker's spirits revive with the next word from Prendergast. It seems that Nick Wilder's patrol has penetrated the Matmata Hills only a short distance before mechanical problems have made it turn back.

'Nick has made a start, nothing more,' declares our commanding officer. 'No one knows what kind of country lies on the far side of those hills, or if it's go or no-go for tanks and guns. No one knows where Rommel is or what fortifications and troops he's thrown into that position.'

In other words, there's still plenty of glory to be won.

Wilder's Gap is some seventy to a hundred miles south of the final passage that will take Monty round Rommel and the Mareth Line. 'Even when the route through the Matmata Hills has been thoroughly explored and mapped, there remains a hell of a long march on the far side, unscouted and unknown. The reconnaissance of that passage is a critical undertaking, upon which depend the lives of thousands of men and the outcome of the entire North African campaign. Here are your orders. Carry them out.'

Prendergast is good. I have only seen him in person once before, but I'm impressed now by his unprepossessing but powerfully focused style. He pilots the WACO himself, alone. Within five minutes he has turned the aircraft up into the wind and taken off back to Hon.

Orders are distributed. Lazarus's, Spicer's and Waetford's patrols will return to base to refit and prepare to move out again as soon as possible. Tinker's patrol, with Popski, and mine will proceed at once to Wilder's Gap and through it, to recce the going on the far side, to Gabès and round the Mareth Line.

Before we start, Tinker, Popski and I take the afternoon establishing a dump of the fuel we've escorted from Hon. We bury three hundred and seventy-five jerry cans and camouflage the site. Tinker hates the fact that another patrol is getting the start alongside his, even though my sector is different from his so there's no direct competition.

As for me, Collie, Punch and Grainger, we at last have the orders we've been waiting for.

Task: To obtain fullest topographical information in the area bounded as follows:

N. COAST – MATMATA-
   KEBILE ROAD
E. TRIPOLI PLAIN
W. CHOTT DJERID
S. LAT. 32°30'

The information is required from the point of view of the advance of a force of all arms on a wide front. It should include the following:

(a) GOING
(b) WADI CROSSINGS
(c) COVER
(d) WATER SUPPLIES –
    WELLS
(e) LANDING GROUNDS

Tinker's orders are identical, but send him to an area farther west and north. Both patrols set out next morning, travelling together. No place is where it's supposed to be on our French and

347

Italian maps but nobody cares, so inspiriting is the flush of taking up a crucial job with comrades we love and trust.

The Hammada el Hamra, across which both patrols now speed with joy, is firm red desert without a scrap of vegetation. Punch floors the accelerator, making as many miles as he can. I feel reborn watching him at the wheel of a new thirty-hundred-weight Chev, christened Te Aroha V, and Collie in his own refitted truck, with Grainger on the wireless and Jenkins on the Vickers as well as serving as medical orderly. Asquith, the navigator replacing Oliphant, seems a sound fellow, as is the jeep driver Holden with whom I ride, and the new lads from the Grenadiers are crack chaps with their tails in the air. Weather is cold but clear. The desert, after a bout of storms, dazzles beneath a mother-of-pearl sky.

On 23 January we rendezvous with Nick Wilder in a wadi forty miles south of Foum Tatahouine. Nick and his patrol are limping home in triumph; they've been instructed by signal from Prendergast to RV with us and Tinker and Popski to impart all intelligence that might be of use.

Wilder's men look worn to the nub. But they're happy. They know what they've done and how important it is. Popski grins, watching Tinker shake Nick's hand in congratulation. 'You're on the map!' says Tinker, showing Nick his own board with hand-printed in chinagraph pencil at point YK.5991.

Nick is gracious but all business. He takes two hours helping us copy his sketch maps and alerting us to the perils that we'll run into on the far side of the Matmata Hills, particularly Axis scout planes.

'The Huns have got birds up everywhere. Rommel knows we're here and he knows what a threat we represent. And watch out for the natives. Jerry's put a price on our heads; every tribesman for a hundred miles will be hunting us like a stray camel.'

Tinker breaks out the brandy. We toast in tin cups. 'I won't lie to you. Nick,' Tinker says. 'I'd have given my left nut to be the one to find that pass through the hills. But if it had to be anyone other than me, I'm glad it's you.'

Half an hour later I'm standing beside Tinker, watching Wilder and T1 patrol pull out for their last leg back to Hon.

'By heaven,' says Tinker, 'there goes a soldier. After Jake, the best there is.'

CHAPTER 33

The gorgeous flat of the Hammada el Hamra, over which we've been happily motoring since Hon, runs out a few miles east of the Tunisian border, where the country rises into a rampart of dunes and sand hummocks. Tinker's navigator finds a break, through which our conjoined patrols slither, crossing the frontier, which is marked by stumpy white pillars, at mid-morning.

There's a good ballasted road, Foum Tatahouine to Nalut, running north-south, but the crossing is so exposed to ground and air that we decide to lie up in a wadi a quarter of a mile east and watch for a safe opening to dash over. Sure enough, just as Tinker's second in command Sergeant Garven is about to probe forward in a jeep, a German patrol of two eight-wheeled armoured cars rumbles into view from the north. The cars are trailed by a pair of Opel 3-tonners, both towing 20mm guns, and preceded by a Flitzer scout car. As we watch, the outfit stops, apparently spotting tracks crossing the road. The armoured cars are SdKfz 234s, as big as tanks but with cork-filled tyres instead of caterpillar tracks, and packing turret-mounted 75mm cannons – twice the size of the 2-pounders in British Crusaders and American Honeys – as well as 7.92 machine guns. Through glasses Collie and I can see an officer sending men to check both sides of the road. 'You don't see the number 288, do you?' asks Collie, making my blood run cold. The Germans search briefly, then mount up and move on. Tinker has us hold up till the midday haze, then dash across the road at points several miles apart.

While we're waiting, a signal arrives from HQ: Tripoli has fallen. 23 January, the 11th Hussars enter the city; Rommel has escaped west.

'What's that mean for us?' Holden asks Sergeant Garven.

'It means Tunis is next, lads.' He points north up the Foum Tatahouine road. 'All eyes are on us.'

By two we've found Wilder's Gap. Nick has warned that the route is no quick sprint through the hills. The passage zigs and zags for almost thirty miles, at first following the floor of several broad, firm wadis, then tracking a disused motor trail through rugged hill and hummock country. The route is a beauty, with frontage five miles broad in places. Winter grass is thick and green, the kind that, according to Punch, is chock full of nutrients. 'A man could carve out a fine sheep farm here,' he says, and indeed we come upon a number of local herdsmen, boys and old men mostly, grazing their stock. Twice Henschels fly over, but cover is good and the planes don't see us. We continue west all afternoon, deploying round bad spots, following Nick's sketches and our own instincts. The place, according to our French maps, is called the Dahar. About ten miles in, an escarpment appears, just where Nick said it would. We locate the track his trucks used to descend. He has marked it with a stone cairn. The patrols halt at the brink. Time to split up. Each will recce the scarp in a different direction, seeking an easier route down, then carry on independently to his assigned search area.

When patrols part in the desert, ceremony is minimal. This time it's different, because we'll be operating in dangerous proximity to each other. Tinker instructs both patrols to be sure they know their recognition signals; he reviews rally points, ciphers and wireless frequencies. Supplies are redistributed so that every truck has its share of fuel, oil, water and ammunition. Popski instructs all hands to be wary of the natives; these are not Senussi Arabs, as in Libya, who are friendly to England, but Berbers whose lands and homes have been despoiled by the French. 'To them, the Jerries are God's finest blokes.'

When it's my turn, I stress to the men the importance of delivering clear, readable topographical maps. 'The left hook we're scouting is not just a jog out and a jog in. If the maps are right, the track'll be a hundred miles long. Over that, traffic has to be able to move six, eight, ten columns across. And that's not light ton-and-a-half trucks

352

like ours, but thirty-ton Shermans on fifteen-ton transporters, twenty-ton fuel and water wagons and heavy guns. An entire armoured division will be using the route we scout. That means vehicle columns ten or fifteen miles long, beating the hell out of whatever track we lay out for them. Make sure it's firm, make sure it's broad.'

Sergeant Garven asks if the divisions will have road-building equipment.

'Probably,' I say, 'but don't count on it. Pick routes that can be negotiated "as is" – and make sure they'll hold up even in a downpour.'

Enough daylight remains for the patrols to get out of each other's range. 'See you, Chap.' 'Luck, Tink.' That's it. I shake Popski's hand and we're gone.

24/1/43. Party separates from T2, proceeds N. through foothills, camping the night at WADI EL AREDJ at YE.1633. Going is rough but passable for all MT. Enemy observation post at hill EL OUTID, dominating wadi and approaches.

25/1/43. All day through torturous going, sandy hummocks, to Arab village of KSAR EL HALLOUF, which OC party recces on foot after dark. Vehicle park is discovered w/ca 20 German and Italian armoured cars and scout cars. Many natives about. Not friendly.

Tinker and Popski are recce-ing the plain to the west; our sector is the hills. Our immediate object is to find a pass north of Wilder's Gap. Nothing. My topo sketches record dead end after dead end.

'This country makes me nervous,' says Punch. He means the hills. 'You can't run away in 'em.'

Grainger agrees. 'We've drawn the rump straw.'

We have expected these uplands to be vacant. No such luck. Our aim of establishing a base camp where we can stash the stores and the wireless truck is frustrated by heavy enemy patrolling activity, including aircraft, and a surprising density of native population, which we take great pains to avoid. This is impossible, however, as every hill and valley is the province of Berber lads and old men tending their flocks. As we pass one toothless gent in a well-ventilated jerd, he clicks his heels and snaps off a Heil Hitler salute. We return the favour, halt and donate a couple of cigs. 'Your friends,' he communicates cheerfully by sign, 'are blowing up the valley.'

For a handful of loose tea, the old fellow agrees to guide us, leaving his grandson to mind the goats. We travel by tracks across a crown called Tel Gomel, the Camel's House, arriving at the village of Matmata in an area of grassy dales from beyond whose shoulder we hear a sequence of muffled blasts. 'Road building,' says Collie. 'That, or fortifications.'

This could be critical. Combined with the Axis outpost at El Outid, it means the enemy are aware of their vulnerability west of the Matmata Hills and are taking steps to shore the sector up. According to our intelligence, the village of Matmata is the inland anchor of the Mareth Line, though from where we are, we see no fortifications. This area is the very sector Monty will aim to outflank. If Rommel is indeed siting gun emplacements and pillboxes, it means the Line is being extended.

Our patrol starts forward during the noon haze, only to have the steering box on the wireless truck cash out. In the halt for repairs, I take the jeep with Jenkins and a Bren gun and work up through overgrown stream beds, then leave the vehicle and continue on foot to the rim of a low spur. Through glasses I make out two Afrika Korps bulldozers, apparently excavating a pit on the reverse flank of the crest overlooking the valley. The blasting continues out of sight on the far side. Jenkins and I can see only a fraction of the valley, which dog-legs round a corner before climbing towards the summit of the plateau. It's apparent, however, that Jerry has got his work boots on. We hurry back to the jeep and down the watercourse to the waiting trucks, which Collie has got under camouflage netting in the interim, to find Punch and Holden in the process of binding our guide's wrists behind his back and tying him to Punch's tailboard. Apparently the old man has worked out that we're not Germans.

'What's the form with this gaffer?' Punch asks.

As chance would have it, Punch has decided to take advantage of the lie-up to clean his revolver. When he produces the weapon, our captive begins to weep. 'No, mate,' says Punch, 'you've got it all wrong.' He seeks to soothe the fellow's fears by producing a cigarette and lighting it for him. Now the old gent is certain his hour has come. It takes Punch ten minutes to allay his terror; by the time he's done, our guest has become a rabid Anglophile. He informs us that a dozen other Inglesi (which turns out to be the SAS party under David Stirling) are camped a few miles south-west at Bir Soltane. Our countrymen have vacated the site for the moment, the old man says, and are off scouting the hills like us.

'Blast these buggers!' says Punch. 'Does anything happen here that they *don't* know?'

We hold the old fellow overnight, signalling HQ to report enemy fortifications under construction – and the locals' knowledge of the SAS camp. By return signal we are instructed to discontinue all mapping activity and concentrate instead on recce-ing the fortifications.

In the morning we make a big show of heading east, then drop our guide off; when he's out of sight we double back west.

Planes buzz overhead all day; it's impossible to move. We net up and lie low. 'It's the lad,' says Collie, meaning the old man's grandson. 'He made straight for the Jerries, bank on it, soon as Granddad didn't show for supper.'

27/1/43. Earth-moving equipt moving along road TOUJANE-MATMATA. Six b/dozers on transporters, plus graders and flatbeds carrying concrete caissons. Two trains of donkeys at VR.8991, ca 20 each, possibly carrying mines. MATMATA-KEBILE road is being reballasted and bitumened between VR.8993 and VR.8995.

That noon, Collie in the wireless truck runs into a party of SAS led by Mike Sadler, the navigator, returning to Bir Soltane from scouting the Jebel Tebaga, a range of hills to the north. Collie warns Sadler that locals know about his camp (which intelligence we have relayed yesterday to HQ, as I said, and Sadler in turn has acquired by signal from HQ last night). That's why he's going back, to pack up and clear out.

'We saw a Mammoth,' Sadler tells Collie, meaning an oversized caravan of the same model as Rommel's own armoured command vehicle. 'Big as life, at El M'dou on the Matmata road. No Rommel, though, more's the pity.'

That night a signal from HQ directs us to get out of the area as well. Tinker and Popski have reported heavy enemy patrolling. We are to move north to reconnoitre the Gabès-Kebile road. This is the key sector of the whole region, the obvious route by which any flanking move by Eighth Army will have to proceed in order to strike the coast behind the Mareth Line. The last thing Sadler leaves with us is the text of a signal received by David Stirling's party just this morning, from Eighth Army at Tripoli.

OKH [German High Command] sends following reinforcements from Europe by sea to Rommel: 10th Panzer Division, 334th Infantry Division, Herman Goering Panzer Division, Barenthin Regiment, Koch Storm Para Regiment, Panzer Detachment 501, plus Italian Superaga Division and German Manteuffel Division already in place. Total: 14 divs, 100,000 men, 76,000 of them Germans.

'Damn,' says Holden, hearing this, 'we've been bloody lucky so far.'

CHAPTER 34

Luck runs out two days later. A signal from HQ reports that Tinker and Popski's base camp at a hill called Qaret Ali has been attacked by Luftwaffe fighters and shot up badly. Every vehicle has been destroyed. Tinker and Popski are missing.

Report of this calamity comes from a third patrol, Lieutenant Henry's S2, fresh out from Hon, which has stumbled on the burnt-out site while recce-ing their own sector west of the Matmata Hills. Two other patrols, Lazarus's and Spicer's, are on their way now from Hon to scout other quadrants north of Wilder's Gap. They could be in this area within days, even hours.

Our orders are changed back to topographical reconnaissance. We're despatched north to that sector – the Tebaga Gap and the Gabès-Kebile road – which Tinker and Popski had been assigned to reconnoitre. Under no circumstances are we to venture near Tinker's camp or attempt to pick up his or Popski's men. Axis air and ground patrols will be saturating the area. HQ fears Tinker and Popski are goners; we and the other patrols are to take over their sector and finish the job they started.

I call a sit-down and walk the men over the map for the hundredth time. 'Have you noticed,' Collie observes wryly, 'how the tone of HQ's signals has changed?'

Indeed it has. We're getting no more 'exercise caution' or 'proceed with care'. Now it's 'a route will be found' and 'you will complete your report within twenty-four hours.'

Tinker and Popski are on their own.

So are we.

I spread the maps on the jeep's bonnet. Due north about thirty miles the plain, which runs north and south where we are now, turns east towards the coast. Along its southern flank lie the hills of the Jebel Melab, on its northern the Jebel Tebaga.

In the middle runs the Tebaga Gap.

That's the one we want.

The Tebaga Gap cuts through to the sea behind the Mareth Line.

'Counting our patrol and Henry's, Lazarus's and Spicer's,' I say, 'we've got about twenty vehicles recce-ing the same sector. Eighth Army only needs one of us to succeed and get the word back to Monty.'

I don't need to add that all others are expendable.

My idea is to descend at once to the plain. But when we scout the approach on the freezing morning of 29 January, we find fresh tracks of German patrols criss-crossing everywhere.

We're forced back into the foothills into the most infernal country yet – a sea of granulated-sugar hummocks, each no greater than two truck-lengths across. Even the jeep mires in these. We sand-channel all day, logging barely two miles. Striking a passable trail near sunset, we hold a quick council and decide to take our chances in the dark on the flat. The trucks descend into sand-hills, which every man would have called hellish if he weren't coming out of even worse. The hold-up now is dense brush, which catches beneath the vehicles' undercarriages and balls up into axle-binding masses that have to be cleared by hand every hundred yards. I probe ahead in the jeep with Punch and the Bren gun. Past one in the morning we strike a track that seems to lead down on to the plain. No time for grub or a brew; we descend, lights out, hoping to strike the Tebaga Gap by sunrise and find a place to nest.

Now the big-end bearing on the wireless truck packs up; we halt to replace it only to find that our only spare is missing. There's nothing for it but, as Punch says, to tow the bitch. We slog on till four, freezing and famished. Suddenly the track dead-ends. We're in a blind wash, butted into the wall of a wadi. I'm afraid if we stop for a kip we'll never get going again. So we make a virtue of necessity, call this site our rear base and leave the disabled wireless truck with three troopers of the Grenadiers and the Bren gun. I backtrack with the jeep and the other two trucks, Collie commanding one and Punch the other.

Dawn finds us camouflaged in the cut bank of a dry watercourse, overlooking a track that snakes down on to the plain. Jenkins prepares a petrol-tin fire for tea but waits to light it till daybreak permits. Suddenly from the flat below comes machine-gun fire. We can hear it, tinny and distant, and see a bright stream of tracers arcing away from us across the lightening sky.

Collie, Punch and I scamper on foot to the shoulder of a ridge that looks over the plain.

Another burst. Another rainbow of tracers.

'Toffee apples,' says Collie, meaning tracer fire deliberately let off to signal the location of the shooters.

'Somebody needs help,' says Punch. 'But who? Us or them?'

Collie points north. A mile out on the plain, two squarish lumps can be seen straddling the track from Gabès. I thumb the focus wheel of my binoculars. Into clarity comes an Afrika Korps half-track, on its side in a ditch, apparently having run off the trail in the dark. A eight-wheeled armoured car protects it.

Half a dozen squaddies hunker round a petrol-tin cooker. A tarpaulin has been rigged from the flank of the 8-wheeler to make a shelter camp. On the car's turret is a black Axis cross and the numeral 288.

We decide to wait the enemy out. Sure enough, within ten minutes engine sound can be heard from the north. An ambulance and a second armoured car appear. The second one is a 4-wheeler. The vehicles halt alongside the disabled half-track; two men and an officer dismount and hurry across. From under the tarp on the 8-wheeler's flank, two soldiers are helped to their feet. I hadn't noticed them before. Both are young and look badly shaken. Their mates help them to the medical vehicle. Meanwhile two scruffy-looking natives have dismounted from the second armoured car; we can see them jabbering to the Germans and pointing up into the hills in our general direction. The officer with the first armoured car comes over from the ambulance. He's tall and slender, nearly as youthful as the two injured troopers, with rimless spectacles and a sober; almost scholarly face. On his left breast pocket he wears an Iron Cross – a decoration for valour.

We watch, forgetting fatigue and hunger, as the two hurt soldiers are settled into the back of the ambulance, which then pulls away north, back towards Gabès and the Tebaga Gap. Now a third vehicle, a repair lorry, rumbles into view from that direction. The second armoured car stays with the first. The fitter's lorry comes up and sets about towing the half-track clear of the ditch. The natives continue palavering. The Iron Cross officer listens patiently. After several minutes he reaches into his trouser pocket, removes several small items and hands them to the two Berbers. Whatever the payoff is, it renders the tribesmen ecstatic. In twenty seconds both have buggered off into the hills. The lorry winches the half-track out of the ditch. Officers hold a brief conference; then the salvage vehicle starts back north, towing the half-track. The two armoured cars crank up, as if to resume their original patrol. By the count of a hundred they've vanished south, round crescent dunes at the base of the hills. By two hundred, our jeep and two trucks are down on the flat, rolling north in the wake of the towing lorry.

'What's the form?' calls Punch into the wind.

I point north. 'Follow them.'

CHAPTER 35

There are decisions you make that you know are wrong the minute you make them.

We roll fast for five miles down the good two-tyre track that the ambulance and the salvage lorry have taken before us. My thinking is this: if we can keep close enough behind these two vehicles without letting their crews spot us, enemy scout planes coming out of Gabès will think we're all elements of the same party. With luck, brazening it out like this will carry us deep into the Tebaga Gap without arousing suspicion.

Sure enough, at about six miles, a pair of Fieseler Storches buzz overhead, giving us the go-by.

The scheme seems to be working.

I'm straining at our dreadful French maps. The northernmost spur of the Matmata foothills, the Jebel Melab, juts into the plain a mile ahead on our right. I can see clearly its bare stony slopes. Beyond the shoulder of the Jebel lies the prize we've been seeking: the five-mile-broad boulevard of the Tebaga Gap.

If we can get in and get out, we'll be telling our grandchildren about this.

But just as the road starts to turn east, the scout planes come back. A Storch is a slow light aircraft, usually unarmed. Two of them pass directly overhead, so low we can see the tread on their tyres and the sunglasses on the pilots' noses. I'm in the jeep in the lead with Holden. Punch in his truck follows. I hear Collie whistle from the trailing truck. He gestures rearwards. When I look back, I see two columns of dust, a mile behind and closing fast.

'The armoured cars!' shouts Collie.

Have we been spotted? Could this be coincidence only?

I turn back to the front. To our immediate right rise the foothills of the Jebel Melab. Left, five miles out, ascends the Jebel Tebaga. In between runs the Tebaga Gap. In the centre of this I see more dust – three, four whirling dervishes – two miles ahead and racing directly at us. From one comes a puff of white smoke. Two seconds later a spout of rock and earth erupts violently thirty yards behind us.

Another shot; a shell explodes the same distance in front.

I point to the hills on the right. Collie and Punch need no more. Trucks and jeep swerve off the road and run for it.

We're in trouble. The hills are bare – no cover. The Storches bank right on top of us. Fighters and bombers will be overhead soon. Holden flattens the accelerator. The jeep pounds upslope over

366

a surface like rutted marble topped with two inches of talc. Collie hammers on our right. I can hear Punch behind on the third truck, loosing a burst at one of the Storches.

The only thing in my head is the mission. One of us has to get away and get back to the wireless truck.

In our favour: our Chevs and jeep are faster and nimbler than the armoured cars on our tail. We've got fuel for hundreds of miles, while all they've got is what's in their tanks. Against us is their armament. In a shoot-out we have no chance. The planes are another problem entirely. The Storches are unarmed, but they can stay overhead all day. Once the Macchis and Messerschmitts show up, our survival time shrinks to minutes if not seconds. But the gravest peril is these dead-end valleys. The hills are a muddle of cul-de-sacs and blind spurs. Our maps are worthless. Every turn could be our finish.

We flee all-out into the foothills. Down below, the armoured cars chase us, grinding in bottom gear. Stakes and fences bound the track we're running on. Signboards with death's head symbols warn

VORSICHT!
MINEN

We speed past a German encampment – engineers laying out a minefield. The troops think we're their countrymen. They wave. When a Storch drops on to our tail and Punch opens up on it with the Vickers, the mine-layers whoop and cheer, thinking it's a drill.

The planes wing away. This is our chance. I signal to Collie and Punch to step on it. For ten minutes we twist and turn at high speed over a labyrinth of goat trails and herders' tracks. The maze works in our favour. Each junction of valleys makes our pursuers guess which track we've taken. We pass two good roads, both demolished by Axis engineers; marked minefields climb slopes right and left. Every valley entrance holds a notice-board:

HALT!
VERMINTES GELÄNDE!

The enemy have dynamited all culverts and retaining walls. Roads have either been under-mined from below or blasted from above. Where valleys come together, the Germans have blown whole hillsides to try to stop further passage. We get round anyway. On a summit I halt and peer back through the glasses. A distance below, both armoured cars have stopped. Smoke pours from the 4-wheeler's undercarriage. A blown head or bearing, who knows? I can see one officer – older, with a dark moustache – urging the other on. The young lieutenant with the Iron Cross.

Here he comes, climbing after us.

The Storches have vanished, replaced by a pair of Me-110s. The fighters scream overhead. They haven't seen us. Punch shouts taunts as the planes bank beyond a crest and vanish. The Messerschmitts, we realise, are too fast to be effective search planes; after one pass it takes them a minute or more to come about and search again. By then we're gone.

We run. For the first time I'm beginning to think we have a chance. If we stay dispersed and use shadows and folds in the earth, we can make ourselves invisible.

We're running down a broad valley with tributary gorges off both sides. Again and again we have to stop to avoid losing one another. Collie's steering box is failing; Punch's clutch smokes so badly it looks as if it's on fire. But the halts help us. Sitting still, spread out, we're hard to spot from the air. We can hear the Messerschmitts scouring a different valley. They've lost us.

Where is the armoured car? At one point, peeping over a ridge, I get an eyeful of the Tebaga Gap below. It's perfect for Monty and Eighth Army. An armoured division could roll through, a hundred vehicles across. If we can get back to the wireless truck, our signal could save hundreds, even thousands, of lives.

But a dead-end valley steals every minute we've gained. No choice but to go back. Can we get clear? For an instant I allow myself to believe we've beaten the odds. But as we emerge at the mouth of the valley, 7.92 machine-gun fire tears into a limestone outcrop fifty feet in front of us. Holden brakes and throws the jeep into reverse. Collie and Punch's trucks plunge for cover to the shoulder. Into view three hundred yards below comes the eight-wheeled armoured car. It stops. Its cannon traverses. It fires.

A 75mm shell ploughs into the ten-foot chalk wall that Punch's truck has ducked behind. Every one of our guns is firing. The turret surface of the armoured car lights up with bullet hits and rebounding tracers. But the car is buttoned up tight. Its cannon fires again. Another chalk slope is blasted into powder.

We can't sit here. The armoured car will simply close and finish us. But if we flee back up the valley, its machine guns will tear us apart out in the open. There's only one chance and we all know it.

We charge. Three hundred yards feels like an eternity under fire. But we're screening ourselves in each other's dust, while the enemy gunners are handicapped by having to peer through narrow gun-slits at moving targets. Our vehicles reach the 8-wheeler and blast past.

We pick an uphill track and bet our lives on it.

The Germans turn after us. A dirt trail mounts the slope. Punch is already on it. Collie speeds behind. Holden guns the jeep in their wake. The armoured car lurches into the pursuit like a monstrous metallic lizard. It takes an angle to cut us off.

A Teller anti-tank mine is the size of a London

phone book; its case is steel and packed with high explosive. The blast of a Teller, or T-mine, can overturn a thirty-ton Sherman or blow a light Crusader tank in half.

Our jeep is a hundred feet upslope when the armoured car's front left tyre strikes one of these mines. In the patrol commander's seat I am flung shoulder-first into the mount of the Browning. Holden wrestles the steering wheel. The jeep heels over on to two wheels, then crashes to earth, facing backwards, and stalls.

No more than five seconds have elapsed since the detonation of the mine. The blast cloud billows already fifty feet into the air and spreads across a hundred more. Uphill, Punch is hooting with joy. Grainger and Jenkins point jubilantly down the slope.

The armoured car lies on its side with its topside wheels still spinning. The mine has ripped its underbelly open like a tin of peas. Flames lick from beneath the surface. I see one man stagger clear. Now comes a second blast, shorter and sharper than the first. It's a German S-mine, what the Americans call a Bouncing Betty. When an S-mine is detonated, a steel case containing three hundred and sixty ball bearings is flung into the air to about waist height; then the case explodes. S-mines are used in minefields as anti-personnel devices, planted round the larger anti-tank mines.

One of the armoured-car troopers, surviving the initial blast, must have trodden or fallen upon an S-mine. That's the second explosion.

Holden has the jeep re-started. I hear Punch's and Collie's trucks revving. 'Go!' I cry. We bolt away up the valley.

When extreme fear is suddenly, unexpectedly relieved, the release can carry one apart from his senses. All I'm thinking is that I want those Germans dead. Behind us, I can hear secondary explosions – ammunition in the armoured car's magazine. I don't look back. To do so might be bad luck. If I turn back, the explosions might stop. I don't want them to. I want them to keep going. I want that bloody car to blow until there's not a scrap of it left bigger than a penny.

Our three vehicles speed away up the valley, round one dog-leg of the rising trail and up another. Suddenly the road runs out. Another dead-end. We brake in a storm of alkali, every eye scanning for a route up and out.

Nothing.

Curses from everyone.

'Back!' I shout. But first I order all the men to clear and test their guns and seat fresh magazines. Other enemy vehicles may have come up in the past minutes. 'Whatever we run into, don't hesitate. Hit them with everything and keep going. We go for the plain and stop for nothing.'

Jeep and trucks are topped out in second gear when we clear the saddle that opens on to the descending slope. Two hundred yards down we see the smoking carcass of the armoured car. No other vehicles have come up. I sign keep going.

We plunge down the track. Holden keeps the jeep in the lead. I'm braced, half standing in the left-hand seat. One foot is wedged amongst the four-wheel-drive levers; the other is jammed into a corner of the dashboard. I'm peering over the bonnet, looking out for enemy reinforcements, when I see a lone figure stagger into the road ahead.

The young lieutenant with the Iron Cross.

I tug the cocking handle of the Browning. I'm about to press the trigger when I see the officer wave both arms held together as if to signal 'Stop, please!' Some impulse makes me hold. My eyes are scanning both sides of the road for any sign of treachery. The young officer has lost one arm below the elbow. With his remaining hand, he presses a wad of material – a shirt or a cap – against the stump. He hops on one leg; the other, bare beneath charred trousers, looks as black as a fireplace log. On the shoulder of the track lie his crew of three, alive but horribly burnt and disfigured.

I hear my voice cry stop.

Holden stares at me as if I've taken leave of my senses.

'Stop, damn you!'

Holden stands on the brakes. Behind the jeep, I can hear Collie's truck slewing sideways with its tyres screaming. The German officer stumbles forward, hopping on his good leg. 'Help my men, I beg you!' he cries in excellent English.

The jeep slides to a stop. I stand behind the

Browning. I don't have to look to know Collie and Punch have got the Vickers and the second Browning all over the enemy. I stare at the men on the ground. All are appallingly burned. One's tunic has been stripped, revealing a chest and belly that look like roasted meat. Another's right arm hangs, turned round backwards. The third's whole left side weeps blood.

Somehow I'm on my feet on the ground. I have taken the Iron Cross officer under one arm, supporting him. I call for the medical kit. My thought is to leave the box for the wounded men and keep moving. But as Grainger brings the pathetically inadequate white case with the red cross on its side, I am seized with such shame as I have never known.

The young officer in my arms has lost the ability to speak. He is in shock and knows it; he struggles to remain conscious and to continue to aid his men.

'Dressing station?' I shout directly into the officer's ear.

'Down the hill.' I can barely hear him. The lieutenant's spectacles have been shattered; shards of glass are embedded in the flesh of his cheek and brow. One eye drains a runnel of blood. He lifts his joined arms, struggling to point towards the plain.

By now Collie and Jenkins have leapt down too. The muzzles of their guns droop on their mounts. Both start towards the maimed soldiers, then draw up. 'Chap, if we bring these poor bastards in . . .'

'I know.'

Collie means we'll be taken prisoner. The mission will fail.

'Take the jeep.' I tell him I'll carry the wounded men on my vehicle. 'You get to the wireless truck.'

Before all else, we must complete our assignment. HQ must learn what we've seen of the Tebaga Gap and of the enemy's dispositions. Nothing can be allowed to compromise that.

But as Grainger and Jenkins kneel beside the wounded Germans, it becomes clear that they can't handle them on our own. Holden steps down from the jeep and comes forward. Collie crosses to Holden's place. He sets one foot inside the jeep and one hand on the wheel. Jenkins and Grainger bend to help the German soldier who looks to be the most desperately wounded.

'Fuck me,' says Collie. He dismounts.

CHAPTER 36

The Afrika Korps dressing station looks just like one of ours: two open-fronted tents with white panels and red crosses on the roofs; tables and chairs out in front under canvas fly sheets. Adjacent: a medical officer's truck, an Opel instead of a Bedford, with its rear doors open and two stretchers set upright against each side. By the time our jeep and trucks have reached it, the German machine guns that have covered us from the moment we broached their forward positions – an engineer company demolishing a road – have long since been lowered.

A dozen men in peaked caps and khaki trousers surround our vehicles; litters are being rushed up. 'Leave the wounded men be!' a medical orderly commands in German. He and others rush aid to their countrymen on Collie's truckbed where they lie, so as not to cause them further pain or injury by moving them. I offer to help but the medics tell me to let them do it. Collie and Punch pull back as well. The stretcher-bearers race up. With exquisite gentleness the medics tend their charred and maimed countrymen. An ambulance speeds from another part of the camp. I can see other trucks approaching.

My intention, when we started in with the wounded soldiers, was to halt within sight of the first German position we came to. From there we would signal distress, then leave the men and flee. But when we reached such a place, the poor fellows in our care were suffering so terribly and needed attention so desperately that instead I simply produced a white handkerchief and drove in.

Not for an instant was there a sense of being captured. The first enemy to approach us immediately became escorts. Following them, we sped into the camp. Now, halted in the centre of the dressing station, we hold our positions as the wounded and burnt men, including the lieutenant with the Iron Cross, are injected with morphine, and made ready to be moved inside the tents. It occurs to me that soon we will we no longer have witnesses to testify to our good works.

Punch and Collie still stand to their guns. Half a hundred enemy troopers pack the space round us. More hurry up every moment. No one speaks. Not a man comes forward. The sense on both sides is of acute embarrassment. The weapons in our hands make us ashamed. No one enquires how we enemy came to bring in these wounded men. No one asks anything. I feel I should speak, break the silence. But nothing comes. Finally a colonel appears, on foot, accompanied by a captain and a sergeant. None carries a weapon. I can't decipher the service devices on their uniforms; almost certainly they are engineers, as there seem to be few line soldiers in this rear area.

The colonel gives instructions to the men surrounding us. He speaks so fast I can't follow. The gist seems to be to detain but not to arrest or disarm us. The colonel's glance finds me. '*Deutsch sprechen?*' Do I speak German?

'*Ein wenig,*' I say. A little.

He feels, I see, as awkward as I do.

The colonel asks my name and what has happened. He does not ask our outfit. This is significant, for the Geneva Convention forbids such a query. Briefly I tell of the chase and the Teller mine. This makes a profound impression. I'm thinking, Am I mad to have brought these men in? Will my own army court-martial me? The transit from the hills has taken most of an hour; one of the soldiers has died, a second seems beyond help. Has the cost to our mission and to my own men been worth it?

The last of the wounded Germans is being settled on to a stretcher on the bed of Collie's truck. The medics set the litter down parallel to the boy's prone form, then rock his body gently sideways until they can slide the stretcher underneath. His wounds have been dressed. The mangled flesh where his right foot had been is now bundled at least in clean gauze and tape.

An armoured car approaches. Round the site, hundreds of Afrika Korps troopers have now collected; they wear boots and jackets like ours, many with sand goggles and the same scarves round their necks to shield against sand and dust. Few are armed.

The armoured car comes up with both hatches open, driver and commander perched high in their stations. The vehicle stops. Behind it brakes an open-sided staff car. Our colonel turns and salutes. All round, soldiers snap to attention.

No one dismounts from the armoured car. From the staff car steps, first, a lieutenant in a dusty greatcoat, then a stocky officer of about fifty in jacket and breeches. The latter officer returns the colonel's salute and comes forward. On his shoulders is the braid of a general. He wears a checked scarf, under which is pinned a Knight's Cross, and an Afrika Korps cap with a pair of sand goggles pushed back over the brim. The officer's throat is bandaged, as one sees so often in this theatre, indicating desert sores or some other campaign malady.

CHAPTER 37

It's Rommel. He comes forward so matter-of-factly and with so little ceremony that he might be your uncle or a professor you admire and who knows you well. I salute. Collie and the others do the same. The lieutenant is apparently Rommel's aide-decamp. A third officer catching up from the staff car must be his interpreter.

Rommel addresses me as Herr Leutnant and introduces himself, including his rank, as if he were just another officer in just another post. The whole thing has come about so suddenly that I don't have time to be daunted. I identify myself. Rommel's ADC indicates that all personnel – Afrika Korps troopers as well as ourselves – may stand at ease.

For long moments the aide speaks privately to his commander. I can barely hear what he's saying but catch enough to know that Rommel is being told the circumstances under which these British and their vehicles have come to be in German custody.

The Field Marshal absorbs this. Throughout, he studies me, my men and our vehicles. The aide finishes. Rommel steps past me towards Collie's truck. His posture indicates that he wishes me to accompany him.

I do.

'Two-wheel drive or four?' Rommel asks in accented but clear English.

'Two-wheel, sir.'

'Indeed?' He confirms this with a glance at the front axle. 'Petrol or diesel?'

'Petrol, sir.'

Rommel eyes the sun compass. He asks if it is the Bagnold version. I confirm this. The general's glance moves to the overflow canister and the hose feeding into it from the radiator.

'Condenser,' I say.

Rommel nods. He steps round to the rear of the truck, taking in the guns and the sand-channels, the spare leaf springs and, under tarpaulins, the load of jerry cans.

'*Deutscher oder Amerikanischer?*'

In just the past month, Eighth Army has started getting American copies of the excellent German petrol container. We prefer the original.

'*Deutscher, Herr General.*'

Rommel smiles. 'A better pouring lip.'

Our captor completes his circuit of the Chevrolet 30-hundredweight. Collie, Punch and the others have formed up into a party, standing correctly but at ease. Rommel stops before them, but addresses me. He speaks in German.

'You are Long Range Desert Group, reconnoitring

a left hook round my position. Is that correct, Lieutenant?'

I respond in German. 'I may not answer that, sir.'

Rommel doesn't smile. But a look constituted of one part amusement and two parts approval softens his otherwise severe features. He takes one step back, then addresses, collectively and in English, me and my crew.

'I shall never forget your kindness to my young men.'

His voice cracks with emotion. There is a short pause; then with a sharp command, the Desert Fox calls for fuel and water to be brought. Afrika Korps troopers respond with alacrity, bringing jerry cans which they load into the back of my jeep and into Collie's and Punch's trucks.

Rommel shakes my hand and that of every man in T3 patrol.

'I will give you an hour's start,' he tells me in English. 'After that, you understand, I must put my hounds on your trail.'

I have no idea what protocol demands. Do I salute? Say thank you? I'm thinking, Get out of here now before anybody changes his mind. I'm about to speak in gratitude when I feel Punch, behind me and to the side, straighten and clear his throat.

'With respect, sir,' Punch addresses Rommel. 'An hour ain't fair.'

Our benefactor turns back.

I shoot Punch a look: shut up!

Punch ignores me. He speaks directly to the general.

'It'll take every bit of an hour, sir, just to get back to where we turned round from. By now your chaps'll be all over the place, where they weren't nowhere near before.' Punch stands taller and meets the Field Marshal's eye. 'We didn't have to help your blokes, sir. We coulda shot 'em all and got a medal for it.'

Rommel's interpreter translates this in its entirety. I listen, making sure he gets it right. Collie and I are both coming out of our boots, expecting all hell to pay back Punch's presumption.

Rommel regards us all for a long moment.

'Till dark then. Will you call that fair?'

'That's square, sir,' says Punch.

I speak before anyone else pipes up with another bright idea. 'That will be most generous, sir.' I salute. Rommel responds and turns on his heel. I have one moment to meet Punch's eye, threatening blue murder. Then we mount up and get out of there as fast as we can.

CHAPTER 38

I dictated my operation report on 6 February from the French hospital at Tébessa in Algeria, where dysentery, not jaundice or pneumonia, at last laid me low. Operation Torch, the Anglo-American landings at Casablanca, Oran and Algiers, had in November put ashore 90,000 men and 450 tanks and this force had by the date of T3's getaway pushed inland as far as the mountains of Tunisia's Western Dorsale.

The Yanks occupied the town of Tébessa, a sizeable and quite charming French colonial outpost, though they were about to get chased out by Rommel when he struck again with his customary audacity, driving the inexperienced American troops back over the Kasserine Pass and nearly out of Tunisia entirely. By then – mid-February 1943 – I and all of T3 had been flown to HQ Eighth Army at Medenine and from there, individually and by various forms of transport, to Cairo and the end of our desert war.

The act of chivalry that liberated us from German custody was by no means without cost to Rommel. By letting us go, the Field Marshal made possible the signalling of our report on the topography of the Tebaga Gap and of his own dispositions within it. In the event, wireless failure prevented us from sending this signal – but Rommel had no way of knowing that when he released us. In addition, our host sacrificed the chance of interrogating us as prisoners of war and perhaps gleaning vital intelligence.

Why did he do it? I believe that, being the man he was, he had no choice. His enemy had performed an act of mercy towards men serving under his colours. By his own imperatives of honour, he could do no less than return the favour. I don't believe he ever thought of doing anything else. Nor, I judge, did any of the onlooking soldiers. In Rommel's boots, I'm sure, they would have done the same.

Our escape proved anti-climactic. We retrieved our Guardsmen waiting with the wireless truck, which had been attacked by Berbers in the interim and its radio put out of commission. Reckoning that our pursuers would track us south towards British lines, we turned west instead. Four days of struggling with mechanical failures and fending off sallies by armed natives got us round the western shoulder of the Chott Djerid, the great salt lake of southern Tunisia. Luck for once stayed with us. We reached the French post of Tozeur a day later and from there made our way to Gafsa, Feriana, and at last to the hospital at Tébessa.

In Tozeur we learnt that Tinker and Popski were alive. They had been in this very town only a day earlier, with all their men, as well as a contingent of SAS and Fighting French, who had linked with them after their camp at Qaret Ali had been wiped out by German aircraft. Tinker and Popski had escaped this calamity by blind luck – being absent on reconnaissance at the time of the attack. Their group, now of over thirty men, had made its escape, as we had, via the Chott. After an ordeal on foot and in several overloaded jeeps, all had at last reached safety on the far side.

The topographical intelligence that our patrol had acquired turned out to be of only corroborative importance. Both Tinker and Popski had reconnoitred the Tebaga Gap before us, as had, within days, the patrols of Lazarus, Spicer, Bruce and Henry. From Tozeur, Tinker had signalled his report to HQ Middle East. In fact he had cadged a flight to Monty's headquarters and there completed delivery of his findings in person.

The discovery of Wilder's Gap, along with Tinker and Popski's reconnaissance of the Tebaga Gap, proved to be decisive in the defeat of the Afrika Korps and the surrender of Axis forces in North Africa. When, on 12–19 March 1943, the 2nd New Zealand Division ran its left hook round the Mareth Line, it was Tinker himself with two NCOs from T2 patrol who guided the formation and its supporting arms.

As for Rommel in that early February, he had by no means shot his final bolt. On the fourteenth, Operation Spring Wind overwhelmed the US forces at Sidi bou Zid. A day later, the Afrika Korps captured Gafsa, the town in which our patrol had been resting just a few days earlier, and pressed north to Kasserine. There on 20 February, Rommel's Panzers fell again upon the unseasoned Americans, capturing four thousand and inflicting a humiliating defeat upon Allied arms.

By 9 March, however, the Desert Fox's good fortune had run out. Racked by jaundice, thrown back by Monty at Medenine, with the Mareth Line days away from being turned, he voluntarily departed for Europe, alone except for his aides. His replacement in Tunisia, General Hans-Jürgen von Arnim, fought on for another month and a half, before finally capitulating at Tunis on 7 May. The despatch from General Alexander to the Prime Minister, Mr Churchill, read as follows:

> Sir, it is my duty to report that the Tunisian campaign is over. All enemy resistance has ceased. We are masters of the North African shores.

This was the end of the Axis armies in Africa and the triumph for which Montgomery and Eighth Army had laboured for so long.

I was returned to Cairo by hospital ship. When Rose reached me, in the 15th Scottish General Hospital, she held in her arms our infant daughter whom she had named Alexandra, after the city in which the child was conceived.

Both Punch and Collie survived the war, though I did not see either until a reunion in Wellington, New Zealand in March of 1963. Punch died on New Year's Day, 1971, of heart failure at his home in Puhoi, north of Auckland. During the time of the patrol described in these pages, I lost four men – Trooper L. Z. Midge, Corporal R. A. Hornsby, Trooper L. R. Standage and Trooper J. M. Miller. To this day I see their faces. Collie and Punch were awarded the Military Medal; Grainger, Oliphant and Miller posthumously were mentioned in despatches. Marks survived his wounds at the flooded wadi. He died in 1986 in Durban, South Africa.

Nick Wilder (DSO) and Ron Tinker (OBE, MC, MM) returned to New Zealand as heroes. I have cited their names over more dinners than I can count. Both have since passed on, Wilder at his sixteen-hundred-acre sheep farm near Waipukurau on 27 June 1970 at the age of fifty-six; Tinker in Christchurch on 16 February 1982, aged sixty-eight. Both retired with the rank of lieutenant-colonel.

Jake Easonsmith (DSO, MC) continued with the LRDG as its commanding officer and was promoted to lieutenant-colonel when the group was reconfigured for partisan operations in the Balkans and the Aegean islands. He was killed by a sniper on Leros on 16 November 1943.

Major (later Lieutenant-Colonel) Vladimir Peniakoff (DSO, MC) authored the colourful and extremely entertaining *popski's Private Army*, which was published to wide acclaim in 1950. He died just a year later of a brain tumour. He was fifty-four.

Major (later Lieutenant-Colonel) Blair 'Paddy' Mayne of the SAS (DSO with three bars, Légion d'honneur, Croix de Guerre) was killed in a motor accident on 13 December 1955 near his home at Newtownards in Northern Ireland. He was the most decorated British soldier of the Second World War, as well as one of the founding pillars and a legend of the Special Air Service.

Now: Rommel.

The end of the Desert Fox's life was attended by bitter irony and by, many believe, even greater honour than that which he had achieved by his feats of soldiering and generalship. Charged by Hitler's henchmen with complicity in the July 1944 plot to assasinate the Führer, Rommel was offered the choice of taking his own life – by cyanide capsule provided by his accusers – or putting the nation through the ordeal of a trial before a Nazi court. More to the point, Rommel was certain that his persecutors would never let him survive to reach trial. He took the poison. He was buried with full military honours at Herrlingen on 18 October 1944.

I was in hospital on Sardinia when I heard the report on the BBC, accompanied by the official German cover story of death from wounds suffered in an American air attack. I believed it. It was not till the publication of Desmond Young's *Rommel the Desert Fox* in 1950 that the truth became clear to all.

Killing Rommel was an aim that we, his enemies, could never accomplish. It took Hitler and the worst of his own countrymen to still the heart of Germany's greatest fighting general. In the end, we who strove against him came to respect Rommel as profoundly, perhaps, as did his own men, whom he led so brilliantly and to whom he was faithful to his final breath.

Stein's novel was published by Gattis & Thurlow in 1947. The book made my career. *The Times* called it 'dazzling' and 'intrepid' and ran a particularly dashing photo of Stein in his RHA uniform, which Rose had taken outside the Bodleian Library. A motion picture was produced based upon the book, with Jack Hawkins and a very young Laurence Harvey. There was even a bit of a Stein cult in Greenwich Village, New York, at the time of the beatniks.

As for my combat career, it continued for eleven months after the German surrender in

North Africa, through the Allied invasions of Sicily and Italy. A fractured hip, acquired not in action but in a traffic accident at home on leave, at last got me out of the line and into the kind of desk job that part of me suspects I was more suited to from the start.

Rose and I still have each other. I remain as deeply in love with her as I was as an undergraduate in 1938. Alexandra has been joined by Thomas, Patrick, Jessica and (so far) six grandchildren.

As for the dream of my mother, I have had it all my life. If the imagery as Stein suggested is about reconciling oneself to death, I have not yet succeeded in doing so.

Last, I must speak of the Italian soldiers we shot down that night at Benina. Over the centuries, countless warriors and thinkers, far wiser than I, have addressed the issue of morality in war and the right and wrong of taking human life. I can speak only for myself. No martial credo, however lofty or noble-sounding, will ever convince me that those men were 'enemy', even though I know that they were and that, had they got the chance, they would have visited upon me and my comrades the same destruction which we loosed upon them. That changes nothing. We took their lives. By wilful violence ordered by me, our guns tore them from wives and children, fathers and mothers; from their country and from themselves. Rivers of tears cannot alter that fact. I have lived with it every day, every hour. Like many of my generation I did not go to war gravely and soberly, as Lao-tzu tells us a wise man ought. But I returned from it that way.

EPILOGUE

C hap's memoir ends with that sentence. What he characteristically omitted to mention was the DSO he won for the operation described in these pages. Chap was awarded the Military Cross at Monte Cassino in Italy, May 1944, this honour joining his mention in despatches from the Gazala campaign, so that the identification line in his obituary in *The Times* of London and the *Guardian* on December 27, 2004 read:

Chapman, Maj. R. L., DSO, MC.

This was the least likely encapsulation that Chap would have chosen for himself in summing up his life, yet I feel certain that his spirit, looking down from heaven, would be warmed to see that 'attrib line', as he would have called it as an editor.

Chap's memorial service was held, as I said, in the chapel at Magdalen College, Oxford. You enter Magdalen through a porter's gate off the High Street. The chapel stands on the right in the first quadrangle. On that morning the space overflowed with mourners filling the quad and lapping round into the adjacent cloister.

The day was dry with a sharp, cold wind. Rose no longer walked well; her son Patrick and a grandson had to support her to her seat. When the service was over, someone produced a wheel-chair, from which Rose greeted guests afterwards at the reception in a pub called the Head of the River. I had flown over alone from California, as my wife had been detained at home by an emergency in her own family; I found myself standing apart for a portion of the evening, just observing.

The guests seemed for the most part to be family, friends, literary colleagues; in other words, those who knew Chap post-war. I watched several elderly gentlemen make their way to Rose. Were any of them old soldiers? Chap and Rose's daughters Alexandra and Jessica greeted those who approached and introduced them to their brothers, who then handed them down to Rose in her chair. Rose must have been tired but she held up like a trooper. You could see her pleasure and gratitude at the words of condolence.

At one point Alexandra presented me to an older gentleman named Guy Bourghart, who was missing his right arm but at eighty years plus still possessed a bone-crunching grip when he shook hands with his left. 'Guy published Dad's first book.'

Bourghart explained that he and Chap had served in North Africa at the same time.

'Chap sold me the book in a casualty clearing station at Sfax in Tunisia, waiting for a hospital ship to take us back to Cairo. They had the sick and wounded stacked on litters, out of doors, in the sharpest gale you can imagine. All we could do was bleed and yarn with one another.'

First book. Did he mean Stein's?

'Chap had the manuscript with him. Incredible. Of course I couldn't read the damn thing. It was all I could do to draw the next breath. But I thought: this young officer is either bloody mad or a hell of a champion for his writers.'

A few minutes later I met the widow of the young lieutenant with the Iron Cross, whose life Chap had saved at the Tebaga Gap. Chap, the lady told me, had tracked her husband down in Frankfurt in the early fifties; apparently there were organizations at that time which provided such services. The couples became friends; they visited each other every summer. 'Now Rose and I,' said the lady, 'shall have one more bond.'

I found Jock, Chap's dear friend and brother-in-law. Jock had given the eulogy. I kept a copy, from which comes this passage:

Chap published, as many of you know, not only serious young writers in English, but also foreign authors. Books in translation. This is rare. Chap was no religious man; I have never seen him inside a church until this day. Literature was his religion. He believed in the written word, in the soul-to-soul communion between writer and reader that takes place in the silence between the covers of a book.

Chap venerated the novel. To him fiction was not merely a medium of amusement or diversion, though he set considerable store by those, but a field upon which the experience of a single individual could be made accessible to others with a power and immediacy that no other medium could reproduce. Chap saw in the novel a universality – a level pitch upon which disparate human beings, entering via the imagination into the experiences and consciousnesses of others, could discover a commonality across the divisions of tribe, race, nation, even time.

Universality. Empathy. These were the qualities Chap worshipped. These were his gods and, if I may declare it of him, he embodied their virtues in his own person in finer and fuller measure than any man I have ever known.

Now I must tell you one final story, of my sister Rose and this man who adored her his whole life long. Many of you have heard of the row Chap and I got into here at university, on the High Street just round the corner, when I caught him with Rose in circumstances that in today's world would be so innocent as to be laughable but in those days were extravagantly flagrant. I seized my sister by the arm and demanded that she come away at once – to which she replied 'Piss off, Jock!' and, breaking free, stalked to Chap's side. I can still see him, setting his arm firmly round her waist and looking me dead in the eye. 'Your sister's with me, Jock,' he said. 'That's it.'

And so she has been for over sixty years. And shall be, I'm sure, for ever.

The reception was ending. I drifted back to the bar. I was looking around, hoping to spot some military emblem, a lapel pin or insignia perhaps, that would indicate an old campaigner. I noticed a toy truck – one of those Matchbox miniatures – sitting on the polished wood in front of a gentleman who appeared to be in his eighties. I crossed to him and asked what type of truck it was.

''Forty-two Chev 30-hundredweight,' the man said, sliding the toy over so I could see it. At once I recognized the workhorse of the Long Range Desert Group. The truck was flawless in detail, down to the sun compass and sand-channels; roof-less, doorless, windshieldless. I introduced myself.

'May I ask your name, sir?'

'Collier,' he said.

'Sergeant Collier? "Collie"?'

Night had fallen; a stiff breeze had got up off

the river. Collier and I immediately repaired outdoors to the terrace where we could talk. I was electrified. I told him about Chap's manuscript, which was absolutely fresh in my mind from my having read it three times in the last several days, and how intimately I felt I had come to know its events, places, and characters – including him, Collie. 'I've got the typed pages in my room; would you like me to make a copy for you?'

'I don't need to read nothing,' said the New Zealander. 'I was there.'

He was a tallish man with a full head of white hair. Though age had whittled his bulk, you could see from the meat of his hands that he still retained a respectable measure of power. He carried himself like a stockman, which is what he was. His pipe was a Sherlock Holmes type, just as in Chap's pages.

He had been visiting his daughter in British Columbia, Collier said, when his wife had phoned from home with the news of Chap's death. The Kiwis who had served with the LRDG were national heroes; an item about any of them, or anyone associated with their wartime service, automatically received featured play in the New Zealand press, particularly in recent years as the surviving veterans grew fewer and fewer. Collie had reserved a flight at once from Vancouver to Heathrow. He had flown in yesterday and was heading back tomorrow. I asked if he had spoken to Rose.

'She's got more important people to talk to.'

It felt oddly exhilirating to be in Collie's presence, as if I'd bumped into a favourite character from a film or a book – which in a sence, of course, I had. Collie felt this, I think. It made him uncomfortable. I was hoping he would open up after a couple of pints. But the old soldier had no such agenda. I asked if he would be returning to the hotel. The party was beginning to assemble for the drive to the inn where the family was staying, in which a suite had been reserved for a late gathering.

'This here's enough,' Collier said.

I could not let his reticence stand. 'If you'll forgive me for asking, Mr Collier, how could you fly all this way, at such expense' – clearly he was no wealthy man – 'and not—'

'I came to see off a mate.'

Collie met my eyes. As far as he was concerned, that said it all.

I was not ready to let it go. 'Collie,' I said. 'I'm going to call you that whether you like it not, because I feel I know you.' I told him of Chap's initial reluctance to show me his manuscript and his even graver disinclination toward having it published. I related Chap's feeling that, because his tenure with the LRDG had been so brief and had been officially Detached Service, he was not a true member of the outfit. 'More to the point,' I said, 'Chap felt that certain actions of his . . . decisions he took or didn't take . . . cost the lives of several good men. He was tormented by that. It was why he—'

'Balls!' For the first time the old man's eyes struck sparks and his voice rang with emotion. 'By Christ, if it wasn't for Mr Chapman we'd have all copped it, not once but half a dozen times. I know he never felt part of the club because he was only with us for that one ride, but so were plenty of others, and they didn't hesitate to grab the glory with both hands. Who earned it more than Mr Chapman? He was just a kid, but he was as thorough a desert hand as any I've seen. And I'll tell you something else . . .'

Collie drew up.

'The Jerry armoured car that hit the Teller mine.' He met my eye. 'Did the skipper write about that?'

'At the Mareth Line, you mean? When you all came back and found the Germans burned and wounded?'

The door opened behind us from the pub's rear room; Chap's son Patrick stuck his head out, calling to tell us that the cars were outside, waiting to take the party to the hotel for brandy. I thanked him and said we'd be with them in a moment. Patrick closed the door; the pub sounds cut off. I asked Collie if he wanted to go back inside.

He was staring out over the frigid river.

'We had an old Vickers .303 on the back of my truck. With fist grips and a thumb trigger.' His hands indicated the posture; he glanced to me to see if I understood. I could picture Collie on his feet in the truckbed with the German armoured car on its side in front of him and the enemy soldiers, grievously wounded but still in possession of their weapons, in various postures before his muzzle. 'I was this close,' he said, 'to blowing those bastards to kingdom come. Believe me, I wanted to. We all did.'

I asked him what Chap had said. Did he give a specific order not to shoot?

'Mr Chapman didn't say a thing. Didn't have to. We knew what kind of man he was. We knew he'd help the Jerries. And we knew we'd back him up.'

Horns were honking out front on the street. Patrick came back and tapped on the pane. I signed that we were coming, then turned back to Collier.

'There ain't a day goes by,' Collie said, 'that I don't thank Mr Chapman for that.'

I convinced Collie to come back to the family gathering. The most gratifying moment was seeing him and Rose engrossed in private conversation. Afterwards I drove him back to where he was staying. Collie didn't want a copy of Chap's manuscript, not even if it were mailed to him in New Zealand. I couldn't convince him even to glance at the parts that singled him out for praise. In the cold outside his hotel – a B&B which Collie said his granddaughter had booked for him on the internet – the old soldier looked worn and frail, but a warrior still. I held out my hand. I told him I considered it an honor to have met him.

He took my hand. 'God speed, mate.'

The next day Rose and the family drove back to London. I stayed on in Oxford for the morning. I had breakfast by myself in my hotel, then walked down to Blackwell's to see if they had Stein's novel. I had never actually seen it. They did, a single copy, in a section called University Authors. The volume I bought was a third edition with the original dust jacket. Stein's photo was inside the back flap. He was a dashing-looking fellow, dark and intense, with the same Ronald Colman mustache that every young sport seemed to fancy in those days. I bought the book to set as a parting token at Chap's grave.

A lecture at one of the colleges was just letting out when I stepped again into the street. The students surged to the great pile of bicycles that sprawled against the side of the building. I watched them wedge their notebooks and texts into the cargo baskets between the handlebars. Apparently bicycles in England didn't have kick-stands, or maybe leaning them against a wall was just the Oxford style. In any event the mob yanked their bikes upright and in an instant were pedalling away in their dark jackets like some swift flight of crows.

The turf over Chap's grave had been staked down with wire mesh to protect it from burrowing animals until the grass had had time to root itself. A wooden cross had been erected to mark the site until the headstone could be carved and delivered. At the base of this sat several candles and handwritten notes, alongside a number of military unit patches and cap badges. I recognized the winged-dagger insignia of the SAS with its motto, 'Who Dares, Wins,' and a 'Fear Naught' badge of the Royal Tank Regiment. Beside these sat a German Iron Cross. I searched the site, seeking the proper niche for Stein's book. Someone had set a bouquet of primroses alongside one of the candles. That looked like the spot. I was just settling the book in place, when my eye was caught by a bright metallic glint.

On the grass, at the foot of the marker sat a tiny toy truck painted in desert camouflage – a '42 Chevrolet 30-hundred-weight. I picked it up and held it for a moment in the winter light. I could see the miniature sun compass and radiator condenser, the .30-caliber Browning and the twin Vickers Ks. Three soldiers in desert garb manned the vehicle: a driver, a gunner, and – standing, with his binoculars pressed to his eyes – a patrol commander.

ACKNOWLEDGEMENTS

Special thanks to Jack Valenti and Rick Butler of the Long Range Desert Group Preservation Society; in New Zealand to LRDG historian Brendan O'Carroll for his wisdom and assistance and to the Reverend Warner Wilder and the Wilder family for their kind support and aid in research; to authors Jonathan Pittaway and Craig Fourie in South Africa; to Peter Sanders and Paul Lincoln of the Desert Raiders Association in England; to Andrew Escott of the First Royal Tank Regiment; to Gunner and military historian John A. T. Tiley of the 263rd Field Regiment, R. A.; and with especial appreciation to Roger Field of the Blues and Royals. My gratitude as well to my American editors Charlie Conrad and Bill Thomas and to Simon Taylor at Transworld in London; to Wilfried and Gisela Eckhardt for their assistance in German-English translation; and especially to my dear friend John Milnes of the BBC, whose contributions, both literary and editorial, went leagues beyond the call of duty. Thanks, you blokes!